A Wedding

Vicki Beeby writes historical fiction about the friendships and loves of service women brought together by the Second World War. Her first job was as a civil engineer on a sewage treatment project, so things could only improve from there. Since then, she has worked as a maths teacher and education consultant before turning freelance to give herself more time to write. In her free time, when she can drag herself away from reading, she enjoys walking and travelling to far-off places by train. She lives in Shropshire in a house that doesn't contain nearly enough bookshelves.

Also by Vicki Beeby

The Women's Auxiliary Air Force

The Ops Room Girls
Christmas with the Ops Room Girls
Victory for the Ops Room Girls

The Wrens

A New Start for the Wrens
A Wrens' Wartime Christmas
Hopeful Hearts for the Wrens

Bomber Command Girls

The Girls of Bomber Command
A Wedding for the Bomber Girls

VICKI BEEBY

A Wedding
for the
Bomber Girls

CANELO

First published in the United Kingdom in 2024 by

Canelo
Unit 9, 5th Floor
Cargo Works, 1-2 Hatfields
London SE1 9PG
United Kingdom

A CIP catalogue record for this book is available from the British Library.

Print ISBN 978 1 80436 719 3
Ebook ISBN 978 1 80436 720 9

This book is a work of fiction. Names, characters, businesses, organizations, places and events are either the product of the author's imagination or are used fictitiously. Any resemblance to actual persons, living or dead, events or locales is entirely coincidental.

Cover design by Becky Glibbery

Cover images © ArcAngel, Shutterstock

Look for more great books at www.canelo.co

Printed and bound in Great Britain by Clays Ltd, Elcograf S.p.A.

As always, to my family:

Mum

Duncan, Jana & Emma

Chris, Katka & Elena

Chapter One

Lincolnshire

March 1943

'Any letters for me?' Thea asked the corporal on duty in the WAAF guardroom. 'Cooper, five five two, Hut Four.' After three years in the Women's Auxiliary Air Force, it came as second nature to recite the last three digits of her service number when giving her name.

The corporal rummaged through the letters. 'Hut Four... Hut Four,' she mumbled under her breath. 'Here we are. Oh, they've all been collected apart from this one for you.' She slid an envelope across the counter. 'Can't think how it got missed out.'

Thea could. She glanced at the letter and recognised her grandmother's handwriting. She stuffed it in her pocket, then looked back at the corporal. 'You're new, aren't you, Corp?'

'That's right. I arrived three days ago.' She gave a self-conscious glance at the stripes on her sleeve, and Thea guessed she was newly promoted.

'Well, give it a few days and you'll find out why no one collects my mail.' The main post office in the camp sorted the post by hut and delivered it to the WAAF guardroom for collection. Here at Fenthorpe, it was considered good form for the first WAAF going to the guardroom that day to collect the post for everyone else in her hut also. In recent weeks, however, Thea's mail had always been missed.

She gave the corporal a cheery grin and left the guardroom. The grin was entirely for show, and she did her best to keep it on her face for the benefit of the other WAAFs milling around the Waafery. It was only once she had collected her bicycle and was riding along the lane to RAF Fenthorpe's main gate that she allowed her smile to slip. She didn't want to give the other WAAFs the satisfaction of knowing how much their treatment hurt.

As she had the morning off, she would have liked to escape Fenthorpe for a while, only she had agreed to meet her sister, Pearl, in the NAAFI later. Together with their friend Jenny, that made a grand total of two people in the NAAFI who would be prepared to speak to her.

Thea gave herself a mental shake. Let everyone whisper behind their hands. See if she cared. It was their loss if they didn't believe in her innocence. She parked her bike behind the NAAFI, then walked in, head held high.

Her spirits lifted when she saw that week's issue of the *Bombshell* had arrived. Until now it had been published monthly and only distributed in RAF Fenthorpe. However, with her sister seconded to work full time on the newspaper, the circulation had been expanded to include all the bomber stations of 5 Group, and it was now also published weekly. From the depleted pile on the counter and the number of people in the NAAFI reading a copy, it was clear that the changes hadn't reduced its popularity. Eager to see how the crossword she'd compiled had turned out, she picked up a copy and paid for it, together with a mug of tea and a wad – the ground crew's name for a rock cake. Knowing it would be a good half-hour before either Pearl or Jenny arrived, she went to sit at an empty table by the window, not bothering to try joining any of the groups at the occupied tables. Unfolding the newspaper, she placed it on the table and began to read.

'Excuse me, do you mind if we join you?'

Thea glanced up, surprised at the interruption, to see a WAAF in a uniform so pristine she must be straight out of initial training. Thea pointed at the chair opposite and was about to invite the newcomer to sit when another WAAF hurried up and grabbed the arm of the girl who had spoken to Thea. 'Not there,' she muttered.

Ignoring the second WAAF, Thea smiled at the new WAAF. 'I'm Thea Cooper. You're very welcome to join me if you'd like. In fairness, I ought to warn you that everyone thinks I'm a thief.' She lifted the lapel of her battledress tunic to reveal the gold and emerald four-leaf clover pin she always wore. 'Apparently I stole this from a dead wireless operator. It's a good story. Gossip's always more interesting than the truth.'

The girl stared at her wide-eyed, but her companion dragged her to another table before she could reply. Pretending to read her newspaper unconcerned, Thea kept half an eye on the two women. Sure enough, hardly had they sat down before the others at their table were leaning towards the new WAAF, speaking behind their hands with many furtive glances in Thea's direction. No doubt they were filling in the newcomer on Thea's many misdeeds.

'Mind if I sit here?' This time it was a male voice.

'Be my guest.' Thea spoke without looking up. 'You might want to hold on to your valuables, though.'

'I'll risk it.'

Thea glanced up, only belatedly recognising the newcomer as a friend. Flight Sergeant James Fitzgerald, commonly known as Fitz, dropped into the chair opposite and regarded her with a quizzical expression. 'Having a bad day? I thought you could use the company, but I'll go if you'd rather be alone.'

He half rose, but Thea, mortified at her offhand greeting, waved him back into his seat. Fitz was the bomb aimer in *C-Charlie*'s crew – one of two Lancasters Thea worked on. Her aircrews were among the few people in Fenthorpe who believed she was not a thief, and she had no wish to alienate them as well. 'No worse than usual. Sorry. I'd like the company if you've got time. Aren't you flying ops tonight?'

Fitz nodded and lit a cigarette with a hand that shook slightly. This didn't surprise Thea; anyone who had flown as many missions as Fitz developed shaking hands or tics. She knew better than to pass comment. 'Just finished our night flying test, so I've got some spare time before the briefing.'

'Ah, and you thought you'd spend it with the station pariah.'

Fitz's blue eyes sparkled. 'So much more exciting than with some dull admin type.' Then his expression grew more serious, and he leaned across the table. 'Look, Thea, you don't fool me. I can see how this nonsense has got under your skin, but it will soon blow over. It has to. Everyone's read the *Bombshell* article, which makes it perfectly clear you didn't steal anything.'

Thea couldn't speak for a moment, taken aback by the apparent ease with which Fitz had seen through her bravado. Everyone on the station – Pearl and Jenny excepted – took her act at face value and thought she didn't care. No one else had bothered to look deeper to see how hurtful she found the treatment. Until now.

Pulling herself together, she rolled her eyes. 'You're forgetting it was written by my sister. Everyone says she's covering up my involvement.'

The thefts referred to had caused outrage in RAF Fenthorpe when the story had broken. The station adjutant, who oversaw the committee responsible for returning dead aircrews' possessions to their families, had been discovered stealing some of these items. Unfortunately, Thea had been involved when the gold and emerald tiepin, a gift from her wireless operator friend Max Turner, had been reported stolen by Max's sister after he had been killed. Thea had no proof that it had been a present, and so most of the base considered her guilty and that her crime had been hushed up because the person who had uncovered the thefts was Thea's sister. They had made their feelings clear by sending her to Coventry, only speaking to her when necessary. There were still a few people who stuck their neck out for her, though – Pearl, her fiancé Greg and their friend Jenny. And now Fitz. She supposed she ought to be grateful.

4

Only… hang on. Fitz was on Greg's crew. She regarded him with narrowed eyes. 'Did Pearl put you up to this?'

'Up to what?' He met her gaze with a wide-eyed innocence that was almost convincing.

'She asked Greg to get his crew to be nice to me, didn't she.' She was struck by a pang of disappointment. For a moment she had actually thought that Fitz's friendliness was genuine.

'So what if she did? I know you haven't done anything wrong.'

He sounded sincere, but that wasn't the point. Pearl was interfering yet again. 'Look, I don't need your pity – or anyone else's, come to that. If that's the only reason you came to speak to me, you can leave.'

He frowned. 'Pity? That's not why I came to speak to you. I—'

At that moment his attention seemed to be caught by something or someone across the room, and he glanced away, frowning. Following his gaze, Thea saw *C-Charlie*'s tail gunner, Jack Knight, hunched over a mug of tea in the corner of the room. He was alone and gazing at his cup with an expression of misery that made Thea's heart twist.

Fitz rose. 'Look, I'm needed elsewhere.' He ground out his cigarette in the ashtray. 'For what it's worth, I didn't sit here because of anything your sister said. I can decide for myself who I speak to, and you seem an interesting person. Maybe next time we meet we can start afresh.'

Thea watched him walk away, feeling like a complete heel. She drained her cup and shoved back her chair, suddenly unable to bear the suspicious looks and whispered conversation any longer.

Once outside, she saw that fog was rolling in from the east, blotting out the pale sunshine and making the prospect of waiting outside far less appealing. There was no way she could face going back into the NAAFI though, so she turned up the collar of her greatcoat and dawdled along the path between the NAAFI and the Watch Office. The Met Office, where Jenny worked, was situated on the ground floor of the Watch Office, so it made sense to wait for her friend nearby. She had just found a spot to lean against the wall when the door was flung open and the new station commander emerged, accompanied by Squadron Leader David Forrester, the medical officer. Thea hastily sprang to attention and saluted; Group Captain Rhodes had only arrived a week earlier, replacing Group Captain Morgan, and rumours already abounded that he was a strict disciplinarian. Forrester returned her salute, acknowledging her with a nod and a smile. Rhodes returned the salute with barely a glance in her direction and without breaking his stride.

'What did you want to speak to me about?' Rhodes boomed to Forrester, his voice so loud Thea could hear even though the two men were walking away.

'We should really wait until we're in your office.'

'Nonsense. I'm a busy man. If we can't talk now, I haven't got time to deal with it.'

'It's Sergeant Wright, sir.'

Despite herself, Thea pricked up her ears. Wright was a gunner on one of the bomber crews, and she'd heard that he'd been showing signs of strain recently and had refused to fly. This was by no means the first time a crew member had buckled under the stress. Considering the terrible danger the aircrews faced, Thea was surprised this didn't happen more often. Although she had heard tales from other bomber stations of men being labelled Lacking Moral Fibre, or LMF, and being publicly humiliated, nothing like that had happened at Fenthorpe. While the men concerned had left the station, as far as she knew, they had been treated with understanding.

'What about him?' Rhodes snapped. 'He's leaving today. I'm on my way to the parade now.'

Parade? Thea frowned. That didn't sound good.

'It's about the parade I wanted to see you. Are you sure it's good for morale?'

6

'Absolutely. What's bad for morale is having a coward on the station.'

Thea felt sick. She hated that a man who had volunteered as aircrew could be labelled with such a hateful term. Part of her work involved meeting the Lancasters returning from bombing operations, and she had seen the holes from bullets and shrapnel and had, on occasion, had to clean blood from the instruments. In her view, it was a wonder any men could be persuaded to fly more than one mission, let alone thirty. Surely there must be a more compassionate way to deal with men who had become overwhelmed by the stress of it all.

The MO evidently agreed, for he said, 'I don't think he's a coward. If I could just—'

'Has he been injured? Does he have a cold or the flu?'

'Well, no, but—'

'Then it's not a medical matter but a matter of discipline. And that's nothing to do with you. We need every available man in the air, so we must set an example. If the aircrews start thinking they can plead flying stress or whatever nonsense is being spouted these days, we'd never have a squadron at full strength again.'

The men's voices had been fading, and now Thea could no longer pick out any words. But what she had heard left her feeling cold and sick. Everyone had been wondering what the new station commander was like, and now she knew. He was a disciplinarian who had more interest in running RAF Fenthorpe like clockwork than the wellbeing of the men and women who lived and worked there.

Chapter Two

Fitz did his best to put the prickly Thea out of his mind as he approached Jack's table. If she didn't want any friends that was her lookout. Although it was true that Greg had asked his crew to be kind to her, that wasn't the reason he had spoken to her. He had thought she looked uncomfortable being subjected to the hostile scrutiny of pretty well everyone in the NAAFI and had wanted her to know she wasn't alone. Her unbothered act hadn't fooled him.

But Jack clearly needed his help more than Thea at the moment. The tail gunner made no attempt to return any of the greetings from anyone approaching his table but gripped his mug as though his life depended on it. No one else bothered to ask what was troubling him, but Jack was a fellow crew member, and to Fitz his crew were like his family.

Jack jumped when Fitz took the chair opposite, as though he hadn't even noticed him approach.

'Mind if I join you?'

Jack barely looked up. 'Suit yourself.'

Fitz leaned across the table so he could speak without being overheard. 'What's wrong?'

'Oh, you know. The usual.' Jack still wouldn't meet his eye.

'If by "the usual" you mean our impending mission while the entire Luftwaffe is intent on blowing us out of the sky, then I can't say I blame you.'

Jack did look up then. 'How can you make a joke out of it?'

'Because I'd go mad if I didn't.' Fitz pulled his cigarette case out of his pocket and offered it to Jack before taking a cigarette for himself. He watched with increasing concern while Jack reached in his own pocket for his matches, then tried and failed three times to strike a match with a hand that shook so badly he seemed unable to make firm contact with the lighting strip. Finally Fitz took pity on him, struck a match and held it for Jack to use. Jack drew on his cigarette and then blew out a cloud of smoke in a long, shaky breath.

Fitz lit his own cigarette and waited until Jack seemed calmer before observing, 'You always used to joke about our situation, same as everyone else. What's changed?'

'Promise you won't breathe a word to anyone else?'

'Cross my heart.' In the circumstances, Fitz left out the *hope to die* part.

'Remember the mission to Mannheim in December?'

'I'm not likely to forget.' *C-Charlie* had been hit by flak, injuring three crew members, Jack included. They had been lucky to make it home at all. 'You seemed fine afterwards, though.' In fact, he had seemed more high-spirited than usual, even going so far as to steal the station adjutant's cap. While he had been wearing it.

Jack took another drag from his cigarette, flicking the ash into the ashtray before replying. 'Yeah, but then we were stood down for a while.' He shook his head. 'Bad mistake. I had too much time to think. Mannheim haunted me. I couldn't forget that if the shrapnel had hit just a few inches to the right, it would have got me in the heart instead of just taking a slice out of my shoulder. Then I'd have never seen my folks or my girl again.'

Fitz had no reply to that. For the most part he was able to lock away the dizzying thoughts of oblivion, but every now and again he would have a night when he was unable to sleep, and then the paralysing fear would strike. He would never admit this to any of his crewmates, though, not wanting to appear weak. Instead, he did his best to forget the danger, and he guessed the others did the same. Jack must be suffering intensely to give a voice to his fears.

'How many ops have you got left – eight? Nine?'

'Eight.'

Fitz nodded. He himself had five missions remaining until the end of his tour, the same as his pilot, Greg. However, his crew had been cobbled together from survivors of other aircrews, and he knew most of the men had a few more to go. 'That's not too long. Once you're through, you'll be able to take a cushy post as an instructor and see out the war as safe as anyone. No one can force you to do another tour.' Although all aircrew were volunteers, those who completed their training were required to complete a tour of thirty missions. Once their tour of duty was over, they would be rotated to safer postings, often as instructors. Worryingly few aircrew actually completed their tour, but Fitz hastily dismissed that thought.

'Don't say that. You'll jinx us.'

'I don't see why. We're an experienced crew, and we've got one of the best pilots in the RAF. If anyone can make it through, it's us.' Fitz did his best to inject a confidence into his tone and expression that he didn't feel. Although the most dangerous time for a crew was during the first five missions, there were so many factors completely outside a crew's control that meant even the most experienced crews couldn't ever say they were safe. Fitz's original crew had completed five missions and he had had every confidence in them. If any crew was going to survive their tour, Fitz had been sure it would be them. But then Fitz had been forced to miss a mission due to injury, and that had been the mission from which *Q-Queenie* had failed to return.

'*You* might make it to thirty, but I've got a bad feeling I won't.' Jack spoke in a low voice. 'Ever since Mannheim, I've had nightmares about that night. I can barely close my eyes without seeing that bloody night fighter come roaring out of the dark, right at me, and not a bloody thing I can do about it because the hydraulics were jammed.' He closed his eyes briefly, and for the first time the dark shadows beneath his eyes registered with Fitz. Fitz also noted with concern the sharp angles of his jaw and cheekbones; Jack clearly hadn't been eating well. He cursed himself for not keeping a better eye on his crewmate. Two other crew members had been badly injured on the Mannheim mission and, as Jack had got away with a less serious injury, Fitz had neglected to consider the psychological effects of the whole experience. Being a tail gunner, Jack spent his missions sitting in the most exposed position in a Lancaster bomber – in a Perspex cupola, situated at the very end of the fuselage. When the hydraulics had frozen, it must have been a horrifying experience to see an enemy fighter approaching and not be able to rotate the turret to return fire, or even escape into the relative safety of the main fuselage. Fitz knew that some senior officers considered the bomber crews – who were mostly non-commissioned officers – to be malingerers if they succumbed to the interminable stress of missions and asked to be removed from duty. It was an attitude Fitz despised. It took an extraordinary amount of courage to climb into a Lancaster bomber every night, knowing you might never see the next sunrise. He wondered if he would have volunteered as aircrew if he had truly appreciated the danger.

'Have you thought of speaking to the MO?'

Jack snorted. 'Not bleedin' likely. I don't want to end up seeing one of those trick cyclists.'

The trouble was, Fitz was starting to think that seeing a psychiatrist was exactly what Jack needed. 'It wouldn't be so bad, would it?'

'Are you saying I'm not man enough to stand being on the crew, is that it?'

'Of course I'm not. The fact that you can still climb into a Lancaster after what happened proves you're braver than most men I know.'

Jack subsided. 'Thanks, mate. That means a lot coming from you.'

The two men sat without speaking for a while, although it was a companionable silence. Fitz gazed out of the window and was startled to see fog rolling in. It was looking more likely that operations would be cancelled, and he didn't know how he felt about that. On the one hand it would give them an unexpected free day and a chance for Jack to recover some peace of mind. On the other hand, it would be yet another delay to the end of their tour. Fitz didn't know if it would be better to end it all quickly or whether they should have more time off in between flights.

It was after all yet another delay, and it meant that they would be spending more time on the endless waiting; and it was the waiting that was, to Fitz, the worst part of being in a bomber crew. When there was nothing to do, he found himself dwelling on all the near misses of previous missions and what might happen on the next. When he was in the air, he was able to push his fears to the back of his mind while he concentrated on looking out for enemy fighters and dropping his bombs on the target. It was a bit like stage fright – the worst part was waiting in the wings for his cue. Once he was in front of the audience, he was able to get lost in the performance.

Fitz had become so lost in thought that he'd almost forgotten Jack was there, and he jumped when Jack spoke again. 'What's that going on in the parade ground?'

Fitz peered out. The fog bank hadn't yet obliterated the view and, as the parade ground was not far away, he could make out the features of a man being escorted out in front of what appeared to be a hastily assembled parade. 'Isn't that Mickey Wright?'

'Looks like it. What are they doing to the poor bloke?'

The words had barely left Jack's mouth before it became all too obvious. Under the stern gaze of Group Captain Rhodes, an NCO stepped up to Wright and ripped off his sergeant's stripes and his aircrew brevet. Fitz watched, dry-mouthed in horror, as Wright was then marched to a waiting truck. Neither he nor Jack spoke another word until the truck had departed.

Finally Fitz took a sip of tea to moisten his lips before saying, 'How could they do that to him? I heard he'd refused to fly, but he was clearly ill. He should be under medical care, not paraded like a criminal. He's flown twenty missions, for goodness' sake. He deserves a medal, not that.'

Jack shrugged. 'I know. I don't think he cares at this stage, though. As far as he's concerned, it's his only way out.'

Fitz could only shake his head, helpless in the face of injustice. It took a moment, therefore, to register that Jack was still speaking.

'Lucky sod. At least *he* won't be flying ops again.'

'Is that what you want? To be treated like a coward and lose everything you worked so hard to achieve?' In his shock, Fitz spoke more sharply than he had intended, and he cursed himself inwardly to see Jack go pale and seem to shrink into himself.

Thankfully a distraction arrived in the form of an announcement, informing aircrew that all operations were cancelled due to the fog.

Jack let out a shaky breath. 'If you'd told me before the war that fog would come to be my favourite weather, I'd have laughed in your face.'

Fitz stubbed out his cigarette. 'Let's go to the pub.' Hopefully there he could forget the cruel scene they had just witnessed and try to come up with the right words to help Jack get over whatever was ailing him.

Chapter Three

'Girls, you'll never believe it!'

Thea, who had chosen a seat in the darkest corner of the snug at the White Horse, put down her drink and stared at her sister Pearl, who had just swept in. Her face was so radiant it was as though a searchlight had just shone into the snug. What could have happened? When they had met in the NAAFI the day before, Thea had been distracted by the conversation she'd overheard between the station commander and the MO, but surely she would have noticed if Pearl was this ecstatic. Thea and her friend Leading Aircraftwoman Jenny Hazleton exchanged curious glances as Pearl dropped into a chair and paused to catch her breath.

'Well,' Thea said after a while, 'are you going to tell us, or are you going to make us guess all the unbelievable possibilities until we hit on the right one?'

Pearl fanned her flushed face and drew a deep breath. 'I've just heard from Section Officer Blatchford about my leave application.'

Jenny bounced in her seat. 'Did you get the same week as Greg?'

'Of course she did. She's hardly going to come bursting in here to say otherwise.' Thea winced inwardly at how grumpy she sounded. She was happy for her sister, she truly was. It was just annoying that yet again Pearl's life was perfect whereas Thea's was, as ever, a mess. But the last thing she wanted was for Pearl to realise something was wrong and put on her older

14

sister act, so Thea made an effort to look cheerful and added, 'Come on, then. I'm dying to know.'

Pearl whipped out the dog-eared exercise book she used to take notes for the *Bombshell* and opened it at the back. 'We've both got the first week in May off, which means' – she turned shining eyes on Thea and Jenny – 'the wedding's on the first of May!'

'That's wonderful. I can't believe you're getting married.' Then Jenny's face fell. 'Although that means you'll be leaving Hut Three and RAF Fenthorpe. I'm going to miss you.'

Pearl's expression sobered. 'I'll miss you, too. And Thea. But I won't be far away, and I'll be in and out of Fenthorpe to gather the news.' Until recently, Pearl had been a radio telephone operator at RAF Fenthorpe, but then the newspaper she had started had been a big hit and she had been seconded to work full time to expand circulation to all the Bomber Command stations in 5 Group, which covered a large area in Lincolnshire. Now she was based at the Haughton Newspaper Group offices in Lincoln, although she would be staying in the Waafery at Fenthorpe until she and Greg wed, when they would move into the married quarters at Fenthorpe Hall – assuming Greg was still at RAF Fenthorpe by then.

Pearl tapped the corporal's stripes on her sleeves. 'It feels like everything is changing so fast. I've hardly been at Fenthorpe for a year and already I've passed my NCO training, got the job of my dreams and met the man I'm going to marry.'

Thea mumbled something she hoped sounded encouraging. She tried not to mind that, although Pearl had only been in the Women's Auxiliary Air Force for just over a year, she already outranked Thea, who had joined in 1939. Thankfully she didn't need to say anything more coherent, because a group of WAAFs on a neighbouring table, who had obviously overheard Pearl's announcement, flocked around the corner table to congratulate her. None of them spoke to or even looked at Thea. It was as though she was invisible.

Jenny clearly felt uncomfortable about this treatment, and she did her best to include Thea in the conversation, but Thea shook her head with a wry smile. 'Don't worry, Jenny. I'm used to it.' She raised her voice. 'Everyone with more than half a brain values me, and I couldn't care less about anyone else.' The other WAAFs seemed to have selective hearing, however, for none of them betrayed even with the flicker of an eyelid that they had heard.

To Pearl's credit, although she graciously thanked the WAAFs, she soon afterwards said, 'You must excuse me. I need to discuss my plans with Thea and Jenny.' Once they had drifted back to their table, she turned to Thea, looking annoyed. 'Honestly, did no one read my report? It proves you were innocent.'

'I know. But some people argue that it's in your interest to clear my name, as I'm your sister. And heaven forbid they should let the truth stand in the way of good gossip.' When Pearl opened her mouth to speak again, Thea silenced her with a gesture. 'Leave it, Pearl. I can fight my own battles. And, as you say, we've got a wedding to plan.'

Pearl eyed her for a while as though contemplating saying more, but finally she pulled a pencil from her gas mask case, saying, 'Fine. You're right, we have got a lot to organise. I'm sure this will soon blow over. Now' — she looked from Thea to Jenny — 'first things first. I find myself in need of bridesmaids. Please say you'll both do it. Blatchford promised to make sure you both get forty-eight-hour passes for the weekend.'

'I'd love to,' Thea said, feeling strangely tearful.

At the same time, Jenny said, 'Of course. I've always wanted to be a bridesmaid.'

'Wonderful. I can't think of anyone else I'd rather have than the two of you.' Then the brilliance of Pearl's smile faded as she seemed to brace herself for saying something difficult. 'The thing is... and don't take this the wrong way, Thea...' She tailed off.

'Out with it.' If Pearl was about to say something unwelcome, Thea wanted it out in the open right away.

'Well, I want to ask Jenny to be my maid of honour.'

Jenny's face lit up but her expression sobered when she caught Thea's eye.

Thea would have laughed if she hadn't felt so snubbed. 'I have to ask myself what's the *right* way to react. I'm your *sister*. What do you expect me to say? I'm—' Thea suddenly noticed Jenny, shrinking away as though wishing herself to be anywhere else. Immediately she shut her mouth, feeling like the worst friend in the world. 'Sorry, Jenny. I didn't mean... You'll make a wonderful maid of honour. Pearl's right.'

'But I don't mind—'

Pearl silenced Jenny with a glance and placed her hand over Thea's. 'You might not believe this, but I was thinking of you. I mean, it's going to be a small wedding, obviously, but there are still things the maid of honour will need to organise. And the way people are treating you at the moment... well, it wouldn't be easy. And besides' – she made a clear effort to lighten the mood – 'Jenny's so well read, I'm sure she's come across a book all about the roles and responsibilities of bridesmaids.'

'Not specifically about bridesmaids, maybe, but I did read a book a few years ago about wedding ceremonies down the ages. There was an interesting chapter on the changing role of— oh, you were joking.'

Jenny started to laugh, and the others joined in, breaking the tension of the last few moments.

'That's settled, then,' Thea said when she had recovered. 'Jenny's the best-qualified maid of honour. And you're right, Pearl. As much as I hate to admit it, the way people are treating me at the moment, they wouldn't cooperate if I asked for help with the arrangements.'

Pearl squeezed Thea's hand, her eyes sending a silent thank-you, before straightening up and saying, 'Well, now that's sorted, we've got a wedding to organise in a little over seven weeks.'

'Have you decided where you're having the service?' Jenny hesitated, then added, 'You are having it in church, aren't you?'

Pearl nodded. 'It's all arranged. There was a brief hiccup when I telephoned the Fenthorpe vicar earlier, only to find he can't fit us in on the first of May, but then he told me that RAF Fenthorpe is actually in the parish of St Margaret's in Elmwick. Anyway, to cut a long story short, that's where we're having the wedding.'

'St Margaret's is lovely,' Jenny said, 'And it's not much farther.'

'I know. Greg and I have walked there sometimes, and the church is beautiful. The churchyard is pretty, too, with trees that should be in blossom at exactly the right time.'

Thea had to smile at the sight of her sensible sister going all misty-eyed.

Pearl quickly snapped back to the present, though. 'Greg and I need to meet the vicar as soon as possible, to make the arrangements. We have to act fast, to get the banns read in time.' Then she faltered. 'Assuming Greg's not flying on the evenings the vicar's free. I mean, here we are, planning seven weeks ahead when we don't even know...' She didn't have to finish the sentence.

'Greg's one of our best pilots,' Jenny said. 'If anyone can complete his tour, it's him.'

Pearl gave Jenny a shaky smile. 'I hope you're right. The closer he gets to the end of his tour, the more aware I become of everything that can go wrong.' And she would know, having worked in Flying Control. Before she had been seconded to editing the *Bombshell* full time, she had been one of the WAAFs who guided the pilots in to land at the end of an operation and had been the first to know how many crews had not returned at the end of the night.

Thea caught Jenny's eye, and in that moment they formed a silent agreement that their main role would be keeping Pearl's spirits up while Greg remained on active duty. If Thea remembered correctly, Greg had just five missions to fly before he completed his tour, the same as Fitz. The thought of Fitz made her smile inwardly. After their chat in the NAAFI the day before, she'd frequently found her thoughts drifting in his direction. 'If any crew's going to make it through safely, it's *C-Charlie*'s,' she said, naming Greg's Lancaster. 'Everyone on the ground crew says how well they work together, and we're all putting in extra hours to check and double-check all of *C-Charlie*'s systems. She's in tip-top condition for every flight. Anyway,' she went on, not wanting Pearl to dwell overmuch on Greg's chances of survival, 'I thought we came here to discuss the wedding. What about clothes? Jenny and I will be in our best blues, of course. I suppose you'll wear your uniform for the ceremony too?' Although WAAFs were expected to wear their uniform whether on or off duty, brides could request permission to wear civvies. The trouble was, clothes rationing made it impossible to buy enough fabric to make a wedding gown, which meant brides were resorting to borrowing and altering gowns from friends or family, or simply wearing their best frock. Pearl was always making the sensible choice, so Thea was sure she would choose to marry in her smartest uniform.

Pearl didn't reply for a moment; instead she drew an expanding spiral beside her list, seemingly unaware she was doing so. She had a dreamy expression Thea didn't typically associate with her sister. 'I know you're going to think I'm crazy,' she said finally, 'but Blatchford said I could marry in civvies, and I do so want to wear something special on my wedding day. Nearly everyone there will be in uniform, and brides are supposed to stand out. When I walk down the aisle, I want Greg to see me looking radiant and beautiful, not wearing the same old thing he sees me in every day.'

'You'll look radiant and beautiful whatever you wear,' Jenny said. 'I know what you mean, though. Is there anyone in your family you can borrow a gown from?'

Pearl shook her head. 'Deedee kept my mother's wedding gown, but she was tiny. I'd never get into it.'

'It's true,' Thea told Jenny. 'I crept into Deedee's room when I was ten and tried it on. It was only a little too big for me even then.'

'What about your grandmother?' Jenny asked. 'I bet her wedding gown would have been beautiful. I love the late-Victorian fashions.'

Pearl frowned. 'You know, I don't think I've ever seen a picture of it. I suppose Deedee must have given it away. She never talks about her wedding. I think it upsets her too much because our grandfather died when she was still so young.'

'You're right. I've never thought about it before, but it is strange she never even mentions him.' Thea tried to think of anything Deedee had told her about their grandfather but could only remember her saying how she had lost him before their mother had been born. Having also lost both her parents before she could remember them, Thea never really thought about it; she was used to having been brought up by just her grandmother and older sister.

'That's a shame.' Jenny's mind was clearly still on the problem of a wedding dress. Then her face lit up. 'I've heard of other brides making wedding gowns from parachutes. There are bound to be enough unserviceable ones on the station for us to use.'

'It's a thought, but how are your dressmaking skills?' Pearl asked, looking gloomy. 'I've never made more than a simple skirt, and I don't know if I can afford a dressmaker, even if I could find time to go for all the fittings.'

Jenny pulled a face. 'Same here. I could never make anything more complicated than a lavender bag. What about you, Thea?'

'Forget it. I might be a dab hand at repairing an artificial horizon, but I never had the patience to learn dressmaking.'

Seeing Pearl was starting to look despondent, Thea hastily added, 'I've got tomorrow off. I'll head into Lincoln and make enquiries with some dressmakers. If we pool our money we should be able to afford it.'

'Good idea,' Jenny said. 'I'll have a word with the parachute packers. If anyone can get us some parachute silk it's them.'

Pearl cheered up. 'That would be a great help. I'll pay you back for any costs as soon as I can, of course.'

'Who are you inviting?'

'Not many people. Aside from the two of you, I'm going to ask Deedee and any of my friends from Flying Control and Hut Three who can make it. Oh, and it would be nice if Mr Haughton can come. Greg doesn't have any family in England. I think he's going to ask Fitz to be his best man and invite his crew, but that will be it. That reminds me – I need to ask Norah if she's got a room Deedee can have for a couple of nights and if we can use the snug for a little gathering after the wedding.' Norah was the landlady of the White Horse.

Pearl made to stand but Jenny beat her to it. 'I'll do it. My maid of honour responsibilities start now. Anyone want another drink while I'm at it?' Armed with orders for more lemonade, she went to find Norah, leaving the sisters alone.

'You know, I never thought there would come a day when I would willingly invite you to the pub, nor that you would only ask for lemonade when there.' Pearl regarded Thea with amusement sparkling in her eyes.

'I didn't think Jenny could afford a double whisky.' Thea grinned at the doubt that now shadowed Pearl's expression. She couldn't explain even to herself why she enjoyed needling her sister so much. Finally she relented. 'I'm joking. I take my duties seriously, you know, and my work requires a clear head.'

'I thought you had the day off tomorrow.'

'I do but, if you remember, I offered to go to Lincoln to try and track down a wedding dress, and I want to catch the first bus from Fenthorpe. I take my responsibilities as a bridesmaid seriously, too.'

'Thea, you know you'd have been my first choice as maid of honour if it weren't for—'

Pearl looked so distressed, Thea regretted winding her up and hastened to reassure her. 'I know. Don't fret. You made the right choice.'

Pearl glanced at the other WAAFs in the bar, who were still ignoring Thea. 'I just wish there was something I could do to help you in return. I've told Blanche she's being an idiot, but she won't listen.'

'It's not just Blanche, though, is it. Most of Fenthorpe has branded me a thief.'

'If you ask me, opinion's turned against you because everyone's horrified about what went on beneath their noses, and they want or *need* to see someone punished.'

'But they did – Sheldrick was jailed.' Ian Sheldrick, who had been the station adjutant at the time of the thefts, had finally been caught and arrested thanks to Pearl and Greg's investigation.

'True, but he was taken away from Fenthorpe before anyone realised what had been going on. Everyone was horrified to hear dead aircrews' personal effects had been stolen, and they wanted to lash out at someone. I think they feel guilty that they didn't realise what had been going on. Take Blanche – she works in admin so she worked alongside Sheldrick. I bet she knows deep down you're innocent but is acting out her guilt for not seeing what he was up to. She'll come to her senses eventually.'

'She'd better come crawling to me on her knees when she does, because I won't accept anything less as an apology.'

Pearl frowned and looked like she was going to give Thea a lecture, so it was a relief to see Jenny return at that point. 'All sorted,' Jenny said, placing the three glasses of lemonade on the table. 'Norah says your grandmother can have the best room, and it's above the storeroom, so it shouldn't be too badly affected by noise from the public bar.'

'Oh, she won't worry about that,' Thea said with a grin. 'Knowing Deedee, she'll be at the centre of any commotion.'

Chapter Four

Thea tramped up Steep Hill, hoping that the top would be free of the smothering blanket of fog. Maybe if she caught a glimpse of the sun she would feel better. She couldn't understand why the way she was being treated was getting her down so badly. Usually she couldn't care less what others thought of her. At least she still had Pearl and Jenny, and the crews she worked with didn't seem to believe the accusations made against her. While she might enjoy letting her hair down off duty, she took her work seriously, and her ground and aircrews all appreciated that.

She emerged from her musings when a shop appeared through the mist with bolts of fabric in the window. The sign proclaimed it to be Rigby's General Draper and Outfitter. Fastened to the window was a sign saying: 'The Latest in Utility Patterns'. Another sign advertised dressmaking services. The last two shops she had visited had not been helpful, so Thea pushed open the door feeling unhopeful. She promised herself a treat in one of Lincoln's cafes or tearooms once she had asked within.

The shop assistant, a woman in late middle age, pursed her lips doubtfully when Thea explained her errand. 'If you can provide the fabric, I could make a simple gown in the time available, but if your sister's set her heart on something in white satin or silk your only hope will be if she's set aside the fabric before the war, because you won't find any in the shops. Most brides these days are wearing dresses or suits that can be worn on other occasions because no one can afford to use their clothing coupons on a dress that will only be worn once.'

Not for the first time, Thea wished Pearl had set her heart on a more achievable wedding dress. 'We're trying to get our hands on some parachute silk. Would that do?'

'Yes. It's very thin, though, so you'd need to give me enough silk for an underskirt.'

Thea wondered when Jenny would be able to speak to the parachute packers. 'Assuming we can get hold of some, how soon would you need it?'

'Your sister hasn't given us long to prepare. I only have time because two of my regular customers have recently joined the ATS and so won't be requiring my services until after the war. I'd need to see her next week to take measurements and for her to choose a design, and I'd need the fabric at the same time.'

After arranging to bring Pearl in for a fitting next week, should any parachute silk be available, Thea's rumbling stomach reminded her that she hadn't eaten since breakfast, so she went to find a cafe. She usually preferred the one above Boots, with its string quartet and lively atmosphere, but, after a tiring morning pounding the streets of Lincoln, she couldn't face the hostility of any RAF Fenthorpe personnel who might be there. Instead, Thea opted for the Bishop's Pal, the WVS canteen at the Bishop's Palace. That had comfy chairs and hopefully a quiet corner to hide if anyone from Fenthorpe was present.

As it turned out, there were no Fenthorpe WAAFs at the Bishop's Pal, and she chose a quiet table where she sipped tea and enjoyed a bowl of vegetable and pearl barley soup. She had brought the letter she had started to Deedee the previous evening, and, once she had mopped up the last of the soup with a crust of bread, she pulled it from her pocket, with the intention of finishing it before catching the return bus to Fenthorpe. As usual, she wrote in a breezy tone, glossing over the unpleasantness of being ostracised and instead regaling her grandmother with entertaining anecdotes about life on the station. Then, hoping Pearl had already told Deedee the news about the wedding, she concluded:

Of course, the big news is Pearl's wedding. She's asked me to be a bridesmaid, can you believe that? I'm going to have to behave myself and act responsibly for a whole day. Pearl's set her heart on wearing a pretty dress on her big day, and I can't blame her. WAAF uniform is hardly the most glamorous outfit. She really wants to wear white, and so I've just spent the morning traipsing around Lincoln, trying to find a dressmaker who can make a dress from parachute silk, assuming we can get our hands on some. It's a shame the wedding won't be in Shrewsbury but I do hope you'll be able to come here.

Once Thea had finished, scrawling her name and a line of kisses at the foot of the page, she folded the letter and put it into an envelope, which she addressed, although she left the envelope unsealed. She would hand it in for censoring as soon as she got back.

Unwilling to leave the cosy cafe and return to Fenthorpe just yet, Thea ordered another pot of tea. She made it last while observing the comings and goings of the cafe and listening in to snatches of conversation.

You'll never guess what our Tony said…

Threepence a pound, can you believe it?

And then I said…

There you go, love. And a little extra, seeing as you've got such a pretty smile.

Thea stiffened, a chill trickling down her spine. That last male voice, with its slight Black Country twang, had sounded horribly familiar. She thought it had come from the other side of the room, and she tried to spot who had spoken. Her gaze fell upon a table occupied by two men in RAF uniform. She could only see the face of one of them, and it was no one she recognised. The other man, who was handing money to a waitress, had his back to her. Thea couldn't tear away her gaze. Holding her breath, she willed him to turn his head

25

so she could see his features. The hair colour was the same shade of dark brown, and the height looked about right. But it couldn't be Billy. She was being foolish. It was simply that writing to Deedee had brought her life in Shrewsbury to mind, summoning Billy to her thoughts.

It couldn't be him. Billy Haywood was in prison.

A hand tapped her shoulder, and she jumped, giving a little squeak of surprise. Her heart thudded against her ribs and didn't ease even when she glanced over her shoulder to see Fitz standing there.

'If it isn't Thea Cooper. Anyone would think you were following me around.'

'What are you trying to do to me?' Thea pressed a hand to her chest, waiting for her pounding heart to slow. 'Anyone with half a brain should know not to creep up on a girl like that. When did you get here?'

'Just now. We waved, but you didn't notice. Sorry if I startled you.'

'You must have knocked ten years off my life.' She released a shaky breath and managed a smile, belatedly noticing that Jack Knight was also there. Remembering her manners, she said, 'Care to join me? You can buy me a slice of fruit cake to make amends.' This was the first time she had spoken to Fitz since she had accused him of taking pity on her at Pearl's request, and she was relieved to see he didn't seem to be holding a grudge.

While Fitz and Jack took off their coats and got settled, Thea glanced back at the table occupied by the man who couldn't possibly have been Billy. But both the men who had been there had now gone. She made an effort to give her full attention to Fitz and Jack, chiding herself for her overactive imagination.

She couldn't help noticing that Jack immediately began to tap his fingers on the table. He didn't look comfortable, and she saw Fitz shoot him a concerned glance. 'Is everything all right?' she asked.

'Right as rain,' Jack replied. 'I'm just fed up with this never-ending fog.'

Somehow Thea wasn't convinced by his reply, but, before she could say anything, the waitress arrived at the table. While Fitz gave their order, she watched him, wondering why he had wanted to join her after the way she had snapped at him in the NAAFI. She was glad he appeared to have forgiven her, though, because it was boring sitting alone and yet she couldn't face returning to Fenthorpe just yet.

'It's nice to see you both,' she said once the waitress had left. 'Especially you, Fitz, because I wanted to apologise for biting your head off the other day.'

Fitz shrugged. 'Think nothing of it. I could see you were having a rough day and thought you could use the company.' He gave a crooked smile. 'I obviously picked a bad time.'

'It was, but that's no excuse.'

Fitz hesitated a moment, then seemed to make up his mind. 'As it happens, I *have* been concerned about you. Not because of anything Pearl's said but because I'm angry at how unreasonable people are being. I don't like to see people treated unfairly.' As he spoke, Fitz glanced at Jack, who had yet to enter the conversation and was instead gazing down at his hands on the table.

'Well, I treated *you* unfairly, and I'm glad you can forgive me.'

She couldn't say more, for the waitress returned and laid spoons and placed tea, pots and cups on the table and removed Thea's empty cup. Once the waitress had left again, Thea opened her mouth to say more but, in an uncharacteristic move, Fitz managed to knock his spoon onto the floor. It was an unusually clumsy accident for someone Thea had always considered to be surprisingly graceful.

Fitz swore under his breath and turned to Jack. 'Don't suppose you could go up to the counter and get me a new spoon?' he asked. 'I'm a bit trapped here between the table and the pillar.'

Jack looked at him, startled, as though he had forgotten where he was, but then he recollected himself, rose and went to do Fitz's bidding without a murmur.

As soon as he was out of earshot, Fitz immediately spoke to Thea in a low tone. 'Can I speak to you about Jack?'

Thea, startled by the abrupt change of tone, could only say, 'Why, is something wrong? I thought he was looking rather jumpy.'

'Jumpy's not the half of it.' Fitz's tone was grim. 'To be honest, I dragged him out to Lincoln to try and distract him. Nothing was working until we got here and saw you sitting in this gloomy corner with a face like thunder. Jack said that he wished there was something he could do to help you. I know you don't want anyone's pity, but it would actually do Jack good to think that he's helping somebody else at the moment.'

His tone when he said she didn't want pity was faintly accusatory, and she couldn't blame him. He was right, after all, and if she wanted any friends she was going to have to stop seeing Pearl's hand behind every offer of support.

'Of course I'll help. What's the problem?'

Fitz shot a quick look at the counter. Following his glance, Thea saw that Jack was still trying to get the attention of the busy waitress. Continuing to speak in an undertone, Fitz said, 'He hasn't been right since that incident when his gun turret got jammed. I'm kicking myself I didn't notice before, if I'm honest. Maybe if I had I could have helped him before he got to this state. In the last few days, the stress really seems to have got on top of him. Possibly all the hanging around we've been doing thanks to the fog has given him too much time to think.'

'What makes you think I can help? I'm not exactly renowned for my sensitivity.'

'Because you were so good with Max.'

Thea swallowed, remembering her friend who had been killed the year before. Her throat was suddenly too tight for speech and all she could do was gaze at Fitz as he went on, his expression sombre.

'The whole crew trusts you because of the way you were with Max. He was a sweet kid with a huge crush on you, and a lot of women would've teased him, made his life unbearable, but not you. You were really good with him. You didn't push him away and you didn't lead him on. He always knew exactly where he stood with you and was grateful for your friendship. And you were the best possible friend. You gave him confidence, knowing that he had such a good friend in you.'

Fitz leaned across the table and held Thea's gaze. For some unexpected reason, she felt her heart give a skip. 'So maybe you're not renowned for sensitivity, but you should be. If anyone can help Jack, you can. I don't mean to pressure you and I'm not trying to pass the buck – I intend to stick with him. But when I saw you here it occurred to me that you would be exactly the right person to try and draw him out. There may be some things that he can't say to me because he doesn't want another member of the crew to think he's not up to scratch, or that he can't be trusted to do his job.' Fitz shrugged, looking suddenly helpless. 'I don't know, to be honest, but maybe he needs somebody outside of the crew that he can be vulnerable with, and I think that person could be you.'

'You do realise that if he's suffering from something like' – grappling for the right word, she could only think of a term from the Great War – 'like shell shock, nothing I can say is going to fix that. He'd need professional help.'

Fitz scowled, nodding. 'The trouble is, he refuses to see a doctor. Talking to you would be better than nothing.' There was a pause, then Fitz added, 'He's thinking of going LMF.'

Thea could only stare at him, aghast. 'Lacking moral fibre? He'd really do that after what they did to Mickey Wright? Is he mad?'

Fitz shrugged. 'I only know what he said, but he seemed serious.' He gazed at the table for a moment before saying, 'It's so wrong. Did you see Wright's LMF parade, then?'

'No, but it's all anyone can talk about in my hut. I saw it once at Warrington, though.' Thea felt sick at the memory. 'It

29

was cruel. I couldn't bear the thought of them doing that to Jack. He's no coward, I know that much.' Then she recalled the conversation she had overheard between the station commander and the MO, and related it to Fitz, rounding it off with: 'If Rhodes found out, he'd see Jack humiliated.' She made up her mind. 'What can I do?'

Fitz chewed his lower lip in silence for a moment. Then he brightened. 'Of course, you've got problems of your own.'

'Thanks for the reminder. Did you have to look so cheerful about it?'

'Sorry. That came out wrong. What I meant is that you should ask him for advice.'

'What good would that do? Anyway, if I wanted advice I'd just have to stand within earshot of Pearl for more than five seconds.'

Fitz's eyes twinkled. 'Something tells me you're not a fan of sisterly guidance.'

'Don't get me started.'

'Okay. Back to Jack. I thought that if you shared your worries with him, it would give him a focus beyond his own fear.'

Thea thought about it. 'It might work for a while, but it wouldn't be a cure. He really needs to see the MO.'

'I know, but if he sees you asking for help it might persuade him to do the same.'

'Why?'

'Because a lot of people regard you as a strong, not to mention stubborn, woman who would never dream of asking anyone for help. If you lead by example, he might see that there's no shame in it.'

Fitz thought she was strong? That gave Thea a glow of pleasure – although she chose to ignore the *stubborn* part. However, there was no time for further reflection, for Jack was returning now, spoon in hand.

Fitz leaned across the table and gripped her arm. 'Please do it, for his sake.'

Jack's arrival made it impossible for Thea to answer. He handed Fitz the spoon, casting wary glances between them. 'This looks serious. Do you want me to leave you two alone?'

Thea shook her head. 'I was just explaining to Fitz how I was feeling about being sent to Coventry. I don't suppose you could do me a favour?'

'Anything,' Jack said, and a spark of genuine interest gleamed in his eyes as he took his seat.

'Well, in that case...' Thea leaned across the table. 'Maybe if the others in Fenthorpe saw the two of you actually speaking to me and being nice to me, it might persuade them that I've done nothing wrong.'

Thea had had only a few seconds to think it over, but had concluded that Fitz had a point. She did find it difficult to ask others for support, probably because she'd spent her life avoiding Pearl's constant interference, but she wasn't going to allow her misplaced pride to deny Jack a much-needed friend. While she wasn't naive enough to think she could solve all his problems, she thought that, if she showed she cared for him, it might give Jack the confidence he needed to seek medical help. Because she hated to think what would happen to him if news of his trouble reached Group Captain Rhodes.

Chapter Five

Two days later Thea's thoughts, inevitably, drifted to Fitz and Jack as she stood in front of the large blackboard in the Instrument Section. Elsewhere in the maintenance hangar — so huge that the Instrument Section occupied only a fraction of its space, at the rear — was a cacophony of clanging metal, drilling, several shouted conversations and the ear-splitting din of at least five fitters whistling conflicting tunes. Thea was used to the noise, though. All her attention was on the board.

The board displayed a chalked alphabetical list of all the aircraft at Fenthorpe, indicating which aircraft would be flying ops that night. The fog had finally cleared, and they were clearly gearing up for a major operation; all of the service-able Lancasters were marked, including *C-Charlie*. The sight gave her a sinking feeling, and she hoped *C-Charlie*'s crew would make it through unscathed. Of course, she wanted *all* the aircrews to return safely, but *C-Charlie* was one of two Lancasters she was assigned to, and she naturally knew 'her' crews better than others. And there was Fitz, of course. He had been on her mind a lot since their meeting in Lincoln; she had been impressed by his concern for Jack. Aircrews tended to react in one of two ways when a member of their team showed signs of buckling under the stress: either they would try to get rid of a man they considered a liability or they would support and encourage him. Thea had been pleased to see Fitz was in the latter group.

'Get your head out of the clouds, Cooper!'

Thea jumped. Somehow Flight Sergeant George Sedman, the NCO in charge of the Instrument Section, had managed to approach without her hearing. She shot him a cheeky grin. 'I was concentrating on the board until you rudely interrupted me, Sarge.' Thankfully, her fellow 'instrument bashers', as the instrument repairers were called, had also refused to believe Thea was a thief. Consequently, she usually found relief from the malicious whispers while at work, and enjoyed bantering with her team.

'It doesn't take that long to read the board. Have you replaced *C-Charlie*'s artificial horizon?'

'Just finished.'

'Good. Now stop daydreaming, refit *C-Charlie*'s blind flying panel and get cracking on your DIs.'

'I bet I know who she's been dreaming about,' said Ted Dean, another instrument repairer, who had joined them at the board. He waggled his eyebrows at Thea. 'She's been spending time with Jack Knight. You going to the dance with him tomorrow?'

'What dance?'

'The one at Fenthorpe Village Hall.'

'Didn't even know there was a dance.' Her social isolation must have prevented her from learning about it. 'Anyway, even if I was going, I'm not interested in Jack that way.'

'Not what it looked like to me. I saw you with him in the NAAFI yesterday.'

'Because he's my friend. And sometimes friends enjoy civilised conversation. You should try it some time instead of spouting innuendoes.' She had seen Jack in the NAAFI the day before, and he had made a show of inviting her over to his table, staring down all who looked askance at him and loudly proclaiming how glad he was to have bumped into her. She had been grateful to have company instead of having to face down disapproving stares all alone, but she wasn't about to let anyone link her romantically with Jack. Fitz on the other hand... She was startled by a totally unexpected thought popping into her head: she wouldn't mind a slow dance with him.

33

Ted threw up his hands in a gesture of surrender. 'Fine. I get it. You're just friends.'

'Good thing too,' Sergeant Sedman said. 'If I were you, I'd stick to seeing the ground crew. If you're not careful, you'll get yourself a reputation as a chop girl.'

'Chop girl?' Thea had been on her way back to her workbench, but now she swung round to face Sedman, hands on her hips. 'You take that back.' Chop girl was a term for a girl who had had the misfortune to have more than one sweetheart killed in action. 'Anyway, I haven't been out with any aircrew who have died.'

'What about Max last year?'

'As I made it clear at the time, he was just a friend. And a good friend at that. It's cruel to suggest his death was anything but a tragedy. That I had anything to do with it.' This was no longer banter, and she knew she could get into trouble for taking her sergeant to task in this way, but she didn't care. She hated hearing WAAFs labelled as 'chop girls'. Wasn't it bad enough to lose someone close to them, without the suggestion that they were somehow unlucky?

'I know, I know.' Sedman held out his hands in apology. 'I was only teasing.'

'Well, it wasn't very funny.'

'Anyway, if you're going to call anyone a chop girl it would be that Blanche from admin,' Ted put in.

Thea pricked up her ears. 'Blanche? Why – was one of her sweethearts killed?' She felt bad for taking an interest, but she was keen to get any information she could on Blanche, considering she was the one who had spread the false rumours about Thea. Not that she would wish for even her worst enemy to have a boyfriend killed in action.

'Oh yes,' Ted said. 'By all accounts, she fell for a gunner a couple of years ago when she was based in Suffolk, and he was killed. Then when she arrived here she got engaged to a wireless operator from RAF Scampton, but he went for a Burton in February last year, not long before you arrived.'

'How awful,' Thea said.

'I know. It's a wonder any of the aircrews will so much as say hello to her now.'

Even though Thea wasn't Blanche's greatest fan, she wasn't going to stand by while one of her fellow WAAFs was being insulted. 'It's hardly her fault if the man she's stepping out with gets killed, is it? Are you really suggesting that a bomber gets hit by flak or shot down by a night fighter because of a girl one of the crewmen was seeing?'

'You're right, Cooper. We'll have less of this kind of talk, Dean.' The sergeant turned his gaze to Thea. 'Now get a move on. We need those DIs completed as soon as possible.'

'Right you are, Sergeant.'

She went to collect *C-Charlie*'s blind flying panel, complete with its new artificial horizon, and soon she was cycling over to the dispersal bay where *C-Charlie* stood, cradling the awkward instrument panel under one arm. Not for the first time, Thea cursed the long distances between the hangar and dispersal bays. The aircraft being grounded with the fog for the last few days had given the team time to complete all the outstanding repairs. Even so, she would still be pressed for time if she was going to fix the blind flying panel in place and then carry out the daily inspections, or DIs as they were commonly known, and get them signed off. The aircrews still needed to take their Lancasters up for their night flying tests and so time was short. All in all, today was going to be a busy day, because there would be more last-minute jobs to do once her Lancasters returned. She would most likely be working until the crews came to board their Lancs, and then she was also rostered to be on duty in the early hours to meet the aircrews on their return. She would be required to make note of any damage or faults that had developed on the flight, and the day's work would start all over again.

And now there was a new worry, quite besides her anxiety on Jack's behalf, for she couldn't get the news about Blanche out of her head. Was Blanche's nastiness a reaction to her misfortune?

C-Charlie's dispersal bay was a hive of activity. Erks were swarming all over the Lancaster, and the air rang with the sound of shouts, hammering and drills. Elsewhere came the ear-splitting roar from other Lancasters having their engines tested.

Although the men in the Instrument Section all treated Thea as a friend, the rest of the ground crew didn't know her so well and had tended to go along with the gossip. While they didn't get in her way – for that would have impeded her work on *C-Charlie* – nor did they actively help her. Thea did her best to ignore the atmosphere and get on with her work. First of all she had to deal with the instrument panel, and so she climbed up the steps and hauled herself inside the fuselage. The blind flying panel belonged with the pilot's instruments in the cockpit, meaning she had to squeeze forward, avoiding various obstacles on the way.

She never ceased to marvel how the crew made it around the inside of the Lancaster, because the interior was extremely cramped, and the men were much larger than Thea. Often when people heard about planes being shot down, they would wonder why the crew hadn't bailed out. But Thea could tell that, once the crewmen had retrieved and strapped on their parachutes, possibly with their plane in a spin, getting to the escape hatch would be nigh-on impossible. She tried to push all thoughts of crashes and conflict out of her mind and sincerely hoped that Fitz and Jack would have an easy mission tonight. Maybe it would put Jack's mind at ease.

Pulling herself over the main spar, she squeezed into the cockpit and eased herself onto the floor beside the instrument panel. When Thea had first made the transition from WAAF driver to instrument repairer, many of the male erks had commented that a woman couldn't possibly handle such technical tasks. Yet Thea soon proved them wrong, excelling at her tasks, and the men had soon come to see that she had one big advantage over them, which was that her hands and arms were much more slender than theirs and so she was able to reach into the awkward corners when working on an instrument or fixing it into the panel. It was still a tight squeeze, but she knew none of the men could have fitted the instruments as fast as she did.

Once that task was done, she set about the daily inspection. She started by inspecting the remaining instruments on the panel, polishing the glass and ensuring that the needles didn't stick, and also checking that there were no loose connections. Then she collected all the portable oxygen bottles from each crew position and set about the laborious task of carrying them back to the Instrument Section, getting them refilled, and then returning them to the aircraft. That done, she had to check the airspeed indicator. This was a task that required two people, so, calling to one of the erks who had just finished repairs to the airframe, she asked him to keep an eye on the indicator. Then she went outside and, after borrowing a scaffold trolley, climbed up to where the pitot tube was located. This served as the air intake for the airspeed indicator. It was a simple test that required her to blow into the tube to simulate the Lancaster moving through the air. Before the rumours had started, this had always provoked a fair amount of ribald comment from the other men. Now there was total silence.

It wasn't that she particularly enjoyed being the butt of a joke, and she had always had to brace herself for the laughter. But on the other hand, everyone had laughed at the men carrying out the same test, so she had known it wasn't just because she was a woman. It was just that the total lack of comment emphasised her social isolation.

However, she tried not to dwell on it too much. She had a job to do, and it was important that she carried it out to a high standard because the aircrew's lives depended upon her. She also knew she could never look Pearl in the eye again if Greg was killed because of a faulty instrument.

After she had finished testing the airspeed indicator – it passed with flying colours – she soon completed the daily inspection. This meant she could sign off the Form 700, clearing *C-Charlie* for its night flying test.

Part of her wished she could loiter to exchange a few comments with the crew when they arrived, because at least they would speak to her, but her other Lancaster also needed inspecting and time was not on her side. Picking up her bicycle, she rode off to the next dispersal bay.

–

Later that night she stood outside *C-Charlie*, watching the crew scramble off the bus. Before Fitz climbed aboard, she grabbed his arm.

'Look after Jack, won't you?' she said, shooting a glance at Jack, who loitered beside *C-Charlie* to smoke a last cigarette before taking his place on board.

'Of course.'

He turned to go, but Thea grabbed his arm again to stop him. 'Take care of yourself as well.'

For a moment a soft smile eased the lines of worry on Fitz's face. 'I'll do my best.'

For the briefest of moments Thea was overcome with an urge to kiss him. She had no idea where that desire had come from; maybe it was because he looked so worried. She refrained, released his arm and watched him climb aboard, praying that she would see him emerge on his own two feet when they returned. If they returned.

Against all common sense, which told Thea she should get what sleep she could and leave now, she felt rooted to the spot. She watched while each of *C-Charlie*'s engines was fired up one by one. The noise of just one engine was deafening; four was an ear-splitting din. The ground shook, and she felt the rumble through her feet and even in her chest. Added to the engines of the other sixteen Lancasters making their way to the runway, she knew, it was a noise that would be keeping the nearby villages awake.

A lump rose in her throat as *C-Charlie* taxied out of its dispersal point and made its way to the runway. She watched as a green light flashed at the far end of the field, and Lancaster after Lancaster took to the air. She would never fail to be moved by this sight, and her thoughts would be with the crews, Fitz and Jack especially, throughout the long hours before their return.

It was only once the din had faded to a distant rumble that she finally went to collect her bike to cycle back to the Waafery.

A recent and welcome addition to the Waafery was a small hut that had been set aside as a recreation room. As many of the WAAFs worked shifts, it had no set opening hours. It housed a simple room containing a variety of chairs of all shapes and sizes, a coke stove, and several mismatched mugs that the WAAFs had supplied from nearby junk shops. Knowing it would be some time before she could settle to sleep, and not wanting to disturb her hut–mates and give them even more reason to dislike her, Thea crept into her hut on silent feet. She only stayed long enough to pick up her mail, which she had left in her top drawer earlier, not having had time to open it. She took it into the recreation room, or the 'rec' as it was known, and put a kettle of water on the stove. She would make some Horlicks, read her letters, and hopefully by the time she had finished she would be calm enough to sleep.

'Is *C-Charlie* flying tonight?' Thea, who had just picked up a mug to spoon Horlicks into it, nearly dropped it. She had thought she was alone. Spinning round, she saw a figure in a shadowy corner. Her sister, curled up in one of the few comfortable armchairs.

'How long have you been here?' she asked.

Pearl shrugged. 'I'm not sure. I got back at seven and heard that ops were on, but I couldn't find out who was flying. I thought I'd wait here.'

'*C-Charlie* is flying. I've just seen her off.' Abandoning her drink, Thea went to sit beside her sister.

'How was Greg? Did he seem all right?'

Thea hesitated, unwilling to admit the truth, which was that she hadn't even noticed him. She had been so concerned with Fitz and Jack's state of mind to look out for any of the others, but she didn't want to admit that to Pearl. 'He'll be fine,' she said. 'Greg is one of our most experienced pilots. I'm sure there's nothing to worry about.' It was what she had told herself, after all, whenever she had thought of Fitz or Jack.

'I know. But I also know I won't be able to sleep a wink until I know he's safe.' Pearl crossed to the stove, picked up a new mug and shovelled Horlicks inside. 'Are you on duty when they come back?'

Thea nodded. 'What about you? Are you going to help out with the tea?' Many off-duty WAAFs would volunteer to make tea for the returning crews.

'I think so, but I'll tell you one thing.' Pearl gave Thea a weak smile. 'If Greg doesn't come back in one piece, I'll kill him.'

Pearl took her drink back to her seat, and, seeing she didn't seem to be in the mood for a conversation, Thea sat nearby and sifted through her mail, immediately seizing upon a bulky package addressed in Deedee's handwriting. It must contain the latest copies of the *Shrewsbury Mirror*. When she had first joined the WAAF, Thea had been much more homesick than expected and had written to Deedee, asking her to send copies of the local newspaper so she could keep up with the news from home. Of course, as Pearl had worked at the *Shrewsbury Mirror* at the time, it would have been simpler to ask Pearl to send her the newspapers. But for various reasons she had wanted to limit her contact with her sister. When the first copies had arrived, she had devoured them from beginning to end, even reading through the classified advertisements, smiling to herself when she saw a familiar name or street she knew well.

She tore open the package and three issues fell out, together with a long letter from Deedee. Thea put the letter aside to read when she knew she could be undisturbed, but seized the papers eagerly. Although she no longer felt homesick, she still enjoyed reading the news from Shropshire, and it meant that, on the rare occasions when she returned home, she wasn't completely out of touch.

After a glance at the dates, she selected the oldest edition and started to read. She quickly skimmed the front page and, seeing it was mainly concerned with national news and news from the war, all of which she already knew. turned over. She spent more time on the next page, which was more concerned with local news. Seeing the name Phillip Meadows on the main article on the next page made her wrinkle her nose as she remembered what Pearl had said about her rival on the paper – the man who had been given the job that should have been Pearl's.

She read it with satisfaction, knowing Pearl would have made a much better job of the article. The news editor must have been away when the article had been published, because the headline was uninspiring and the article took too long to make its point. 'Should Blackout Be Eased?' the headline asked, making Thea roll her eyes. Of course not. Not unless the people of Shrewsbury wanted to invite all the enemy bombers in Europe to drop their bombs on its streets. The opening paragraphs were clumsy, with needlessly long words and convoluted sentences. Thea's lips curled as she read on, looking forward to telling her sister about her erstwhile rival's less-than-spectacular impact upon the paper. It was only when she reached the third paragraph that she clutched the paper, creasing the pages, rereading it to be sure she hadn't misread it.

> *Unfortunately, blackout restrictions have caused more than one life to be cut off before its time. Only two nights ago, a man was killed when he was hit by a car while crossing Abbey Foregate. The man was later identified as Corporal John Haywood, 29, of Longner Street, Frankwell.*

Thea had to read it three times before she could be sure her eyes weren't playing tricks on her. John Haywood was Billy

Haywood's brother. What were the odds of reading this only two days after thinking she had seen Billy in Lincoln?

Or had she simply noticed the article because she had felt a lingering sense of dread ever since that day? Yes, that had to be it. She read on. And her blood froze.

> *Aircraftman William Haywood, the deceased's brother, told the Shrewsbury Mirror...*

Thea couldn't read any more. She felt sick. *Aircraftman William Haywood.* So Billy was out of prison and in the RAF. Perhaps he really had been in the Bishop's Pal.

Pearl's voice cut across her horrified thoughts. 'I see Deedee is still sending you the *Shrewsbury Mirror.* Anything interesting?'

Thea cleared her throat and did her best to appear nonchalant. 'Nothing much. The usual. You know the sort of thing.'

Evidently her attempt to mask her reaction wasn't working, for Pearl was studying her curiously. 'Are you sure? You look like you've seen a ghost.'

She forced a smile. 'Nothing like that. If you must know, I was wincing on your behalf because I was reading a poorly written article by your best friend, Phillip Meadows.'

Pearl pulled a face and snatched the paper from Thea's hands. 'Let me see.'

'It's on page two.' Thea tensed as Pearl ran her eyes down the page, even while she told herself not to be an idiot. Pearl had never known of Thea's relationship with Billy, for Thea had been careful never to let the two meet, knowing how Pearl would disapprove of him. Quite rightly, too, as it turned out.

Pearl's gaze settled on the article, and her lips curled into a sneer as she read. 'Good grief. If this is the kind of tosh Meadows is turning out, Mr Kingsley must be regretting choosing him over me. I'm itching to take a pencil to this. The fact that a man was killed should have been the headline, not mentioned in the third paragraph. I always thought

Phillip Meadows was a waste of space, and it's nice to have it confirmed.' Then her eyes narrowed. 'Wait a minute. William Haywood? That name rings a bell.'

Thea's blood ran cold. Maybe Pearl had known more than she had let on at the time?

A moment later, Pearl snapped her fingers. 'I've got it. He was convicted for burglary or something. I remember typing up the article. He was sent to prison for five years. I suppose he must have been released early.'

It was on the tip of Thea's tongue to give all the details – he had broken into a stationer's shop, attacked the owner and stolen considerable amounts of cash and valuables. Fortunately for the owner, Billy had been caught leaving the property, thanks to a vigilant member of the public who had seen him breaking in and telephoned the police. If the owner hadn't been found so soon, it was likely Billy would have been tried for murder as well. However, she didn't want Pearl to know that she had been involved with Billy, and knowing all the details of a crime that had happened nearly four years ago was suspicious for anyone who hadn't either known him or been involved in the case in any way. She caught the words in time and merely nodded.

Pearl was still engrossed in the article. 'His brother is quoted here. Listen.' She rustled the paper and read, 'Aircraftman William Haywood, the deceased's brother, told the *Shrewsbury Mirror*, "I was looking forward to spending time with him after serving away from home for some years."' Pearl snorted. 'He makes it sound as though he'd been in the forces instead of in prison. If Phillip had an ounce of journalistic sense he'd have remembered William Haywood's name from the case in 1939. It was big news for Shrewsbury and even got a mention in the national papers. Instead, he just takes what William fed him. Oh, listen to this. He goes on to say: "The people of Shrewsbury are now asking themselves if such stringent blackout regulations are necessary in this part of the country."' She rolled her eyes. 'Honestly, that man is impossible. Phillip Meadows has had a bee in his bonnet about the blackout ever since he twisted his ankle stepping off a kerb. You'd think he would rather avoid having Shrewsbury flattened by bombs, but apparently his minor inconvenience was far more important. And, yes, it's tragic that people have been killed in road accidents, but you only have to look at places like London, Liverpool and Coventry to be thankful Shrewsbury's not considered a strategic location.' Pearl gave a slight shake of the head. 'Anyway, sorry for the rant but my blood still boils whenever I think of how that idiot got the reporter's job instead of me.'

Thea, however, was not sorry for the rant at all. It meant she could steer the conversation away from Billy to safer ground. 'But look what you've achieved since you've been here. You started up a newspaper that's going from strength to strength.' She grinned. 'You should send a copy to your old editor to show him what he missed.'

Pearl's eyes sparkled. 'You and Deedee think alike. She sent Mr Kingsley the first edition that went out to all of 5 Group.'

'Good for her!'

Pearl placed her empty mug on a table and sat up straighter. 'I was mortified, to be honest.'

'Go on. Admit that a bit of you hopes he regrets letting you leave.'

'Maybe a bit.'

And Pearl went on to tell Thea of the lovely letter of congratulations she'd received from Mr Kingsley's secretary, who told Pearl she'd taken great delight in pinning her copy of the *Bombshell* above her desk. Thea listened with half her mind, relieved that Pearl had no inkling of her past involvement with Billy Haywood.

Strange to think she had once been fascinated by him, drawn in by the air of danger that surrounded him. She had never told Pearl of him, knowing her sister would order her not to see him again. Looking back, Thea wondered if half the attraction had been the knowledge of Pearl's disapproval, because she couldn't imagine what she had ever seen in him. She hoped with all her heart that it had not been Billy she had seen at the Bishop's Pal, because the thought of him being nearby filled her with dread.

And what if Pearl met him? Thea shuddered at the thought. She never wanted her sister to learn about one of the darkest times in Thea's life; the reason she had joined the WAAF and left Shrewsbury behind.

Chapter Six

'Essen's straight ahead, Skip.' The navigator's voice, sounding tinny over the intercom, rang in Fitz's ears.

The mission had been mercifully straightforward so far, and Fitz, who had been manning the front gun, had had nothing to do but gaze into the darkness, searching for night fighters that had failed to materialise. Looking ahead, he could now see searchlights stabbing the air and an orange glow on the horizon. The first wave of bombers had already struck, and now it was their turn.

Releasing his gun, Fitz scrambled down the ladder, through the hatch into the bomb aimer's compartment, right in the nose of the aircraft. He settled himself on his stomach on the padded flooring and made a last-minute check of the bombsight and fusing switches, sparing a thought for Thea as he did so. Assuming he came out of this night in one piece, he was going to ask her to the dance in Fenthorpe as a thank-you for keeping the instrumentation in excellent working order.

If there hadn't been a war on, Fitz might have enjoyed the experience of looking down from the bomb aimer's compartment. Set in the lower portion of the Lancaster's nose, it ended in a circular Perspex blister that gave him an excellent view of the ground. Of course, it was dark, but what with Pathfinders' flares, fire from the incendiaries, and the searchlights, there was plenty to see. He closed his eyes briefly, trying to visualise the photographs of the target that he had seen in the navigation and bomb aimers' briefing, then he looked through the bombsight.

'Two minutes till bomb run,' Edwin, the navigator, called.

This was what Fitz was here to do. He pushed all thoughts and worries from his mind. He consciously closed his mind to any lingering memories of Thea, and also didn't allow himself to wonder how Jack was doing in the rear gunner's turret, right at the other end of the Lancaster. It was his responsibility to drop the bombs on target, in this case the Krupps factory in the west of the city. He refused to let himself dwell on the human cost of what he was doing. It had been impressed upon the aircrews in every briefing that hitting their targets would strike a blow against Nazi Germany and would shorten the war. He only allowed himself to think about that.

Through the bombsight, he could see flak bursting all around: vivid, orange explosions that made him flinch. Forcing himself to ignore them, and *C-Charlie*'s violent rocking, he focused on the target.

Don't think about the flak. Don't worry about it. That's Greg's problem, and you know you can trust him. Drawing a shaky breath, he blinked his eyes to clear them. He needed all his concentration now, because it was his job to line *C-Charlie* up precisely over the target, and only release the bombs on top of the Pathfinders' marker flares. If he couldn't see either them or the target for any reason, Greg would have to bank and return to the start of the bombing run, increasing the risk that they would be caught in searchlights and either shot down by night fighters or brought down by flak. The key to survival was to get over the target, drop the bombs and get out as quickly as possible. That's what had kept them alive so far and that's what would keep them alive now.

Edwin's voice continued to count down the time to the bombing run and now they were there: 'Thirty seconds to target!'

It was time for Fitz to take control, and to his relief he had a clear view of the crimson marker flares. He had to trust that the Pathfinders had dropped them in the correct position, for smoke from the fires obstructed his view of any buildings. He called out instructions to Greg: 'Left... left... steady.' Fitz held his breath as he watched the target draw closer to the inter-section of the bombsight graticule. There it was! He pressed the release. 'Bombs away!' he called. Immediately his stomach lurched as *C-Charlie*, free from the weight of the bombs, soared upwards. There followed a tense wait for the photo flash. As soon as it had gone off, and the camera had taken its shot, Fitz had to fling out a hand to steady himself as the Lancaster banked sharply and dived.

'Bombs gone. Jettison bars across. Close bomb doors,' Fitz called.

A trail of anti-aircraft fire followed their erratic course, buffeting the aircraft like an autumn leaf caught in a gale. From Fitz's position, the explosions were happening right in front of his face, making him feel horribly exposed. Beams of white light reached out for them, and Fitz tensed when one search-light passed right in front of the nose. How Greg managed to evade it, Fitz couldn't imagine, but suddenly the searchlights angled in a new direction, and *C-Charlie* had soon left them behind. Fitz felt the tension drain from his shoulders as the flak receded into the distance, and he had just shifted position to reach the bomb bay inspection hatch when a disorienting crash, accompanied by a blinding orange flash, made him fling his arms across his face. Certain the aircraft's nose had been shot out from under him, he grappled for a handhold, expecting to feel himself tumble through the air. Then, as his vision cleared, he saw he was still lying in his prone position safe in the bomb aimer's compartment, with a nasty hole in the Perspex in front of him, but no other damage.

'Fitz, what happened? Talk to me, Fitz.'

Over the ringing in his ears and the wind shrieking into the compartment through the damaged Perspex, it gradually dawned on him that Greg was calling to him via the intercom. 'I'm okay. Boy, that was close. Flak exploded right under the nose. There's a hole in the Perspex.' Levering himself onto hands and knees, feeling more shaky than he cared to admit, he lifted the inspection panel and peered at the bomb racks. 'Bomb bay's empty. I'm coming back up.' Still blinking from the blue zigzags dancing in front of his eyes, his took his position at the front gun. Vaguely aware of Greg ordering the flight engineer to check for any damage, he gazed out into the night sky, waiting for his galloping pulse to settle.

He leaned his head against the Perspex, taking slow, deliberate breaths, forcing himself to calm down. That could have been worse, he said to himself over and over again, still rattled at the narrowness of his escape. It could have been so much worse. He half listened to the talk over the intercom, voices becoming more cheerful the further from Essen and the closer to the North Sea coast they got, although he didn't feel up to joining in himself. He couldn't remember when he had felt more shaken. However, he was glad to hear Jack's voice sounding cheerful and confident. Apart from the freak explosion just now, it had been a remarkably straightforward mission, and Fitz sincerely hoped that this would have reassured Jack, calmed him and convinced him that he could stay the course.

That he wasn't going to crack up.

He didn't know how much time had passed – it could have been a few minutes, or it could have been an hour or more – when he felt a touch on his arm. It was Allan Doughty, the flight engineer. 'Everything seems to be in working order,' he said. 'Looks like you had a lucky escape. When I heard that great bang, I thought the whole front of the plane had blown off.'

'You and me both.' Fitz twisted his head to give Allan a grin, only to be faced with the other man's expression of horror.

'Good grief, what happened to your face? You're covered in blood.'

Fitz raised a hand to his cheek, and was shocked when his fingers came away sticky. He looked at his hand in disbelief. It was gleaming with blood.

'You must've been struck by a splinter when the flak exploded,' Allan said.

Fitz could only shake his head in disbelief. 'I didn't feel a thing.' Funnily enough, now he knew he was bleeding he was suddenly aware that his face was stinging badly.

Alan handed him a handkerchief. 'Hold on a sec and I'll get the first-aid kit.' He moved off, cursing the cramped interior, climbing over the spar and disappearing from view. As the first-aid box was located near the tail, it took him a minute or two to get there and back. 'You're not going to charm the girls with that face,' he said when he returned. Then he opened the first-aid box and started the process of mopping up the blood from Fitz's face.

'Well,' he said finally, once he'd got rid of the worst of the blood and fastened a dressing over the wound, 'it's just a flesh wound, but you should probably get it checked out when we get back.'

Reassured, Fitz felt well enough to return to his gun.

Greg grinned at him. 'If a cut face is the worst that happens on this mission, I'll settle for that.'

Fitz nodded in heartfelt agreement. His crewmates were his family, and his main concern with every op was for them all to return safely. 'At least it means you won't be asking me to take over this time.'

Fitz had initially trained as a pilot and had passed the early stages of the course. However, when it came to night flying he had hated being reliant on the blind flying instruments, and it had been a relief when he had failed that part of the course. He much preferred being the bomb aimer. Yet when Greg learned that he knew how to fly, he occasionally asked him to take over for a few minutes on longer runs, insisting that Fitz get used to the feel of flying the Lancaster in case Greg was ever incapacitated. Fitz prayed such an emergency never arose.

As it turned out, Fitz's injury was the only mishap and they made it to the Lincolnshire coast with no further incident. A golden dawn chased them to Fenthorpe, and Greg executed a perfect landing that made Fitz want to cheer with relief. Once Greg had switched off the engines, Fitz grabbed his parachute and shuffled towards the hatch, feeling as though he wanted to sleep for a week. Despite his exhaustion, his heart gave a little bound when he peered out and saw Thea waiting to greet the crew. He seemed to summon extra energy from somewhere, and climbed to the ground with a spring in his step. He was about to approach Thea when someone grabbed his arm.

He twisted to see who it was, and the curt insult died on his lips when he saw it was Jack. He hadn't seen him for the whole of the flight, which wasn't a surprise considering he was stuck in the rear turret for the entire time. Jack had been grinning but, when his eyes fell on Fitz's face, his expression froze. 'Christ almighty, what happened to your face? Where did all that blood come from?' The colour drained from his own face.

'It's nothing. Just a splinter that hit my cheek when that flak exploded in front of the nose. It looks worse than it is. You know how it is when you cut your face. I nicked myself shaving the other day, and the ablutions looked like an abattoir by the time I'd managed to stop the bleeding.'

Jack gave a smile, but it looked forced. 'It looks pretty bad to me. You should see the medics.'

In truth, Fitz was feeling shaky, although he put it down to reaction from the shock rather than anything serious. But it would be foolish to ignore an injury, so he nodded and promised Jack that he would report to the MO as soon as debriefing was over. He was upset to see that all of Jack's good humour seem to have faded, and did his best to cheer him by adding, 'And after breakfast, of course. You won't catch me missing out on real eggs and bacon.'

Thea's reaction was hardly reassuring. When she saw him, her eyes went wide. 'Good God, what happened to you?'

The only excuse he could give for what happened next was that he was drunk with relief. He wrapped an arm round her shoulders and planted a kiss on her lips, only slightly hampered by the dressing on his face. 'It's serious, I'm afraid. Only one thing can save me now.'

Thea shrugged away his arm. However, he was delighted to see her gaze linger on his mouth before settling on his eyes. 'If you tell me it's another kiss, you'll end up being carried away feet first.' But she was smiling a smile that made the events of the night fade to insignificance.

'I would never be so crass,' he assured her.

Her smile deepened. She had lovely dimples. 'I'm glad to hear it. So tell me what you *do* need.'

'The pleasure of your company tonight, at the village dance.'

–

Thea hummed to herself as she wandered through the cook-house carrying her tray, looking for a place to sit. Seeing Pearl and Jenny, she plonked her tray down on their table and sat on the bench beside Jenny.

'You're looking cheerful this morning.' Pearl herself looked happy, although the smudges beneath her eyes betrayed her lack of sleep. Thea guessed she must look even worse, having been required to wait a long time for the return of her other aircraft, *D-Donald*. The Lancaster had finally limped in with the strag-glers. None of the crew had been killed or injured, although the aircraft had sustained significant damage, and it had taken a long time for Thea to write up a lengthy list of items needing repairs. She had only returned from the Instrument Section a few minutes ago, having been released by Sergeant Sedman to go and get breakfast. Despite the heavy workload, she had been singing to herself all morning, thanks to the unexpected although not unwelcome kiss from Fitz.

Now she gave Pearl a grin. 'I've got a date this evening. Assuming ops aren't on tonight.' Aircrews weren't generally given another mission the same day they'd arrived back from the last one, but Thea decided to make sure. She turned to

Jenny. 'What do you think the chances are? Are we going to get snowed in this afternoon?'

Jenny looked as though she was seriously considering the question. She chewed her mouthful of porridge thoughtfully before saying, 'I don't think it's going to snow. On the other hand, the last forecast I saw predicted the wind would pick up, and we might even see gales.'

Both Thea and Pearl perked up. If the wind got really strong, flying was bound to be cancelled.

'I suppose I shouldn't be glad if ops are scrubbed,' Pearl confessed. 'Greg's got to complete thirty missions, whether it takes another week or a month or a year. And I do so want him to have finished his tour by our wedding.'

'Well, I'm not sorry. I want to have fun tonight – I deserve some every once in a while.' Thea scowled at the food on her plate. 'It would certainly make up for having to eat this slop every morning. I don't know what's worse, the lumpy porridge or the powdered eggs.' She stuck her fork into the eggs, electing to start with the runny goo before it went cold.

Pearl was looking at her with raised brows. 'Who are you seeing? I don't remember you stepping out with any of the men from Fenthorpe.'

'Fitz,' she said, her thoughts drifting yet again to the kiss. The mere thought of it made her lips tingle, and she surreptitiously examined her reflection in her spoon to check there wasn't some tiny insect crawling over her mouth. 'He's taking me to the village dance.'

She had thought Pearl would be pleased. Instead, she muttered, 'Oh, Thea.' It was never good news when Pearl said her name like that. 'Are you sure that's a good idea?' she added.

Thea's good mood evaporated. 'Seriously? Is there anything in my life you don't feel the need to interfere with? What's wrong with Fitz? I thought you liked him.' She dropped her eating irons with a clatter as a thought struck. 'Or is the problem that you *do* like him, and you think I'm going to hurt him. Is that it?'

'Of course not.'

'Then why shouldn't I see him?'

'It's not that I think you would do anything to hurt him, or that he would hurt you for that matter, but he's aircrew. I want you to be happy, and I speak from experience when I say I don't want you to go through the same worry as I do every time they fly.'

'Do you honestly think I would worry any less even if I wasn't seeing Fitz?' Thea demanded. 'I care about everyone on *C-Charlie*'s crew. And *D-Donald*'s, come to that.' Pearl looked like she wanted to speak, but Thea wasn't going to let her. Not until she had said her bit. 'They're my crew, my responsibility. I would feel that way if I wasn't going out with any of them. Or if I was seeing them all.' Then, seeing Pearl's expression, she hastened to add, 'Not Greg, of course. Why shouldn't I go out with whoever I like and have fun? I work long hours, as we all do, and when I'm off duty I want to enjoy myself.'

'I suppose you're right.' Pearl's tone didn't quite back up that comment, but at least she was trying. Thea knew Pearl found it difficult not to interfere in her life; as the elder by six years, she was too used to taking responsibility for Thea. Yet while the sisters had had plenty of arguments on the subject over the years, Thea felt that on the whole Pearl was now much improved and had finally accepted Thea was an adult. Even so, she had found it tough sharing a base with her sister after three years of freedom, and she had to admit that she was glad that Pearl was now working in Lincoln and would move out of Fenthorpe altogether once she was married.

'You know,' Pearl said a moment later in an all-too-innocent tone of voice, 'Greg was taking me out to Lincoln tonight, but maybe we should go to the dance. It sounds fun.'

'Don't you dare—' Thea subsided when she saw how Pearl's eyes sparkled from suppressed laughter. 'Oh, ha ha, very funny. Try and scare me like that again, and you might find yourself with a wedding bouquet full of nettles.'

'I wish I could go, but I'm on duty tonight,' Jenny said.

'I'll tell you all the gossip tomorrow,' Thea promised her. 'Anyway, I don't suppose it will be all that exciting. It's only Fenthorpe, after all, not London's West End. I expect Fitz won't be able to dance for toffee and he'll spend the evening stepping on my toes.'

Chapter Seven

For once in her life, Thea didn't mind being proved wrong. As Fitz whirled her through their first dance together, leading her with startling confidence and skill, she felt all her worries fade away. She forgot everything but the mellow swing music, the blur of lights and faces and the heat of Fitz's hand upon her back. She could almost imagine she was dancing at the Ritz instead of in the cramped village hall, and that the couples occupying the tables were dressed in their finest evening wear and sipping champagne cocktails instead of a decidedly suspect punch that tasted like a mixture of Cherryade and ginger beer.

'Tell me something about yourself that I don't already know,' Fitz murmured in her ear, turning them just in time to avoid a collision with another couple.

Thea was momentarily stumped. 'Like what? I hope you're not expecting me to share my deepest, darkest secrets on our first date. A girl's got to keep an air of mystery, you know.'

'Okay, we'll start with something simple, like your name. What's Thea short for — Dorothea? Theodora?'

Oh, great. He had to start with that one. No one had asked her before, and she'd managed to keep the hideous truth from her friends until now. 'Guess. What name do you think suits me best?'

'Let me see.' Fitz twirled her, taking his time and making a show of looking her up and down with narrowed eyes. When she was securely back in hold, feeling slightly breathless, he said, 'You don't look to me like a Dorothea. Dorotheas are too ordinary and sensible — tweedy. On the other hand, you don't look like a Theodora, either. For some reason, the name Theodora brings to mind a Valkyrie in full armour.

Thea couldn't help herself; she burst into giggles.

Fitz looked alarmed. 'What have I said? Don't tell me you really are Theodora.'

'No, but my Sunday school teacher when I was eight was a Theodora, although she looked nothing like a Valkyrie.'

There was another pause in the conversation while Fitz steered them round a table that jutted into the dance floor, but any hope that the distraction might make him forget the subject died when he said, 'How about Anthea? No, that doesn't look right either.' He chuckled. 'I feel like a character in *Rumplestiltskin*. Give me a clue. It can't be that awful.'

'It is. I'm afraid if I tell you, *you'll* run away.'

'Now why would I run away from the most intriguing woman in Fenthorpe?'

Intriguing. Thea liked that. If he'd called her beautiful, she'd have dismissed it as mere flattery, but his more original choice of word persuaded her that he meant it. She leaned back a little so she could study him. He looked very dashing in his best blues, and the healing cut on his face didn't spoil his looks but only made him more interesting. While he was not particularly tall – he matched her five foot eight inches – with his lithe, athletic figure and long legs he appeared taller. He had grey-blue eyes that contrasted with his dark brown hair and were a perfect match for his uniform, and, when he caught and held her gaze, her insides performed a little swoop. Although she had always thought of Fitz as good-looking, now this knowledge struck her with an almost visceral blow.

'So' – his lips tilted upwards in a lopsided grin – 'do I get to find out your real name?'

'Thea *is* my real name.' Then she relented. After all, there was nothing stopping him from asking Pearl what her name really was, so there was no point in hiding it. 'Let's trade secrets. I'll tell you my full name if you tell me where you learned to dance like this.'

Was that an expression of alarm that crossed his face? But at that moment the song drew to a close, and Fitz dipped her expertly as the last liquid notes of the clarinet faded away. By the time Thea glimpsed his face again, he was smiling with no sign of unease. 'It's a deal.'

'You go first,' she said.

'All in good time. I think you might need a drink for this, and I don't mean that disgusting punch. If you find us a table, I'll get us some real drinks.'

There was a quiet table free in the corner of the hall, and she made a beeline for it. If she was going to be saying her full name out loud, she didn't want anyone else overhearing. Blanche would have a field day if she found out.

Fitz soon returned with lemonade shandies for them both. 'It was that or more punch,' he said, clinking his glass against hers. 'Cheers.'

She took a gulp of her drink, grateful for the refreshment after the dance. 'Now, fess up. I want to know where you learned to dance like Fred Astaire.'

Fitz grimaced and muttered something under his breath. Thea thought it sounded like, 'Wish they'd had whisky.'

'Why? You make it sound like it's some shameful secret.'

'I'm not ashamed. I haven't exactly kept it a secret, although I am worried about how my crew might react if they found out.'

'Why?'

'Because—' Fitz winced, as though he were a driver who had lost control of his car and was now anticipating a crash '—I was a ballet dancer.'

'What – with the tights and make-up and... and the tights?'

Fitz's expression had relaxed as Thea spoke, and now his eyes sparkled. 'You already said that.'

'I know.' For Pearl's twenty-fifth birthday, Deedee had taken both sisters to London to celebrate and had managed to secure them tickets to see the Ballets Russes. While Pearl had enthused over the music and the discipline of the corps de ballet, who had moved in perfect synchrony, Thea's abiding memory was of the tights. The men's tights. Or, rather, what they contained. The performance had been highly educational. Now all she could think of was Fitz, with his long legs encased in clinging fabric. She sincerely hoped he couldn't read her mind, although, judging from his lopsided grin, he had probably guessed the direction of her thoughts.

'Yes, I wore tights. I even wore make-up during performances.'

'Performances? So you were in a company?' Thea made an effort to get her mind off Fitz's legs and associated regions and take an interest in what he was telling her. When he nodded she asked, 'Which one?'

'The Vic-Wells in London.'

Thea was impressed. Even she, with her limited knowledge of dance, had heard of the famous company based mainly at Sadler's Wells. 'I've heard of them. You must have been good.' After the trip to see the Ballets Russes, Deedee had expressed a wish to see more ballet, but then the war had started, putting an end to all such plans. Thea explained this to Fitz now, saying in conclusion, 'Pity we didn't manage another visit to London. I might have seen you.'

'Maybe. I would have been in one of the lesser roles, though.'

'Still, you must have been good to have earned a place at the Vic-Wells.'

'I like to think I was. I'd just made it to principal dancer when the war started.' Fitz's eyes clouded. 'I'd just achieved my dream only to have it torn from me.'

'Did you volunteer straight away, then?'

'Yes. It was a few months before my call-up came through, but I knew I couldn't stay out of the war, even if conscription hadn't been introduced.'

'Do you miss it?'

'Every day, but I don't regret joining the RAF. I need to feel like I'm taking some kind of action to end the war.'

'Have you really told no one on the crew?'

Fitz shook his head. 'I made the mistake of admitting I'd been a dancer during initial training.' He grimaced. 'There were a couple of lads in the group who made my life a misery. Were forever tripping me when we were marching, called me names, that sort of thing. Thankfully I've never run into any of them again. After that, I swore I'd hold my tongue. If I'm honest, it was probably that experience that persuaded me to volunteer as aircrew.'

'That's awful. But your crew isn't like that, I'm sure.' Thea could understand that some men would feel the need to bully anyone who didn't conform to their idea of masculinity, yet she didn't think anyone in Fitz's crew felt that way.

'I'm sure you're right. Maybe I'll pluck up the courage to tell them one day.'

'Will you go back to dancing when all this is over?' Assuming Fitz came through in one piece. But that was a horrible thought, and Thea pushed it away.

Fitz shook his head looking doleful. 'Dancing requires dedication. You have to practise every day. I haven't danced a step or exercised since the day I first put on this uniform. Even if the war ended tomorrow, there would be no going back for me.'

Thea didn't know enough about ballet to dispute this, but she wished she could think of something to cheer him up. After a brief pause, the answer came to her. 'Well, I think it's wonderful you were a dancer, and when Fenthorpe holds another dance I know who'll be top of my list for partner. Anyway, you've fulfilled your side of the bargain, so I suppose it's time to make good on my promise. Shall I tell you my name now, or do you want to try more guesses?'

Fitz's face lit up. 'I nearly forgot. No, I'm all out of guesses. Come on, tell me.'

'Promise you won't laugh?'

'Promise.'

'Very well. I feel like I should ask for a drum-roll. My actual name is' – she paused, milking the moment for all it was worth – 'Athena.'

Fitz choked on his drink. He put down his glass and made an obvious effort to keep a straight face. 'As in the Greek goddess?'

'Sadly, yes. You can imagine the teasing I got at school. And that was just from the teachers.'

'But Thea isn't even short for Athena.'

'I know, but Pearl started out calling me Thena, and it eventually turned into Thea.'

'Were your parents fans of Greek mythology, then?'

'My mother was, apparently.'

'Why apparently? Didn't you ask her?'

'Never had the chance. She died not long after I was born.'

'Oh. I'm sorry. You must miss her.'

Thea shrugged. 'It's hard to miss someone I never knew. Same goes for my father. He died before I was born, which I know sounds suspicious, but it's true.'

'Was he killed in the Great War? That's how I lost my father.'

Thea nodded. 'That's something we've got in common, then. My father was killed a week after he'd returned from leave, but not before he'd left me as a parting gift for my mother.'

'Who took care of you after your mother died?'

'My grandmother. Also Pearl, who acts more like a mother than an older sister most of the time.'

'Ah, that explains a lot about Pearl. It must have been hard for her, losing two parents in such a short space of time. She must have been terrified of losing anyone else.'

Thea stared at him while she struggled to process what he had said. How had that never occurred to her before? Deedee, in her rather vague way, had tried explaining exactly that, she remembered now, but Thea had never truly grasped what she'd meant until now.

There was no chance to ponder it, though, for Fitz spoke again. 'Hang on, how come your sister's called Pearl?'

'What do you mean? It's the name my parents chose for her.'

'I know that. I mean, if your mother was such a fan of Greek myth that she'd call you after a goddess, how come Pearl got such an ordinary name?'

'Ah.' Thea raised her eyebrows significantly. 'Well, it might interest you to know that Pearl is actually her middle name, chosen by our father, who insisted she have a more normal middle name that she could use if she preferred. Sadly, he wasn't around to make the same provision for me.'

'And her first name?' Fitz leaned across the table, his eyes alight.

'That's Pearl's secret to reveal, not mine.' And Thea rather thought Pearl would choose not to. Pearl detested her first name even more than Thea hated Athena.

–

Fitz's heart gave a huge thump when Thea's lips curved into an impish grin. 'You're not even going to give me a clue?'

'Absolutely not. Pearl knows an awful lot of stuff about my childhood that I wouldn't want to become general knowledge. If you want to know her name, you'll have to ask her yourself.'

Fitz couldn't remember the last time he'd enjoyed himself so much. While it was Thea's looks that had first drawn him to her, it was her sense of fun tempered with compassion that made him hope with all his heart that this wouldn't be their last date. He hadn't known what to expect when he'd told her of his dancing career, but her straightforward acceptance had surprised and pleased him. Having her know the truth was a load off his mind.

He realised that he'd drifted off in his own thoughts and noticed Thea giving him a quizzical look. 'So?' she asked. 'Are you going to ask Pearl about her real name?'

'No fear,' he said, recovering himself. 'Although I have to wonder if Greg knows. Won't she have to give her real name when she's making her wedding vows?'

Thea's smile widened. 'You're right! Oh, I can't wait to see her face when I remind her.'

And so the rest of the dance passed in laughter, conversation and more dancing. Fitz had never known an evening like it, where he had so much he wanted to say to her while simultaneously also wanting to drink in every word she said. Thea told him more about her childhood, which seemed mostly to have consisted of escaping school and Pearl's clutches, and he laughed until his sides ached over the stories of the various scrapes she had got herself into. In turn, Fitz described his own childhood with his mother, who was a former dancer herself and now a dance teacher. He spoke of his pride when he had been accepted into Sadler's Wells ballet school and then into the company, and how much he had sacrificed because of having to spend so many of his waking hours in training.

Before he knew it, the last dance had ended and the band started to pack away their instruments.

Confused, Fitz looked at his watch. 'I can't believe it's that time already.' Then a thought struck him. 'You did get a late pass, didn't you?' He had organised one for himself but it hadn't occurred to him to suggest Thea ask for one.

'No, I didn't get a chance.'

'But it's already eleven.' Those without a late pass had to sign in by ten thirty.

Thea was pulling on her coat, looking unconcerned. 'Don't worry about me.' She tapped the side of her nose. 'I never bothered to sign out, you see. There's a hole in the fence behind the Waafery. I'll get in there. Piece of cake.'

Fitz was starting to see that Thea's habit of getting into scrapes hadn't ended when she had left school. He opened his mouth to suggest that maybe she might find her time in the WAAF easier if she didn't break the rules, but then changed his mind. Why spoil a perfect evening? He shrugged on his own coat, then said, 'Come on, Cinderella. Let's get you back before anyone reports you missing.' He offered her his arm.

They strolled up the dark road, chatting about the dance, and, despite the chill wind, Fitz felt cocooned in warmth. The minutes sped by and all too soon he could just make out the dim outline of RAF Fenthorpe's perimeter fence. A little farther on they drew level with an ancient oak tree at a junction with a narrow lane. Its roots must have stretched as far as the edge of the road where they were walking, for Fitz caught his foot on one. He had been holding a torch in his free hand, and the light zigzagged upwards, briefly illuminating a large hollow in the oak's gnarled trunk before he recovered and pointed the torch back by their feet.

'This is where I have to leave you. The hole in the fence is up here.' Thea pointed up the lane.

Fitz couldn't bear the evening to end. 'I'll see you safely in.'

'Oh, but I don't want to make you late.'

'Let me worry about that. I won't have you blundering around these lanes in the pitch dark all alone.'

'Seriously? None of the other men I've been out with were worried about my safety,' Thea said, although she made no more attempts to dissuade him as they turned up the lane.

'Then you ought to choose them with more care.' Fitz was surprised by the flash of jealousy he felt. It was none of his business how many men Thea had gone out with, yet he felt a sudden urge to punch each and every one in the face.

–

Thea wrapped her arm more securely round Fitz's, smiling to herself at the note of jealousy in his voice. 'I feel I should clarify that I haven't been out with many men since coming to Fenthorpe. And I can only pull stunts like staying out late when there are no ops on.'

'Hey, I wasn't implying you shouldn't see anyone else.'

Now it was Thea's turn to feel a twinge of unease. Did that mean Fitz wasn't bothered if she went out with anyone else? Because she suddenly realised that she would care if he carried on seeing other girls. Why was that? What made him different from any of the other young men she had been on dates with? Then it hit her. Fitz hadn't been trying to impress her with talk of his bravery in action or how important he was. Nor had he spoken down to her as though she was nothing more than a pretty face to him. They had talked about real things, such as his career and her parents. And when it had been her turn to speak, he had actually listened instead of waiting for a chance to tell her more about himself.

Thea was starting to realise that she had indeed been seeing the wrong kind of men.

Oh well. In for a penny in for a pound. 'Why would I want to see anyone else,' she asked now, 'when I've met a man who's not only good-looking but also cares enough to see me safely home? Well, safely back to the hole in the fence, anyway.'

Talking of which, here they were. The cluster of hazel bushes behind which the hole was concealed was looming up out of the darkness. In the high wind, the branches, weighed down by heavy leaf buds, rattled like waves crashing on shingle.

Acting on impulse, she grasped both of his hands and faced him, even though she couldn't see his face and he was no more than a dark shape against the starry sky. 'I've really enjoyed this evening and I'd like to do it again if you feel the same way.' Not giving him a chance to answer, she leaned in and kissed him. It started awkwardly, for she missed his lips in the dark, and they ended up bumping noses. But then her lips were on his. A moment later, his arms wound round her back and pulled her close, and for a glorious while nothing existed in the darkness apart from his mouth, hot upon hers, and his hand stroking her spine through the thick layers of her uniform and her coat.

When they finally parted for air, Fitz spoke, and she could hear the smile in his voice. 'Next time I won't spend the walk wondering how to engineer a kiss.'

'You mean there will definitely be a next time?' She felt surprisingly breathless, and hoped she didn't sound as dazed as she felt.

'You can count on it. I can't remember the last time I enjoyed myself so much. Now, where's that gap in the fence? I want to see you safely through before I leave.'

'It's right here.' Thea directed her torch beam to reveal the narrow space between the hazels and the fence. A well-trodden path showed that Thea was not the only one who knew of the existence of the break in the fence. Although she had taken care not to pay the place too much attention in the daylight, when she had first learned of the gap from a WAAF in her hut, in the days before she had been ostracised, she had walked past casually to ensure she knew where to find it and inspected it with surreptitious glances. It had been created by a fallen branch and was concealed by bushes on both sides of the fence, which probably explained why it had survived for so long. It was now possible for an enterprising WAAF to hitch up her skirt and scramble into the Waafery over the collapsed tangle of twigs and wire – as long as she was prepared to risk torn clothes.

On the point of climbing over, Thea turned back, grabbed Fitz by the collar and planted one last kiss on his lips. 'A down payment on what you can expect if you ask me out again,' she said. Then, with Fitz's torch lighting her way, she climbed over. 'Now, run before you get marked down as a late arrival,' she hissed. 'I don't want to wait for you to finish a stint on jankers before we can see each other again.' And she hurried to Hut Four feeling happier than she had done for a long while.

Chapter Eight

If anything, the next day the wind was even stronger. Cycling to the hangar after breakfast, Thea battled a fierce headwind that made it feel as though she was going backwards. When she finally reached the refuge of the Instrument Section, she was alarmed by the creaks and groans emanating from the hangar's structure as the storm tugged it this way and that, and every now and again there were rattles overhead as flying debris struck the roof. It was no surprise that all flying was called off by mid-morning. When Sergeant Sedman announced the news, Thea felt the tension seep from her muscles. Her crews would be safe for another day. *Fitz* would be safe, and perhaps she would see him later.

'NAAFI up!' Corporal Dean called a short while later. Although there was a NAAFI hut at RAF Fenthorpe, it was a long way from the maintenance hangar, and so there was also a NAAFI van that did the rounds of the station, visiting the remoter sections, delivering tea and wads to the personnel who couldn't make it to the NAAFI hut on their breaks.

Sometimes Thea still cycled elsewhere on her breaks, especially if she had arranged to meet a friend such as Jenny. But not even the promise of caviar and champagne in the NAAFI would have induced her to make the cycle ride in this storm. She rushed out with the others and joined the queue.

'Char and a wad, please, Bet,' she said to the fierce-looking lady in the window when it was her turn. Then she took her tea and rock cake back to her bench. As she sat at her bench, dipping the wad into her tea to soften it enough to chew, she wondered what Fitz was doing. She had never been so fascinated by a man before. Until now, dates had meant going to dances or a nightclub, having fun. She had never dreamed that she would enjoy simply sitting and talking to a man before. Or maybe she had never met the right man until now.

She waited with impatience through the rest of her morning for her dinner break. She had already decided not to eat at the cookhouse but to spend some precious money on sausage and chips at the NAAFI. As Fitz was a sergeant, he wouldn't be eating at the cookhouse with the lower ranks but would have his meals at the sergeants' mess. Unless he also chose to eat at the NAAFI. For the first time she was jealous of Jenny who, working in the Met Office, which was situated in a central location, got to see the crews more frequently, especially the navigators and bomb aimers, who would be interested in finding out more about the forecast weather conditions for each mission. Then she remembered that Jenny would be forced to go round all the weather stations on the base to take hourly readings, whatever the weather, and her jealousy faded. At least she was safe and sheltered in the hangar.

Much to Thea's disappointment, there was no sign of Fitz in the NAAFI when she was finally released to have dinner. Thankfully she spotted Jenny sitting at a table by the window with her nose in a book, looking decidedly windswept. 'Mind if I join you, or are you too engrossed by' – Thea squinted at the title of Jenny's book – '*The Principles of Flight*?' She pulled a face. 'Seriously, is that the best way of spending your precious dinnertime?'

'Oh, it's fascinating.' Jenny marked her place with a bookmark and put the book aside. 'Did you know that a wing's cross-section is flat on the underside and curved above to force the air to travel faster over the top of the wing than beneath? It creates an area of relative low pressure over the wing so the air beneath pushes the wings up, creating lift?'

'No, I' – Thea's innate honesty compelled her to amend her answer – 'well, yes, actually I did. I went on a date with a pilot a couple of years ago, and he spent the whole time trying to impress me by explaining it to me. I wasn't impressed, and I never went out with him again.'

'But you do understand the science behind flight, so it wasn't time wasted.'

Thea opened her mouth to argue, only to close it with a snap when she realised Jenny was laughing. 'Actually, lectures on physics aside, I'm glad to see you here. I didn't fancy eating my dinner in silence and being ignored by everyone else. I thought you'd probably be in the cookhouse, but I couldn't face the slop they usually serve.' She pointed at Jenny's plate of sausage and chips. 'I see you had the same idea as me.'

Jenny stabbed one of her sausages and nodded. 'I've spent the whole morning battling through the gale to take the readings, and each round took so long that I had about thirty seconds to plot the data before it was time to go out again. Worst of all, I got hit in the face by a Stevenson screen door when I was trying to open it.' She pointed to a purpling bruise on her cheek. 'After a morning like that, I thought I'd treat myself to an edible meal for a change.'

Thea winced in sympathy at Jenny's bruise. 'I've got some arnica back in my hut. Drop round later if you want to borrow some.'

'Thanks. I will.' Jenny loaded her fork with a generous mouthful of food and chewed with relish. Thea tucked into her own meal, and the two friends ate in appreciative silence for a few minutes.

Finally, Jenny put down her fork with a sigh. 'That's better. I'll have to eat here more often now I've got my promotion.'

'Promotion? I didn't know you were going for it.'

'I wasn't keeping it a secret, but I never got round to mentioning it what with all the fuss around Pearl's wedding. But I had my board the other day, and today I found out I earned my props.'

'That's brilliant! Congratulations. Not that I'm surprised with all the reading you do.' Thea pointed to her own propeller badge on her sleeve, the indicator that she had achieved the rank of leading aircraftwoman, or LACW for short. 'Now we'll have matching uniforms when we're Pearl's bridesmaids.'

Jenny looked pensive. 'It's funny. I've been looking forward to getting this promotion for so long, but now it's happened I feel flat.'

'You shouldn't. You've done really well. Next time you, me and Pearl get a night off together, we'll go out to celebrate.' To Thea's dismay, her suggestion only seemed to make Jenny look more glum. 'Why? What did I say?'

'You said we'd go out with Pearl. But Pearl won't be at Fenthorpe much longer, and I'm going to miss her.'

'So am I.' Thea was shocked by her own admission. Having spent most of her life trying to evade her sister, it was surprising to realise that she actually enjoyed Pearl's company and looked forward to their get-togethers at mealtimes and in the evenings. Then she brightened. 'We'll just have to have the best ever night out with her before the wedding.'

A small smile tugged at the corner of Jenny's mouth. 'I suppose that would be fun.'

'Talking of the wedding, though, how far have we got with the preparations? My Lincoln trip wasn't very successful, although there is one dressmaker who said she would make a dress if we could get material.'

Jenny perked up. 'I nearly forgot. I spoke to one of the parachute packers, and she says the only parachute available at the moment has been bagged by another WAAF for her sister's wedding.'

'How does that help?'

'I found the WAAF who's taking it, and she says her sister's quite petite, and we can have the surplus silk. There'll be enough to make some nice underwear.'

'Great – so as long as Pearl doesn't mind walking down the aisle in her undies, we've got everything sorted.' Thea made a mental note to telephone the dressmaker in Lincoln to cancel the appointment with Pearl. She could simply take in the silk along with Pearl's measurements next time she was in Lincoln. There would be no need for a full fitting to make a simple camisole and French knickers. 'I'm sure Greg wouldn't mind, though.' She stabbed her fork into her last chip. 'So what you're saying is that, apart from underwear, we're no further forward.'

'I suppose not.'

'What are our options?' Thea asked. 'I've been all around the possible dressmakers and shops in Lincoln and there are no second-hand gowns for sale anywhere.'

'I suppose we could try further afield. We might get to Newark or Grantham on a day off.'

'But they're even smaller than Lincoln. If we can't find what we need here, we're unlikely to get anything from there. It's a shame we don't know anyone who would lend Pearl a dress— Ow, what was that for?'

For Jenny had gripped Thea's arm, her eyes blazing. 'Not lend, but hire. I'd forgotten all about it, but I'm sure I read something a while ago in one of the local newspapers. I think there might be someone in the area who has collected a selection of wedding gowns that she's hiring out to brides.'

Thea stared at her friend in exasperation. 'Why didn't you say something before? It would have saved me a wasted day in Lincoln.' Not to mention the unsettling experience when she thought she'd seen Billy Haywood. On the other hand, the day had led to her spending more time with Fitz, so maybe it hadn't been a completely wasted day. 'Oh well, it's good you've remembered it now. Where do we find this person?'

'That's just it – I don't remember. It was just an advert I happened to notice when I was using newspaper to light the stove in the hut. It must have been a few months ago, which is why it didn't really register, because it was before Pearl got engaged.'

Now Thea was regarding Jenny with awe. 'What must it be like to have a brain like yours? I wish I could remember an advert I happened to glance at months ago. It would save me all the studying I have to do every time there's a change to the Lancaster's instruments.'

Jenny's cheeks turned pink. 'It's fine as long as you don't mind having a head stuffed with useless information. Anyway, it doesn't really help, because I can't remember the name of the woman or where to find her.'

'But since it was an advertisement, she might have put it in more than one newspaper.'

'Of course!' Jenny's face lit up. 'There's a whole pile of newspapers in the rec.'

'Excellent. I'll be free this evening, so we can go through them all later. You bring the Ovaltine, I'll bring a slab of Deedee's fruit cake.'

–

Later that evening, Thea sat with Jenny in the rec, mugs of steaming Ovaltine on the table beside them, while they leafed through a stack of newspapers. Two plates bearing nothing but cake crumbs sat beside the mugs. Pearl wasn't there, as she was busy writing an article.

'I never knew it was possible to fit so many advertisements in a single page,' Jenny complained as she ran her index finger down a column. She gave an exclamation of disgust. 'Look how black my fingers are. Archie-vists must spend their lives washing their hands.'

Thea, used to Jenny's habit of mispronouncing words she had only ever read, silently spelled out 'archie-vists' in her mind. Thanks to her brain becoming fixated upon images of arches, it took longer than usual before she hit upon the correct word. 'You mean archivist. Yes, it must be grubby work. Give me a job repairing aircraft any day.'

Jenny snorted. 'I'd rather have blackened fingers than the torn fingernails you're always getting.'

Thea couldn't deny it. She was forever breaking her nails, thanks to her habit of using them to undo tiny screws instead of hunting for a suitable screwdriver. She opened her mouth to reply but then her eyes fell on a small item about two-thirds of the way down the page she was reading. 'Here it is! Listen. "Wedding dresses available for hire. No coupons required. Call Miss Honeycroft on Lincoln 773".'

Jenny snatched the paper from Thea's hand. 'We should call now.'

'But we don't know when Pearl will be free. She's the one who needs to choose the dress.'

'Quite right, too.' Pearl walked in and flung herself into the chair next to Thea. 'If I leave the choice of dress to Thea, I'll end up getting married in some low-cut, slinky scarlet number.'

Thea arched her eyebrows at her sister. 'You'd thank me for it later. Anyway, it depends on how irritated I am with you when I'm choosing. If you'd been interfering too much, I'd go full shepherdess, complete with crinoline, hundreds of layers and flounces decorated with ribbons. Oh, and a bonnet.' She gave an exaggerated shudder. 'It would solve the problem of not being able to get hold of flowers for the bouquet, though, because we could just decorate a shepherd's crook for you with pink and blue ribbons.'

Pearl's response was to give Thea a withering look. Then she turned her back on her sister in a pointed manner and addressed Jenny. 'Dare I take it that you've found somewhere that supplies wedding gowns?'

Jenny handed her the paper, pointing out the advertisement. 'It sounds like she's got a collection of gowns from before the war. It would solve all your problems if you can hire one from there.'

'Wonderful!' Pearl, looking energised, sprang to her feet. 'I'm going to call her right away.' Then she glanced from Jenny to Thea. 'I'd love it if we could all go together. It wouldn't feel right choosing my gown alone.'

'I have a free evening the day after tomorrow,' Jenny said. 'What about you, Thea?'

'That depends if they're flying ops. How's the forecast looking?'

As if in answer, a huge gust of wind shook the hut. Jenny gave the roof an anxious glance before replying, 'There's your answer.'

Pearl dug a handful of coppers from her pocket. 'I hope the telephone box is still standing. Wish me luck.'

About ten minutes later she was back. Her hair was windswept, but she was beaming. 'That's all sorted. I've arranged to see Miss Honeycroft at seven on Tuesday.' She sank back into her chair. 'It'll be a weight off my mind to have a dress organised. I hadn't realised there was so much to do.' She counted off on her fingers. 'I've still got to get underwear, shoes and a veil, and what about a photographer? And a ring?' Her voice was becoming increasingly strained as she went on. 'On top of that, it's nearly a week since we settled the date, yet Greg and I still haven't met the vicar, and there's so much we need to discuss, like hymns and readings, if we're going to have the perfect wedding.'

Thea pulled a face. How could they ever hope to arrange a perfect wedding at short notice and when the whole country was in upheaval because of the war? Pearl had seemed to understand that when she and Greg had first decided to get married, so why the change? At least she had one piece of good news. 'Jenny's managed to get hold of enough silk to make underwear. The dressmaker I found in Lincoln has agreed to do it.'

'Wonderful. Give me the silk and I'll take it myself. I suppose some things are moving forward.' But Pearl's smile quickly faded. She bit her lip, then added in a low voice, as though to herself, 'I just wish I knew for sure when Greg would be free to visit the vicar.'

And suddenly Thea understood Pearl's need to ensure every detail of the wedding was exactly as she wanted. It was because the most important detail – whether or not Greg would survive the last few missions of his tour – was completely out of her control. Organising the wedding was her way of distracting herself from the fear. She squeezed Pearl's arm. 'Tell you what. Why don't I give the vicar a call now and arrange a time? I'll explain Greg's situation and say you'll go alone or with one of us if Greg's flying that night. At least you'll be able to get the ball rolling.'

Pearl gave her a weak smile. 'That's actually a good idea.'

'Don't sound so surprised!' Then she added, 'But have you got any coins left? I spent the last of mine at the NAAFI van earlier.'

'Nice to know some things don't change.' Pearl fished out a few coppers and handed them over. 'Thank you, Thea. I suppose I really ought to start thinking of you as a grown-up.'

Grinning, Thea hurried to the phone box. It was occupied by another WAAF, who seemed to be discussing the entire plot of *War and Peace*. Thea waited as patiently as she could, buffeted by the wind, until she finally snapped and tapped on the glass. The WAAF glanced at her, then, acting as though no one was there, returned to her conversation. Thea was starting to get seriously fed up with being ignored.

Eventually the WAAF must have run out of money, for she replaced the receiver and emerged from the phone box. Thea smiled at her sweetly and said a cheery, 'Thank you!', knowing it would annoy her. Then she went inside, glad to be out of the wind for a while. Picking up the receiver, she spoke to the operator. 'Elmwick Vicarage, please.'

A short while later, she was speaking to the vicar. He proved very understanding when Thea explained the difficulties, and agreed to meet Pearl alone if necessary. 'My son's in the RAF too, so I know how it is,' he told her. 'I'll do everything in my power to make it the happiest of occasions.'

Thea returned to the rec to find Pearl looking happier, thanks to a hefty slice of Deedee's fruit cake. 'It's all arranged,'

Thea told her. 'He can see you tomorrow evening. All you have to do is drag Greg there as soon as possible so you can get the legal stuff out of the way. You know,' she added with a grin, 'give him your names. Your *full* names. You'll have to tell me how Greg reacts when he hears yours.'

Jenny sat up. 'Why?' She grinned at Pearl. 'Have you got an embarrassing middle name?'

'No, she's got an embarrassing first name. Pearl's her middle name.'

'What is it? I'm dying with curiosity here.'

'I can't bring myself to say it,' Pearl said with a pained expression. 'You'll just have to wait and see on the day.'

Chapter Nine

The wind dropped the next morning, and, when Thea returned to the maintenance hangar after completely reinstalling *C-Charlie*'s instrument panel, she was met by Sergeant Sedman. 'Ops are on tonight. Is *C-Charlie* ready for her test flight?'

'Yes, Sarge.'

'Good. I need you on the flight.'

Thea nearly skipped out of the hangar. While some of the other erks complained about joining the crews on their test flights, saying they got airsick, Thea loved the sensation of being in the air. It was a pity, then, that Sedman seemed reluctant to allow her on the test flights, probably because most WAAFs were barred from flying. Even though an exception was made for instrument repairers like Thea, Sedman evidently felt a need to protect her. Thea chafed at his reluctance, knowing as she did that she was better suited to the work than most of the men because she was slighter and more agile, meaning she found it easier to work in the cramped conditions.

When she got back to *C-Charlie* she found the crew already there. Her gaze immediately sought out Fitz, as though there was a magnetic pull between them, and when their eyes met a thrill coursed through her veins. She took a step towards him, hoping for a moment, but the other erk who would be flying with them pulled her aside.

'I'm checking the hydraulics on the rear turret,' he told Thea in an undertone. 'I've told Knight over and over that they're in perfect working order, but he won't accept it. I think he's got the wind up him good and proper.' Then the man grimaced.

'Can't say I blame him. I hate these test flights, don't you? I can never get it out of my head the number of test flights that end in crashes.'

Thea rolled her eyes. 'Not that many. Anyway, I have the greatest confidence in our ground crew. All our Lancs are in tip-top condition.'

'Yes, but there's always pilot error.'

'You're a real cheerful Charlie, aren't you.' She looked for Fitz, and scowled when she saw him climbing into the Lancaster. 'Just concentrate on your work. It'll keep your mind off the likelihood of a mid-air collision.' With that she climbed into the fuselage, glad that she would be working at the other end of *C-Charlie* from the gloomy erk. And closer to Fitz.

She scrambled towards the cockpit, cursing herself for letting the excitement of her budding relationship with Fitz make her forget to look out for Jack. At least now she was on the same flight for half an hour or so, she could try to judge his state of mind.

She stowed her parachute and navigated around the various obstacles and made it to the forward section of the Lancaster, where Greg grinned at her. 'Nice to have you on board. We can find you a paper bag if you think you might need it.'

'You know me. I'll be fine.'

'We should have you on all our test flights,' Fitz called. 'You're the only erk I know who doesn't spend the flight throwing up.'

Thea did her best to ignore the way her heart gave a little thump, and tore her gaze from Fitz. She had a job to do, after all, and she knew that, if anyone complained she had been flirting with one of the crew, Sedman would never let her fly again.

'Strap in,' Greg ordered. 'I don't want the WAAF CO on my case if you injure yourself getting thrown around on take-off.'

Obediently, Thea squeezed back past the navigator's and wireless operator's positions and strapped herself onto the rest bed. Then came the ear-splitting roar as the engines were started up one at a time. The roar only grew louder as Greg taxied to the runway, then opened the throttle, while waiting for the signal to take off. From where Thea was sitting she couldn't see the signal, but suddenly they were speeding down the runway, and she was pressed against the back rest as the speed increased.

'Hold on, Thea,' Greg called. Then they were in the air, and Thea was flung against her harness as *C-Charlie* rose in a steep, climbing turn.

From her seat between the wings, Thea couldn't see out, so she was glad when they levelled out and she could release her harness and go forward to carry out the instrument checks. Her nerves singing, she took a moment to admire the view, with RAF Fenthorpe just one more shape within a broad patchwork of fields, coloured in shades of green, brown and yellow. It was a good thing she was immune to airsickness because *C-Charlie* was being buffeted by the wind, which seemed to be picking up again. As she worked, she was aware of the other crew members carrying out their own checks. The radio operator sent out a stream of Morse into the ether, and, once they reached the coast, Greg gave permission for the gunners to test their guns. Once Thea was satisfied that all the instruments were correctly calibrated and in optimal working order, she returned to her seat. Now her work was done, she paid attention to Jack and how he was getting on in the tail.

'I've put it through its paces,' the other erk was saying, referring to the rear turret, 'and it's in perfect working order.'

'Keep trying,' Jack said. 'There's something wrong, I'm telling you.'

Even across the intercom, which distorted voices, Thea could detect the growing anxiety in Jack's voice. She exchanged glances with Fitz.

'Perhaps I should go back and see what's the matter, Skip.'

He raised his brows, giving Greg a significant look, which told Thea that he must have spoken to him about Jack's state of mind. He would, of course. Greg was not only *C-Charlie*'s skipper but also the oldest crew member, meaning the others tended to take their problems to him. Thea often thought that this trust the crew showed in Greg was one of the reasons why they worked so well as a team and had survived so many missions. Of course, luck was a factor as well, and she could only pray that their excellent teamwork and luck both held out long enough to see them safely through to the end of their tour.

'Go on,' Greg told him.

–

Fitz hesitated when he edged past Thea's position. On the one hand, it would be pretty crowded at the tail end of the aircraft with the extra erk already there. On the other hand, Thea understood the problems Jack was having and might be able to calm him down better than any of the other crew members. 'Actually, Thea, I could use your help... er... checking the valves work on the portable oxygen.' This was the oxygen crew members plugged into when leaving their positions and moving around the aircraft, and it wasn't in use on this flight as they hadn't climbed to a high enough altitude.

Thankfully, Thea didn't question him. Her eyes flashed with understanding, and she unfastened her harness. 'Of course.'

Fitz felt a swell of gratitude that Thea understood him so well.

They found Jack in the rear of the fuselage, still arguing with the hapless erk. 'I'm telling you, it's going to stick. I can feel it in my bones. It will be just like last time.' His fists were clenched at his sides, and Fitz was scared Jack might actually strike the erk in his panic. Panic verging on hysteria.

Greg's voice came over the intercom. 'I need some of you to come forward. There's too much weight at the rear.'

Thea stepped between Jack and the erk and put her hands on Jack's shoulders. 'Come with me, Jack. Let's leave the fitter to give the system another check. He's a good engineer. You know you can trust him.'

Jack pulled himself from her grasp. 'I know nothing of the sort. I've been telling everyone for weeks that there's a fault, but no one will listen.'

His voice was rising, and Fitz knew the rest of the crew must surely realise Jack was in trouble. That wasn't good. The moment the crew suspected one of their number wasn't up to the job, there was a danger that mistrust would creep in, which could have fatal consequences in a life-or-death situation. He knew he had to do something fast.

'You trust me, don't you, Jack?'

Jack, who had looked to be on the verge of shouting at the erk, looked at him in surprise. 'Of course I do.'

'Good. So you go with Thea and give her a hand checking the oxygen valves. I'll take a turn in the rear turret and put it through its paces. If I find something wrong, the engineer will have to believe us.'

Jack's breathing eased fractionally, and he nodded.

Thea tugged his arm. 'Come on, then. I could really use your help.'

Fitz flashed her a grateful look as she led him forward. Then he turned to the erk. 'Let's give this one last thorough test.'

He crawled into the cramped interior of the rear turret and settled onto the seat. Fortunately, he and Jack were of similar heights, so the seat was set at the right height to allow him to see out. It was a lonely feeling, stuck out here at the very rear of the aircraft. He was even facing away from the rest of the crew. Although he had known how exposed a rear gunner must feel, it hadn't truly hit home until now when he was sitting in the turret on a flight. He wondered if the isolation exacerbated Jack's stress. Fitz felt alone when in the bomb aimer's position, but he only had to remain in the belly of the aircraft while on the bombing run. For the remainder of a mission he either manned the front gunner's position, which was close to the pilot and flight engineer, or assisted the navigator. Poor Jack had to stay separated from the crew for the entire flight.

Grasping the control handles, he first rotated the turret to its limits to port and starboard, then elevated and lowered the guns, firing off several rounds as he did so. Seeing no problems – not that he'd expected to – he repeated the process, this time swivelling the turret and raising and lowering the guns at greater speed, trying to imitate the rapid reactions of a gunner in a genuine combat situation. He kept it up for far longer than he considered necessary, ensuring that he had covered all possible combinations of gun and turret rotation. At no point did the hydraulics stick, not by even the tiniest judder. The mechanisms worked smoothly at all times.

In some ways, he wished he could have found something wrong, something he could tell the erk to fix. Jack had become so convinced there was a fault, Fitz doubted he would ever trust the turret completely, and that might lead to a fatal hesitation when they were under fire. He crawled out of the turret with a heavy heart and went to find Jack.

He found him sitting on the rest bed, talking to Thea. He stiffened when his gaze met Fitz's. 'Well? Did you find out what's wrong?'

Fitz shook his head. 'I tried every manoeuvre, Jack. It's all moving perfectly.'

Jack thumped the thin mattress. 'That's bullshit, and you know it.'

Thea moved to intervene, but Fitz stopped her with a hand to the shoulder. 'It's not. I promise you, I tested everything to its limits and I couldn't find anything wrong. You know I wouldn't make this up if it wasn't true. I feel pretty helpless in the bomb aimer's position, you know, so I do know how it feels. The engineers stripped down the entire mechanism after Mannheim, remember, and they're the best at their jobs.'

But Jack wasn't having any of it. 'We were flying much higher when the hydraulics jammed. Maybe it was a fault that only happens above a certain altitude. We should get the skipper to climb.'

Greg must have heard, for he said over the intercom, 'No can do, Jack. You need to trust the engineers. Anyway, we're approaching the airfield, and the wind's really blowing up. Strap in, everyone, this could get bumpy. Fitz and Thea, stay on the rest bed.'

'Whatever you say, Gramps.' Fitz wasn't surprised by the order. The bomb aimer often stayed in this position for safety during take-off and landing; the only difference was that he didn't usually get to hold the woman of his dreams in his arms while doing so. Jack went back to strap into his seat, looking very unhappy. Fitz would speak to him later, but for now he would enjoy the opportunity to sit with his arm round Thea.

They were in a steep descent by this time and, although Fitz couldn't see out from this position, he knew Greg would be lining them up with the runway. Just at the moment he was expecting to touch down, the aircraft swung violently to the side. Thea gave a startled cry as she was flung against Fitz. Fitz tightened his grip on her, not feeling too happy himself. The next second, the wheels made contact with the ground, bounced, then struck the ground again. The Lancaster swerved again, then finally continued in a straight line along the runway and came to a controlled stop. Fitz let out a shaky breath.

'Sorry about that,' came Greg's voice, sounding cheerful and not at all sorry. 'We caught a bit of a crosswind there.'

'Understatement of the year,' Thea muttered as she extricated herself from Fitz's hold, although he was reluctant to let her go. 'Good thing we weren't carrying any bombs.'

When they descended from the aircraft, Fitz was torn between making sure Thea was all right and checking on Jack. His mind was made up when he caught a glimpse of Jack's pale, strained face as he disappeared through the hatchway. After squeezing Thea's arm, he hurried after Jack, who clearly wasn't in the right frame of mind for that night's mission. He just wished he could think of the right words to say, ones which would help.

Before he could catch up with Jack, the crew were greeted with the news that operations had been scrubbed again, thanks to the rising wind. Even though Fitz usually hated it when a mission was called off at this late stage, this time he couldn't help but be grateful. Now maybe he could use the time to persuade Jack to seek help.

Before getting on the transport back to the operations block he hurried to speak to Thea. 'I was hoping we could spend our next free evening together, but I don't want to leave Jack on his own.'

Thea pulled a face. 'I think you're right.' Then she brightened. 'Look, why don't we get everyone together at the Piebald Pony tonight? That way Jack won't be alone, and he won't feel like he's intruding on a date, either.'

'Good idea. I'll ask the others. I'll leave you to invite some WAAFs.'

'I can ask Pearl and Jenny, but no one else is speaking to me, remember?'

'Sorry. I forgot. We really need to do something about that.'

'One thing at a time. Let's see what we can do for Jack first. We'll worry about me later.'

Chapter Ten

This time Thea signed out properly at the guardroom, so there would be no sneaking through the gap in the fence later on. As far as she was concerned, that took half the fun out of the night, but Jenny, who she was with, refused to use the 'back door', as the WAAFs in the know had christened it. Pearl and Greg had their appointment with the vicar of St Margaret's that evening but promised to pop into the pub later if they had time. The rest of *C-Charlie*'s crew, Fitz included, were already at the pub, making the most of an unexpected night off. Thea and Jenny had grabbed a quick bite to eat at the cookhouse when they came off duty and then walked down to the village. On the way, Thea filled Jenny in on her worries about Jack.

'That's terrible,' Jenny said when Thea had finished. 'I wish there was something we could do to help.'

'I don't suppose there's anything in one of those weighty books of yours that would help?'

'Not really. I did read something about shell shock in the last war, but I don't think the lower ranks who suffered were treated well. The officers were diagnosed with shell shock and sent back to Britain for treatment. The Tommies were accused of malingering and shot. It's the same old story. The working classes are always treated as though they have no feelings.'

There was such bitterness in Jenny's voice that Thea stopped and stared at her friend. 'I've never heard you speak like that before.'

'You should try being born into a mining family in the Forest of Dean. I worked in a local mine office, and you should hear how some of the mine owners spoke about the workers, as though they had no more feelings than the pack animals.'

Thea carried on walking, feeling pensive. 'I've always thought of myself and Pearl as working class, but now I see I took so much for granted growing up. I complained when Pearl insisted I stay on at school to do my higher cert, and now I feel guilty because I know you would have given your eye teeth for the chance. Yet you work so hard to make up for the learning you missed out on, and you put me to shame, you really do.'

'What did your grandmother do for a living? I don't think you or Pearl have ever said.'

That gave Thea pause for thought. 'You know, I don't remember Deedee ever working. I mean, she's often got involved volunteering for local charities but I don't think she's ever done paid work. Why has that never occurred to me before?'

'I suppose you take for granted how things are when you're a child.'

'But it should have occurred to me when Pearl left school. Deedee tried so hard to persuade her to stay on after she'd finished her school cert, insisting she didn't need Pearl to start earning money, but she never said where her income came from.'

'Maybe your grandfather left it to her in his will.'

'I suppose he must have done. I've no idea what he did, though. I really must ask Deedee more about him next time I see her.'

'That won't be long, if she's coming for the wedding.'

'She is. I got a letter from her yesterday saying how much she was looking forward to it.' And Thea looked forward to seeing Deedee. She had lived away for over three years now, so she was taken by surprise for the sudden yearning she felt for home. For Shrewsbury's winding streets and the sparkling horseshoe curve of the Severn, and most of all for the comfort of Deedee's company. She longed to curl up on the rug by the fire in Deedee's little cottage and pour out her hurt at the way the other WAAFs were treating her and her worries about Jack and, yes, her hopes about her fledgling relationship with Fitz.

The conversation moved on to wedding business, and Jenny described the parachute silk she'd procured. 'I'll give it to Pearl later, so she can take it to the dressmaker in Lincoln. There might even be enough to make a nightdress.'

Thea half listened, still enveloped in homesickness. The wedding talk did serve to remind her that she would see Deedee at the wedding, and she comforted herself with that.

When they got to the pub they found only Fitz and Jack in the snug; the rest of the crew were in the public bar. They were gathered around the piano, arms round one another's shoulders, singing a rowdy version of 'The Lambeth Walk'. However, when Edwin Holland happened to glance up and saw Thea and Jenny, he nudged his crewmates and they filed out to join the group in the snug. Thea went to the bar to buy herself a ginger beer, then squeezed into a seat at the corner table where Fitz was sitting with Jack.

If anything, Jack looked even more nervy than he had done that morning. An untouched half-pint of beer sat in front of him, and he was picking at a loose button on his jacket, scarcely seeming to notice he was doing it. However, he brightened when he saw Thea, giving her hope that she would be able to distract him from whatever dark thoughts he had sunk into.

That hope was squashed with his first words. 'Thea, you tell him. No one believes me when I say there's something wrong with that rear turret, but you believe me, don't you?'

Thea exchanged glances with Fitz, lost for an answer and feeling helpless.

The look evidently wasn't lost on Jack. He gave the table leg a savage kick, and drinks slopped onto the polished wood. 'I thought you were on my side. I thought you believed me.'

'I *am* on your side. So's Fitz. So's the whole crew, come to that.' Knowing she was bound to regret it tomorrow, she hurried on before Jack could interrupt. 'Look, I promise to speak to our best engineer tomorrow and get him to check out every possible cause for the turret to stick. I'll get him to strip down the whole turret if necessary.'

Jack's fingers closed over the loose button. 'How will you persuade him? You heard the erk today. He said there's nothing wrong.'

Thea twirled a strand of hair around her finger and waggled her eyebrows. 'I'll use my feminine wiles. He'll be putty in my hands.' It was a good thing the flight sergeant she had in mind was one of the few members of the ground crew who was still talking to her.

Jack's scowl faded. Now it was Fitz who looked less than happy.

'What?' she said to him. 'Jack wants my help, and if I have to flirt with every erk on the base to get it that's what I'm going to do. I'd do the same for anyone on the crew.' If it had been any other man she'd been out with, she'd have also pointed out that they'd only been on one date, and neither of them had mentioned anything about not seeing others. Yet Thea felt as though their relationship was deeper than just the one date suggested and, if she was honest, she wouldn't be happy if he flirted with other women, so she held her tongue.

To his credit, Fitz relaxed and said, 'Of course. I'm being a pig. Just… promise you won't enjoy it too much.'

She relented and kissed his cheek, noticing as she did so that the cut he had received over Essen was healing nicely. 'I won't enjoy it at all.'

'You'd really do that for me?' Jack asked. 'I don't want to get you into trouble.'

'I won't. But I'd do it even if it did get me into trouble. Anyway, I manage to get into trouble on my own account enough times, so I'm used to it.'

Jack had released the button now, and looked more at ease. He even managed a faint smile at Thea's comment. 'Thank you.'

He sipped his beer and sagged back in his seat, closing his eyes briefly. 'I can't tell you how much it means to know you and Fitz take me seriously.'

'We all do,' Fitz told him. 'The fact that you can climb into a space no bigger than a barrel every mission makes you one of the bravest men I know. I nearly wet myself the few minutes I was in there this morning, and that was without fighter planes and flak coming at me from all directions. I'll do anything it takes to help.'

Jack gave the first real smile Thea had seen on his face in ages. 'Even flirt with every erk on the base?'

'Absolutely. But I'd keep it a secret from Thea.'

After that, Jack relaxed enough to be lured into a game of darts – *C-Charlie*'s gunners against *D-Donald*'s. This left Thea alone with Fitz in their quiet corner. She did what she'd longed to do all evening and took his hand, threading her fingers through his. Jack responded with a smile, wrapping his arm round her shoulders without letting go of her hand, pulling her to his side. With a happy sigh, Thea rested her cheek against his shoulder.

'Thank you for your help with Jack. It means a lot.'

Thea shifted so she could see his face. 'You take it personally, don't you? Jack's problems, I mean. Why?'

'I'd do the same for any member of the crew.'

The way he said it kindled Thea's curiosity. 'Your crew is really important to you, isn't it?'

'All aircrews are close. We have to work well together or we'd never make it.'

'Yes, but I get the feeling that closeness means even more to you than the others, and I wondered why.'

Fitz gazed into the distance for a moment before replying. 'I've never really thought about it before but I suppose you're right. I think it must be something to do with missing the dance company when I joined the RAF.'

Thea snuggled back against him. Usually when she was going out with a man she craved the excitement of going out dancing and being wined and dined. She'd never expected to find simply sitting and talking as enjoyable as this. 'What was life like in the Vic-Wells?'

'It was like having a family for the first time in my life. I've got my mother, of course, but no siblings. I never really realised it until I joined the company, but I'd been a lonely child.'

Thea considered this. 'I suppose I was lucky to have Pearl. Not that I appreciated it growing up, but it meant I had someone closer to my age than my grandmother.'

Fitz nodded. 'Anyway, joining the Vic-Wells was wonderful. I was with other young people, all working towards the same goal.'

'You must really miss them.'

'I do. But now I have a family again.'

'And you don't want to lose them,' Thea finished for him. It certainly explained why Fitz was so worried about Jack and determined to take care of him.

She would have pursued the subject but, before she could say more, Pearl and Greg arrived, having finished their meeting with the vicar of St Margaret's. They took their places at Thea and Fitz's table.

'It's all arranged,' Pearl said, her face glowing. She snuggled against Greg's side and smiled up at him with an expression that looked far too doe-eyed for Thea's sensible sister. 'I can't believe this is actually going to happen. And do you know what?'

'The vicar's going to take the service dressed as Widow Twankey?'

'Idiot! No, the vicar's next-door neighbours have got a horse and cart they're prepared to let us use on the wedding day. So Thea, Jenny and I can ride in it on the way to the church. I was worried about how we were going to get there.'

After that, Jenny also joined them, and the conversation was dominated by wedding news, and Thea resigned herself to the fact that she and Fitz wouldn't get any more time alone that evening.

However, while she, Pearl and Jenny were deciding the best way to get to Miss Honeycroft's house the following evening, she felt Fitz's warm hand enclose hers under the table and squeeze. She shot him a sidelong glance, and her heart gave a little flip when he smiled a crooked smile that was meant for her alone.

A while later, Jack rejoined them looking much more cheerful, having led *C-Charlie* to a sound victory over *D-Donald*. 'I haven't forgotten that you asked me for help about your problem with the WAAFs,' he said, leaning across the table and addressing her directly.

Thea was forced to disguise a start of surprise by brushing an imaginary strand of hair out of her eyes, for she had completely forgotten about Fitz's request to involve Jack in the problem. Now she smiled at him. 'That's kind, but there's really no need—'

'There is. I said I wanted to help and I will. I've been thinking about it a lot these past few days, and do you know what I've realised?'

This time Thea managed to bite back a sarcastic retort and simply shook her head.

'It was Blanche Dalby who started the rumours, wasn't it?'

'Yes, but she hasn't been as bad as some of the other WAAFs, to be honest.'

'I know, but where she leads others follow.'

'So what do you suggest I do about it?'

'You need to make friends with her.'

'Oh, yes, simple. If she wanted to be friends with me, she shouldn't have spread lies about me.'

'I didn't say it would be simple, but I think if you can win her round she'll use her influence to persuade the others to be friends with you again.' Before Thea could think of any more objections he added, 'I've promised to trust you over the rear turret. The least you can do in return is trust me in this and make an effort with Blanche.'

Put it like that, she could hardly refuse. 'Fine, I'll be nice to her.'

'Good. You never know, she might turn out to be a good friend.'

'And the RAF will fly to Berlin on the back of armour-plated pigs.'

At the mention of flying to Berlin, all the light seemed to drain from Jack's face, and she could have kicked herself. So much for trying to take his mind off flying ops.

She freed her hand from Fitz's and reached across the table to grasp Jack's arm. 'Listen, Jack, do yourself a favour and go and see the MO.'

'Why? I'm not sick.'

Thea didn't have the expertise to try explaining illnesses of the mind, so she tried another tack. 'Look at it this way: Greg's your pilot, right?'

'He was the last time I checked.'

'So the lives of the whole crew depend upon him.'

'Yes, but I don't see what—'

'How would you feel going on a mission if you thought he was on the verge of a breakdown?'

Jack flinched. 'He wouldn't— I'm not—'

She ignored his telling denial and forged ahead. 'You would want him to get help. Partly because you wouldn't be happy knowing your pilot wasn't well enough to fly but mostly because he's a member of the same crew, and you're like family. And nobody would blame him, knowing what he goes through. And the MO wouldn't blame him. He's a good bloke.' She was starting to lose the thread of her argument now. She was finding it hard to make her point without implying that she thought Jack was unfit for duty. In the end she decided to grasp the bull by the horns. 'Look, I'm not saying you're cracking up. All I'm saying is that you've been under extraordinary pressure, doing probably the most dangerous job in the RAF. I'm sure the MO could help you if you let him.'

Jack's gaze dropped to his hands as he appeared to consider her words. He took so long she started to hope she had got through to him, and he would agree to see the MO.

Then he gave a shake of the head and looked up, although he wouldn't quite meet her gaze. 'No,' he said. 'We're all finding it difficult. My problems are no different from anyone else's. I can't expect to be treated any differently.'

'Jack, I—'

It was his turn to cut her off. 'I've only got seven missions left. I can do it. Then I'll be able to take a training job somewhere and have a break from it all.' He smiled, but it looked completely forced. 'In a month or two, we'll all be able to look back on this time and laugh.' He drained his drink, then rose. 'Where are *D-Donald*'s gunners? I can feel a rematch coming on.'

Chapter Eleven

The wind continued to tear through Fenthorpe the next day. Coming straight from Siberia, as Jenny informed them. It brought with it a sharp cold, making everyone forget the early promise of spring and huddle into their greatcoats as they scurried between buildings. There was also something about its unrelenting nature that put the whole base on edge. In the maintenance hangar, people dropped their tools and made more mistakes, and the generally good-natured cursing and banter that Thea had become accustomed to took a more irritable turn. Arguments broke out, and the NCOs were frequently called upon to intervene. Thea herself found her usually nimble fingers were chilled and stiff, making delicate tasks take longer than usual. Sergeant Sedman hovered over her, telling her to get a move on, until she was tempted to snap at him. The only thing that made her hold back was the threat of punishment and being confined to base. That would have meant not seeing Fitz, and Fitz was the one bright light amidst all the gloom. Because the continued gales meant operations were cancelled yet again, and all aircraft grounded, which meant she didn't have to work so late and Fitz would be off duty that night. Even though she had promised to go with Pearl to help choose her wedding dress, she hoped they would be finished in time to meet Fitz later.

Another reason for being glad operations were cancelled was Jack. She hadn't forgotten her promise, and spoke to the flight sergeant in charge of *C-Charlie*'s fitters, persuading him to go over every inch of the rear turret. As she had expected, he found nothing wrong with it, although Jack had not been happy when she told him. His refusal to see the MO and his insistence that he could see out the remainder of his tour worried her deeply. She couldn't forget his agitation on the test flight, and dreaded to think how he would react if anything went even slightly wrong during a mission. Hopefully the continued break would give Jack time to recover his equilibrium, or even allow her and Fitz enough time to persuade him to see the MO.

Overall, though, the enforced break in operations was having a negative effect on the station, and people were increasingly irritable with one another. Probably not the best time to take Jack's advice and attempt to befriend Blanche, Thea mused as she walked into the NAAFI that afternoon to wait for Jenny. Yet she had promised Jack, and she knew it would be easier to have another go at persuading him to see the MO if she could show that she took *his* advice seriously.

As she looked for a free table, she half hoped Blanche wouldn't be there. Her heart sank when she saw her least favourite WAAF sitting next to another WAAF Thea didn't recognise. If they had been deep in conversation, Thea would have held back, knowing an interruption would be unwelcome. However, they were both reading a copy of the *Bombshell* and only making the occasional comment to each other.

With no excuses remaining, Thea squared her shoulders and took a seat opposite Blanche, pretending she had only just recognised her after she had sat down. 'Oh, hello, Blanche. Anything interesting in the paper?'

Blanche didn't so much as glance her way. She turned a page and studied the crossword. The crossword Thea had compiled. After a few seconds of uncomfortable silence, Blanche turned to the girl beside her. 'I wouldn't bother with the crossword if I were you. It's far too simple.'

I won't let her get to me. I won't let her get to me. Thea rose, forcing her frozen features into a smile. 'You know, I've just remembered I told Jenny I'd meet her outside the Watch Office. Sorry to run out on you. It's been a blast.'

How was she supposed to befriend Blanche if the snooty cow wouldn't even speak to her?

She put that question to Jenny once they were on the Lincoln bus. 'I wouldn't bother with her, only Jack seemed so sure making friends with her would be the answer to all my problems,' she concluded.

'He's got a point,' Jenny replied. 'Whatever we might think about her, she's got a lot of cronies who follow where she leads. If she makes up with you, the others are bound to be nicer to you too.'

As this was so similar to what Jack had said, Thea had to acknowledge the idea had merit. 'So I suppose you think I ought to try again?'

Jenny seemed to consider it. 'I do, but you obviously need to come up with a different approach if she won't speak to you at all. What are you going to try next?'

'You're the one who reads all the books. What do *you* think I should do?'

'It's tricky. I mean, I don't understand why she's taken against you in the first place. She works in the admin section, and I'm sure I've heard her say she does the administration for the Committee of Adjustment. So if anyone knows you're innocent, it would be her.' The Committee of Adjustment was the group that took responsibility for removing the personal effects of the aircrews killed or missing in action and returning them to their families. It was Ian Sheldrick, the camp adjutant, who had taken advantage of his position as head of the committee and stolen the money and valuables.

'I had no idea Blanche was responsible for their admin.' Light was dawning in Thea's mind. 'This changes everything!'

Jenny frowned. 'You can't think she had anything to do with the thefts?'

'No. She's far too straight-laced. Much as I would love to see her marched away by the police, I don't believe she's a thief.'

'Then what?'

'Don't you see?' Thea belatedly glanced around the bus, reassuring herself that there were no WAAFs within earshot. 'Having the thefts take place under her nose must have made her uncomfortable. For a start, if she was in charge of typing up the inventories of personal effects sent to relatives, she must be feeling pretty embarrassed that she didn't notice that Sheldrick had fiddled with them. On top of that, along comes Pearl, who's only been on the base for five minutes, and she discovers what's going on and catches the thief. Pearl gets all the glory, and Blanche is left feeling stupid, not to mention scared that people might start wondering if she was also involved.'

Jenny was nodding in understanding. 'And so she pointed the finger at you to keep attention away from her.'

'Someone who is, after all, a known troublemaker,' Thea finished for her.

Jenny's eyes blazed. 'You might get into scrapes, but stealing from the dead? You would never stoop so low. I can't understand why people have swallowed her lies.'

'Well, not everyone's as intelligent as you,' Thea told her, more grateful for Jenny's staunch support than she could say. 'Anyway, I heard she was engaged to a wireless operator from another base who was killed last year before you two arrived. Grief can do funny things to people. Maybe she wasn't thinking too clearly.'

'I still think it's big of you to be so understanding. I don't think I could be, given the same circumstances.'

'I'm doing it more for Jack than for her, but I'm hoping the insight will give me an idea of how to approach her next time.'

There was no more time to discuss her theory, because the bus was now arriving in Lincoln. When they climbed down, Jenny glanced uneasily at the huge cathedral tower that dominated the town from atop the hill. 'I hope the wind doesn't get any stronger. I could almost believe it would bring down the tower.'

Thea patted her arm. 'Don't worry. It's withstood centuries of storms. I don't think it's going to fall down just yet. Come on, let's collect Pearl.'

Pearl had been working in the newspaper offices in Lincoln that day, so they went to wait for her in the foyer, as arranged the previous night. The first person they saw when they walked into the impressive reception area was Thomas Haughton, owner of the Haughton Newspaper Group and the man who funded the *Bombshell*.

'Pearl will be down in a moment.' He smiled at the girls, eyes twinkling. 'Today's a big day. I do hope she finds the perfect gown.'

'I hope so too. We're getting short on time. Not only have we got Pearl panic-stricken with dreams of walking up the aisle, wearing her scruffiest clothes, I've also got Deedee – that's my grandmother – writing just about every day, demanding to know why we haven't organised a dress yet. And believe me, coming from my grandmother that's unusual. She never gets in a tizzy about anything.'

'I think Pearl said your grandmother is coming to the wedding?'

'That's right. I'm really looking forward to seeing her, actually. I haven't been home much since I joined the WAAF.'

'I look forward to meeting her. What did you say her name was again?'

'Deedee. Well, it's really Edith but everyone calls her Deedee.'

'Edith.' Mr Haughton tilted his head with a frown, as though he'd expected to hear another name. As ever when Thea met Mr Haughton, she thought he looked at her as though trying to recall an elusive memory. However, he soon shook off whatever was bothering him and said, 'It was a pleasure meeting you both again. Enjoy your evening.' And he left.

Pearl joined them soon after, and they strolled together up the hill, following the directions Pearl had scribbled on the back of an envelope.

Miss Honeycroft's house was an elegant townhouse near the cathedral. They all glanced at each other, overawed by the size of the house, until Pearl straightened her shoulders and marched up to the door. 'I suppose as this errand is for my benefit...' She grasped the heavy brass ring and knocked three times.

A maid who looked to be no more than sixteen answered the door. 'Have you come to see the wedding dresses?' she asked before Pearl could introduce herself. When Pearl said she had, the girl clasped her hands in delight. 'Oh, this is my favourite thing about working here.' Then she blushed, seeming to remember herself. 'This way, please.'

She led them up a broad staircase that wouldn't have looked out of place in Buckingham Palace, then through a set of double doors into a large drawing room. Several mahogany armchairs, upholstered in green velvet, were arranged around an imposing fireplace. There was also a matching settee with highly polished arms and legs. Although Thea was no expert, she guessed these were genuine antiques. In a large space in front of a wide bay window stood a tall clothes rail on wheels, draped with a huge sheet.

An elegant woman of about fifty rose to meet them as they entered the room. She wore a silk blouse and a calf-length woollen skirt in a dogtooth check that, although simple, screamed class. 'Do come in, my dears, and take a seat.' She waved a long-fingered hand at the armchairs.

Pearl perched on the edge of a chair. Thea did likewise, terrified that the valuable chair would break under her weight.

'I'm Miss Honeycroft. Which one of you is Miss Cooper?'

'I am,' Pearl and Thea answered in chorus.

Pearl laughed and explained, 'We're sisters. I'm Pearl, and my sister is Thea. And this' – she indicated Jenny – 'is our friend, Jenny Hazleton.' Even as she was speaking, her gaze drifted from their hostess to the covered clothes rack.

'A pleasure to meet you all. Now, Pearl, you're the bride, am I right? Stand up, dear, and let me take a look at you.'

Pearl, looking relieved to get out of the chair, sprang up and stood while Miss Honeycroft eyed her up and down, then walked in a circle round her, saying, 'Very good. A nice, trim figure and a small waist. Yes, I've got several gowns that would suit you.' She glanced up at the maid, who hovered in the doorway. 'Anna, please fetch us all some tea.'

Once the maid had left, Miss Honeycroft smiled at Pearl. 'I expect you'd like to see the dresses.'

'Yes please.' Thea got the sense that Pearl would have needed to be physically held back from the gowns if the other woman had delayed any longer.

Miss Honeycroft led them over to the clothes rail and removed the sheet. Pearl and Jenny gave murmurs of appreciation, and even Thea, who had never been one to go starry-eyed over weddings, felt a shiver of excitement at the sight of the gowns. While they were too closely packed to pick out individual details, the sight of flowing lace, silk, chiffon and satin in all shades of white, ivory and cream was a sight to inspire anyone with even the tiniest romantic streak.

'Let me explain how this works,' their hostess said, running loving fingers over a satin ribbon. 'Two years ago, when clothes rationing was introduced, a friend's daughter had terrible difficulty finding a wedding dress. I made enquiries around the city and eventually found a woman who was prepared to lend her a dress. Before I knew it, other friends were asking me to use my contacts to find wedding gowns, and that's when the idea of this service came to me. I've gathered together quite a collection, as you can see, and each gown is available for hire at a very reasonable rate.' She gave a self-deprecating smile. 'I have no need to make money out of this, as my late father provided for me very well. All I really ask is for each bride to cover the costs of cleaning and any alterations required.'

'That's very generous,' Pearl breathed. Then, because she never seemed to stop being Pearl, she said, 'I would love to write an article about you for the *Bombshell*, the newspaper I run for the local RAF bases.'

'I'd be flattered.'

Anna arrived with the tea, so Miss Honeycroft left them to browse through the gowns while she poured a cup for each of them.

'These are all so beautiful, I don't know how to choose,' Pearl said, unhooking a 1920s flapper-style dress and holding it against her.

'Anna's bringing an empty rail in,' Miss Honeycroft called. 'Anything you want to try, hang there. We've got a dressing room set up next door.'

'I almost wish I was getting married,' Thea murmured, examining the flapper dress. 'I quite fancy wearing that one.'

Pearl grinned and put the dress on the empty rail that Anna had just wheeled in. 'Find yourself a fiancé first. Speaking of which, how are things going with Fitz? You two were looking pretty cosy on the walk back from the pub last night.'

Despite the warm glow that enveloped her at the thought of Fitz, faint irritation prickled Thea's skin. Pearl's comment felt a little too much like interference, wanting to know at this early stage how the relationship was progressing. At any other time, she would have snapped at her sister, but she held back, not wanting to spoil Pearl's excitement. 'Things are going well,' she said. 'Although we've only been out on one actual date together, so talk of fiancés is somewhat premature.'

'Who'd have thought it?' Jenny said. 'Thea the tearaway is actually glowing.'

'Put a sock in it, before I talk about you and Edwin. Don't think I didn't notice the two of you together in a corner all evening.'

'He was explaining about astronavigation.'

Pearl rolled her eyes. 'The sad thing is, that's probably quite true.'

'Anyway,' Thea put in, 'we're supposed to be helping Pearl choose her wedding dress.' And definitely not discussing Fitz. Then she caught sight of a gown that completely took her mind off Pearl's meddling. She suppressed a giggle. 'What about this one? I'm sure we can find a crinoline to go with it.' She held up a gown that perfectly matched her 'full shepherdess' description.

'I don't think I'd get through the door in that.' Pearl took the Bo-Peep dress and replaced it on the rail. 'I prefer a more streamlined silhouette.'

Fortunately, there were several that fitted this description, mostly dresses from the 1930s. Miss Honeycroft, who had apparently despaired of the girls joining her for tea, returned to inspect the gowns Pearl had set aside to try. 'All very elegant,' she said. 'You'll look wonderful in any of these. But there's one more you might want to try. Now, where is it?' She searched the rack, a furrow forming between her brows as she evidently failed to find what she was looking for. 'Anna, where's the Edwardian lace gown?'

Anna clapped a hand to her mouth. 'I quite forgot, Miss Honeycroft. I took it into the sewing room to mend a seam and then left it there. One moment, and I'll fetch it.' She scurried out.

'Bring it to the dressing room,' Miss Honeycroft called after her. 'Miss Cooper might as well start trying on her other choices.'

'I feel like a fairy-tale princess,' Pearl said a few minutes later as she gazed at her reflection in one of the several full-length mirrors arranged artfully to give her an all-round view of herself.

Thea was surprised to find herself blinking back tears. 'You look beautiful,' she said, when she could trust herself to speak.

Pearl was wearing a sleeveless gown of sheer white satin. It crossed over the bust and then skimmed her hips before the skirts flared out and pooled in a train around her feet.

Pearl turned in a slow circle, and Thea admired the way the skirts swished around her.

'Is it a bit long?' Pearl asked, taking a few experimental steps.

'It depends on what shoes you wear,' Anna replied. She had returned and hung a dress at the end of the rail, although Thea had been too busy helping Pearl step into the gown to see what it looked like.

'Goodness, I never even thought about shoes. I'll have to do something about that, or I'll end up getting married in my sensible WAAF lace-ups.'

'Oh, we have shoes too. Choose your dress first, then we'll find you shoes to go with it.' Miss Honeycroft came to stand beside Pearl at the mirror. 'You look lovely, but how do you feel about this one?'

'It's gorgeous but I don't think it's quite me. Maybe it's the satin, but it feels too... slinky.'

'Not to worry. There are plenty more to try. I know they'll all suit you, so it's just a matter of picking out one you feel most comfortable in.'

'I can't believe I actually have a choice,' Pearl said while Thea and Jenny unbuttoned her at the back.

'Forget the fabric for a moment, but what did you think about the shape of this one?' Miss Honeycroft asked.

'I love it. Very simple. Very chic.'

'Good.' Miss Honeycroft picked out a dress in oyster chiffon, cut on similar lines to the satin dress. 'Try this.' She looked as though she was having the time of her life.

They worked through the gowns in this way. Pearl looked stunning in all of them, and liked three enough to put them aside on what she called the 'maybe' rack. Yet Thea had the feeling none of the gowns had jumped out at her as being the perfect one. She was sure that Pearl, being Pearl, was telling herself that, with the constraints of clothes rationing, she should be grateful that she had found three dresses she liked well enough to be seriously considering them for her wedding, yet Thea couldn't forget the longing look in her sister's face, and hoped with all her heart that she would find the perfect dress to wear on her wedding day.

Miss Honeycroft seemed to be enjoying herself more and more as the fitting continued. Thea noticed that although she had sent Anna to fetch another dress, she hadn't mentioned it since the maid had returned with it. Thea got the sense that she hadn't forgotten, but was saving it, in the way a child would save her favourite sweets for last.

Only when Pearl had tried all the other gowns, and put four on the 'maybe' rack, did Miss Honeycroft exclaim, 'Oh, did you try the Edwardian lace one yet?' It was said with such glee that Thea knew her suspicions were correct. When Pearl shook her head, Miss Honeycroft said, 'Where did you put it, Anna?' She rummaged through the remaining gowns, even though Thea was positive she knew exactly where it was. Finally she flourished it with a triumphant, 'Here it is.'

Pearl gazed at it, transfixed, and simply said, 'Ohhh!' It was more an exhalation than a word. 'I think that's the one. I *have* to try it on.'

When she finally stood before the mirror and looked at herself in the dress, tears came to her eyes. Thea knew exactly how she felt. The dress was exquisite. It was composed of a mixed lace overdress with a sleeveless silk slip beneath. Thea could have spent hours examining all the patterns in the lace. Some panels were six-petalled flowers in a very open weave, others were of the finest mesh, sprigged with tiny versions of the same flowers. The intricacy of the lace complemented the simplicity of the cut. As Miss Honeycroft had said, the style was clearly Edwardian. The bodice had a high square neck, and the close-cut sleeves fell to just below the elbow. It was high-waisted, with a silk ribbon cunningly woven into the lace and tied below the bust. The skirt hugged Pearl's hips, then gently flared, ending just above the ankle in front and fanning out behind in a short train.

But more beautiful than the gown was Pearl's radiant face. While the colour, a delicate shade of ivory, brought out the warmth of her flawless skin, the glow was all her own. Thea knew she was picturing walking down the aisle in this dress, her eyes on Greg's face.

'This is it,' Pearl said in a husky voice. 'This is the one. I don't need to try the others again.'

'I knew it.' Miss Honeycroft clapped her hands, looking suddenly almost girlish in her delight. 'As soon as I remembered it, I knew this was the perfect dress for you. I do so love to match the right bride to the right gown.'

Pearl's eyes widened. 'Bride. I'm going to be a bride. In this dress.' She reached out to grasp Thea's hand, and Thea, swallowing the lump in her throat, squeezed tightly in response.

Chapter Twelve

'Everything is starting to feel real now,' Pearl said once they were walking back down the hill, arm in arm.

Thea gave a mock scowl. 'You mean you'd been ordering us around on imaginary errands until now?' But she was genuinely happy to see her usually sensible sister almost giddy with delight.

'You know what I mean,' Pearl said. 'Anyway, I can't thank you two enough for finding out about Miss Honeycroft. I couldn't have found a more perfect dress even if I'd chosen the design myself and had it made especially.'

For the dress had fitted perfectly and needed only a minor alteration at the hem. Miss Honeycroft had instructed Pearl to walk around while still wearing the lace gown, then got her to sit and even kneel on a cushion fetched by Anna. 'It's one thing to try on a dress and see how you look standing up, but you'll be moving around, sitting and even kneeling for the blessing,' Miss Honeycroft told Pearl. 'The last thing you want is for a seam to give when you kneel down. Young Anna here is a wizard with a needle, so she'll have no trouble getting the fit exactly right.'

As it turned out, the dress had fitted as if it had been designed for Pearl. It was only when she had picked out a pair of shoes – cream satin peep-toe sandals, decorated with seed pearls – that Anna declared she would need to let down the hem a little to accommodate the three-inch heels. It would be ready in a week, and then Pearl was welcome to collect it, together with the sandals and a veil, which had a headband also decorated with seed pearls that matched the shoes.

Now Pearl tucked her arms through Jenny's and Thea's and declared, 'I think we should celebrate. Where shall we go?'

This was Thea's department, and she knew exactly the right place. 'The Albion Hotel,' she said. 'The bar is nice and classy and will be the ideal place to toast your wedding gown.'

'Not literally, I hope,' Jenny said with a giggle. 'I got a sudden image of us holding the dress up to the fire on a huge toasting fork.'

'Don't even think such a thing.' Pearl looked horrified. 'I can't bear to think of anything happening to something so beautiful.'

'It won't.' Thea led the way to the hotel. 'I knew all that reading was bad for you, Jenny. It's turned your mind.'

When they walked into the Albion, Pearl looked around with approval at the impressive entrance hall with its high columns and sweeping staircase. She was even more delighted with the bar, which was spacious and allowed in light through a glass dome in the centre of the ceiling. 'This is just right, Thea. Thanks for bringing us here. A pub would have been too rowdy, and I did want to celebrate with the two of you before we have to go back to Fenthorpe.'

They ordered tea and, while they waited, Pearl chattered away happily, first about her excitement at finding the dress and then about her ideas for an article featuring Miss Honeycroft's dress hire service. Thea's attention drifted and she let her gaze wander around the room. It was, like most venues in Lincoln, dominated by men and women in air force uniform. As her gaze travelled idly over the men, her heart gave a little skip when she saw the back view of someone who she thought was Fitz, but when he turned she would feel a surge of disappointment as she realised it was a stranger.

This was no good. She was supposed to be enjoying a mild flirtation, not mooning over every man who bore the tiniest resemblance to the man she was seeing. What was happening to her?

But before she could examine her feelings too closely, her heart gave another lurch for an altogether different reason; she saw Blanche sitting at a corner table with another WAAF.

'What's the matter, Thea?' Jenny's voice snapped Thea's attention back to her own table.

Thea gave a discreet nod of the head in Blanche's direction. 'Over there. It's Blanche.'

Jenny's face settled into a determined expression that Thea didn't like at all. 'This is your opportunity. You've got to speak to her.'

Pearl was looking from Jenny to Thea. 'What's all this about?'

Thea, recalling that Pearl hadn't been present when she had explained her theory about Blanche, filled her sister in, finishing with: 'And the thing is, Jack told me I ought to try making friends with her. If it was anyone else, I would have told them where to go, but Fitz and I think Jack might be more willing to seek help for himself if I can give him some confidence by showing him how much I respect his advice.' She winced inwardly when Fitz's name slipped from her tongue. She braced herself for Pearl to say something about how she couldn't go five minutes without saying his name.

But, 'Makes sense,' was all Pearl said. 'Off you go. It's the best opportunity you're going to get.'

'I can't. We're here to celebrate your dress. And anyway, she's with a friend. I should speak to her alone.'

The words were hardly out of her mouth before the other WAAF, the treacherous so-and-so, murmured something to Blanche, left the table and made for the ladies' powder room.

The corner of Pearl's mouth twitched. 'You couldn't ask for a clearer sign than that. Go on, it won't take you long. And there'll be plenty of time to celebrate when you get back.'

Thea made her way towards Blanche's table, thinking that she'd like to give her unknown friend a piece of her mind for leaving the room at that exact moment. She needed time to prepare, to decide the best way of approaching Blanche. But before she knew it, she was standing at Blanche's side, knowing that, whatever humiliation was to come, her sister and Jenny were about to get a grandstand view.

'Hello, Blanche.'

She must have taken Blanche completely by surprise, for she glanced up with a start and, instead of ignoring Thea, she blurted, 'What do you want?'

'I just want to talk.' Seizing her opportunity, she took the newly vacated seat and leaned across the table, compelling Blanche to meet her gaze. Now Blanche had acknowledged her existence, it would be harder for her to ignore Thea. 'I think it's time we ended' – she gave a vague wave of the hand, unable to think of a suitable word to describe the state of their relationship – 'this feud,' she finished. *Feud* wasn't exactly right, for it implied a state of active warfare, but Thea couldn't think of anything better.

Blanche leaned back in her chair as though trying to put as much distance between them as possible and eyed Thea coldly. 'Why would I want to do that?'

'Because you know full well I didn't steal anything. You just don't want to admit to all your cronies that you were wrong.'

If Thea hadn't been sure of herself before, the flicker of unease that flitted across Blanche's expression would have confirmed it. She pressed on, aware that Blanche's friend could return at any moment, and wanting to have her say before they were interrupted. 'The truth is, you're ashamed that Sheldrick was stealing dead men's possessions right under your nose and you hadn't realised it. What's more, you're jealous at all the attention Pearl got when she and Greg caught him, and making me suffer was the only way you could think of getting your own back on Pearl.'

'How dare you! That's a filthy lie. Take that back this instant.'

'No. Because it's all true. And what's more, I think you're ashamed, deep down, because you're not a bad person at heart. You just don't know how to stop now you've started.'

Another twitch at the corner of Blanche's eye, and Thea knew the barb had struck home.

But if she had thought Blanche would cave and beg Thea's forgiveness, she discovered her mistake now.

Blanche rose, shoving her chair back with a force that made the legs screech upon the polished wooden floor. Thea was aware of heads turning in their direction. Blanche pointed a shaking finger at her, and, in the sudden hush that had settled upon the lounge, every word she spoke next could be heard clearly by everyone present. 'Get away from me. I don't want anything to do with you, you... *thief.*'

While Thea wasn't averse to being the centre of attention, she didn't enjoy the walk back to where Pearl and Jenny were sitting, feeling an itch between her shoulder blades as though the gaze of everyone present was burning a hole into her back. 'That went well,' she observed as she dropped into her seat.

–

'She said that in front of everyone?' Fitz was outraged. 'I wish I'd been there. I'd have told her a few home truths.'

Thea opened her mouth to reply, but instead glanced up as a particularly violent gust of wind shook the NAAFI roof. 'I'm relieved ops have been scrubbed again tonight. I hate the thought of anyone going up in that.'

Fitz pulled a face. While it was good to be able to spend time with Thea – he had come straight to the NAAFI on hearing that there would be no flying that day and had been lucky enough to bump into her on her dinner break – he chafed at the inactivity. And whatever the stress of endless waiting was doing to him, that was nothing compared with the strain Jack was displaying. 'I'm certainly thankful to be on the ground during this gale, but I wish I could get these last four missions over with. I'm starting to think we're going to break the record for the longest tour in history.' He bit the corner off his flapjack. 'Anyway, it's not as if I can enjoy all the free evenings when my girlfriend is too busy on duty or dealing with wedding preparations to come out with me.'

Thea's eyes opened wide. 'Is that what I am – your girl-friend?'

Fitz could have kicked himself for blurting that out. He had started to think of Thea as his girlfriend, although he should have asked her how she felt about their relationship rather than assume she felt the same way. He studied her face and was relieved to see that, while she looked startled, she didn't seem displeased. To his relief, the corner of her mouth tilted up in a slow smile. 'That was silly of me,' he said. 'We've never really spoken about it. But I—'

Thea clasped his hand. 'I'd love to be your girlfriend if that's what you really want.'

He couldn't stop his own smile from spreading across his face. 'It is.'

'I'm going to have to keep an eye on you at the wedding then. I don't want the best man sneaking off with the maid of honour.'

'I wouldn't dream of it. Anyway, I've got my eye on the other bridesmaid. Rumour has it she's a bit of a tearaway.'

Thea punched his arm. 'Beast.' But she was laughing, and she took his hand again.

He squeezed her fingers and simply gazed at her in silence for a while, hardly able to believe his luck that Thea, who could go out with any man she wanted, would choose him. It took him a moment to recall what they had been talking about before he had made the girlfriend comment. 'Anyway, back to Blanche. Do you think anything you said got through to her?'

'I doubt it.' Then Thea, who had drawn breath as though on the point of saying something else, broke off and looked at the door. 'Although we might find out. Here she comes.'

Fitz followed her gaze and saw Blanche walking their way. Was it his imagination, or did she colour slightly when her glance wandered in Thea's direction? She swept past, her nose in the air, and, once she was out of earshot, he murmured, 'If it makes you feel any better, I thought she looked embarrassed. She probably realises she's in the wrong but doesn't want to lose face.'

'Her lose face? She's not the one being treated like a thief.'

'I know. I'm sorry.' Fitz dabbed up the crumbs on his plate, wishing he had the solution to her problems. 'I could have a word with her if you think that would help?'

Thea sighed. 'No, but thanks for offering. I think this is something I have to work out myself.' Then she brightened. 'The people who matter stuck with me, and that's all I care about. Anyway, I *am* always getting myself into trouble, so she could just as well have sent me to Coventry for something I *did* do.'

'Like getting in and out of the station through a hole in the fence?'

The smile she gave him in return made his insides do a little swoop. 'Ah, but I haven't been caught doing that yet.' She glanced up at the clock and grimaced. 'Oops. Time to get moving if I don't want to end up on a charge.' She crammed the remains of her flapjack into her mouth and mumbled something that might have been, 'See you later.'

'Wait. Want to come into Lincoln with me tonight? There's a dance at the Assembly Rooms. I don't know who else will be there. Maybe a load of old people, but—'

Thea, who was already on her feet, waved him into silence. Then, once she had swallowed her mouthful, she said, 'I'd love to. And I don't care if we're the only couple under ninety, there's only one man I want to dance with.' She blew him a kiss and walked off, hips swaying. Fitz, his stomach in free-fall, watched her until she had disappeared through the door.

–

Later that evening, after a frantic wash to get the grease from her fingernails, Thea was dressed in her best blues and waiting in the NAAFI for Fitz to meet her. Although she sat alone, this time it was by choice and not because no one would talk to her. She had a crossword to compile and, if she didn't have it ready by dinnertime tomorrow, Pearl was going to be furious.

When she had first volunteered to compile a crossword for each edition of the *Bombshell*, she hadn't known what she was letting herself in for. She had to draw up a grid, find words to fit into each space and then make up a clue for each word ranging from easy to downright fiendish. She wanted to ensure that people attempting her crosswords felt a sense of achievement when completing them, yet didn't get frustrated by having too many difficult or ambiguous clues. To her surprise, she had found that she enjoyed the work, as it helped her forget the stresses of working on an operational bomber station for a while.

Now, with her exercise book open in front of her, she sat with her pencil poised over the page, trying to come up with a good clue for 'Harvest'. A sensation of being watched by hostile eyes made her look up, and she wasn't at all surprised to see Blanche settling at a nearby table. Although Blanche wasn't looking her way, Thea had the feeling she had only just glanced away. Blanche, it seemed, had not forgiven her for the little scene at the hotel.

While Thea noticed several people looking from her to Blanche and back again, as though waiting for the explosion, one man had eyes only for Blanche: Sam Drinkwater, *D-Donald*'s flight engineer. Interesting. It looked like Blanche had an admirer. And judging from the way Blanche blushed when she caught Sam looking, she felt the same way about him.

Fitz's arrival cast all other romances in the shade, and she smiled up at him joyfully, focusing all her attention on her own happiness. Fitz, however, had evidently picked up on the continued tension between her and Blanche. 'You two still haven't buried the hatchet, I take it?'

'Not yet, although Blanche looks like she'd like to bury it in my head.' She rose and wove her fingers through Fitz's.

'Anyway, we have an evening to ourselves, and who knows how long this weather will last, so let's make the most of this time. And I promise to sign out officially this time, so there'll be no sneaking in through the back door. I even managed to wangle a late pass.'

–

The next morning, Thea hummed a cheerful tune as she lay in a contorted position on the floor of *D-Donald*'s cockpit, checking the connections behind the instrument panel. The wind had dropped, and the station was abuzz with preparations for a mission. Around her she could hear erks whistling and shouting comments to one another as they filled the fuel tanks, replaced the ammunition and worked on the engines. Thea tried not to worry about the coming mission and how Fitz would fare, but fixed her thoughts on the more uplifting memories from their date the evening before.

Even though there had been plenty of other young men present, she had been true to her word and danced only with Fitz. Although she had never felt like the most graceful dancer, in his arms she felt like Ginger Rogers. There was clearly an advantage to going out with a former ballet dancer. In the slower numbers he had held her close, and, obeying the words of one of the songs, they had danced cheek to cheek and Thea had, indeed, felt like she was in heaven.

The feeling had remained with her, and even now, accompanied as they were by the sounds of hammering, rivet guns and the rattle of ammunition, the melting sensation in her stomach remained, and she couldn't stop smiling.

What was it about Fitz that made him stand out from all the other men? Until now, dates had always been about the thrill of the night out – the dancing or the high spirits that always abounded when a group of airmen got together at a pub or club. But with Fitz, she wanted to see *him*. She didn't care if they were together in a club or a cinema or simply out walking. The pleasure of being with him added colour to any activity.

Maybe it was because they were both misfits. Despite Pearl's efforts, Thea had never felt the need to conform to society's idea of how a young woman should behave. In this she had been encouraged by Deedee, who had always told her to follow her heart, as long as she wasn't hurting anyone, and that forcing oneself to fit in did more harm than good in the long run. And Thea suspected that Fitz never felt as though he truly belonged among men who had done so-called normal jobs before the war. It was comforting to be misfits together.

Perhaps that was why they were both determined to help Jack, because he was struggling to behave in the way expected of aircrew.

'Thea, is that you down there?'

Thea sat up too quickly and bumped her head against the pilot's seat. 'Ouch. Yes, it's me.' She blinked to clear the stars from her eyes and saw Sam Drinkwater leaning across the seat. With him being *D-Donald*'s flight engineer, Thea knew him well enough to talk to, though they had never really mixed socially. 'How can I help?' She levered herself off the floor and perched on the pilot's seat.

She expected a question about the fuel gauges or some other technical query. Instead, Sam snatched off his cap and rubbed his forehead, looking awkward. 'It's nothing to do with the instruments. I just wanted to ask you…' He tailed off, muttering something inaudible.

'Spit it out, Sam. It can't be that bad.' Although Thea had a horrible suspicion that he was trying to ask her out.

'I wondered if you could help me with something.'

'I won't know unless you tell me what it is.'

Sam rubbed his nose. 'The thing is, there's this girl.'

Here we go, Thea thought. He would start by praising her auburn hair and her beautiful eyes before finally confessing that the girl in question was, in fact, her.

Sam's face was aglow, and he carried on. 'She's the most beautiful woman in Fenthorpe, and I've been trying to summon up the courage to ask her out for weeks now, but I can't get the words out.'

The most beautiful woman in Fenthorpe? Sam must have it bad. While she was happy with her looks, Thea wasn't deluded enough to consider herself the most beautiful by any means. 'That's sad but I don't understand what you expect me to do. If you can't tell her, why not write her a letter?'

'That's what I wanted your help with.'

'You did?' It was dawning on Thea that perhaps Sam wasn't trying to ask her out. 'Whatever I can do, I'll be happy to help. You're a good-looking bloke and one of the nicest people on the base. She'd be mad to turn you down.'

'I knew I could count on you. The thing is, she loves doing crosswords, and she always does the one in the *Bombshell* without fail. I thought you could organise the solution of the next one to form a message to her.'

Thea was intrigued. 'That would certainly get her attention. What's her name?'

Now Sam looked embarrassed, and mumbled something Thea was sure she must have misheard.

'I'm sorry. Can you repeat that? For a moment, I could have sworn you said Blanche.'

'I did.' Sam fiddled with the harness on the flight engineer's seat. 'It's Blanche.'

Thea stared at him. 'Blanche Dalby?' Only then did she recall the way she'd seen Sam gazing at Blanche in the NAAFI. Her blissful memories of dancing with Fitz had temporarily driven it from her mind. Still, she couldn't imagine why Sam would request help from her of all people. She spoke with all the patience she could muster, like a teacher explaining long division to a recalcitrant child. 'You do know Blanche thinks I'm a criminal? Why should I help her?'

A flush had crept up Sam's throat and it now reached his face, staining his cheeks with bright pink spots. He had clearly understood the words she had refrained from saying: *why would you want to go out with her?* 'I know it's a lot to ask, but I think it might help you too.'

'How?' While Thea liked Sam and wanted him to be happy, she didn't think she'd be doing him any favours by helping him get together with Blanche.

'I think deep down she feels bad about spreading rumours she knows are untrue. It all got out of hand.'

'Maybe, but she didn't exactly try explaining that to any of the WAAFs in my hut who act like I don't exist. How can you want to be with a girl who can be so spiteful?'

Sam winced. 'She's not spiteful, not at heart. But I think she'd let herself get bitter, and for a while she couldn't see her way out.'

Thea reflected on this, remembering what she'd heard about Blanche's losses. 'And you think you're the man to help her?'

'I don't know, but I'd like to try.'

It was Sam's honesty that made up Thea's mind to help him – not that she was going to put him out of his misery just yet. 'So what is it about her spiteful, bitter exterior that makes you think there's a kinder, more loving woman inside?' She braced herself for a detailed description of Blanche's good looks.

'A few weeks ago, I was sitting at the next table to hers in the NAAFI.' Sam had gone all misty-eyed, and Thea knew he was no longer in the cramped cockpit but back in the NAAFI, gazing at Blanche through a haze of cigarette smoke. 'She was on her own, doing the *Bombshell* crossword, and suddenly she started laughing. She looked up and saw me watching her, and said, "Ten down." And I started laughing because I'd found ten down funny too. I remember thinking how well we would get on together because we shared the same sense of humour. And she's very pretty, of course.'

This was not at all the answer Thea had expected. Sense of humour – Blanche? 'Who'd have thought my crosswords could bring people together? And there was me thinking that Blanche didn't appreciate my crossword-setting skills.'

'Blanche?' One of the fitters working farther back in the fuselage must have overheard their conversation, for now he stuck his head into the cockpit from the navigator's position. 'Are you talking about the girl from admin? You want to stay away from her, pal.'

'Why? I think she's lovely.' Sam might not be able to string two words together when he was around Blanche but at least he could defend himself against one of the men.

'She probably is, but she's a chop girl, that one. Seen off two men already.'

Thea bristled and opened her mouth to defend Blanche. While she and the other woman might never see eye to eye, she wasn't going to stand back while one of her sister WAAFs was being insulted. Especially over something as cruel as the loss of two men dear to her.

However, before she could say anything, Sam spoke up. 'You know what? Even if I did believe that superstitious nonsense, it's a risk I'm prepared to take. A girl as classy as Blanche is worth it. As it happens, though, I don't believe it. If I get shot down tonight, it'll be because of a night fighter or the tons of flak being fired into the air.'

The erk pulled a face. 'Suit yourself. Don't say I didn't warn you.' This was followed by the sound of him scrambling back towards the exit hatch.

Thea could have hugged Sam. 'Well said. Although I don't understand how you can give that erk a piece of your mind and not be able to say a word to Blanche.'

Sam gave a wry smile. 'Probably because I find her much more attractive than him. Whenever I find myself within ten feet of her, my tongue sticks to the roof of my mouth, and every thought I've ever had leaks out of my brain. I couldn't even tell her my own name, let alone say something witty and entertaining that would grab the interest of a girl like Blanche.'

'Well, if there's any justice in the world, she'll want you once she's solved the next crossword.'

A spark of hope lit up Sam's eyes. 'Then you'll help?'

Thea nodded. 'But if you still can't speak to her once she's read your message, then I'm washing my hands of you.'

Chapter Thirteen

'Where do you think we're going tonight?' Jack asked Fitz as they strolled towards the operations block.

'My money's on Happy Valley.' Fitz glanced sidelong at Jack, trying not to make it look obvious that he was studying him. Jack had become increasingly agitated as the morning wore on and operations were announced despite what Fitz still considered to be very strong winds. The constant waiting over the past few days had taken its toll on Jack, and, although he hadn't lost his temper again as he had over the gun turret, Fitz knew he had hardly eaten. His restlessness at night had also kept his hut-mates awake until Fitz feared none of them was in a fit state to endure a gruelling mission. Operations had been scrubbed for eight days in a row, and Fitz couldn't help reflecting on the probability that his tour would now be over if they hadn't had so many missions cancelled. Over one way or another, at any rate. Fitz didn't like to think too deeply about the likelihood of surviving his final missions. He also thought Jack might have overcome whatever fears were plaguing him if he had had less time to dwell on them.

Now they were about to go on their first test flight since the storm, and he would have to keep a close eye on Jack's behaviour. It was a shame they were stationed at opposite ends of the plane. He knew the wireless operator and mid-upper gunner would also look out for him, but he wished he could be there himself. He would try to persuade Greg to let him go aft during the flight so he could see for himself how Jack was faring.

However, all his plans were thrown awry when Squadron Leader Price marched into the locker room as everyone was digging out their gear. His face was grim. 'Sorry, lads. The Met Officer has revised his forecast and says the wind is picking up again. All ops are scrubbed and flights are grounded.'

Groans echoed around the locker room, interspersed with a few cheers. The men flung their kit back into their lockers and filed out. Jack, however, slammed his locker door, then slid to the floor and rested his head on his knees, his arms wrapped round his head. It was a posture of utter hopelessness.

Fitz crouched beside him. 'What's wrong?' He'd have thought Jack would have been relieved not to have to fly when he was still trying to convince the ground crew that his gun turret was jamming.

'I don't know if I can take this much longer.' The words were muffled, as Jack's head was still cradled in his arms. Even so, Fitz couldn't miss the despair in his voice.

They were now the last two people in the locker room, so Fitz settled himself on the floor beside Jack and patted him awkwardly on the shoulder. 'Take what? Tell me what's going through your mind.'

'All this waiting. Waiting around the operations block to see if we're flying ops that day. If we are, then we still spend a lot of the time hanging around, guessing where we're going – if it's a place we've been before or somewhere new. And in the back of my mind, I'm thinking, is this the one – the mission that will claim my life? And all the time, I remember those awful moments when the rear turret jammed and there was a bloody great night fighter zooming straight for us. It was so close I could see the flames spitting from the guns and the stream of tracer fire. All I could do was watch as the stream got closer and closer to me.' Jack shuddered. 'I still don't know how I wasn't hit.'

He raised his head. There was a red line down his cheek where it had been pressed against a fold in his sleeve, and to Fitz he looked so much like a child whose face was rosy from sleep that he thought his heart might burst from pity. 'I'm useless. No one else seems to be afraid.'

'That's not true. You're not useless, and every one of us is terrified. No sane man wouldn't be.' But even as he said it he knew that, while every single member of the crew went through the same fears as Jack described, everyone responded differently. Greg, for example, tended to let off steam after a difficult mission by tearing through the countryside at high speed on his motorcycle or accepting a dare such as placing the adjutant's cap on the highest branch of a tree. He knew it had caused friction between him and Pearl, although they had managed to work it out. Edwin, the navigator, threw himself into his studies, which he said helped take his mind off everything other than the wonders of the cosmos. Fitz himself used a technique he had developed to help him through stage fright, which was to imagine a huge trunk with a strong lock. Any thought that led to anxiety he locked away inside. Back in his dancing days, those thoughts had been things such as the size of the audience or an irrational worry that he would trip on stage. Obviously these days there was nothing irrational about his fears, but he could deal with them in the same way and, once he had locked them up, they tended to stay there.

Jack, though, didn't seem able to put his dread to one side in the same way. Maybe it was something to do with having so little control over his fate when they were up in the air. Greg, piloting the plane, had the most control, of course, and Edwin as navigator was constantly at work to guide them to and from the target. While Fitz's main role of bomb aimer only took up a small part of the flight, at least he was at the front of the plane near the pilot and navigator, so he was more aware of the decision-making involved during each mission. Even though every crew member could hear what the others were saying through the intercom, Fitz took extra reassurance in being able to see with his own eyes when Greg was at ease or if he was worried by any situation.

Jack drew a shuddering breath. 'I think it's these endless days of doing nothing that are wearing me down. If it hadn't been for this wind, you'd have finished your tour, and even I would have been nearly there.' He swallowed. 'Or dead. Either way, I wouldn't be suffering from this endless dread.' He turned tormented eyes upon Fitz. 'I don't know how much more I can take.'

His voice shook, and Fitz could see that he was, indeed, at the end of his endurance. 'You don't have to go through this alone,' he said. 'If you'd only go to the MO—'

Jack pulled away from Fitz and pushed himself to his feet. 'You know how I feel about doctors. My dad went into hospital when I was ten. His doctor told him it was a routine operation, and that he'd be up and about within a week.' Jack's face twisted. 'The day after the operation his wound festered, and he died a few days later.'

'I'm sorry. That must have been awful. But the doctor wouldn't have operated if he hadn't thought it necessary. I had to have treatment when I injured my knee. Not surgery, thankfully, but if I hadn't received proper medical treatment, it would have ruined my career.'

'Why – what did you do?'

Fitz could have kicked himself. He'd kept quiet about his dancing career for so long and now he'd carelessly let that slip. Still, if he was expecting Jack to trust him and act on his suggestions, he ought to show Jack some trust in return. 'I haven't spoken about it because I wasn't sure how the rest of the crew would react, but I was a ballet dancer.'

'You're having me on.'

'No, really.'

'What – you mean prancing around in a tutu?'

Fitz gritted his teeth. This was precisely why he hadn't told anyone apart from Thea before. 'You do know only the women wear tutus?' Then he realised Jack was grinning. Not in mockery but in the light, teasing way their crewmates used to show that they were only joking.

The exchange seemed to have given Jack brief respite from whatever his inner demons were telling him, for he looked a mite more cheerful. 'I'm only kidding. I always wondered why you were able to spring out of *C-Charlie*, as limber as anything at the end of a long flight while the rest of us stumbled around as stiff as ninety-year-olds.'

'You won't tell the others, will you? They might not be so understanding.' Fitz could hardly believe Jack was treating his confession so lightly when it had been weighing on his mind ever since he had come to Fenthorpe.

'Why not? No one cares a fig what anyone was doing before the war. All they care about is if we hold it together while we're on a mission. No one who's heard you would doubt that you've got nerves of steel. Your voice stays steady as a rock while you steer us over the target, never even flinching when there's flak exploding all around us. Not like me.' Jack's own voice shook once again, and now Fitz could see that, while his expression had lightened, his eyes were still the eyes of a tormented man. 'I wish I had your nerves, I really do. I did at the start of our tour, or I thought I did. But it's like something broke that night when the turret jammed. I thought I'd feel better if I gave myself time, but nothing's changed, and I'm no good to anyone like this.'

'That's not true.'

'You know it is. I can't do my job like this. I'm going to see the CO and tell him I'm going LMF.'

A chill ran down Fitz's spine. 'You can't do that. You saw the parade Rhodes forced poor old Wright to go through. You're... unwell. Why won't you see the MO?'

'I told you. I don't trust doctors.'

'But you trust me, don't you?'

'You know I do.'

'And you trust Thea?'

'Of course.'

'Then please don't reject our advice. You're one of the bravest men I know, and—'

'How can you say that when I'm this utter wreck?'

'You're not a wreck. I've told you, you're ill, and I think the MO could help if you let him. But you are brave, and that's why I don't want to see Rhodes humiliate you. You're no coward. You volunteered as aircrew and you've flown twenty-three successful missions, carrying on even after Mannheim.'

'I don't feel brave.'

'But you are. You prove it every time you climb aboard *C-Charlie*. It's easy for Group Captain Rhodes to call a crewman a coward while he sits behind his safe desk. I'd like to see how he'd respond if he was forced to fly to Happy Valley night after night.'

'But what good would it do to see the MO?'

Fitz remembered the conversation Thea had overheard. 'The MO tried to stop Mickey Wright's LMF parade. He stood up for him and told Rhodes that Wright was ill and needed treatment, only Rhodes wouldn't listen. That's why you need to go to the MO, not the CO. The MO will try to help you.'

Jack had sat straighter while he'd listened to Fitz's explanation. 'The MO's on our side?'

'Yes. That's what I've been trying to tell you.'

'All right. I'll go.' Jack scrambled to his feet, looking suddenly very young and vulnerable. 'Will you come with me?'

–

'How's your latest crossword coming along, Thea?' Corporal Dean asked, levering a lid off a packing case. The lid came loose with a splintering sound, revealing the 750-litre oxygen cylinders inside.

Bracing her back, Thea heaved the first cylinder out before replying. 'Not too badly. I'm a bit stuck on a good clue for "Blanche" though.' She had to shout to be heard over the noise in the hangar. A new delivery of oxygen cylinders had arrived for installation in the Lancasters and, while Ted and Thea were opening crates, other erks were bringing more into the hangar and stacking them in a teetering pile. The air resounded with their shouts and the rattle of chains, as a hoist lifted some crates to the top of the pile. Thea glanced up warily. She didn't feel entirely comfortable working below the stack that was now nearly twice her height. It was probably her imagination, but it seemed to be leaning towards her.

'Blanche?' Ted called back. 'I didn't know you were such good friends you were dedicating crosswords to her now.'

'I'm not. I'm doing a favour for Flight Sergeant Drinkwater.'

'What's he got to do with it?'

'He's sweet on Blanche and wants to send her a message via the crossword.'

'You'd do that for the girl who's making your life a misery?'

'I'm doing it for Sam. But if it makes Blanche happy, she's less likely to annoy me again, so we all win.' It was this thought that had compelled her to devote most of her free time over the last four days to the crossword.

Ted laughed. 'I like the way you think. Good luck with that.' He reached for another crate that was being winched down to him.

The hangar shook as a violent gust of wind struck, shrieking like a banshee. One of the men at the top of the pile clutched the crate beside him, his white face turned to the roof as though expecting to see it ripped off. The whole stack wobbled.

'Should they be up there?' Thea eyed the wooden boxes. They had been stacked like a giant staircase, allowing the erks to scramble up so they could winch the topmost crates down to Ted and Thea. The recent delivery meant the stack was higher than usual, and that, combined with the way the whole hangar was being shaken by the gale, made her uneasy.

'The sooner they winch down the highest crates, the better,' Ted said. He pushed the now-empty crate aside, ready for collection, and reached up to steady the next one that was being lowered. 'A little to the right,' he called up to the winch operator.

Thea stepped forward to help, and that was when she saw the stack really was leaning.

'Get back!' She reached for his arm. 'I think this lot's about to fall.'

As she spoke, the wind howled again, and Thea didn't think Ted had heard her. She opened her suddenly dry mouth to shout again but the suspended box swung towards the precarious pile and struck it. The topmost boxes wobbled, and Ted turned, mouth wide in a silent yell. He gave Thea a shove.

An instant later, something struck her hard on the elbow. She stumbled and fell, and all she could do was fling her arms over her head as the air rang with cries of horror.

Chapter Fourteen

Something heavy landed near her head with a splintering crunch, and she flinched as her arm was struck, stinging like fury. She lay there, ears ringing and heart pounding, for what felt like an eternity but in reality was probably only a few seconds.

'Lift those crates,' someone was yelling. 'Hurry!'

Someone shook her shoulder and she rolled over, gasping, and found herself looking up into Sergeant Sedman's concerned face.

'Thea, are you okay?'

'I... yes, I think so.' She grasped Sedman's offered hand and pulled herself to her feet. Now she could see where all the crashes had come from – the topmost boxes from the pile had toppled to the ground and lay in heaps of fractured wood and oxygen cylinders close to where she had fallen.

Several erks were working on the stack to make it secure, but another group was clustered around the largest heap on the floor. 'Ted,' someone was saying. 'Ted, say something.'

'No.' She was hardly aware she had spoken; the voice seemed to come from a distance. She took a step forward, but Sedman held her back.

'Let them work. You'll only get in the way.'

Although she didn't approach the pile of crates, she refused to move any further away. She could tell from the urgency in the men's voices that Ted Dean must be under the crates, and she needed to watch, to reassure herself that he would be all right once he had been freed. Worryingly, she couldn't hear his voice, only the increasingly anxious words spoken by the rescuers.

'Ted, speak to me.'

'Help me move this crate.'

'I can't find a pulse.'

'Try his throat.'

'Nothing. No, wait. I've got it but it's very weak.'

One of the men turned to Sedman. 'Call for an ambulance.'

'Already have. It shouldn't be long now.'

The last crate was moved aside, and Thea could tell from the sudden hush and in-drawn breaths that Ted's injuries were severe.

Thankfully the ambulance arrived at that point, pulling up inside the hangar as close to the scene of the accident as possible. Thea felt helpless as she watched the ambulance driver and her helper lift Ted onto a stretcher, assisted by as many of the erks as could get close enough to the stretcher.

While the others carried Ted to the ambulance, the driver approached Thea. 'You should come along too. Get the MO to take a look at your arm.'

'What? I'm not—' Then Thea glanced down at her arm and saw that her sleeve was torn and stained with blood. Her mind refused to process what she was seeing. 'I don't remember doing that.'

It was as though seeing her injury mended the connection between her arm and her brain, because the arm suddenly started to throb. Unable to disguise her wince, she allowed the WAAF driver to coax her to her feet and guide her to the ambulance.

Sedman's gruff voice followed her. 'Don't even think about returning to duty until the MO clears you. And make sure they take good care of Ted.'

Thea perched on a stretcher for the short journey to Sick Quarters, unable to take her eyes from Ted's chalk-white face. She heard the WAAF taking care of him say that he had a severe head injury and crush injuries to his right leg. Although he needed care beyond what could be administered in Sick Quarters, they would stop there before going on to the hospital so the MO could attempt to stabilise him for the longer journey. While Thea was no medic, she knew this meant Ted's injuries must be life-threatening. She couldn't understand how he could be laughing and joking one minute and close to death the next. It occurred to her that this must be what it was like for the air crews, and she felt fresh admiration for the men who willingly flew into danger night after night, never knowing if they would return.

The MO, Squadron Leader Forrester, had clearly been alerted to their arrival, for he ran out to meet the ambulance the moment it drew up outside Sick Quarters.

'Take him to the crash room,' he snapped. 'He's going into shock.' The crash room was where badly injured aircrew were taken for urgent treatment until they were stable enough for transport to hospital.

Thea followed them out of the ambulance, not sure what to do. There was no way she was leaving until she knew how Ted was. Not to mention, her left arm and elbow was very painful by this time, so she knew it would be foolish to leave before she got it treated.

She was following the stretcher-bearers into the building when a hand grasped her shoulder, making her swing round with a start.

It was Fitz, his face pale and worried. 'Thea, what happened?' Then his gaze dropped to her arm. 'You're hurt.'

'It's not bad. But Ted…' Her throat suddenly felt too swollen for her to squeeze out any more words, and to her embarrassment she felt tears roll down her cheeks.

'Come inside. Let's find somewhere to sit down.'

She nodded and for the second time that day allowed herself to be led. It was only when she was sitting on a chair just inside the door that she realised Fitz wasn't alone, for he looked past her and said, 'See if you can find a blanket, Jack. She's cold.'

Only then did it occur to her to ask, 'What are you doing here?'

Fitz glanced after Jack, who had disappeared into a room a few yards down the corridor. Only when the door closed behind him did Fitz reply in a low voice, 'I expect you've heard flying's off again today.' When she nodded, he continued, 'I don't really understand it, but Jack practically broke down when we got the news. I think he was all keyed up for the mission and something just seemed to snap when it was called off. I finally managed to persuade him to see the MO, only it looks like we chose a bad time.'

'It might be a bad time for Jack, but I'm glad you're here.'

At that point Jack returned armed with a blanket. She studied his face and saw he looked almost as pale as Ted had been. She shuddered at the memory of Ted's blood-streaked face, and accepted the blanket gratefully when only a few seconds earlier she would have protested that she didn't need it. Anyway, while there was nothing she could do to help Ted she could, at least, show Jack she appreciated his help.

She hadn't noticed how cold she had been feeling until the warmth of the blanket seeped into her muscles, and she shot him a smile. However, she forgot the words of encouragement she had intended to speak when another doctor and two nurses hurried out of a room farther down the corridor and rushed into the room where Ted had been taken. Thea craned her neck, desperate for a glimpse of Ted, but one of the nurses closed the door behind her before she could see in.

Fitz's anxious voice recalled her. 'What happened, Thea?'

Taking a deep breath, Thea explained about the accident. 'It all happened so fast,' she finished. 'I still can't really believe Ted's badly hurt.'

Fitz, too, seemed to be having trouble taking it all in. 'I always thought you were safe, working in the Instrument Section. I never dreamed something like this could happen.' He pointed to her arm. 'How bad is it?'

'I don't think it's too bad. I remember something hitting me on the elbow. I suppose I must have caught a glancing blow from one of the crates.'

Gritting her teeth, she eased off her jacket and rolled back the torn sleeve of her shirt. Both sleeves were bloodstained and, when she angled her arm to inspect the damage, she heard Fitz's indrawn breath. She soon saw why. Although her elbow was already scabbing over, it had clearly bled a good deal, and the skin surrounding the cut was already swelling.

'You've got some nasty splinters in there, and you're going to have a whopping bruise by tomorrow,' Fitz told her. 'I would help with the splinters but I'm afraid of making it worse. Best to wait until a doctor or nurse can take a look.'

He pulled a folded handkerchief from his pocket. 'Use this. It's fresh from the laundry and completely clean, I promise.'

Thea took it and gingerly dabbed at the cut, wincing when she inadvertently pressed where a splinter was digging in. 'It'll be a while before anyone's free.' She nodded at the closed door, through which low voices could be heard, too muffled to make out any words.

'Here. Let me see if I can help.' Fitz took the handkerchief back and folded it to make a pad. 'Have you got another hanky I can use for a bandage?'

Thea shook her head. 'Mine's covered in oil. I wouldn't let it anywhere near a cut.'

'What about you, Jack?'

Jack didn't respond. Fitz frowned. 'Jack?'

Thea twisted so she could see Jack, and forgot all her own aches and pains when she saw he was sitting hunched over in his seat, his arms wrapped round his stomach. His gaze was fixed on the door and his face was as white as though he were the one injured. He didn't give any sign of having heard Fitz at all.

Thea placed a hand on his shoulder, and he flinched and then looked at her as though he had forgotten her presence. 'Jack? What's wrong?' she asked.

Before he could answer, the crash room door swung open, and the MO emerged, his face grave. Thea's eyes were drawn irresistibly to the room beyond to where Ted lay on a bed. His eyes were closed, and his face was a ghastly bluish-grey. Noticing the MO was approaching her, she opened her mouth to ask him how Ted was, but then another movement within the room made her mouth go dry. The nurses were pulling a sheet over the bed, covering even Ted's face.

'No.' She glared at the MO. 'There has to be something you can do.'

The MO shook his head. 'I'm very sorry. We did everything we could but he had lost too much blood. He'd sustained severe crush injuries to both legs. If it's any comfort, he'd have probably needed to have them both amputated.'

Thea glared at him. 'I'm sure that will be a great comfort to his wife and young children, who have just lost their husband and father.' Taking this tone with an officer was inviting a severe reprimand and a week on jankers if not something worse – Pearl would be having a fit if she could see her now – but she couldn't seem to stop herself. 'I don't think they would care if Ted's legs were flesh and bone or made with tin, they would just want him with them.'

The flow of words stopped, the silence in the room heavy, and she braced herself for a reprimand.

However, when the MO spoke it was in a chastened voice. 'You're right, of course, and I'll be sure to bear that in mind when I write to his widow.' Then, in brisker tones, 'Now, what about you? I gather you were hurt too.'

However, Thea's thoughts were on another wounded man. 'I can wait,' she said. 'I think you ought to see Jack first.'

Glancing Jack's way, she saw him staring into the room where Ted lay. He didn't seem able to drag his eyes from the shrouded figure on the bed. Then he belatedly seemed to register that Thea had spoken his name and finally turned his head towards her, although his gaze kept sliding back towards Ted. 'What did you say?'

The MO took over. 'You wanted to see me?'

'Me? No!' Jack leaped to his feet, startling Thea, as she would have sworn only a few seconds earlier that he would have been unable to stand. 'I mean... it's nothing. I thought... but no. It's nothing, really.' While he spoke, he had been backing towards the main door. Now, he turned and bolted and the door slammed behind him.

'I'm sorry.' Fitz rose and cast an apologetic glance at Thea. 'I'd better go after him. Get yourself patched up, and I'll catch up with you later.' So saying, he set off after Jack.

Thea hesitated, wishing she could help Jack too, but then her elbow gave a vicious twinge, reminding her that it would be foolish to leave it untended. After a last look towards the door through which Fitz had just departed, she held out her arm to the doctor.

—

Fitz ran after Jack, feeling torn. He hated leaving Thea alone when she was injured and had seen a colleague and friend killed, but Jack seemed so distressed he knew he couldn't leave him alone either. As Jack hadn't had much of a head start, Fitz soon caught sight of him, making a beeline for the NAAFI. He had slowed his initial panicked flight and was walking in a brisk march. However, he must still be looking distressed, for Fitz saw several people shoot him concerned glances as he hurried past.

Fitz expected to see Jack go into the NAAFI. Instead, he veered past the entrance and made his way around the back of the hut. There he slumped to the ground beneath a tall elm tree and sat with his back against the trunk, arms wrapped round his knees, which were pulled to his chest.

Fitz broke into a jog and quickly reached him. Jack glanced at him when he sat down next to his friend. 'I thought you'd be with Thea,' he said.

'The MO's taking care of her.'

'Is she badly hurt? I'm sorry, I didn't even notice.'

Fitz took Jack's concern as a sign that he was starting to emerge from whatever fearful state had seized him earlier. 'She'll be fine. She's bruised and shaken but no worse than that, thank God.'

'Not like Corporal Dean. What happened to him?'

Fitz briefly outlined what Thea had told him, taking Jack's question as proof that Jack had closed in on himself while in Sick Quarters, for Thea had been sitting beside him while she had described the accident.

'It's hard to believe.' Jack was still hugging his knees to his chest, rocking slightly. 'I'd started to envy the erks, thinking they had safe jobs. But now it seems like no one's safe.'

Jack looked like a terrified child, and Fitz wished there was something he could say or do that would take his fears away. 'Why don't you come back to Sick Quarters?' he asked. 'We can see how Thea is and then you can speak to the MO about how you've been feeling.'

Jack shook his head. 'You go. You should check on Thea. I'll stay here.'

'Thea was worried about you. At least come along so you can set her mind at rest.' Fitz clung to the hope that, if he could get Jack back into Sick Quarters, he'd be able to persuade him to speak to the MO.

But Jack was having none of it. 'I told you. I don't trust doctors. My dad went into hospital and died, and now it's poor old Ted's turn.'

'But Forrester's a good doctor. You saw how he was with Thea. He had every right to throw the book at her for speaking to him the way she did, but he understood she was upset. He even admitted he'd been wrong to say what he did.'

'But he thought it, didn't he. When he saw the state Ted's legs were in, he thought Ted would be better off dead. Face it, that's how the officer class thinks. They view those of us from the working class as no better than draft animals, to be put out of their misery when they're no longer of use. He didn't consider how Ted might have felt, or what his family might have wanted. Not until Thea spoke up for him, and then it was too late. How do we know what happened in there? Maybe Ted's life might have been saved if the MO had gone ahead and amputated his legs on the spot. What if he just stood back and let Ted die?'

'He wouldn't have done that. He's a decent bloke.' The trouble was, Fitz knew Jack had a point. Not that he thought the MO would have casually stood by and let Ted die, but there was definitely a section of the senior officers who seemed to regard the lower orders as lacking the finer feelings of the upper classes. Group Captain Anthony Rhodes was one of these people. However, that was all the more reason to persuade Jack to see the MO and get himself signed off sick before Rhodes found out about Jack's state of mind. Because while Rhodes might allow an officer a certain latitude, and think he was suffering from shattered nerves, he would never allow a working-class man the same consideration. He would always condemn a man such as Jack as a coward and see him punished accordingly.

Seeing Jack's mouth set in a stubborn line, Fitz tried once more, although with less hope. 'At least come with me to see Thea. She was worried when you ran off like that.'

'I can't. You go. I'll stay here.'

'You can't stay here in this wind. You'll have a branch falling on your head.' In fact, now he came to take notice of the weather, he realised the wind had dropped significantly. The tree still swayed and creaked overhead, the swollen leaf buds rattling, but not in the wild way it had earlier. He was struck by the crazy idea that the storm had been like some vengeful ancient god, and now it had finally been appeased by the sacrifice of Ted's life. He gave himself a mental shake. Clearly his head was too full of the sort of fantastic stories that got made into ballets.

Jack shook his head. 'I'll be fine.'

'You don't sound it. Anyway, if a branch does fall on your head, you'll end up in Sick Quarters or hospital, and I thought you didn't trust doctors.' Inspiration struck, and Fitz pulled a few shillings from his pocket. 'Look, I'm sure Thea will need something to eat when she's finished having her arm dressed. Go to the NAAFI and buy us some cake and a pot of tea, and we'll meet you there.'

'If you think that would help.'

'I know it will.'

Fitz satisfied himself that Jack really was inside the NAAFI before he went to find Thea, then, once back in Sick Quarters, he found the corridor empty. The door to the room where Ted had been treated was closed, but he didn't think Thea would be in there, as that room was reserved for emergencies. Ted's body was probably still inside, while the MO made arrangements for an ambulance to take him to the mortuary. For a few moments he hovered uncertainly, caught between going to search for Thea and waiting where he had sat earlier. He had just decided to sit and wait when a door opened further up the corridor and Thea emerged. She held her jacket over her good arm, and her injured elbow was now wrapped in a white dressing.

She hurried to meet him. 'Did you find Jack? Is he okay?'

'Yes, I found him. He's in a bit of a state, though. I tried to persuade him to come back here but he refused. What about you – how are you feeling?'

'I'm fine. Bruised but fine. But, Ted… I can't believe it.' Her face crumpled, and Fitz caught her in his arms. Thea buried her face in his shoulder and shook with sobs. It was as though she had held herself together, determined to appear strong in front of the doctor, and now she was finally letting her grief pour out. Deciding it was best to wait out the storm, Fitz guided her to the chairs and supported her, patting her back, until her tears subsided.

'Sorry,' she muttered once she had regained control. 'I must look a fright.'

'You look beautiful.'

'Liar.' She gave a watery smile. 'But it's just like you to try and make me feel better. That's why I love you.'

137

Chapter Fifteen

Thea jerked out of his arms as though she had received an electric shock. In other circumstances, her horrified expression would have been comical. 'I mean… I…'

Fitz decided to put her out of her misery. 'I have no idea what you just said,' he lied, 'being suddenly struck by temporary deafness. Even if I had heard, I would have completely disregarded it, putting it down to delayed shock.'

Thea gave a shaky laugh. 'That's all right, then.'

There were times Fitz wished he wasn't such a gentleman, because he yearned with all his heart that he could find out if Thea had really meant what she had said. Did she love him? Because he was starting to think he was in love with her. But pressing her to explain herself over what was clearly a slip of the tongue felt ungentlemanly. He was sure she wouldn't have said it if she hadn't still been in shock. If they ever were to declare their mutual feelings, he wanted it to be natural and spontaneous, not a result of clouded judgement. Pretending he hadn't heard, even though they both knew he had, was the right thing to do.

To ease the momentary awkwardness, he said, 'Anyway, we're supposed to be meeting Jack in the NAAFI. He's buying us tea and cakes.'

'Good,' said Thea, 'because I'm famished.'

–

Thea wished she could sink into the ground and never emerge again. How could she have made such a blunder? It must be the shock and reaction to the events of the day. If she hadn't seen Ted killed in front of her eyes she would never have blurted anything out about her feelings.

She kept her mouth firmly shut as they made their way into the NAAFI, although she shot several sidelong glances in Fitz's direction. He hadn't said he loved her in return. And that was what she wanted, wasn't it – to carry on as before, enjoying each other's company without feeling the need to deepen their relationship? It must be what Fitz wanted, at any rate, for he had practically fallen over himself to make it clear he hadn't heard when he obviously had.

Anyway, she had long ago made up her mind that she had poor judgement when it came to men. The whole episode with Billy Haywood had taught her that. Pearl was right, although Thea would sooner attend church parade in nothing but her underwear than admit it to her sister: she was foolish and unreliable and couldn't be trusted not to make a decision that would harm herself or others. That was why the WAAF was so good for her – being forced to comply with the rigid restrictions imposed upon the young women in its ranks kept her out of trouble. Well, deep trouble, anyway. She supposed she would always get herself into minor scrapes. Half the fun of being in the WAAF was finding out how far she could push the boundaries before she got caught.

Fitz seemed to shake off his awkwardness long before Thea managed it. Once in the NAAFI, he led them to a table where Jack was already waiting and handed her a mug of tea, saying, 'Strong, sweet tea is supposed to be good for a shock.' He peered into the sugar basin and wrinkled his nose. 'If you can make tea properly sweet with just one lump.' He picked up the tongs and dropped the last sugar lump into her cup.

Thea would have protested – Jack looked as though he could use a boost – but she was starting to feel the aches and pains from her accident, not to mention cold and shaky, so she stirred her tea and drank without objecting.

'How's your arm, Thea?' Jack asked.

Thea, grateful for something to talk about that wasn't either her feelings for Fitz or Ted's death, grasped gratefully at the topic and found herself gabbling. 'Oh, it's not too bad. It had pretty much stopped bleeding by the time the doc looked at it, so he just removed the splinters, applied a dressing and gave me an aspirin. He told me to stay off work tomorrow, and to see him in the afternoon before he'll clear me for duty the next day.' She paused for breath. Trying not to think about what she had said to Fitz only meant she was dwelling on Ted's death. She couldn't seem to forget the image of his still form on the bed in Sick Quarters, just before the nurse pulled the sheet over his face. Her bout of tears in Fitz's arms had helped, yet the image persisted.

Another thought struck, and she rose to her feet.

Fitz frowned at her. 'Where are you going?'

'I just realised. I have to write to Ted's wife. I was with him when the accident happened. She'll want to know how he… he…' She swallowed, her throat suddenly thick. She couldn't say *died*. It was too horribly final for the cheerful, lively soul that Ted had been.

Fitz's expression softened. 'I agree she'd appreciate a letter, but give yourself a chance to take it in yourself. You're still in shock. In fact…' He appeared to make up his mind, and also rose. 'Let's get the gang together – *C-Charlie*'s crew, you, Jenny, and Pearl if she's around. We're going to the Piebald Pony to add Ted's name to the roll of honour.'

'Seriously? But I thought that was reserved for aircrew.' The roll of honour was what RAF Fenthorpe's aircrews called the patch of ceiling in the public bar at the White Horse in Fenthorpe. Whenever a crewman was killed in action or declared missing, the remaining men would write his name on the ceiling.

Jack too was on his feet, and he nodded. 'Ted was part of the team,' he said. 'It's only right that his name should be honoured.'

Now Thea really did think she would start crying again. 'Thank you. That means a lot.' She knew that adding the names of the lost aircrews was not just a way of honouring them but also a means to help the remaining men say goodbye and then put them out of their mind enough to carry on flying. It might appear harsh, even brutal, to outsiders, yet Thea appreciated that the crews would barely be able to function, let alone fly over Europe night after night, if they carried the burden of all the men they had lost. Maybe Fitz and Jack were right, and honouring Ted in this way would help her face her daily work again without sensing his ghost peering over her shoulder. She turned to Fitz and Jack. 'You round up the crew, I'll see what Jenny's doing. I think Pearl's still in Lincoln, though.' It was probably for the best. She wasn't sure if Pearl would approve. Understand, maybe, but not approve.

An hour later, Thea and Jenny walked into the public bar at the Piebald Pony and were greeted by cheers from the crew of *C-Charlie*, who had arrived a few minutes earlier. Thea shot Jenny a concerned glance, unsure how her younger and very inexperienced friend was coping with the attention. They always sat in the snug when they visited the pub, and even here in Bomber County, where the WAAFs had proved they were equal to their male counterparts and accepted as such, it was considered not quite the done thing for a woman to set foot in the rowdy public bars. Jenny, however, was smiling and seemed undaunted, even when Fitz handed her a brimming half-pint mug.

'Don't worry – it's shandy,' he said with a wink. 'I know you're on duty tomorrow morning. It wouldn't do to have all our Lancs flying into a thunderstorm because you misread the weather instruments.'

'I hope you got me a real drink,' Thea told him. 'I'm suddenly off duty tomorrow, and I want to give Ted a proper send-off.'

'I read your mind.' Fitz handed her another half-pint mug, with not a hint of lemonade or ginger beer. 'And not forgetting the most vital piece of equipment.' He handed her a pencil. 'You might want to stick it behind your ear.'

'I... what?' Thea looked at the pencil, uncomprehending.

Reality only sank in when Fitz crouched down in front of her with his back to her. 'Climb aboard,' he called over his shoulder. The other crewmen started to clap and cheer.

'You can't be serious.' Surely they didn't expect her to actually write on the ceiling? She had imagined one of the men would do it.

'No one better qualified,' Fitz said. 'He was your corporal, after all. You're the one who knew him best. I mean, I'll do it if you're scared of heights.'

'No. I'll do it.' Sincerely hoping no one would tell Pearl, she handed her glass to Jenny and tucked the pencil behind her ear, seeing the sense in having her hands free. Then she hoisted herself onto Fitz's shoulders. 'Are you sure you can manage?' Being tall, she was aware she must be heavier than most girls, and she didn't want him to injure himself.

He grinned up at her, making her suddenly aware of her stocking-clad legs being revealed as her skirt bunched up around the tops of her thighs. 'I could lift you with one hand.' And she had a sudden image of him as a dancer, hoisting his partner high into the air, making her look as light as a feather.

He put his hands on her knees to steady her, and never had she been more glad she'd chosen to wear the nylons she'd managed to buy for herself instead of the thick lisle monstrosities that were supplied to all WAAFs. Then, rising as smoothly as if she were no heavier than a child, he stood, and Thea felt herself soar through the air. The next moment, her head was skimming the heavy oak beams and she had a clear view of name after name scrawled upon the ceiling.

Feeling as solemn as though she were about to give the reading in church, she groped for the pencil.

'Wait!' Greg called. 'If you're going to do this properly, you have to drain your glass first.'

Standing on tiptoe, Jenny handed over her beer.

Greg frowned. 'It's supposed to be a pint.'

Edwin Holland came to her rescue. 'She's only about half your weight, so a half-pint is fair.'

Greg conceded with a nod, and gestured to Thea to continue. She had seen the lads do this several times, so she knew what was expected. Raising her glass in a toast, she cried, 'To Ted!'

The others raised their glasses in return. 'Ted!'

'Wishing you soft landings, wherever you are,' Greg said. As skipper, he seemed to have taken on responsibility for overseeing the impromptu ceremony. He grinned at Thea. 'Over to you. Down in one!'

The others took up the chant, and Thea raised her glass to her lips and started to drink. Although a half-pint wasn't as bad as a full pint to drink down, she still struggled, and prayed she wouldn't expire from lack of oxygen before she finished. After draining the final drops, she gasped with relief and flourished the empty glass, to more cheers.

Now for the final part of the ritual. She tossed the glass down, and Jenny caught it. Then she grabbed her pencil and searched for an empty patch of ceiling to write Ted's name. 'Can you move left three steps?' she asked Fitz.

At which his crewmates all laughed and chanted, 'Left, left, left, steady.' Thea couldn't work out what the joke was but she reached out and scrawled *Ted Dean* just below the name *Max Turner*. Max had been a friend of hers, and it felt appropriate to write Ted's name near his.

'Bombs away!' the airmen yelled and, before she knew what was going to happen, she was falling. Before she had time even to cry out, she was caught in the waiting arms of Greg, Jack, Edwin Holland and George Hepple, the wireless operator. They lowered her to the floor, and she spent a flustered few seconds checking her skirt was hanging round her knees and not still hitched up round her thighs.

'You've never done that before,' she gasped.

'We had to improvise for a member of the ground crew,' Fitz told her, so straight-faced it took her a moment to work out that he was joking. 'How do you feel?' he asked once the rest of the crew had wandered back to the bar.

Thea considered this. 'It helped,' she said finally. 'I mean, it's going to be awful the first time I go on duty and he's not there, but now I know I can do it because we gave him a proper send-off.'

—

Pearl arrived soon after and seemed genuinely upset to hear of Ted's death. 'What a tragedy,' she said once they were in the quieter snug, leaving the men in the public bar. 'When we set up the In Memoriam column in the *Bombshell* I always imagined it would just name aircrew. I never dreamed anyone on the ground would be affected.'

Thea nodded. 'It's only just sinking in, really,' she said. 'I can't stop thinking of Ted's wife, either, and wondering what to say when I write to her. She must have been reassured to have him assigned to the ground crew. I can't imagine how she must be feeling now. I assume she's already received the telegram.' She shuddered. 'It's funny the things you think about at times like this, isn't it,' she said after a pause.

'Like what?' Pearl asked.

'As I said, I can't get Ted's wife and family out of my mind and how they're reacting to the news. I mean, if Ted had been aircrew she would have lived in daily dread of his death, but knowing he was a fitter and on the ground she must have been grateful that he'd got a safe posting. What do you think is worse – hearing bad news after months of suspense, or the shock of it arriving out of the blue?'

'The first,' Pearl replied without a moment's hesitation. Then she gave a wry smile. 'Although I suppose I would say that, seeing as that's my reality at the moment.'

'Sorry,' Thea said. 'I didn't mean to remind you.'

Pearl shrugged. 'It's not something I'm likely to forget.'

There was something in her tone that made Thea study her anxiously. However, before she could say anything else, Jenny put in, 'I think both options are equally bad. Either way, the wife and family has lost someone dear to them. I don't think any amount of anticipation can truly prepare you for it.'

'But if it comes out of the blue, they haven't suffered sleepless nights trying to prepare themselves for the event.'

'But—' Jenny broke off and gave Pearl a searching look. Apparently abandoning her line of argument, she asked, 'Are you having second thoughts?'

'Absolutely not. But I suppose this talk of Corporal Dean's wife is making me wonder if I've fully considered how I'd cope if Greg... if the worst happened.'

Thea thought someone had to say it. 'It's not too late to back out.'

But Pearl shook her head with a smile. 'It is for me. I love him with every inch of my being. While I might have no idea how I would cope if' – she squared her shoulders – 'if he died, one thing I know for certain is that, if I hadn't married him, I'd regret it for the rest of my life.'

Pearl met Thea's gaze, and her expression reassured Thea that she really didn't have any doubts. 'That's what you need to remember when you write to Mrs Dean. Nothing you write can possibly take away the pain she's feeling now, but later on she'll treasure any words that will give her a picture of the man she knew and loved. Because memories are all she'll have left.' Then she glanced at Jenny. 'What are the chances of the wind dying down enough for ops to start again tomorrow?'

'It's hard to say.'

'You're usually right. Don't tell me what the forecasters are saying. What do *you* think?'

'I *think* the wind will still be too strong tomorrow, but there are signs we're finally reaching the end of these storms, and I think the bombers will be cleared to fly the day after.'

Pearl paled. 'That's good enough for me. It gives Greg over a month to fly his last four missions. So by the time we're married, he'll have finished.'

Or he would be dead. Even Thea wasn't careless enough to put that thought into words. Anyway, as Fitz flew in the same crew as Greg, their fates were entwined. It occurred to Thea that maybe it wasn't a good idea for her to be seeing a member of Greg's crew. For if the worst happened, it was likely to be because *C-Charlie* had been lost, Fitz along with everyone else. How would she be able to support her sister if she had also suffered a terrible loss?

And it would be a terrible loss. Whether or not her slip of the tongue had been the truth and she was actually in love with Fitz, Thea couldn't be sure. However, she was sure that losing Fitz would be a tragedy she'd never fully get over.

Pearl sat up straighter and made a visible effort to appear more optimistic. 'I thought the whole point of these little ceremonies was to help us put aside morbid thoughts. Let's talk about something more cheerful.'

'Like your wedding?' Jenny asked with a smile.

'Actually, yes. I had some good news today. I got a message from Miss Honeycroft that my dress and shoes will be ready to be collected on Saturday. I can't wait to see them again.'

'Jenny and I both have Saturday off,' Thea said. 'We can make a day of it and then have a trying-on party in the evening. I'd love to see Blanche turn green with envy when she sees it.' As soon as the words were out, she felt a twinge of guilt, remembering that Blanche had lost two sweethearts, one of them her fiancé. Seeing Pearl so happy must be hard. It made Thea more determined to finish the crossword to give Sam the push he needed to ask Blanche out.

'I'd like that.' Then Pearl grimaced. 'Bother. I forgot I'm spending Saturday at RAF Waddington, collating their latest news.'

'No problem. Jenny and I can collect it, and we can still have the trying-on party in the evening. It'll make up for having to spend a couple of days under the MO's eye.'

Pearl frowned. 'Wait. The MO?' She looked Thea up and down. 'Were you hurt too? Why didn't you say?'

Thea knew the only way to put Pearl's mind at rest was to tell her everything. She had already removed her jacket in the heat of the snug, and now she rolled back her shirt-sleeve to reveal the dressing. 'I was caught in the same accident as Ted, but I only got a minor bump.'

Some of the worry faded from Pearl's face, but she said, 'The MO must have a reason for signing you off duty. Perhaps it's not such a good idea for you to go into Lincoln. I'm sure he intended you to get some rest.'

'Honestly, I'm fine. The MO only wants me to take tomorrow off. Do you think he'd turn me loose on our Lancasters' delicate instruments if he thought I wasn't up to it?'

Pearl looked mollified. 'I suppose you're right. Anyway, you'll be with Jenny, so she can keep an eye on you.'

It hurt that her sister trusted Jenny more than Thea. 'You do realise the age difference between me and Jenny is nearly as much as the age difference between the two of us? You might want to consider that next time you treat me like a ten-year-old.'

Pearl looked shamefaced. 'You're right. I'm sorry. I really am trying to improve, but I can't seem to get it through my head that you're an adult.'

'You're much better than you were. This time last year you'd have insisted on tucking me into bed with a teddy bear the moment you heard I'd been hurt.'

'That's not true.' But Pearl's grin belied her outrage. 'I'd have given you a cup of cocoa too.'

The girls' laughter was the best tonic Thea could have asked for. As little as a year ago, she would never have believed she and Pearl could become such good friends, having thought it impossible with someone who seemed determined to cast herself more in the role of interfering mother than a sister. Now she raised her glass to Pearl. 'You know, Greg's been so good for you. I know you always used to be on at me to act my age, but it's been a real eye-opener to see how his influence has helped you act *your* age. Like a young woman instead of someone middle-aged before her time.'

Pearl gave a wry smile. 'If we're trading backhanded compliments, now's the time for me to say how much I like seeing you with Fitz. You seem a lot steadier since you started seeing each other. Dare I hope it's getting serious?'

And in three sentences, Pearl had undone everything she'd just said. Thea gritted her teeth. There she was interfering again, hinting that Thea ought to be settling down. Yet she felt too disheartened to pick up the argument again, so she tried to make light of it. 'Oh, you know me. I'm never serious.'

But behind her renewed resentment, there was a flicker of panic. People seemed to think she and Fitz were on the verge of engagement. Had she really got over her old mistakes? Was she ready to get serious?

Chapter Sixteen

'This is nice, isn't it?' Jenny said once they'd stepped off the bus in Lincoln and were walking towards the shops. 'We don't often do things just the two of us.'

That was true, Thea reflected, and a shame, because she treasured Jenny's friendship. 'We'll have to make more of an effort to take time off together,' she told her. 'I suppose I've been rather wrapped up in Fitz. And Jack's troubles, of course.'

'It's understandable, and I don't mind.'

'But I do. You're a good friend, and I've neglected you. I'll do better in future, I promise.'

'I appreciate that, but promise you won't neglect Fitz. He's good for you. Anyway, given half the chance I'd be going out at all hours with—' Jenny broke off, biting her lip.

Thea leaped on the opportunity. 'With who? It's Edwin, isn't it? Go on, I won't tell anyone else, even Pearl.'

Jenny sighed. 'I suppose I haven't hidden it very well. I do like him. Not that it makes any difference, because he obviously doesn't feel the same way about me, and I feel so foolish for having worn my heart on my sleeve.'

'What do you mean, he doesn't like you? Fitz tells me he's always finding excuses to visit the Met Office when he knows you're on duty, and, if your opinion on the weather differs from the forecast given during the briefing, he usually goes along with yours. Apparently your wind speed estimates have saved him from going wildly off course on more than one occasion.'

Jenny's cheeks turned pink. 'He's really said that?' Then she shook her head. 'It doesn't make any difference, though. I know he enjoys my company and values my opinion, but that's as far as it goes, it seems. If his feelings ran deeper than that, I'm sure he would have said something by now.'

'I suppose so. I'm sorry, though, Jenny. I would never have teased you about him if I'd known.' Thea was glad she'd mentioned making more time for Jenny before her friend's confession. If she'd only brought it up now it would have sounded like pity. 'I meant it, though, about making more effort to spend time with you. Especially once Pearl leaves Hut Three. In fact, I wonder if Blatchford would let me take Pearl's bed once she moves out?'

'I'd love that. Only won't you hate sharing a hut with Blanche?'

'I'll survive. She might even start speaking to me if this cross-word stunt works.' Thea had told Jenny and Pearl about Sam's request, and both had shared her hope that getting Blanche and Sam together might soften Blanche's attitude towards Thea. As the crossword was in the latest edition of the *Bombshell*, which had gone on sale that day, she hoped the business would be settled soon.

Thea hadn't been paying much attention to their progress and only belatedly noticed that they had crossed the river and were now on the high street. 'Anyway, I don't want to spoil our day in Lincoln with thoughts about Blanche. What shall we do first – collect the dress, or shopping?'

'We should leave the dress until last,' Jenny said. 'I'm going to be terrified while it's my responsibility. Imagine how awful we would feel if it got dirty or damaged.'

'I suppose you're right. Knowing me, I would leave it somewhere.' Thea had a sudden picture of arriving back in Fenthorpe only to discover she'd left the dress on the bus. Not the way to persuade Pearl she was mature and responsible. 'Shops first, then. Where shall we go?'

'I could do with your advice, actually. Here we are with only a little over a month to go, and I haven't got Pearl and Greg a wedding present yet. What are you getting them?'

'A wedding present?' Thea felt herself go cold. There went any hope of being considered mature and responsible. A truly grown-up young woman would have remembered to get her sister a wedding present. 'I don't believe it. I completely forgot about it. I've no idea what to get. Some sister I am.'

Jenny was undeterred. 'We've got all day. I'm sure we'll find something good.'

'Let's have a wander and see if we get any inspiration.'

But as time wore on, it was clear there was no obvious answer. Thea had thought Pearl might like a pretty frock to wear on her honeymoon, but that would need clothing coupons, which neither had. Traditional wedding gifts such as a dinner service or silver teapot were pointless, even if they'd had enough money. For the foreseeable future, Pearl and Greg might not even be living together. Even if they were, it would be in officers' married quarters, where all meals would be provided.

Finally, feeling disheartened, they retired to the cafe above Boots to gather the strength for a second assault on the shops and to think through any other ideas.

They sipped tea to the soothing accompaniment of the string orchestra while they gathered their thoughts.

'I'd like to get them something special,' Thea mused, 'only I don't have much money.' Although as an LACW in a skilled trade she had received several pay rises since joining the WAAF, it still wasn't much. What really irked her was that she only got paid two-thirds of the amount given to the men doing exactly the same work.

'Pearl will understand,' Jenny told her. 'You send money home to Deedee too, don't you?' When Thea nodded, Jenny added, 'From what I know of Pearl, she'd rather you spent your money on your grandmother than anything fancy for her.'

'She doesn't know. I asked Deedee not to tell her.'

'Why on earth would you do that?'

'I don't know. I suppose Pearl seemed to have such a low opinion of me when I ran off and joined the WAAF, I didn't want her to think I was sending Deedee money as a way of earning back her love.'

Jenny rolled her eyes. 'Honestly, I used to wish I had sisters instead of only brothers, but now I'm starting to think I'm better off without. Do you two ever communicate?'

'We're getting better.'

'I should hope so.' Jenny muttered something under her breath that might have been, 'You can't get any worse.' Then, after clearing her throat, she said, 'I think the first thing you do when you see her is explain that you would like to give her and Greg a lovely present, but you're going to have to defer the proper gift until they are actually setting up house together. Then you can get them something you are sure they will need. You will also explain that you're going to get them something now, but it will only be small because you are, after all, sending a fair proportion of your wages to Deedee. If you say it like she should already know, you won't be making it into a big issue.'

'I suppose that would work. And it's a good idea about waiting until they set up home for their real present. We don't have any family apart from Deedee, and Greg's family are all in Australia, so they don't have a load of relatives able to lavish them with gifts.'

'I never thought of that,' Jenny said, looking suddenly thoughtful. 'That Greg's family is in Australia, I mean. I wonder if he'll want to move back there after the war?'

'That's a point. Greg used to work for a charter company. He might be expected to return there when it's all over. Over here, companies are keeping jobs open for the men who join up. Do you think they do the same over there?' Thea was surprised by the pang of loss that had struck at the prospect of her sister moving to the far side of the world. After years of trying to escape from Pearl's interference, it was strange to think how much she would miss Pearl should she move far away.

'I don't know. I never thought of it.'

'I wonder if Pearl has.' Somehow Thea didn't think she had. She was sure she would have said something if they'd made the decision to move to Australia once Greg was released from his service to the RAF. After all, Greg had been averse to talking or even thinking about making future plans, and even his engagement to Pearl had been a decision to make the most of the present. Somehow she didn't think Pearl and Greg had spoken much about the future. 'Can you believe it?' she said now. 'All this time Pearl has pressed me to think ahead more, and I don't think she's thought ahead at all concerning the biggest decision she'll ever make.' She forced a grin, determined to see the light side. 'Please let me be the one to bring this up.'

'Rather you than me. Although as Pearl's never going to change her mind about marrying him, you should probably leave it for now. No point in upsetting her and spoiling her big day.'

'I suppose you're right.'

'Anyway, we still need to work out what to get them for now.' Jenny's eyes wandered over the table and to the tiny sprigs of wild flowers arranged in a delicate china vase. 'I know – how about a vase?'

'Good idea. Pearl always liked to arrange flowers from our garden at home. I doubt wherever she ends up next will be any prettier than our huts, so she'd like something to brighten the place up. Maybe I could get her a photo frame.'

'Yes.' Jenny's eyes were shining. 'She'll be able to use it for her wedding photograph.' Then she frowned. 'Have they arranged a photographer? If not, Edwin's got a Brownie camera, and I've seen his photographs. They're really good. We could ask him to take the photos.'

'I don't think Pearl's thought of a photographer, so using Edwin would be a good idea, assuming he's free that day.'

'He's done the same number of tours as Greg and Fitz, so he should be finished by then. I presume they'll get leave before being sent to an OTU or wherever they'll go next.'

OTU stood for Operational Training Unit, and it was likely that the crew would be needed in one as instructors once they had finished their tour. If they finished their tour. Thea promptly banished that stray thought.

She drained her cup and pulled out her purse to pay for their drinks. 'Right, we'd better get a move on. We've got presents to buy!'

As it turned out, they were able to find a vase and a picture frame in the same shop, an antiques shop near the top of Steep Hill. The girls could have spent hours wandering around the display cases crammed full of mismatched china teacups and plates. However, aware that time was passing and they still needed to collect the dress, they focused on the cases containing vases and picture frames. Jenny couldn't choose between a pretty fan-shaped glass vase and a china one decorated with exquisite rosebuds. However, when Thea found an art deco oak picture frame, Jenny immediately opted for the glass vase. 'It's Art Deco too, so they'll match,' she told Thea happily.

Once they had their purchases wrapped, they went to collect Pearl's gown, veil and shoes. Thea emerged from Miss Honeycroft's house cradling a large, flat cardboard box in her arms with as much care as she would hold a newborn baby. 'I'm scared the slightest movement will rip the lace to shreds,' she told Jenny, who had charge of the smaller boxes holding the veil and shoes and looked as though she was holding an unexploded bomb. 'Come on, let's get to the bus before something terrible happens.'

They followed the most direct route to the bus station and were approaching the bridge when Jenny happened to glance into the stationery shop they were passing. 'I nearly forgot – I'm almost out of ink. Wait here. I won't be long.' She hurried inside, leaving Thea on the pavement holding all the boxes.

Thea held them against her body in a protective gesture and turned to gaze into the shop window, more to protect the dress from being jostled by any passers-by than out of interest in the window display.

The doorbell jangled, and Thea glanced up automatically to see who was walking out. She went cold all over when she saw

154

a man with a slight figure and dark brown hair. This time she could see his face and there was no mistaking Billy Haywood. She turned away, but not fast enough.

'I don't believe it. Thea Cooper. Long time no see.'

There was no escape. 'Billy. Out of prison, then.'

'Yeah, they let me out early so I could join up.' He indicated her uniform. 'I see you didn't escape conscription, even if you managed to evade arrest.'

'I didn't *evade arrest*, I didn't do anything wrong—' Thea caught herself from saying more. This wasn't a conversation to have in public. Instead, she said, 'I heard what happened to your brother. My condolences.' She glanced into the shop, praying Billy would leave before Jenny emerged.

Billy, however, gave no sign that he wanted to move. 'It was the first time we were going to see each other since my release.' His eyes hardened. 'He was knocked down on his way to the pub where we were going to meet. I never got to see him.' There was an accusatory tone to his voice, as though he thought Thea had been driving the car that hit his brother.

Thea shot a desperate glance at the shop doorway. She needed to end this now. 'That's awful. I'm really sorry.'

'How sorry?'

'What?' Was he expecting her to grade her level of sorrow?

At that point the shop bell jingled and Jenny walked out, brandishing an ink bottle for Thea to see. 'Got it!'

Thea, her stomach in knots, made one last effort to make her escape. 'I must dash – I'm late for my bus.'

She took a step towards Jenny, but her progress was halted when Billy grasped her arm. 'Not so fast. We still have unfinished business.' He lowered his voice. 'Or do you want your pretty friend to find out what you're really like?'

There was no opportunity to answer him before Jenny got close enough to overhear. Thea hitched a smile on her face even while she watched with growing despair as Jenny sailed up to them. She cast an enquiring glance at Billy. 'Hello, are you one of Thea's friends from RAF Waddington? I'm so glad she came to join us in Fenthorpe, but I'm sure you must all miss her.'

'A friend from home, actually.' Billy held out his hand to Jenny. 'Billy Haywood. I expect Thea's told you all about me.'

'Jenny Hazleton.' She shook Billy's hand, and seeing her touch him made Thea feel sick. 'She hasn't mentioned you, but Thea doesn't generally talk about her home much.'

'Why doesn't that surprise me? So you're at RAF Fenthorpe now?' Billy shot Thea a significant glance. 'I'd forgotten where you'd moved to. It's nice to know you're settling in well and making friends.'

Although his tone was smooth, there was a definite threat there, and Thea wondered if he suspected what she had done on the night he had been arrested.

Jenny appeared oblivious to the undercurrents. 'It was lovely to meet you, but we've got a bus to catch.' She moved away, clearly expecting Thea to follow.

Billy, however, intervened. 'I won't keep you long, but I was hoping to have a quick word with Thea. In private.'

Thea wished more than anything she could get away, but, now Billy knew she was at Fenthorpe, there was a real risk that he would show up there and make trouble for her. It hadn't escaped her that Billy had evaded the question of where he was based, but it seemed likely he was also near Lincoln. If she left now, she would be living in constant fear of seeing him again soon. 'Just give me a minute, Jenny. Take the boxes and I'll catch you up.'

Jenny didn't look happy, but took charge of the packages and headed off for the bus station. Once she was out of earshot, Thea turned to Billy. 'Tell me what you want.'

'What I want? You make me sound so mercenary. Isn't the pleasure of your company enough?'

Thea simply folded her arms and glared at him.

'Oh, very well. I think your friends at Fenthorpe would be very interested to learn just what you got up to in Shrewsbury that had you running to the WAAF.'

Thea felt sick. This was clearly an attempt at blackmail, and, while she knew giving in to him once would only be inviting him to return for more, she couldn't think of any other way of getting rid of him. 'How much do you want?'

'I'm a reasonable man. Shall we say twenty pounds?'

Thea gaped. 'You've lost your mind. I haven't got anything like that kind of money.' This was nearly a third of her annual income.

'I said I was reasonable. I can take it in instalments.'

But in a flash of insight, Thea knew that if she agreed now she would never see the last of him, and she decided to take her chances. 'Forget it. You'll have to top up your wages elsewhere, because I can't afford it.'

Before Billy could respond, she stalked away, and joined Jenny in time to scramble onto the bus just before it departed. She was able to distract Jenny from asking about Billy by changing the subject to Pearl and her reaction when she saw the wedding gown. Yet although Jenny seemed to quickly put the new acquaintance out of her mind, Thea couldn't shake off a growing unease that she hadn't seen the last of Billy Haywood.

Chapter Seventeen

RAF Fenthorpe was on high alert as everyone was preparing for the first mission in a fortnight, thanks to the gales. The wind today was nothing more than a playful breeze that frisked through the hedgerows, rustling the unfurling leaves. It was hard to believe that only yesterday Fitz had feared it would rip the roof off the NAAFI.

After so long confined to the ground, Fitz would have enjoyed the test flight, if he hadn't been so worried about Jack. If only he had been able to persuade Jack to speak to the MO, he would probably be on sick leave now instead of preparing to fly another mission. Fitz could only hope the mission would be straightforward, and preferably to a nearby target so they wouldn't have to endure a long flight to get there. The longer it took to reach the target, the more chance there was of something going wrong, and with Jack's fragile state of mind Fitz was worried how he might react.

By the time the crew filed into the briefing hut, Fitz's heart was in his mouth. He made sure he was sitting with Jack, and kept half an eye on him as he placed his pencil and notebook on his desk. Although the hut's walls were covered in posters warning the aircrews of the perils of passing on sensitive information, all eyes were glued to the red curtain drawn across the board upon the platform at the front of the room. Behind this curtain was the all-important map, showing that night's target. The knot in Fitz's stomach that he'd been able to forget about for most of the day now seemed to increase in size and pull impossibly tight. He became aware that he was tapping his pencil on the desk, beating out the rhythm to the waltz from *Coppélia*. He put down the pencil and clasped his hands behind his back, only to snatch up the pencil again when Squadron Leader Price rose from his seat. A hush fell on the room, and the only sound in the room was Price's measured footsteps as he walked to the platform.

Let it be an easy run. Please give us an easy run. Fitz thought he might be physically sick as Price drew breath to make his announcement.

'Good afternoon,' he said in his cultured accent. In another life he could have got work as a BBC news presenter. 'I trust you are all feeling rested after our enforced break.'

There was a ripple of uneasy laughter.

Just tell us where we're going. And make it somewhere close. From the rather strained expressions of the men in his line of sight, Fitz knew they must all be thinking the same as him. If the combined wishes of nearly one hundred men could affect the location of the target, 505 Squadron would be on their way to drop leaflets over Skegness.

Price placed a hand on the curtain cord. There was the faint hissing noise of ninety-eight indrawn breaths. 'Our target tonight is Berlin.'

The target announcement was usually greeted by a groan, especially when the target was in the Ruhr Valley, or even cautiously hopeful nods when the target was one generally regarded as a 'milk run' – a safe mission. Today, the CO drew back the curtain to dead silence. Fitz gazed at the revealed map in desperation, praying he had misheard. But there was no mistaking the course the bright red cord took, from Lincolnshire all the way into the heart of Germany, ending right over Berlin. Price said something Fitz couldn't quite catch through the ringing in his ears – no doubt something along the lines of how vital their mission was to the war effort and taking the war to the Germans – then he handed over to the navigation officer. Fitz tried to concentrate on the course instructions but was distracted by a tight grip on his arm.

He glanced aside to see Jack staring at him, his face a deathly white. Jack swallowed twice before whispering, 'They've got to be out of their tiny minds.'

Fitz said nothing, although he had to agree. How many men would lose their lives tonight for the sake of 'taking the war to the Germans'? He, for one, had never before questioned where they were sent but had willingly done his duty, proud to feel he was playing his part in shortening the war. But this felt unnecessary. He couldn't understand the reasoning behind it.

He couldn't let Jack see his fears, though, so he forced his face into a smile and murmured, 'We'll be fine. We've got the best skipper in the squadron. He'll see us through.' He only wished he believed it.

–

Later, when the briefing was over and there was nothing more to do but wait, the crew went to eat. Although both Edwin and Greg were now officers and took most of their meals in the officers' mess, it had become their habit to join the rest of the crew in the sergeants' mess for the meals immediately before and after a mission. Fitz firmly believed it helped them work well as a team and was one of the reasons why they had survived for so long. He could only hope it would see them through their last missions as well. He felt bad for the remaining crew, who would have to take on a new pilot, navigator and bomb aimer once Greg, Edwin and himself had left, but thought it likely they would get experienced men rather than aircrew fresh from training.

It was becoming known that the first five and last five operations in a tour were the most dangerous. A crew that survived the first five had gathered enough experience to avoid making 'rookie' mistakes. The survival rate for their next twenty operations was significantly better. But aircrews were now starting to notice that the most experienced crews – the ones at the same stage as *C-Charlie*'s crew – also seemed to be lost at a higher rate than those on their middle twenty missions. While no one was quite sure why this should be, most thought it was down to two reasons. First, that these crews were losing concentration as they started to get too confident about completing their tour. Second, and Fitz firmly believed this was the main reason, was that the cumulative stresses of so many operational flights became overwhelming, and the crews stopped functioning so efficiently. As he looked round at his crew now, he could see signs of strain on his friends' faces that hadn't been there before. Even Greg, who Fitz regarded as one of the most easy-going men he knew, had developed a slight hand tremor. Fitz could only pray they could all hold it together for their remaining missions. For Greg, Edwin and himself that was just four nights' work before they would be moved to non-operational duties. Put like that, it didn't sound impossible.

—

Thea's mood lifted somewhat when they got back to Hut Three to find Pearl just returned from her day at work. It was fun to see her normally calm and unruffled sister tremble with excitement as she removed the lid from the box and lifted out the gown. The other WAAFs in the hut also gathered round, and gasped in awe as the beautiful lace dress emerged from its covering of tissue paper.

Even Blanche looked impressed. She had arrived, her crisp new edition of the *Bombshell* folded under her arm, at the same time as Pearl, and her curiosity to see the gown had clearly overcome her reluctance to be in the same place as Thea. 'It's quite pretty for such an old-fashioned style,' was her verdict.

'High praise indeed,' Thea muttered. She was tempted to ask if Blanche had done the crossword yet, but decided to wait, not wanting to detract from Pearl's big moment.

'After three years in uniform, I'm almost tempted to find myself a husband if it means I could wear a gown as gorgeous as that.' Helen, the hut corporal, reached out a hand to the scalloped edge of one of the sleeves, then drew back before she touched the delicate lace. 'I'm terrified I'll spoil it. You'd better cover it up quickly before someone spills tea over it or something.'

Thea, who had suffered similar qualms ever since collecting the dress, breathed a sigh of relief when Pearl folded it back into its box. It was bad enough being afraid that Billy Haywood would turn her life upside-down without having to worry about Pearl's dress. One worry at a time.

Helen cast one last glance at the dress before Pearl secured the lid, then gave a wistful sigh. 'Well, I'd better return to duty. Ops are on tonight, so I expect the office is full of navigators wanting the latest weather reports.'

All Thea's fears concerning Billy and Pearl's dress shrank to the size of a grain of sand compared with the granite cliff that was her dread over Fitz. 'They're flying tonight?' Now she came to think back, there had been increased security on the gate, and she was cross with herself for letting her own worries cast out thoughts of the crews. Before the aircrews were briefed, all phone boxes on the base were locked and personnel were forbidden from leaving without permission, to avoid word getting out of that night's target. She glanced at Pearl. 'Is *C-Charlie* flying?'

'I presume so. I don't know. I only just got back.' Pearl was looking as pale as Thea felt, with no trace of the happy flush that sight of the dress had produced. She drew a deep breath and made an obvious effort to appear composed. 'We knew they were likely to be flying today, after such a long break. I just hope it's a straightforward run.'

Blanche looked self-important. 'All available aircraft are flying, so *C-Charlie* will be included.'

'Do you know where they're going?' Pearl looked as though she was holding herself back from seizing Blanche by the collar.

'Well, no.' Blanche looked pained to have to admit it. 'But from all the buzz among the senior officers, it's clearly a major operation.'

Pearl put a trembling hand to her chest, and Blanche, to do her justice, looked concerned. 'I'm sorry, maybe I should have kept my mouth shut.'

'I could have told you that,' Thea muttered.

Pearl, however, shook her head. 'It's fine. I've had a long time to wonder if I'd prefer to know when Greg is flying or if I'd rather remain in blissful ignorance. On the whole, I've decided it's better to know. This way I can think of him and the rest of the crew. I know it doesn't make any difference, but if anything happened and I hadn't said a prayer for him and his crew that night, I don't think I could forgive myself.'

Thea was reminded of the conversation they'd had after Ted Dean's death and realised Pearl must have done a good deal of thinking since then. She decided she felt the same way. If her thoughts and prayers were with Fitz, Jack, Greg and the rest of the crew that night, she felt that she was playing her part.

'Do you want to see them off?' she asked Pearl then.

Pearl nodded. 'And I'll help out with the tea for when they return,' she added. 'Let's face it, I won't get a wink of sleep tonight, so I might as well do something useful with my time.'

'I'll come too,' Thea told her. 'What about you, Jenny?'

'Of course. You don't think I'd let you worry alone?'

Thea gathered her belongings. 'I've got some darning that needs doing, so I'll see you later.'

'Wait.' Pearl picked up the box containing the lace gown. 'You should look after this. I don't trust myself not to try it on every five minutes.'

'But shouldn't Jenny—?'

'I want you to do it. I trust you, and it's time I acted that way.'

Thea took the box, swallowing to ease the sudden lump in her throat. 'I can't tell you how much this means. I'll take the very best care of it.'

Once she was back in her hut, she stowed the box safely under her bed, awash with gratitude over the new closeness between her and her sister.

The rumble of aero engines was already filling the air when they went to collect their bicycles. Pearl looked at the sky anxiously. 'They're preparing to leave early, aren't they? Won't it still be light when they reach Europe?'

Thea glanced at her watch and frowned. 'You're right. That's strange.' The bombers usually left after dark, to minimise their chances of being sighted by enemy fighters and anti-aircraft batteries. What with the earlier start and the lengthening daylight hours, thanks to the arrival of spring, it would still be some time before the Lancasters were flying under cover of darkness.

'They must be going a long distance,' Pearl said, grim-faced.

There was a grassy area not far from the start of the main runway, where the WAAFs stood when they wished to wave goodbye to the departing bombers. There was already a cluster of WAAFs gathered, and the girls added their bikes to the pile already there and went to join them. Blanche was in the group, and pointedly turned away from Thea. Either she hadn't yet completed the crossword, or she had and was not amused. Then a Lancaster taxied to the head of the runway, and all Thea's attention was taken up with that.

'B-Beer,' Thea muttered, seeing the Lancaster's markings.

The roar of the Lancaster's engines rose to a bellow as the pilot held it against the brakes, waiting for the signal to take off. Thea strained her eyes, seeking out the caravan near the downwind threshold of the runway, knowing the pilot would be doing the same, waiting for the flash of green light giving the go-ahead to take off. She could almost feel the snap of the waiting pilot's tension as the signal came and B-Beer lurched forward, slowly at first and then gathering speed. Thea waved with the others, although she doubted if the pilot or any of the crew would be able to see them. She held her breath as the wheels lifted off the concrete. With a full load of bombs and fuel, any error now could be disastrous. It was a little like watching swans taking off from water – an apparently endless run-up, where it seemed impossible that something so huge could ever haul itself into the air. *B-Beer*, after appearing on the point of crashing back to the ground, suddenly lifted higher, its wheels skimming the treetops as it gained height. Then it was banking and climbing, disappearing from view.

Another three Lancasters repeated the process, then Thea's breath caught in her throat as *C-Charlie* arrived on the runway. A chilly hand clutched hers. Glancing around, startled, Thea saw Pearl. She blinked back tears at this rare evidence of her sister's vulnerability. 'He'll be fine,' she assured Pearl. '*They'll* be fine.' Because her thoughts had drifted from her future brother-in-law to Fitz. 'They're a good crew. The best. They'll all be there at your wedding, you mark my words.'

Pearl didn't answer, simply nodding, tight-lipped. When *C-Charlie* hurtled down the runway, her grip tightened until Thea suspected it would take a while to get the circulation going through her hand again. She didn't complain, though, for she understood Pearl's fears more than she was willing to admit. Fitz was on that plane. Would she see him again?

'You've only got to do this three more times,' she said to Pearl now, as much to reassure herself as her sister.

Pearl drew a deep breath and relaxed her grip. 'That's what I've been telling myself all evening.' She gave a hollow chuckle. 'At what point did our positions become reversed? I thought *I* was supposed to be the one doling out the sisterly advice.'

'I overtook you years ago. You were just too full of yourself to notice.'

The next Lancaster to depart was *D-Donald*. Was it Thea's imagination, or did Blanche's attention sharpen? She certainly seemed to be following *D-Donald*'s progress into the sky more closely than she had with the other aircraft. Was it possible that Sam Drinkwater's affections were returned?

Jenny must have also noted Blanche's interest, for, when the Lancaster was safely away, she asked, 'Is there anyone particular you're watching for?'

'Maybe,' Blanche replied. Then, in a rush, she added, 'Do you know any of *D-Donald*'s crew? Do you think he—I mean, they'll be all right?'

Thea bit back a smile, convinced she knew the identity of the 'he' that had slipped out. She placed herself so that she was out of Blanche's line of sight, enabling herself to watch her reactions.

'I know the navigator, and he really knows his stuff,' Jenny said. 'The rest of the crew must be good too. They've survived fifteen missions, after all. They couldn't have done that unless they all pulled together.'

Blanche's expression relaxed fractionally. 'Good to know.'

While Blanche remained coy about the identity of the man who had caught her interest, Jenny must have known Thea was burning to know. She asked, 'So, tell me. Which member of *D-Donald*'s crew are you sweet on?'

Blanche sighed. 'Was I really that obvious?'

'So there *is* someone. Go on, who is he?'

'It's Sam Drinkwater. Do you know him?'

'Not well. He seems nice, though.'

'More than nice. He's wonderful.' Blanche's eyes drifted out of focus, and her mouth curved in a soft smile. The roar of another Lancaster speeding down the runway seemed to recall her to herself, and the smile slipped from her face. 'I don't think he likes me, though.'

'Why not?' Jenny caught Thea's gaze and rolled her eyes.

'He came to see me earlier today and said he had something important to tell me. I got my hopes up, and was waiting for him to ask me out, but do you know what he did?'

'No, what?'

'He gave me a copy of the *Bombshell*! I mean, it's not exactly every girl's dream, is it?' A spot of bright colour glowed on each of Blanche's cheeks.

'That… doesn't sound romantic, certainly.' Jenny hesitated, and Thea could tell she was trying to decide how to proceed. 'Did he say anything else?'

If Sam hadn't mentioned the crossword, Thea would throttle him next time she saw him.

Blanche's brow furrowed. 'He *did* say something else, now I come to think of it. What was it?'

Thea just about managed to refrain from screaming: *anything to do with the crossword?* If she was truly enamoured with Sam, wouldn't she have drunk in every word he spoke and replayed it in her mind over and over ever since? That's what Thea did with Fitz.

After an infuriating pause, Blanche continued, 'I feel awful now. I should have been paying him attention, but he came haring up to me in the NAAFI when I had just taken my first sip of tea in hours. I'm always terribly busy the days we fly ops, and hardly have time to think, let alone take ten minutes to myself. I wish I'd paid him more attention, though. He deserved it.'

'I'm sure he understands. Think back to exactly what you were doing.' Jenny's voice was persuasive. 'I bet you paid him more attention than you think.'

'Let me see.' Blanche's eyes lost their focus again. 'Like I said, I'd just taken my first sip of tea when Sam burst into the NAAFI' – Blanche's face was instantly transformed and seemed to glow from within – 'and he was so eager to speak to me, I felt all flustered. I was sure he was going to ask me out, you see. But then he just handed me the paper. What was I supposed to say to that? I mean, I know our friendship started over the crossword, but really.' Her eyes opened wide. 'Wait, I remember now. The crossword! He said something about the crossword.'

Thea waited, burning with impatience while Blanche drifted back into her thoughts.

'That's it! I remember now. He said I ought to solve the crossword, because I might find a message. Why didn't I remember that before?'

'Because you were busy and tired?' Jenny gently suggested.

'Well, yes.' Blanche frowned. 'Wait.' She craned her neck to look past Jenny, her eyes boring into Thea's. 'You compile the *Bombshell* crossword. Do you know about this?'

Thea was too startled at being directly addressed by Blanche to evade the question. 'Well… yes. But it was Sam's idea.'

'Is it some kind of trick?' Blanche's narrowed gaze didn't waver.

Pearl, who had stayed out of the conversation until now, took a step closer to Blanche, her sisterly indignation obviously getting the better of her. Thea caught her arm to silence her, knowing she needed to deal with Blanche herself. 'It's no trick,' she said. 'Look, I know you don't trust me, but just do the crossword. Where's the harm in that?'

Blanche's internal battle was clear to see, doubt warring with hope. Finally she gave a curt nod. 'Fine. I suppose it won't hurt. But if this is your twisted idea of a joke…'

'You'll turn all your friends against me?'

Blanche had no reply to that, and turned away.

By this time the last Lancaster was climbing into the air, and the gathered WAAFs were dispersing. 'Well, that was interesting,' Thea said to Pearl and Jenny. 'If Blanche doesn't apologise once she and Sam are happily together, my next crossword will have the words "Blanche", "ungrateful" and "cow" in the solutions.'

Chapter Eighteen

When Thea had climbed into bed, she had supposed she wouldn't manage to get any sleep, and it did take her a while. On top of the usual worry concerning the aircrews, she also couldn't forget Blanche's accusations. She sincerely hoped Blanche would manage to complete the crossword, or at least the clues making up Sam's message, before it was time to greet the returning crews. It would be one less worry if Blanche could be civil to her for a change.

Thoughts of Blanche and Sam inevitably led to herself and Fitz. She had judged Blanche unfairly for not immediately recalling what Sam had said about the crossword, but that was because she could remember all her conversations with Fitz. Not only the words but also each expression as it played across his expressive face, and the way her gaze lingered on his lips, and how she longed to kiss them.

There was no avoiding the truth any longer. Whether or not Fitz simply thought of her as a fun diversion, she had fallen head over heels in love with him. How had she allowed it to happen? She had been so careful after Billy.

But what if Fitz *did* love her? Was she going to break the heart of a man who was risking his life in service for his country? That would be a cruel way to treat him. Despite these thoughts churning through her brain, sleep eventually caught up with her and she drifted off, only to jerk awake when she heard another WAAF climb out of bed in the darkness. There followed the rustle of clothes, and Thea knew it must be time to get up.

It was a relief not to see Blanche at the bike stand when she went to meet Pearl and Jenny.

'We haven't seen her,' Pearl said, when Thea enquired after her whereabouts. 'I think she went to the rec to do the crossword.'

'I hope she stays out of my way. It's bad enough waiting for the crews to come back without worrying about getting a knife in the back.' Thea climbed on her bike and set off.

There wasn't much talking as they cycled along the road separating the domestic side of RAF Fenthorpe from the operational side. In the blackout, they had to concentrate on the pale circles of light cast by their shielded headlamps, which never gave much warning of potholes or obstacles. At the same time, they had to listen out to make sure they weren't getting too close to another cyclist. For the most part, therefore, the WAAFs rode without speaking, and there was nothing to hear apart from the whir of bicycle chains and the screech of brakes, punctuated by the occasional distant yelp of a fox from across the fields.

Only when they had left their bikes behind the operations block and gathered outside did they resume unfinished conversations as though they hadn't been interrupted by a bike ride of over a mile.

'Anyone know where they went tonight?' Thea looked around the group of WAAFs who had arrived before them. There was no sign of Blanche.

A WAAF Thea vaguely recognised replied. Thea thought she worked in Flying Control. She said just one word. 'Berlin.'

Thea, who had started to pace, stopped short and stared at the WAAF. 'You're joking.'

'Wish I was. When 505 Squadron's CO came into Flying Control earlier this afternoon, he was looking positively green around the gills. He didn't say anything, of course, but I got the impression that he thinks the top brass must be suffering from temporary lunacy. Of course, he had to appear to support them, so he spouted something about "Taking the war to the Germans."'

'Funny,' Pearl muttered, sounding not at all amused. 'I thought that's what they'd been doing every time they've gone off to bomb the Ruhr Valley.'

The Flying Control WAAF shrugged. 'I know, but there must be a good reason.'

Pearl appeared to have recovered from the initial shock. 'I hope you're right. Anyway, the main thing now is to make sure we're ready with hot tea when the crews get back.'

It was a long wait, but finally the longed-for sound of aero engines could be heard in the distance. The drivers who were waiting to collect the returning crews and ferry them back to the operations block hastily stubbed out cigarettes and returned to their buses, and the runway lighting was switched on. Thea, who had waited like this many times, knew this was the worst time. There would be no knowing which crews were safe until they climbed out of the buses.

The din of aero engines increased. 'How many in this group, do you think?' Jenny asked, her head cocked to the sky.

Thea was used to estimating numbers from the noise. 'Three, I think. Here's the first one now.' As she spoke, the navigation lights of the first Lancaster to arrive blinked into view, and pretty soon two more sets of navigation lights could be seen, circling at different heights. Thea knew the WAAFs in Flying Control would be directing each returning Lancaster to join the circuit at set heights, and bringing them in to land, prioritising those with low fuel or injured men. Bombers had been known to limp back seriously damaged and even on fire, and Thea sincerely hoped there would be no such drama this time.

She held her breath as the first Lancaster touched down, but there had been no need for anxiety. It made a perfect landing and quickly taxied off the runway to its dispersal point, allowing the next aircraft in the queue to make its approach. All the while, the waiting WAAFs were listening out for more.

'I think there's another one in the distance,' Pearl said only a minute or so after the first three Lancasters had landed. 'Wouldn't it be wonderful if *C-Charlie* was in the first group?'

'It would certainly save a long, anxious wait,' Thea replied. 'Promise you won't break off your engagement if she's the last one back, though?'

This earned more of a laugh than the feeble joke deserved. Last year, Pearl had broken up with Greg after a particularly long wait. Although Pearl had insisted there had been more to the break-up than the frayed temper resulting from the agonising suspense, Thea persisted in teasing her sister at every given opportunity. And at times like this, it reminded them both of how their fears had come to nothing.

When the buses brought the first crews back, Thea felt as sick as Pearl must have been when *C-Charlie*'s crew weren't there. 'Although it was unreasonable to expect them,' she said, trying to persuade herself as much as Pearl. 'They didn't take off as early as any of these crews.'

Then they were kept too busy handing out mugs of hot, strong tea to the exhausted men to think for a while. This was why Thea liked to volunteer when she wasn't on duty, and she knew Pearl and Jenny felt the same way. If they hadn't come to hand out the teas they would, in all likelihood, be lying awake in their huts, counting each Lancaster as it flew over.

She was delighted to see that the fourth crew to return was *D-Donald*. Although having Fitz on the crew meant *C-Charlie* was the Lancaster Thea always looked out for first, *D-Donald* was also 'her' Lancaster, and she would be devastated if anything happened to her. She watched the men as they climbed out of the bus. While all looked tired – not surprising after the long flight to Berlin and back – she was relieved to see that none had been hurt.

The pilot winced when he saw her. 'Afraid the compass stopped working. Think it must have been hit by a bullet or some flak.'

Thea gave her best impression of an irate schoolmistress. 'I swear you boys are determined to make more work for me.'

But what the pilot might have said in return was cut off when Sam Drinkwater jumped down and a squeal came from the back of the group of WAAFs. There was the sound of running footsteps, then Blanche launched herself into Sam's arms. Thea supposed she must have been staying out of her sight. Sam, looking both startled and delighted, recovered from his initial awkwardness and hugged her in return.

'Did you do the crossword?' he asked her, gazing into her eyes as though he couldn't believe he was actually holding her in his arms.

'Of course,' Blanche replied. 'You don't think I routinely throw myself at airmen, do you?'

Thea was forced to bite her lip to suppress the sarcastic retort that was just crying out to be spoken. She didn't want to trigger a new feud.

Neither Sam nor Blanche were paying her any attention, though, so probably wouldn't have heard her even had she spoken. They had eyes only for each other. Sam, clutching his tea in one hand, had his free arm wrapped firmly round Blanche's waist. 'Do you have an answer for me?' he asked.

'Yes. I'd love to go dancing with you, tonight or any other night.'

At that, Sam apparently lost all his shyness, bent his head and kissed her. Thea half-expected Blanche to feign outrage and slap him as though she were a heroine in a melodrama. To her credit, she didn't seem bothered what anyone else might think and kissed him back with enthusiasm, not stopping even when Sam's crewmates cheered them both.

They finally emerged for air, looking slightly flushed and rumpled. Despite her usual jaded nature, Thea had to admit they looked sweet together, and was happy to have helped them get together.

Blanche caught her eye. She hesitated a moment then, to Thea's surprise, released Sam's hand and walked right up to her. 'Thank you, Thea.' She bit her lip. 'I owe you an apology.'

'Yes, you do.' Thea wasn't going to let her off easily. 'This isn't a good time, though.' She couldn't pay Blanche any attention when her every sense was reaching out, looking for any sign of *C-Charlie*'s return.

'How about I buy you lunch later in the NAAFI?'

'If you can bear to be seen with me.'

Blanche bit her lip. 'I suppose I deserved that.'

'You suppose correctly.' Maybe if Thea hadn't been so concerned with *C-Charlie*'s whereabouts she would have enjoyed seeing Blanche squirm, but as it was she couldn't keep this up. 'Oh, very well. See you in the NAAFI at 1300. I'll want sausage and chips, mind.'

'It's a deal.'

Once Blanche had departed, Thea's thoughts inevitably turned to the whereabouts of *C-Charlie*. Thankfully there wasn't long to wait before she caught a glimpse of Fitz's face through the window of the next bus to draw up.

Pearl clutched her arm. 'Oh, thank God. There's Greg.' The whole crew had returned in one piece. Like the others, they looked exhausted, as though they had walked the whole way to Berlin and back, but even Jack was smiling, even if his smile did look somewhat strained.

Despite Thea's somewhat cynical response to seeing Blanche and Sam kiss, she forgot all about that now and, before Fitz had finished stepping down from the bus, she had pulled his face down to hers and planted a kiss full on his lips. 'Welcome back,' she said. 'Did you really go all the way to Berlin?'

'Yup,' was the terse reply. 'I can't tell you how good it feels to have my feet back on the ground. I don't want to repeat that run in a hurry.'

She let him go reluctantly, after arranging to meet him that evening.

'Thanks for coming.' Blanche gave a nervous smile as she took a seat opposite Thea. Thea was aware of a murmur of interest around the crowded NAAFI, and heads turned as word spread that the mortal enemies were together at the same table.

'They're probably waiting to see which one of us gets carried out on a stretcher.' Thea paused on the point of tucking into her sausage and chips, bought by Blanche. 'You didn't put arsenic in the salt, did you?'

Blanche tossed her head. 'I wouldn't do anything so obvious.'

Thea was surprised by the light of mischief in Blanche's eyes. Sam was right – she *did* have a sense of humour. 'I think Sam's going to be good for you. I'm glad you two are together.'

'I— thank you.' A furrow appeared between Blanche's brows as she peered at Thea's face, studying her. 'I was expecting you to be angry with me,' she said in the end. 'You'd have every right.'

'I'm not sure how to react. You said you wanted to make your apology. I'm waiting.'

Blanche nodded and gazed down at her plate, pushing the peas around with her fork. After a drawn-out pause, she spoke in a rush. 'You were right, what you said at the hotel the other evening.'

'Which bit?' After the way Thea had been treated, she was in no mood to make this easy for Blanche. 'I seem to remember saying quite a lot.'

'All of it. You can't imagine how awful I felt, being forced to listen to you telling me exactly what I'd done wrong. But most of all, I feel like such an idiot for not realising what Sheldrick was up to. I should have seen it. I should have—' A look of horror crossed her face. 'You don't think I helped him, do you?'

'No, I know you wouldn't do anything like that.'

Thea's reassurance seemed to make Blanche feel worse. She bit her lip and addressed her next words to her right thumbnail.

'Deep down, I always knew you wouldn't steal anything either. You were right when you said I was jealous of Pearl, too. I was jealous that she'd barely been at Fenthorpe for two minutes and already she'd uncovered the truth behind such despicable thefts. I really should have noticed what was going on.'

To her credit, she didn't attempt to excuse her oversight by explaining that she'd recently lost her fiancé, and that made Thea more willing to meet her halfway. 'You shouldn't blame yourself for that. What about all the other members of the Committee of Adjustments, or Sheldrick's CO, come to that? Anyway' – Thea grinned at Blanche – 'personally, I think Pearl only got involved because she was trying to impress Greg, the shameless hussy!'

That had the effect Thea had aimed for – it made Blanche giggle. 'I can't believe you're being so understanding. I don't think I would be, were our positions reversed.'

'Life's too short to hold grudges.'

Blanche's mouth tightened. 'You can say that again.' Thea knew she must be thinking of her dead fiancé. 'For what it's worth, I'll be sure to tell all my friends I made a mistake and that I've apologised to you.'

'Thank you.' Thea nodded at the others in the NAAFI, many of whom were making a show of being engrossed in conversation even though it was clear they were all curious to know what Blanche could be saying to Thea. 'I think they probably already know.'

Chapter Nineteen

Thankfully there were no ops on that night, which was a good thing as most of the Lancasters seemed to have returned damaged, to a greater or lesser degree. No crews had been lost from Fenthorpe, although, when Thea had met Fitz for a brief catch–up in the NAAFI, Fitz said they had seen more than one Allied bomber go down on what Thea could tell had been a harrowing mission. They hadn't had much time to talk, as Thea had needed to return to work. *D-Donald*'s compass had needed extensive repairs after it had taken a hit from a piece of shrapnel; she was under pressure to complete the repair by the end of the day, as rumours were rife that ops would be on again the following day. Thea thought it highly likely – according to Jenny the weather was set fair, and, after a long break caused by the gales, she was sure Bomber Command would be anxious to make their presence known to the Germans again as soon as possible.

Therefore she hadn't been able to spend as much time with Fitz as she would have liked before having to dash back to the Instrument Section.

Life in the Instrument Section was strange without Ted. Thea missed his banter, and several times looked up to make a comment, only to see an empty stool at the bench where he had always sat. She had heard they would be getting a new corporal in another week, and, while she looked forward to the ease in workload, she knew it would be difficult to come to terms with seeing someone else occupying Ted's place.

Still, the lack of distraction meant that Thea finished the repairs to *D-Donald*'s compass rather sooner than anticipated, and was even able to make a start to some minor instrument checks needed by *C-Charlie*. She therefore had no trouble ensuring she had a free evening and could go to the pub with Fitz.

'It's good to know we can simply enjoy the evening and not have to write anyone's name on the ceiling tonight,' she said, hugging his arm as they made their way to the pub.

'Definitely,' Fitz said, although he seemed distracted.

'Is something the matter?' she asked.

He drew a deep breath. 'I've got a horrible feeling we're going to be sent back to the same place tomorrow night.' He spoke in a low voice, low enough not to be overheard even if there was anyone lurking in the hedgerow.

In her horror, she couldn't trust herself to keep her voice low. 'You're kidding.'

'I wish I was. At the debrief I could tell that the Pathfinders had marked the target short, and it doesn't seem as though we achieved what we set out to do.'

'I wish they'd give you a couple of nice, easy missions to finish your tour on.' Then a sudden thought struck. Although she knew both Fitz and Greg had completed the same number of ops while in different crews before they had lost their original aircraft and been moved to *C-Charlie*, she had never questioned if the other crew members had completed the same number as well — but now she remembered a conversation she'd had with Jack a few weeks ago; she was sure he had told her he'd had eight ops remaining, and it only just occurred to her that Fitz had only had five ops to go at that time. 'Will you all finish after another three ops, or is it just you and Greg?'

'It's a bit of a sore point with the crew,' Fitz said. 'Edwin finishes at the same time, but the others all came from the same crew, and they lost their Manchester after only two complete missions. So they will need to fly another three before finishing their tour. Not that they begrudge us finishing before them, but it's a real shame that we won't all finish together. Also, having to get used to three new crew members when they're right at the end of their tour won't be easy for any of them. We're all praying they'll at least draft in an experienced pilot rather than sending in a complete sprog.'

There was a long pause while Thea pondered what this would mean for the crew. She hoped for all their sakes that *C-Charlie* would also get an experienced bomb aimer and navigator to give them the best chance of completing their tour. 'I expect that's what will happen,' she said finally, hoping to comfort Fitz. 'After all, just because the crew will be changing, *C-Charlie* will carry on flying. Do you know what we say about the crews and the planes in the ground crew?' When Fitz shook his head, she explained, 'We say that the crews only borrow their aircraft. Hopefully *C-Charlie* will carry several crews before the war's all over.' Then she paused, thinking how what she had said could be misunderstood. 'I said hopefully because I want *C-Charlie* to survive, not because I want her to lose loads of crewmen or because I want the war to drag on for years.'

'I know what you meant.' Fitz suddenly tugged Thea to a halt and his face was serious in the golden evening light. 'Thea, we've managed to skim over the subject whenever it comes up, but, assuming I complete this tour, what then?'

'What do you mean?' Although she had a pretty good idea what he was trying to say. He wanted to know if they had a future after he left Fenthorpe. And, even though she had always promised herself she wouldn't fall for Fitz and wouldn't expect anything of their relationship beyond enjoying the here and now, she found that her mouth went dry at the prospect of him leaving with no assurance that they would meet again.

'Taking each day as it comes isn't enough for me any more. If I'm still alive this time next week or month or even year, I want to have you in my life, no matter where in the world

I might be. I want to believe that maybe we could even start hoping and planning for a time when we might be together.'

In that moment, Thea understood exactly why Pearl had agreed to marry Greg despite the uncertainty surrounding their lives. Because they wanted to be together for as long as they could. Thea had never imagined she would feel the same, but now she did.

Though she hadn't uttered a word, something of her feelings must have shown in her expression, for Fitz smiled and brushed a strand of hair back from her face, looking like a man who has just won the pools. 'I was sure you were going to tell me I was deluded,' he said.

Thea wrapped her arms round his shoulders and moved closer. 'Now, why would I do that when I can do this instead?' And she kissed him.

When they broke the kiss, he rested his forehead against hers, and Thea had no desire to move away or continue their walk. Moments of peace like this were few and far between, and she found herself relishing their closeness and breathing in the peace.

'You know, when I heard we were going to Berlin yesterday, I was so sure that *C-Charlie*'s fate had been sealed. I couldn't imagine getting all the way there and back in one piece, and I regretted not making clear my feelings for you.'

'Maybe it gave us both the kick up the backside that we needed,' Thea put in with a light laugh. 'I've been lying to myself for a while, telling myself that what we have is just a bit of fun, that if either of us get transferred to another part of the country we'd separate with no regrets.' Even now, with Fitz's openness about the prospect of death, she couldn't bring herself to talk about his dying and how she would feel. 'When I went to help with the tea last night, and one of the WAAFs told me you'd gone to Berlin...' She shuddered and couldn't continue for a while, instead pulling him closer and clutching his shoulders, reassuring herself that he really was there. 'Well,' she said eventually, recovering her ability to speak, 'if you... hadn't come back, I would have always regretted not being honest about my feelings.' She gazed into his eyes, close enough to see the darker flecks of grey in the blue eyes. 'I love you, Fitz. That time I blurted it out, I tried to brush it off, pretend it was a slip of the tongue. Well, I'm sorry. If I was being honest back then I'd have told you I meant it. I don't care if you can't make any promises about the future, but I want you to know that I love you, and, if we have a future, I want us to spend as much of that future together as possible.'

It was some time before they resumed their walk, and even longer before Thea remembered why she had asked about when the rest of *C-Charlie*'s crew would complete their tour. 'I nearly forgot. How was Jack last night?'

'He was actually fine.'

'That's good, isn't it?' Fitz's tone had not been positive, which puzzled her.

'Yes and no.'

'Are you going to explain what you mean, or are we going to talk in riddles for the rest of the night?'

This earned a reluctant chuckle. 'Fine. I mean, of course it's good that Jack managed to hold himself together last night. But we had an unusually smooth run. The trouble is that now he's trying to persuade himself that he's over whatever problems he has and everything will be fine from now on.'

'So he won't go back to the MO?'

'No. He says he doesn't need to.' Jack sighed. 'It doesn't help that he's got no faith in doctors – he told me his father died in hospital. And just when I'd persuaded him the MO was a good bloke, and he ought to confide in him, he sees a dead body the moment he steps through the door. It's reinforced all his old fears. I don't know if I'll be able to persuade him to go back, but if we have another bad run I'm terrified he'll declare himself LMF and allow himself to be humiliated.' Fitz's voice shook, and it took a moment for Thea to realise it was with anger. 'I'll never understand the pettiness and cruelty of the LMF ruling. Even if a man doesn't complete his thirty missions – for which, I might add, he volunteered – it can never take away the fact that he risked his life in the skies over Europe many times over. He should get a medal, but instead he'll be mocked and treated like a criminal and a coward.'

Thea placed a hand on his arm. 'He won't. Because we're still going to do everything we can to help him, aren't we?'

He gazed at her, eyes wide, as though he'd forgotten she was there. Then he relaxed and smiled. 'Yes, we are.'

The sun was low in the sky by the time they reached the pub in the middle of the village, and it cast long shadows across the street. The glare meant that Thea had to shade her eyes and was only really aware of passers-by as silhouettes. Therefore, she didn't pay much attention to the figure leaning against the pub's porch wall until it placed itself between her and the doorway.

'Hello, Thea. Got a moment?'

Thea froze. While she couldn't make out the man's features in the glare of the low sun, she'd know that voice anywhere. It had haunted her ever since she had heard it in Lincoln. Billy Haywood.

'Oh hello, Billy,' she said with a show of indifference. 'Maybe another time. I'm busy at the moment.'

Billy didn't budge. 'I've got something to say that you won't want to miss.'

While Thea refused to be intimidated, the last thing she wanted was to get into an argument with Fitz present. 'Fine. Go on in, Fitz. I won't be long.' Feeling she needed to add some kind of explanation, she added, 'Billy's an old friend from Shrewsbury.' She avoided Fitz's gaze, knowing her eyes would betray her uneasiness.

Fitz gave Billy a long look, then said, 'Are you sure you'll be all right?'

'I'll be fine. See you in a minute.'

As soon as Fitz disappeared inside, Thea snapped, 'Now you listen to me, Billy Haywood—'

'No. *You* listen to *me*.' Billy grasped her arm and pulled her, none too gently, away from the entrance and round the corner to a deserted spot in the angle between porch and main wall. When he spoke again his voice was a low murmur, although the menace in its tone was unmistakable. 'I know what you did, Thea. You owe me.'

Chills trickled down her spine. He couldn't possibly know. She raised her chin. 'I don't know what you mean.'

'I mean, you're the reason I got caught. And I deserve compensation.'

'That's a long word for you. Are you sure you know what it— Ow!' For Billy had tightened his grip. She glared at him. 'Let me go, or I'll scream.'

'You wouldn't.'

'Try me. I'm sure the police would be very interested to learn that a former prisoner was attacking women.'

She had no idea what the police would actually do, but Billy must have decided he didn't want to risk it, for he released her. She took a step back, rubbing her bruised arm, and decided to brazen it out. 'I don't know what you think I've done, but you were the one who broke into an old man's shop and attacked him. It's your fault you ended up in prison, not mine. Now, if you'll excuse me, I'm going to join my friend before he comes looking for me.'

She edged away, taking one hesitant step then another, expecting him to haul her back at any moment.

'I wouldn't leave if I were you.' Billy's voice was mocking. 'You see, I know exactly what you did, because my brother saw you. Shall I come with you and tell all your friends? I bet they'd be interested to hear what you were like back then.'

An icy hand seemed to squeeze Thea's heart. 'You wouldn't. Anyway, I didn't do anything wrong.'

Billy shrugged. 'That's a matter of opinion. Why don't we ask your friends and see what they think?'

Still Thea hesitated. She *hadn't* done anything wrong. She wanted to scream it to the skies. *Yet you went around with Billy,* a voice whispered deep inside her head. *What would Fitz say if he heard you were infatuated with a man who nearly beat an old man to death? He'd never be able to look at you again.*

She slumped against the wall. 'I suppose if I paid you the money you want, you could be persuaded to leave my friends alone?'

'You've got the idea.'

She had never hated anyone as much as she hated Billy at that moment. Nor had she ever felt so helpless. She pulled out her purse. 'It will take me a while to get hold of twenty pounds, but I can give you something to get started with.' She offered him her last ten-shilling note. It was a wrench to let that go, and she had no idea how she was ever going to raise twenty pounds, but she'd manage it somehow. Anything to keep Fitz's good opinion. His love.

Billy gave a smile that she itched to punch. 'Oh, twenty pounds was what I asked for before you so rudely refused me. The price has gone up to thirty now.' He took the banknote and used it to fan his face. 'I'll take this as a down payment, though.'

Thea could only stare at him. Twenty pounds had been an impossible amount. How was she ever to raise half as much again? 'You know I don't have that kind of money.'

'Maybe there's a little job you can do for me that would make us even.'

Thea's heart sank. Knowing Billy, a 'little job' probably involved theft, and there was no way she was prepared to sink so low. On the other hand, if she didn't buy herself some time there was nothing to stop Billy marching into the pub and giving her away, and she couldn't bear to lose either Fitz's love or Jenny and Pearl's high regard. 'What kind of job?' she asked.

'Not here. We don't want to be overheard. Are you free any time tomorrow?'

Thea shrugged. 'Maybe I could slip out for an hour at around eleven.' She usually got a break then, and, if ops were on, the base wouldn't be locked down until later. How Billy would be able to get from where he worked to Fenthorpe at the drop of a hat, she couldn't imagine.

Billy, however, seemed unbothered. 'Very well. I'll meet you in the lane outside the main gate. We can enjoy a romantic walk together in the pretty Lincolnshire countryside.'

Thea's flesh crawled at the mere thought. 'Are you based nearby, then?'

'Oh, I got a forty-eight-hour pass, starting this evening. Don't worry. Nothing's going to prevent our meeting.' He sauntered down the path with a casual wave.

'Nothing apart from a solid kick in the crotch,' Thea muttered to herself as she pushed open the pub door. While she had no intention of paying Billy any more money and certainly wasn't going to be manipulated into getting mixed up in whatever nefarious scheme he was up to, she had no idea how to get out of it. Not if she didn't want him turning the whole of RAF Fenthorpe against her just when people were speaking to her again.

The moment she stepped into the snug, her eyes fell on Fitz. He was sitting with Jenny, Pearl, Greg and a few of his other crewmates. He seemed to instinctively know she was watching him, for he glanced up and met her gaze, giving her a smile that made her insides swoop. Here was the man she had just declared her love for. The only man who could have encouraged her to overcome her misgivings and make a real commitment. How would he feel if she told him what she was truly like?

That would be the sensible thing to do – sit down with them all now and explain what had just happened. Between them they could find a way to fend off Billy's threats, and they could probably report him for blackmail.

Thea's gaze drifted to Pearl, who was leaning against Greg, laughing at something Jenny had just said. Then she glanced over her shoulder to shoot a smile at Greg, and, although the love in her expression was undeniable, there was also a tension that Thea could read only too well. It was a fear that Pearl had struggled to suppress, with only limited success. In that moment, it was as though Thea could hear Pearl's thoughts: *Will you still be here this time tomorrow?*

Inadvertently, Thea's gaze drifted back to Fitz, and she wondered the same thing.

She knew all about Pearl and Greg's determination to accept whatever happiness they could have and not to worry too much about the future. But if she sat down now and told them what had just happened, she would destroy this peaceful scene. Times like this were rare and precious and should be preserved, not shattered with one swing of the hammer that her news would be. Even Blanche and Sam looked blissfully happy, sitting in the quietest corner, holding hands across the table. Evidently they had abandoned any idea of dancing, and seemed content to simply drink in each other's company. They were both laughing and talking, seeming to trip over their words in their hurry to say what was in their hearts. Thea didn't want to disturb that cosy scene either.

At that moment, Pearl looked up, saw Thea and beckoned. Taking a deep breath, she went to sit in the seat Fitz had saved for her, between himself and Pearl. If she was going to say anything it had to be now.

'Is everything all right?' Fitz asked. 'What did that bloke want?'

Pearl leaned forward. 'What bloke?'

This was it. She could confess everything now while she had the attention of the whole table. That way she would only have to explain herself once and would only have to face everyone's anger or disbelief or disgust once.

She hesitated a moment too long. 'Well, he—'

'Oh, it doesn't matter,' Pearl said at exactly the same time. 'I did promise not to be an interfering older sister and to stop poking my nose into your life. I really ought to start living up to my word. Anyway, Jenny's just had a really good idea about the flowers. Tell Thea what you said, Jenny.'

And the moment was gone. Thea didn't have the heart to burst Pearl's happy bubble, and, the longer Jenny chattered away about collecting cow parsley and moon daisies from the verges, the faster Thea's resolve faded. She muttered something to Fitz about catching up with an old friend and then joined in with the wedding talk. She would have to get herself out of trouble, as she always had before.

Chapter Twenty

Fitz went down to breakfast in the sergeants' mess the following day with an extra spring in his step. It was hard to believe that, after what felt like an eternity of hoping that he and Thea wanted the same thing out of their relationship, he had finally plucked up the courage to tell her honestly how he felt. And although he hadn't expected her to say she returned his feelings, by some miracle she had done just that.

Three more operations. That was all he had left. If he got through those then perhaps he would even ask her to marry him. He didn't expect her to leave the WAAF, and he had no idea where he would end up being posted – probably not in Lincolnshire. He doubted he and Thea would end up close enough to live together, but he wondered if she would agree to marriage so they could at least see one another when they got leave.

He gave himself a mental shake. Thea had only just admitted that she loved him and could see a future with him in it. Talking about marriage was probably a step too far for someone as independent as she was. She had said she loved him, and that was all that mattered for now. That and getting through the next three missions in one piece.

Seeing Jack at a table beside the window, Fitz went to join him, uncomfortably aware that he had not paid him much attention since that awful day when they had seen Ted Dean's dead body.

'There's a buzz in the air,' Jack said when Fitz took a seat opposite. 'Something tells me we're flying ops tonight.'

Fitz decided to have one more attempt. 'Look, Jack, you don't have to do this. Why not come with me to the MO after breakfast?'

Jack, however, set his jaw and shook his head. 'You know my feelings about that. Anyway, I'm feeling better now. I thought I wouldn't be able to get through another mission, but the Berlin op proved I can do it.'

This was what Fitz had feared. That Jack would deny he had any problem. While he was relieved Jack was no longer threatening to go LMF, he hated to think what might happen if he panicked or froze if anything unexpected happened. Speaking in a low voice, he tried to explain his worries to Jack, but the other man brushed them off. 'I'm fine, honest. You can depend on me.'

'And what about when Greg and I complete our tours? How will you feel about flying another three missions with a new pilot and without me to keep an eye on you?'

'You're worrying about nothing.' Although Fitz could have sworn he caught a flicker of unease in Jack's eyes.

Fitz only gave up when they went to the operations block and saw that *C-Charlie*, complete with her usual crew, was on the list to fly, together with all the serviceable Lancasters. *D-Donald* was also on the list, and Fitz knew the ground crews must have worked around the clock to get her back into good repair. He knew Thea had put in long hours to get the compass fixed.

When he went to do their flight test, he half hoped Thea would be among the ground crew members sent into the air with them, but he saw no sign of her. She was probably carrying out extra checks on *D-Donald*.

They were among the first group of Lancasters cleared to make their test flights and, when Fitz tested his guns over the sea, he hoped and prayed today's mission would be so straightforward he wouldn't be required to fire a single shot. When they made their return approach to the airfield, he wondered where Thea was and if she was looking out for them. He looked forward to landing after their mission, when hopefully Thea would be waiting for him. Then he and Greg would only have two more missions to fly.

Greg made a perfect landing. As the test had gone smoothly, they now had some time to kill before the briefing. The crew split up, all intent on filling the next few hours with the various pre-mission rituals they had devised for themselves. Greg went off alone, and Fitz knew he would be writing a letter to his parents in Australia that he would leave in his locker in case of his death. He had done this for as long as Fitz had known him, always burning the letter when he returned to the locker room in the early hours of the next morning. Fitz wondered if he now wrote to Pearl as well.

Fitz had a similar routine, writing to his mother, putting down the words he knew he would want her to read should he not survive the mission. As it was a sunny day, he collected his writing case from his hut and then retired to a shady spot under a tree not far from the main gate. At the moment the gates were open, but they would close soon before the briefing and that night's target was made public. With his writing case open on his knees, he drafted his letter in pencil, knowing that using his fountain pen in this position would most likely end with his getting ink all over his uniform. With the fresh long grass and unfurling leaves swaying in the breeze, he wrote, telling his mother that he was proud to serve his country and, whatever happened, he didn't regret volunteering as aircrew.

After all, he jotted down after tapping his pencil on his chin while groping for words, *if I hadn't joined C-Charlie's crew, I would never have met Thea. I hope you will be able to meet her soon, because I'm sure you would love her. I'm so lucky to have her, and even if I die tonight and we've only had this brief time together, I'd rather it be like this than never having met her at all.*

He meant every word, and hoped his mother would take comfort in them should she ever receive this letter. For, like

Greg, he destroyed each unsent letter. It was one thing his mother reading such an emotional outpouring if these turned out to be his last words to her, but he would probably die of embarrassment should he survive and send her the letter by mistake.

When he had finished, it was still too early to return to the sergeants' mess for dinner, so he pocketed his letter and signed out at the gatehouse, deciding to go for a stroll to clear his mind. This was something else he liked to do before a mission when the weather was fine, and today was perfect, with the promise of spring in the air. It felt too good to hole himself up in the smoky NAAFI.

Once out of the gates, he turned in the direction that led away from the village and let his mind wander as he strolled along the lane. Now the storms had passed, the weather seemed to be making up for lost time, and signs of spring were on every tree and bush. The ground crews were still testing engines, and Fitz relished the interludes when there was no roar emanating from the dispersal points and a hush fell over the site. Then he would become aware of the birdsong and even the hum and buzz of insects. At one point he saw a tiny wren perch upon a hazel twig and pour out a song that seemed ridiculously loud considering the tiny body producing it. He took comfort from knowing that, whatever happened to him, the wren would still be there tomorrow, singing to anyone who passed.

The sound of voices came from somewhere a short distance ahead. As he was approaching a bend in the lane, he couldn't see who was there, although he heard a man's voice raised as though in anger. The wren stopped its song, cocked its head, then flew off in a whir of feathers. Then he heard a woman's voice and stopped dead, straining his ears, his heart speeding up. Surely that was Thea. He would know her voice anywhere.

The voices had dropped again, and he couldn't make anything out. He had been sure it was Thea, though. Or was it just that his thoughts had been with her, conjuring her voice?

His curiosity restoring the power of movement to his limbs, he approached the bend in the road. Some instinct told him to stay out of sight, although he couldn't really explain why. Maybe it was the note of either anger or fear he had heard in the woman's voice. Staying close to the hedgerow, he peered round the corner. The first person he saw was Thea. She was pushing her bike, keeping pace with a man in RAF uniform. He couldn't be sure, but he thought the man was the one who had stopped her outside the White Horse last night. He hadn't liked the look of him, but had no reason to disbelieve Thea's assertion that he was an old friend.

Now, however, Thea didn't look happy, and Fitz couldn't understand why, if she didn't want to speak to the man, she didn't simply climb on her bike and ride off. He dithered, unsure of his next actions. Should he intervene and risk Thea's ire for interfering in something that wasn't any of his business or should he accept she had things under control and leave her alone?

He studied the pair for a while longer. Something about the man roused his protective instincts – the way he sneered at Thea as though he held some kind of power over her. Fitz didn't like that at all; one of the things he admired about Thea was her strength and independence. He couldn't imagine her in any man's power, yet here she was, clearly disagreeing with him yet apparently unable to be rid of him.

Then she shook her head firmly and said in a voice loud enough to carry to Fitz, 'Get lost. I'm not doing it.' Lifting the bike by its handlebars, she pivoted it until she was facing back the way she had come and, placing her left foot on the pedal, pushed the bike into motion. The man was too fast for her, though, and managed to close a hand round the rear rack, bringing Thea to a halt with a jerk.

Fitz had seen enough. He broke into a run and waved his arms at the man. 'Oy! What are you playing at? Leave her alone!'

The man let go of the bike and straightened. He snarled a few words at Thea that Fitz couldn't catch, then hared down the lane a short way before flinging himself over a stile and taking off across the fields.

Fitz ignored him as soon as it was clear he wasn't bothering Thea any longer and concentrated on her instead. For a moment she wobbled precariously on her bike, as it had jostled alarmingly when the man had grabbed it and then released it. Thankfully Thea managed to get it under control and put her feet down. She eyed Fitz, looking wary.

Fitz quickly caught her up. 'Are you all right? Who was that man?'

He knew Thea well enough not to expect her to throw herself in his arms, weeping with gratitude for rescuing her. Even so, her reaction shocked him. 'What are you doing here? Were you spying on me?'

'No, of course not. I was out for a walk and happened to see that man. I thought he was going to knock you off your bike. What did you expect me to do?'

'I can look after myself.'

'I know.' Fitz was mystified. Surely anyone would have intervened after seeing what he had witnessed. 'But you can't expect me to walk away when I see someone being attacked.'

Thea snorted. 'He wasn't attacking me.'

'No? Then what was he doing? You didn't look like you wanted to be with him. I thought you'd be grateful for some support.'

'Well you thought wrong.' Gripping her handlebars so tightly her knuckles turned white, she started to march down the lane.

Fitz took heart from the fact that she hadn't simply ridden her bike away, leaving him behind. He walked alongside her, wondering at her flare of temper. It was almost as though she were on the defensive, feeling guilty and lashing out at him. But he couldn't imagine why she felt guilty. It wasn't as if he had caught her having a cosy walk with another man – she clearly hadn't wanted to be with him. 'Look, yesterday you told me

193

you wanted to be a part of my life for however long we could be together, and I don't believe it's unreasonable to think that helping you get away from strange men is a part of that.'

Thea caught her foot on her bike's front wheel and stumbled, muttering under her breath. Fitz took the handlebars, meaning to push the bike for her, only for Thea to snatch it back.

'I don't need you to do everything for me,' she snarled. 'You're as bad as Pearl, constantly checking up on me.'

Now Fitz was completely baffled. 'Thea, I wasn't checking up on you. I told you. I had a couple of hours to kill before the mission briefing, so I decided to go for a walk. I had no idea you were out here.'

'But when you saw me with Billy, you couldn't resist poking your nose in.'

Billy. Fitz filed away the name. Not that it was much help, considering there must be hundreds of men called Billy in Lincolnshire. 'No, I left you alone at first. I only came to help when I heard you tell him to go away.'

He knew he had said the wrong thing the moment the words slipped out. Thea's eyes narrowed. 'So you *were* spying on me. You were listening to us.'

'No, I—'

But it was as though she had been waiting for him to slip up. 'I knew I shouldn't have agreed to go out with you. You were spying on me. You don't trust me. Well, I can't go out with a man who doesn't trust me. We're finished.'

'You're kidding, right?'

But doubt crept in when Thea didn't laugh it off, and the half smile on his lips gradually faded in the face of her stony gaze. When she spoke there was no humour or warmth in her tone. 'It's just not working, Fitz. I thought' – Her voice became a little rough, and she paused to clear her throat – 'well, that doesn't matter now. You're not the man I thought you were. It's over.'

So saying, she swung herself into the saddle and started to ride away. Fitz couldn't take in what had just happened and watched her go, expecting her to turn round at any moment, her eyes gleaming with delighted mischief, and tell him of course she was only joking. But she carried on, and it slowly dawned on him that, for whatever reason, she really had meant to break up with him.

'Thea, wait!' he called after her. But she didn't look back.

Fitz couldn't understand what had just happened. She was gone, and she hadn't been joking. Had last night been a lie? She had told him she loved him, yet less than twenty-four hours later she was accusing him of interfering when he clearly hadn't, and had refused to even listen to him.

For some minutes after Thea had ridden out of sight, he remained standing on the verge, gazing at nothing. He couldn't even tell how he felt; his emotions flitted from one state to another before he could get hold of them. One moment there was a flare of anger, the next bewildered hurt. She had gone without a word of explanation, just when they had seemed to be getting so close.

An army truck rattled past, tooting its horn, and Fitz staggered back, startled into an awareness of passing time. Whatever had happened with Thea, he needed to try putting it out of his mind, because he was flying tonight and would need his full concentration for that. After one last glance towards the field where the stranger had made his escape, he reluctantly turned and trudged back to the gate.

He had taken only about a dozen steps when he was seized with an anguish that struck like a physical pain. He doubled over, gasping. Thea was out of his life, gone, and he had no idea why. While they might not have been together long, he was staggered by the sudden sense of loss and wrongness. It was as though his heart had been ripped in two and Thea had disappeared, taking her half with her. What was left didn't feel strong enough to sustain him.

If he hadn't had anyone else depending on him, he might have stayed there for hours, trying to force his brain to comprehend the incomprehensible. But he had a crew and a squadron.

He had his orders. If there was no longer any love in his life he would try to fill the missing pieces with duty, because he couldn't let his crew down.

With a heavy heart, he trudged back to the gate.

Chapter Twenty-One

When Thea heard Fitz call after her, she nearly turned back. All she wanted to do was fling herself into his arms and beg his forgiveness. But then she remembered what had just happened, and she hardened her heart. She was bad news. She always hurt the people she got close to. Take Pearl – her sister had given up on her own hopes and dreams to support her through school, to enable her to have the education she'd denied herself. And how had Thea thanked her? By getting involved with men like Billy Haywood.

And look how that had turned out. Billy had ended up in prison, and then his brother – wholly innocent of any crime – had been killed on his way to meeting Billy for the first time after his release. While she couldn't deny Billy had deserved prison, John Haywood would still be alive had she not taken the action that had resulted in Billy's arrest. While she had acted with the best of intentions, she had caused a man's death. She was bad news.

That was why she had finished with Fitz. She had leaped at the first excuse, even though she was secretly grateful his appearance had sent Billy running. Fitz would only suffer if he stayed with her, so she had done the kind thing and given him the push herself.

Yet if she was doing the right thing, why didn't she feel better? Despite the signs of spring all around, she felt as though the world had been draped in cold, grey fog.

It was a good thing all the tasks she had to work on that afternoon were routine, because she doubted she could have coped with anything that required much thought. Not that she didn't pay attention to her work — she was always too aware of the lives depending on her to get things right — but while she was tightening screws and arranging instruments back into their correct place in a panel, glimpses of Fitz's bewildered, pained expression kept appearing before her. She hated what she had done yet couldn't think of a better way to keep him safe from her.

That's right. Because breaking up with him only hours before he's due to fly off on a mission is bound to put him in the right frame of mind. She hastily squashed that thought.

She *had* been relieved when Fitz's shout had scared Billy away, though. She had gone to meet him expecting to be able to bargain him down to a more reasonable sum of money. But instead of agreeing to a lower amount, he had started telling her of a job he wanted her to do in place of paying him.

'Nothing you can't handle, I'm sure,' he had said with a nasty grin. 'A girl with your abilities.'

'Cut the flattery. Just tell me what you want me to do.' Thea kept her voice even, although her stomach was twisting into knots. She was starting to feel she had been manipulated into this situation, with Billy demanding an amount of money he must have known she couldn't afford. What had she got herself into?

'Nothing much. It's just that a friend of mine would like to get certain messages out of Fenthorpe sometimes.'

'Why can't he come to the main gate and ask like anyone else? If he has legitimate business, they'll let him collect a message.' She put a stress on 'legitimate', knowing that any friend of Billy Haywood was unlikely to have a lawful reason for wanting to get onto a Bomber Command station.

'Because he doesn't want the authorities poking their nose into his business. But there are always unofficial ways in and out, and I'm sure a resourceful girl like you never takes long to find them.'

'And why do you think I'm going to help? I'd have thought my actions last time made it pretty clear that I don't want to get involved in anything illegal.' Because whatever Billy was up to, it was obvious it *was* illegal, and something that would get Thea arrested or court-martialled if she was caught.

'You know why. It would be a terrible shame if your friends learned about your past. They'd probably want nothing more to do with you.'

'Look, I don't care what you think you're going to do, but Pearl would never want me to get myself arrested for a lowlife like you. Get lost. I'm not doing it.' Then she had attempted to ride away, only for Billy to grab hold of the rear luggage rack, and she had been afraid he would tip her off the bike. That was when Fitz had appeared, and she had been so glad to see him.

Until she realised she would have to explain what Billy wanted.

Now, as she fixed the last screw into the instrument panel, her vision blurred with sudden tears. Was it only last night that she had been so happy, that she had thought she and Fitz had a relationship as strong and reliable as Pearl and Greg's? How dare Billy think he could ruin that for her just because it suited his own plans?

And that led to another thought that made her blink away her tears and sit up. He had wanted her to help sneak messages out of the base. What on earth was he planning?

She still hadn't come up with a satisfactory answer when it was time to get dinner. Deciding that she needed a pick-me-up that she would never find in the cookhouse, she opted to spend the last of her money on bangers and mash in the NAAFI. She had also thought that she might be left alone in the NAAFI, but instead the first thing she saw when she walked through the door was Jenny waving at her. Pearl was also there. Once she had a tray laden with sausages, mashed potato and plenty of gravy, she squared her shoulders and went to join them. She was sure the camp grapevine would soon be buzzing with the news that she and Fitz had broken up, so she might as well tell Pearl and Jenny herself rather than face their shock and disappointment that she hadn't told them.

As she was putting down her tray she happened to glance out of the window, just in time to see a man in RAF police uniform fastening a padlock to the phone-box door. Her appetite suddenly deserted her. They always locked the phone boxes when the aircrew briefings were about to start, to prevent the news of that night's target being mentioned accidentally during a phone call. Her thoughts immediately flew to Fitz, who would be about to go into the briefing and discover where he and the other crews would be flying to that night.

Pearl must have also seen the door being locked for, when Thea glanced at her sister, she saw she had gone a shade paler than usual.

Jenny had noticed too, and put a hand on Pearl's arm. 'They'll be fine. They're the best crew in the squadron, and they're going to come back tomorrow, just as they always have.'

Pearl pressed her hands to her stomach and released a shaky breath. 'I hope you're right.'

'Are you going to wait for them to come back?' Thea asked them both. 'I'm on duty, so I won't be able to help with the tea, but I'll join you once I've finished.'

Pearl, making an obvious effort to lighten her sister's mood, gave Thea a nudge. 'Are you sure you'll be able to tear yourself away from Fitz?'

The words were like a blow to Thea's stomach. Her break-up was at the forefront of her mind, to the extent that she felt like she had been preceded into the NAAFI by her own personal town crier, ringing his bell and announcing, 'Oyez, oyez! At eleven thirty, on the twenty-ninth day of March in the year of our lord, nineteen hundred and forty three, Thea Cooper did cruelly cast off the only man she'd ever truly loved.' She'd completely forgotten Jenny and Pearl couldn't see her internal turmoil and wouldn't know she and Fitz were no longer together. She really didn't want to say it. That would make it real. But she couldn't keep it from them either.

Doing her best to keep her voice light, as though remarking on the weather, she said, 'Actually, I'm not going out with Fitz any more.'

Jenny's face crumpled in dismay. 'Oh no! I thought you were perfect together.'

'Why – what did you do?' Pearl asked at the same time.

Ah well, she *had* wanted to distract her sister from the upcoming mission. 'Thanks, Jenny. And thanks for the vote of confidence, Pearl. Who says it was because of anything *I* did?'

'Sorry. But I did think you were well suited. What went wrong?'

Thea cut the remainder of her sausage into three equal slices before replying. 'I suppose it *was* my fault.'

'Oh, Thea. Why? Fitz is a lovely man.'

'I know he is. That's why—' Thea hastily bit back the words before they slipped out. She couldn't afford to let slip about Billy. Not until she had worked out what to do about him. 'Things just didn't work out, okay? I can't really explain it, but it wasn't meant to be.' She shoved a forkful of sausage and potato into her mouth, even though she didn't want any more.

Pearl eyed her doubtfully but held her tongue. Soon after, Jenny announced she had to go back on duty, prompting Thea to glance at her watch and realise she needed to get back to the Instrument Section.

'Jenny and I have already arranged to help with the tea again,' Pearl said, collecting the pile of notes she'd been working on. 'Come and find us once you've dealt with your Lancs.'

There was no mention that they might not return, because neither of them could bear to contemplate that.

–

'Bombs away!' Fitz announced, gritting his teeth at the sudden upward surge of *C-Charlie*, now relieved of the weight of the bombs. There was the usual tense wait for the photo flash, and then he felt the nose go down and had to brace himself to prevent himself slipping to one side as he felt the Lancaster bank. As soon as he recovered his balance, he checked that the bomb bay was empty, then scrambled up the ladder out of the bomb aimer's compartment and took his seat at the front gun.

For the second time in three days, they were in the skies above Berlin, and Fitz was every bit as unhappy to be there as he had been the first time. Still, he had done his job and dropped the bombs directly over the markers, so he could only pray that they got home in one piece.

Where Thea would be waiting. He knew she was rostered to meet the returning aircraft. Perhaps he would have a chance to speak to her, try to persuade her to give him another chance.

Another chance at what, though? He had no idea what he had done wrong. He had thought things were going well between them, right until they weren't.

And who was the strange man he had seen her with? Although he couldn't be sure, all his instincts told him the man had something to do with Thea ending their relationship. If not everything to do with it. Only the night before, she had told him she loved him with all of her heart. As far as he could tell, the only thing that had changed since then was that she had met the stranger. He was convinced the man in the lane was the same man who had spoken to Thea outside the White Horse. Thea had told him he was an old friend from Shrewsbury, but she hadn't looked pleased to see him.

'Night fighter, six o'clock!' The shout — Fitz recognised Jack's voice, even with the distortion from the intercom — roused him from his daydream. Fool! He was going to get everyone killed, being caught on the hop like that. He heard gunfire from the rear of the aircraft, then Jack's voice came over the intercom again. 'It's gone underneath us.'

Fitz tensed, bracing himself for the impact of bullets upon the fuselage. He swung his gun this way and that, straining his eyes for any sign of the fighter. Having an enemy plane below them was a dangerous situation, for the Lancaster had no guns that could fire beneath the fuselage or wings. It was a vulnerability that enemy fighters exploited mercilessly.

Even as he scanned the air, *C-Charlie* dived and turned, and he knew Greg would be struggling with the heavy controls as he heaved the Lancaster through a series of evasive manoeuvres.

'Everyone keep your eyes peeled,' Greg ordered. 'Shout out if you see it.'

There followed a few seconds of silence from the crew, and Fitz knew they were all doing the same as him: searching this way and that, scanning every inch of the sky that was within their view.

Without warning, a fighter appeared out of the darkness, flying straight for Fitz's position in the nose. Fitz yelped, then shouted, 'Enemy aircraft twelve o'clock,' firing at the same time. He had no idea if it was the same one Jack had seen; he could only hope it was, because if they were being stalked by two fighters they didn't stand a chance. It was still heading straight for them, and Jack saw glowing orange lines of tracer shooting directly at them. He felt a judder as the bullets hit, and still *C-Charlie* didn't change course.

'What are you doing, Skipper?' he yelled, still firing back at the enemy.

'We're bigger than him. He can swerve,' came Greg's reply, and he sounded no more anxious than if this were some kind of playground game.

Fitz held his breath and then at the last possible moment the fighter banked, and he had the satisfaction of seeing a line of his bullets pepper the fuselage. 'I got it!' he cried. 'Nice one, Gramps.'

'It's on fire,' the mid-upper gunner reported. 'Going down. Nice shooting, Fitz.'

There were a few cheers, but then Greg said, 'Stay alert. There are bound to be others.'

There followed a tense fifteen minutes in which the crew said little. The only words spoken were the navigator's directions and Greg's acknowledgements. Fitz was starting to hope they had got away completely unharmed when George Hepple, the wireless operator, spoke. 'I think I've been hit. Just a graze, I think, in my upper arm.'

'Fitz, go back and take a look.'

'On my way, Skipper.'

George's position was just behind the navigator and, although it wasn't far, it was a scramble to climb over the bulkhead while the plane was in motion. When he got there, he found George clutching his left arm, looking pale. Fitz hurried to get the first-aid box and then bent over George. 'Why didn't you say anything earlier?'

'I didn't feel it. I only just noticed the blood on my sleeve. I don't think it's bad.'

A quick examination confirmed that it was just a flesh wound. The bullet had scored a groove in the fleshy part of George's upper arm, missing all major vessels. 'You'll live,' he told George once he had applied a dressing. 'You'd better see the MO when you get back. He might sign you off for a day or two.'

'Lucky bastard!' This was Jack, over the intercom. Fitz couldn't tell if he was joking.

'Any damage to the aircraft?' he then asked George. 'Thea— the erks will need to know if we need any repairs.'

'I think it's just a few holes in the fuselage. We'd know if there was any serious damage.'

'What about the hydraulics?' Now there was a definite edge to Jack's voice. 'He might have got the hydraulics!'

'It's fine. He didn't.'

But Jack clearly didn't believe him, and the sound of the rear turret motors whirring reached Fitz's ears. He cursed under his breath. Jack had seemed to be keeping his fears in check despite the length of the last two operations, and Fitz had started to hope he would make it to the end of his tour without any more trouble.

Once he had assured himself George was all right, he went back to the tail, cursing as he stumbled over the ammunition boxes. He saw that Jack was, as he'd suspected, putting the turret through its paces, swinging it left and right, taking the rotation to the limits in both directions. While this wasn't necessarily a bad thing – the gunners needed to stay alert and keep watch for the entirety of the flight – Jack's attention seemed fully focused on the controls and not at all at the sky.

'Jack! Stop it! Everything's fine!' He hammered on the rear of the turret, taking care not to get his fingers caught in the moving machinery. 'Jack, it's all working. Relax.'

Whether his words got through to Jack or whether Jack came to his senses of his own accord, Fitz didn't know. But the turret stopped its aimless swinging. A moment later, Jack scrambled out backwards, wiping sweat from his face. One look and Fitz knew Jack was in no state to man the rear turret any more this flight. Speaking over the intercom, he said, 'Skipper, this is Fitz. I'm sending Jack forward to cover the front gun. I'll take over in the tail.'

Jack was wiping his face with his handkerchief. 'Do you really mean that?'

'Course I do. I've always wanted to have a go in the rear turret.' Fitz wished he could spend longer with Jack, get a better idea of his state of mind, but at the moment there were two guns unmanned, and they couldn't allow themselves to be caught on the hop. 'Get a move on, before Greg complains about the trim.'

So saying, he disconnected himself from the portable oxygen and plugged himself into the turret's oxygen supply. Then he squeezed in and eased himself onto the seat. The first thing he noticed was how cold it was. Jack had requested that the erks cut away some of the cupola's Perspex panelling, to avoid it getting fogged up. Most experienced tail gunners did this, the result being that although they might get a clearer view, and thus save the lives of their crew, the wind buffeted them unmercifully. Now Fitz shivered as the cold bit through the layers of his flying suit, battledress and long johns, and hoped they would get back to Fenthorpe before he froze to death.

However cold it was, it was better than flying. As he operated the hand controls and slowly rotated the cupola from left to right, he comforted himself with the thought that, at least here, Greg couldn't ask him to take over as pilot for any length of time.

After what felt like hours, Edwin announced that they were crossing the coast. They had managed to avoid setting off any anti-aircraft defences once they had left Berlin behind, probably thanks to Edwin's expert navigation, and now that they were over the North Sea Fitz felt his tension drain away. Although he knew they had to remain vigilant for enemy fighters, the closer they came to friendly shores the less likely it became that any of the feared night fighters would find them. While he didn't relax his vigilance, Fitz once more allowed his thoughts to drift to Thea, and rehearsed the speech he would make that would show her the depth of his love and commitment. He spared a thought for Jack, too, listening out for his voice as the crew exchanged banter over the intercom.

He had already known how lonely and exposed it must feel to occupy the rear turret, but he had never truly experienced it before. He could hear the rest of the crew, but he felt completely isolated from them. His usual position being in the aircraft's nose, Fitz spent most of a flight close to Greg and Allan Doughty, the flight engineer, and so could always see what was going on and read from the others' expressions how confident or otherwise they were feeling. Even when he was in the bomb aimer's compartment and slightly more isolated, he was effectively in charge of the Lancaster by that time and so in control. Back here he had nothing but the intercom chatter to go on. He was even facing away from the direction of flight and the other crew. Fitz hadn't realised how out of control Jack must feel. No wonder he was feeling the strain after so many missions. He wished he had suggested swapping positions before; it would have given him a better understanding of Jack's state of mind and how to get through to him. As well as speaking to Thea, Fitz determined to make a serious effort to persuade Jack to see the MO. He'd drag him there if necessary.

–

Cold and weary, Fitz had never been so glad to reach the end of a flight. He was so stiff after what felt like hours cramped in the tiny rear turret that, once he'd climbed down to the ground, he needed to pace up and down to get the circulation moving again and try to get some warmth back into his frozen limbs. He could hear Thea speaking to Greg and Allan, asking if any repairs were needed. She must have walked right past him without even speaking to him. A chill crept into his heart that had nothing to do with the brisk dawn air. Why wouldn't she even speak to him? Was she truly that uncomfortable in his presence? He needed to speak to her, though, and, once Greg and Allan moved away, he took a step towards her. He couldn't let her leave without letting her know how much he loved her.

He opened his mouth to speak, then saw Jack blunder past, his face a mask of distress. For another second or two he was torn two ways. Then his mind cleared. Thea could wait but Jack needed him now. His crew were his family, and he couldn't bear to see any of them suffer. He followed Jack onto the bus.

–

'Welcome back,' Thea said to Greg, aware all the while of Fitz standing a few yards behind her. 'Pearl's waiting by the operations block. She'll be overjoyed to see you.'

She should speak to Fitz. She longed to see him, to reassure herself that he was unhurt. She'd thought her heart might stop when an ambulance had roared up to meet *C-Charlie* at the dispersal point, and even now she knew the only injury was a flesh wound to the wireless operator, her heart hadn't stopped pounding. Wasn't Pearl always urging her to behave more like an adult? The mature thing to do would be to speak to Fitz like a friend, tell him she was glad to see him back safe and sound. She would do that the moment she had finished taking note of any repairs. Thankfully *C-Charlie* had come off as lightly as the crew, with only a few bullet holes in the fuselage requiring patching and no damage to the instruments or inner workings. Once both Greg and Allan had made their reports, she finished taking notes at high speed, then turned on her heel to find Fitz, only to see him climbing into the crew's bus. He didn't even look back.

She was tempted to grab her bicycle and ride to the operations block, hoping to intercept Fitz before he went to the debriefing. However, at that point, *D-Donald* taxied up to its dispersal point, and she was required to go and deal with that. By this time the sun was rising above the hedgerows, casting a golden light on the scene. She could immediately see that *D-Donald* had been through far worse than *C-Charlie*. One of the engines was smoking, and the wings and fuselage were pockmarked with holes from flak and bullets. Worse, an ambulance was also racing towards the aircraft, so the pilot must have radioed through a request for medical assistance.

She stood back while the crew climbed out, praying no one was seriously hurt. She couldn't see Sam, and had a horrible few minutes imagining breaking the news to Blanche, before she saw him scramble down the ladder, helping a man who had his arm in a sling. Breathing a sigh of relief, Thea did a quick head-count and saw all seven crewmen had emerged more or less on their own two feet. She dashed up and began the usual routine of welcoming them back and asking for details of repairs needed.

It was half an hour before she had finished and could cycle to the operations block. She immediately saw Pearl and Jenny and went to join them. 'Have *C-Charlie's* crew already gone through to debriefing?'

Pearl nodded, looking happy despite the shadows of exhaustion under her eyes. 'All safe and sound.'

Thea didn't know whether to feel disappointed or relieved. She wouldn't see Fitz now, because the crew would go straight to breakfast after their debrief and would then turn in for some rest.

'I can't believe they were sent to Berlin again,' Pearl said. 'I hope they get somewhere easier for their last two ops.'

Only two more. After that, Fitz would be posted away from here to a non-operational unit and she would never see him again. Apart from the wedding, of course. Even though she had broken up with him for his own good, it didn't give her the peace of mind she'd thought she be rewarded with. Instead she felt empty and cold.

'How many more bombers are we expecting?' she asked to try to distract herself from the ache inside.

Jenny grimaced. 'One from 505 Squadron and another two from 642.'

That put things into perspective for Thea. She and Fitz might no longer be together, but he was alive and well and, although he didn't know it, was safer without her.

A scream sent a ripple of alarm through the waiting WAAFs, and Thea looked round frantically to see who had been hurt. Her gaze fell on Blanche, who was running towards them from the operations block, flapping her hands in front of her eyes as though she had burned them.

'What's happened?' Pearl demanded the moment Blanche joined the group. Now Thea could see tears pouring down her face. A horrible thought occurred to her that Sam had been hiding an injury and had collapsed.

'You'll never believe it,' Blanche gasped, when she'd recovered herself enough to speak. 'Sam asked me to marry him and I said yes!'

Thea had been so convinced a terrible tragedy had occurred, it took a moment for her to take in Blanche's news.

Before she could say anything, Jenny exclaimed, 'How wonderful! Congratulations!'

Thea recovered herself enough to add her congratulations to those of the other WAAFs, although it was still hard to accept, considering Blanche and Sam had only been together a short while.

Thankfully, Blanche was prepared to do all the talking, so even if Thea's congratulations had sounded less than whole-hearted she didn't seem to have noticed. 'I know what you're thinking,' she said. 'Sam and I hardly know each other.'

Thea opened her mouth to utter a platitude, but Blanche chattered on without allowing anyone else a chance to speak. 'It's true, of course, that we've only been going out a short while, but sometimes you know right away when you've found the man who's right for you. Sam and I have a real connection I've never known with anyone else before, even—' She bit her lip, and Thea, convinced she'd been about to name the fiancé who had been killed, regretted her cynical thoughts. On observing Blanche with Sam, she had been convinced they made a good couple, and if they had decided to take a chance and claim some happiness from these terrible times then she wished them well.

'I think you and Sam make a good couple,' she told Blanche. 'I'm happy for you both.'

Blanche beamed at her. 'Thank you. And we both owe you so much, after you helped bring us together.'

Thea, startled at how easily Blanche seemed to have accepted her as a friend, muttered something about being happy to help, then added, 'Have you set a date?'

'Not yet, because we need to get permission and then organise leave, but we want it to be as soon as possible.' Blanche gave a little skip. 'Oh, I forgot my parents won't know yet. I must write to them straight away. Or maybe a telegram? But no, getting a telegram would probably scare them out of their wits. Oh, this is so exciting. I must dash. See you later!' And she raced away, leaving Thea with a spinning head.

Chapter Twenty-Two

Two more missions. That was all Fitz and Greg had left before they finished their tour. After the two missions to Berlin, there was another lull in operations, and once again the crews were left kicking their heels, doing no more than training flights each day. A few crews were sent on minor missions such as mine-laying, but *C-Charlie* wasn't included. Thea could see Pearl grow more and more agitated with each passing day, and she sympathised because she felt the same way. She was torn between longing for the next two missions to be over with and dreading them. They were so tantalisingly close to knowing Greg and Fitz would be safe, yet that only seemed to make the fear that something would happen to them more intense.

Finally, just over a week after the second Berlin mission, the hum of expectancy around the camp told Thea that there was a big operation on that night. Annoyingly, it was her day off, so, instead of being the one to make the final checks on *C-Charlie*'s instruments and reassure herself everything was in tip-top working order, she could only pray that was the case.

Pearl was working in Lincoln that day, so she at least was spared the worry of knowing Greg would be flying that night. Jenny also had a day off. 'Why not go into Lincoln?' Jenny suggested. 'Anything's better than hanging around here when we've got nothing to do.'

This sounded like a good idea to Thea, so the two friends set off for the bus after breakfast. Despite being off duty, Jenny wanted to know what the latest weather charts contained, 'In case anyone asks me.' Thea rather suspected that by 'anyone'

Jenny meant Edwin, but she said nothing and arranged to meet her outside the main gates. Accordingly, she signed out at the guardroom and paced outside the gates, wishing she could get Fitz out of her mind.

Ironically, the distraction, when it arrived, was not welcome.

'Finally managed to catch up with you,' came Billy Haywood's sneering voice.

Thea cast her eyes up to the heavens. 'For goodness' sake, Billy, don't you ever take no for an answer?'

'Not when I know you don't really mean it.'

Thea flung out her arms. 'I'm never going to agree to help you. You can tell anyone you like about my past, I don't care.' After all, now she was no longer seeing Fitz, what harm could the truth do?

Billy took a long drag from his cigarette, then flung it onto the road and ground it with his heel before answering. 'What would your sister think? She's getting married, isn't she?'

'What about it?' Thea tried to ignore the chill trickling down her spine. How did Billy know about that?

'It would be a shame if anything happened to spoil the ceremony, her getting married to a dashing pilot and all. Most unfortunate.'

He was bluffing. He had to be. 'Don't be an idiot. There's nothing you can do, and you know it.'

'Oh, really?' He reached into his pocket and pulled out a scrap of torn newspaper. Thea's unease coalesced into real horror as he unfolded it and read aloud. 'The staff of the *Shrewsbury Mirror* would like to offer their congratulations to Pearl Cooper on her engagement to Pilot Officer Greg Tallis. The wedding will take place on May 1st at eleven o'clock at St Margaret's Church, Elmwick, Lincolnshire. We wish them all the happiness in the world.' He folded the scrap and replaced it in his pocket before giving her a smug smile.

Thea remained rooted to the spot throughout, unable to work out what to do. 'You wouldn't dare do anything. I'll report you to your CO.'

'Oh yeah? And who might that be?'

'It's—' Thea bit her lip in frustration. No wonder Billy had evaded any questions about where he was based, although it couldn't be far considering the frequency with which he turned up like a bad penny.

Billy gave an unpleasant laugh. 'You don't know, do you, and I aim to keep it that way. Anyway, I've arranged for leave to cover the date of the wedding, so there's nothing to stop me being there. The only way you'll stop me is by doing what I say.'

He seemed determined to make her suffer for the wrong he perceived she had done him, and Thea rued the day Billy had discovered where she was. She could only suppose he spent every second of his off-duty hours hovering around Fenthorpe, which did rather point to him being posted nearby. She wondered how he had got there, and glanced around, looking for a vehicle. She didn't even know his trade, and wondered if he was a driver. If so, he was using the car for his own personal business and she would be sure to report him – if only she knew where he was based.

She couldn't see any sign of a car, though, and decided he must have caught the bus to Fenthorpe and walked here. She cursed the fate that had led to her running into him, when surely he must have only limited time to loiter around RAF Fenthorpe looking for her.

Aware that Jenny might emerge through the gate at any moment, Thea opted to appear to agree to his request to get rid of him. 'Fine. Tell me what you want me to do.'

'Like I said, there's a message someone wants getting out of your base this afternoon, at around four. Information about a business deal, if you must know.' Billy tapped the side of his nose. 'Only the whole camp will be locked down if you're flying ops tonight.'

Thea frowned. 'And what exactly is my part in all this?'

'Oh, nothing too difficult. All you have to do is wait in the NAAFI at half past three, and someone will pass you a message.'

'Who? And why can't this WAAF get the message out herself?'

'None of your business. And she's on duty all afternoon and can't get away.'

'How will she know who to give the message to?'

'Take a pencil and place it beside your teacup. That will be your identification. You'll know when you've got it. I've heard whispers among the WAAFs of Fenthorpe that you've got a "back door" – a way out through the Waafery fence.'

'Even if we have, what makes you so sure I know where it is?'

'I know you, Thea. If there's a way out of the Waafery, you'll know where it is. You were never a stickler for the rules.'

'Maybe I've changed.'

'And maybe I'm the Shah of Persia.' Billy lit another cigarette. 'The question you have to ask yourself is this: do you want to see me at your sister's wedding? It would be fun, don't you think, if I arrived and said I had an objection? What would the vicar do if I claimed to be Pearl's long-lost husband?'

'You wouldn't!' Thea stared at him in horror. She had no idea if he'd be expected to produce evidence. Would the vicar be forced to postpone the wedding while he investigated Billy's claims? It had been difficult enough for her and Greg to arrange their leaves at the same time. Who knew when they would be able to marry if that happened? She knew she couldn't risk it.

Billy's smile widened, and she knew he had accurately deciphered her inner turmoil. 'You know I would.'

Thea looked at him, torn between contempt for him and a surge of protective love towards her sister. Pearl had sacrificed so much for Thea, yet most of the time Thea had flung that sacrifice back in her face. She deserved to have a perfect wedding day, unspoiled by any of Thea's past mistakes. She could understand now why Pearl had asked Jenny to be maid of honour instead of Thea. Thea always found a way to ruin things.

'Fine. I'll do it.'

'Good. I'll be checking up on you. Once you've got the message, come to the junction where this road meets the lane to Fenthorpe. I'll meet you there at four. If you deliver the message – unread, mind – I'll spend my leave elsewhere and stay away from your sister's wedding.'

She wanted to ask what this was all about, but saw Jenny in the corner of her eye and knew her time was up. 'I'll see you later. Now push off.' She hurried to meet Jenny, praying her friend hadn't noticed Billy.

—

The trip with Jenny did nothing to soothe Thea's inner turmoil. What was she to do? She longed to share her dilemma with her friend, but she had got enough people into trouble in her life and didn't want to get Jenny involved in something that, to Thea, appeared highly suspect. When they got back to Fenthorpe in the early afternoon, Jenny said, 'What do you want to do now? We've still got hours before it's time to see the aircrews off.'

'Actually, I've got some work I need to do.' It wasn't a lie as such – Thea was constantly needing to keep up to date with changes to instruments, and had a notebook stuffed with information that she would occasionally flick through to test herself.

Jenny's face fell. 'I understand.' Then she brightened. 'I've got a book that Mr Haughton sent to me via Pearl. I can read that. I've been looking forward to it but never found the time.'

Despite herself, Thea smiled. 'What's the title? No, don't tell me – *A Guide to British Snails*.'

Jenny grinned. 'Actually it's *Sense and Sensibility* by Jane Austen. But I'll have to look out for *A Guide to British Snails*. It sounds really interesting.'

The pair parted after arranging to meet at the rec in time to wave off the aircrews. Relieved to have shaken off Jenny without hurting her feelings, she glanced at her watch and saw there was still an hour before she was supposed the meet the mysterious messenger, so she paced around the stretch of grass behind the NAAFI, trying to work out what to do. She wasn't sure she bought Billy's tale of a business deal, although if anyone was likely to be involved in dodgy dealing or the black market it was Billy. Nevertheless, something had felt off.

She still hadn't decided what to do when she went to the NAAFI at the appointed time, ordered a pot of tea and found an empty table. Remembering Billy's instructions, she took a pencil out of her pocket and placed it beside her teacup. It all seemed ridiculous, like the kind of thing that happened in the spy novels she had loved to read as a teenager. Perhaps this was an elaborate hoax.

It happened so fast that she barely noticed it. Someone brushed against her as they walked past, and, although Thea was irritated, it happened often enough in the crowded NAAFI for her not to think too much of it. Then she felt a hand slip into her pocket.

She had just enough wits about her not to cry out, and only looked up to see who it was. However, she only caught a glimpse of a WAAF's back. She was medium height with a medium build, and her hair was hidden under her cap. There was no way Thea would recognise her if she saw her again. Craning her neck, she tried to spot the WAAF from a different angle, but whoever it was strode out of the door and out of sight before Thea could pick out any distinguishing features.

Slipping her hand in her pocket, her fingers encountered a slip of folded paper. Although Billy had told her not to look at it, Thea couldn't rein in her curiosity. After a quick glance around to make sure she was unobserved, she surreptitiously smoothed out the paper on the table in front of her, placing her ginger beer bottle so it hid the message – assuming there was a message – from inquisitive eyes.

There was only one word, written in precise block capitals, clearly intended to disguise the handwriting. One word that froze her blood. It said: *DUISBURG*.

Thea shoved back her chair and rose on shaky legs. This was no longer a joke or a mild inconvenience. Duisburg was one of the main cities in the Ruhr industrial region – a major strategic target for RAF Bomber Command. Was it that night's target? If so, by getting this information outside the camp she might possibly be aiding the German defences. Practically everywhere you looked, there were posters warning them that careless talk costs lives, and here she was being instructed to hand this vital piece of information to Billy. While she hated to think that any British man would be willing to betray his country, Billy had proved time and again that he would do anything for money.

She hurried outside, hardly aware of what she was doing. One thing was certain – she would not deliver this message. It occurred to her that she could deliver a different piece of paper on which she had written another German city, but she dismissed the idea. For Billy to accept it, she would have to pick another likely target, and there was always the chance that Bomber Command had another mission on that night to the place she had picked. No. She had to tell someone and worry about disruption to Pearl's wedding later. Who should she tell?

As if by divine intervention, Fitz appeared at that moment, strolling with Jack towards the NAAFI. Forgetting that she was trying to avoid him, she ran to meet them. 'Have you just come out of your briefing?' she asked, cutting off whatever greeting Fitz might be about to make.

Fitz nodded, looking wary.

'Where are you going?'

'Thea, you know we can't—'

'Is it Duisburg?'

Fitz grabbed her arm. 'How the hell do you know that?'

Thea felt as though she had swallowed a lump of lead, the last hope that this was some innocent prank fading away. 'There's something fishy going on, and I don't know who I should tell.'

'You can start by telling us.'

This was what she had been afraid of. She didn't want Fitz to know about Billy. He had stood with her through the whole horrible time while she was being shunned. Although she had been innocent of the accusations, neither did she feel entirely blameless. Yet it was in her past and she wanted to keep it that way. Still, she didn't have a lot of choice, and she really wanted Fitz and Jack's help. Choosing her words carefully, she explained about Billy's threat to spoil Pearl and Greg's wedding, saying only that Billy had been someone she knew in Shrewsbury who had been a troublemaker and had ended up in prison, playing down how well she had known him.

Fitz's expression hardened as she told her tale, making her heart shrink. He clearly despised her and was glad she had broken off their relationship; there was no way he would want to be involved with someone like her. Someone who couldn't seem to stay out of trouble.

'What should I do?' she asked finally.

Fitz and Jack exchanged glances, both seemingly lost for words. Eventually Fitz said, 'This needs to go right to the top, but we'll start with our CO.'

'Yes, of course.' Thea couldn't imagine why she hadn't thought of that herself. They'd had the chain of command drummed into them from their earliest lectures as new recruits. She could only think that her agitation had driven all sensible thought out of her.

'No slight meant to the WAAF CO,' Fitz continued, 'but this is urgent, and our CO will be able to get things moving more quickly.'

'That's fine. Where will we find him?'

Fitz stared down at his hand as though only just noticing he was still holding her arm. 'Sorry,' he muttered, releasing her. 'We'll try his office first, although whether he'll be there at this stage in the day is another matter.'

Fortunately Squadron Leader Price was in his office and, after an irritable greeting, due, Thea was sure, to everything that needed his attention before the aircrews left later that evening, he had given them his full attention.

When Thea told him what was written on the paper and handed it to him, he leaped to his feet. 'Good God! What time are you supposed to deliver it?'

Thea glanced up at the clock and grimaced. 'In ten minutes.' How she was supposed to get to the Waafery and through the 'back door' unseen in that time was beyond her.

'That doesn't give us much time,' Price muttered, although whether this was directed at anyone other than himself Thea couldn't tell. He chewed his lip and then appeared to come to a decision. 'There's no time to tell the station commander. This is on me.' He ripped a piece of paper from a notebook, making it roughly the same size as the paper Thea had given him, and wrote a name in block capitals. 'I know for a fact that we're not sending any aircraft here tonight.' He handed it to Thea.

Thea took it, uncomprehending. Glancing at the paper, she saw Price had written *PILZEN*. 'What do you want me to do?'

'What you were asked.'

'But I'll never get there in time.'

'You will if you use the back door. I'll drive you to the main gate myself and authorise the guards to let you out. Myself and these two gentlemen will follow you at a discreet distance and attempt to grab him once you've handed him that paper.'

'It's too dangerous. What if he attacks her?' Fitz looked surprisingly pale.

Price gave a heavy nod of the head. 'Believe me, if we had time to come up with an alternative plan, I'd jump at it. But I'm sure you agree this is a serious breach of security, and we have to act now.'

Fitz made no further objection, though he didn't look happy. Without further ado, Price led them to his car, which was parked nearby, and soon, after he had had a word with the guards at the gate, had driven them through and then continued for about half a mile until they were close to the junction Billy had named. Then he pulled onto the verge.

'Get out here, Cooper. You'll have to walk the last hundred yards or so. If he's already there, I don't want him to see you getting out of the car. Don't worry, we'll be following.'

Thea's heart was in her mouth as she made her way to the junction. A glance at her watch showed her she had just three minutes before the meeting time. She had to walk round a sharp bend before she could see the junction, but she expected Billy to be already waiting for her. When she rounded the corner and didn't see him, she wasn't too surprised, deciding he was probably concealed behind a bush. However, when she reached the junction, she looked all around, and there was no sign of anyone. Looking at her watch, she saw it was exactly four. Maybe her watch was fast. She paced up and down, looking in all directions. She wondered what Price, Fitz and Jack made of it, but she didn't dare go to them in case Billy arrived and drew his attention to them.

Time ticked by, and Thea was getting seriously worried. Not about Billy – for all she cared, he could have fallen under a bus – but for Fitz and Jack, who should be focusing on that night's mission.

Above all, she wanted this to be over with, to have seen the last of Billy. Now she wouldn't be able to go out without worrying he was going to appear again.

Finally, after half an hour had passed, the purr of a motor engine made her glance round, and she saw Price's car with the three RAF men inside.

'No sign?' Price asked.

Thea shook her head. 'No, sir. I'm sorry I've wasted your time. I don't know what's happened.'

Price told her to climb in. 'We've got a mission to fly, and we can't wait any longer. I'll brief the senior staff, though. I still think this is very serious. If you hear from this Haywood fellow again, you're to report to me straight away. Understand?'

'Yes sir. Of course.' Thea climbed into the back, very glad that Fitz was occupying the passenger seat so she only had to look at the back of his head. She didn't think she could have coped with even the short journey back to Price's office with Fitz beside her. While she remained convinced that she had done the right thing in ending their relationship, it didn't stop her aching to touch him and to see his face light up and the smile that seemed reserved just for her.

The return drive passed in silence, the only sound to be heard above the engine the sound of Jack picking his nails. She glanced at him and saw he looked even paler than usual, and the dark shadows under his eyes gave his face an almost skull-like appearance.

Thea felt a surge of pity and berated herself for letting her own concerns make her forget Jack's struggles, which must be so much worse. Of course, Fitz had always kept her updated about Jack's wellbeing, and, as she hadn't seen him for over a week, Jack had slipped her mind.

So preoccupied was she with Jack's state of mind that she failed to notice Price had parked the car until she realised the others were getting out.

'Are you on duty, Cooper?'

'What—? Sorry, I mean, no, sir.' Thea felt heat creep up her face and was relieved to see Squadron Leader Price's lips twitch. Most of the RAF officers – and the WAAF officers, come to that – didn't stand on ceremony, many of them having been promoted from the lower ranks. But a few of them were sticklers for the correct etiquette, and Thea was always wary around them until she had worked out what kind they were. Price, it seemed, was more interested in getting the job done than being saluted, and she relaxed a little.

'Good. I need to report this to the station commander, and it would save time if you could be there.'

The tension immediately returned. The station commander was known to be a stickler for the formalities. However, she couldn't very well refuse and, sensing she had an ally in Price despite the waste of his time that afternoon, she nodded. 'Of course, sir.'

'Good.' Price addressed Fitz and Jack. 'Thank you for bringing this to my attention. I'm sorry to have taken up so much of your time. I suppose you'd better go and get yourselves ready.'

Jack made an odd noise in the back of his throat. Fitz immediately frowned. 'What's the matter?'

Jack started to pick his nails again. It was a nervous gesture that Thea didn't think he was even aware of. 'I can't. I can't do it.' He was shifting from foot to foot now, and to Thea's eyes he seemed to be working himself up to something big.

Fitz frowned and put and hand on his shoulder. 'I think—'

But whatever Fitz thought, none of the others would ever know, because Jack burst out, 'I can't go up in that... that thing again. I'm going LMF.'

'What did you say?' These words boomed from a new arrival that no one had noticed. Standing just outside the door of the admin block, the station commander himself scowled at the group still standing beside the car.

Chapter Twenty-Three

Her heart pounding, Thea snapped out a salute along with the others. Why did Group Captain Rhodes have to show up at that exact moment? From the favourable opinion she had formed of Price, she thought he would have tried to help Jack, not condemn him. But Rhodes was another matter.

Fitz looked as though he were about to speak but Price cut him off with a look and said smoothly, 'I'm glad to see you, sir. I've had a rather disturbing report that you should hear right away. Flight Sergeant Fitzgerald and Sergeant Knight have been good enough to help me, but Sergeant Knight has been taken ill and needs to report to the MO.' He glanced at Fitz. 'Make sure he gets there. Tell your skipper I'll take over as rear gunner tonight. It's about time I got out from behind my desk.'

'Yes, sir. Thank you, sir.' Fitz put his hand on Jack's shoulder. 'Come on, let's get you sorted out.'

Thea wished she could go with them, but she admired the adroit way Price had handled the situation and not attempted to explain what Rhodes may or may not have overheard. By not reacting to Jack's announcement that he wanted to go LMF, he had hopefully made Rhodes believe he had misheard. At Price's invitation, she followed him and Rhodes into his office.

–

'I can't believe you got hauled in front of Group Captain Rhodes.'

Thea scowled at her sister. 'You make it sound like I was being punished.'

224

Thea, Pearl and Jenny were standing yet again under the dark pre-dawn sky, outside the operations block, waiting for the aircrews to return. Thea had been in two minds about waving the Lancasters off earlier that night and had eventually concluded that Fitz wouldn't welcome seeing her. Despite helping her over the mysterious message, he hadn't attempted to speak to her alone. He hadn't appeared to care that it had been the first time they had spent any time together since the day they had split up. She had to admit that, even though she remained convinced he would be better off without her, her ego was wounded at how easily he seemed to have accepted it. *Maybe*, a little voice whispered in her head now, *you didn't see the crews off because you didn't want to see his indifference towards you.*

She had also avoided Pearl and Jenny since she had returned from being grilled by the senior staff, the main reason being that Thea had yet to confess to Pearl that she had seen Billy Haywood, and hadn't looked forward to it. However, she had lain awake all night, worrying about Fitz and the other aircrews, and had been unable to stay away from the operations block now they were expected home. To pass the time when she had seen Pearl and Jenny, she had given them an edited version of events, glossing over exactly why Billy had thought she would help get the message out of Fenthorpe.

'Sorry,' Pearl said now. 'I just find it incredible that Group Captain Rhodes actually deigned to speak to a mere WAAF.'

'Well, it wasn't really me he was speaking to, it was Squadron Leader Price. But Price wanted me there in case Rhodes wanted to ask me anything.'

Jenny, who had listened to the tale in silence, had been looking more and more thoughtful. Now she asked, 'What I don't understand is why this Billy person would think you'd be willing to help with something that's clearly illegal.'

Pearl saved Thea from having to think up an excuse. 'I expect he thought Thea was still the same tearaway she was when she was a teenager. We know she's changed, but Billy wouldn't.'

Thea listened in amazement. 'You think I've changed?'

'For the better, yes. I mean, I know it took a while to get through my thick skull, and I admit I was unfair to you when you were younger, expecting you to act and think like an adult when you were still in your early teens. But I really admire the person you've become and I trust you. Why else would I give you the responsibility of looking after my wedding gown?'

Thea swallowed the sudden lump in her throat. 'I thought it was just because my hut is conveniently next door to yours.'

'No. It's because I know you take your responsibilities seriously. It might have taken me way too long to understand that going out to let off steam after an arduous day is not being irresponsible, but I know now. I think I've learned more from you this past year than you have from me, and if you'd told me that when you arrived I'd have laughed in your face.'

Now Thea felt really awful. Because she had never told her sister the truth about why she had left home and joined the WAAF, and she still hadn't told the complete truth now. The trouble was, she didn't want to cause any alarm about the wedding. When it was all over, she would confess and hope Pearl still felt the same way about her then. 'That means a lot. Thank you,' was all she could say in response. Deciding it was time to steer the subject away from her involvement with Billy, she hit on a subject that was bound to make Pearl forget everything else. 'Have you been able to get your wedding ring yet?'

Pearl's face was instantly transformed into one of glowing delight. 'I nearly forgot – I was in Lincoln earlier and I popped into the jewellers on the off-chance, and it was ready.' She grimaced. 'Poor Greg was disappointed not to be the one to collect it, but' – her face shadowed – 'there's no knowing when he'll be able to get away, and I did so want to have it safe and sound.'

'Where is it now?' Thea asked.

'Shut up in my bomb-box, safe under my bed.' Bomb-boxes were handy wooden containers with rope handles. As the name suggested, they had originally been used to transport bombs. However, the WAAFs had soon discovered that they were ideal for additional storage, and nearly every WAAF in Fenthorpe now had a bomb-box of her own tucked under the bed.

'What does it look like?' Jenny asked. Even in the dark, Thea could see the dreamy expression on her face. 'When I get married, I'd like a rose-gold ring, maybe with a pretty verse inscribed on the inside.'

'You'll have to wait till after the war, then,' Pearl told her. 'Unless you find an antique ring, I suppose. Mine's a utility ring, so it's quite thin and most of the inside is taken up with hallmarks. It's not pretty, but Greg did buy me a beautiful engagement ring, and I decided we ought to save our money for when we set up house together.' Then she faltered and glanced up at the sky, even though there was nothing to see.

Thea, knowing she would be wondering if it was premature to be planning on setting up their own house when Greg had still not completed his final two missions, tried to think of something else to distract her. 'You know, I've just had an idea about the ceremony. I know you were planning to walk down the aisle with just Jenny and me, but why don't you ask Mr Haughton to give you away? He's done so much for you, I'm sure he'd love to be asked.'

'That's a wonderful idea.' Pearl pulled Thea into an enthusiastic hug. 'I can't believe it never occurred to me. You're right, he's the closest thing to a father I've got. I'm seeing him tomorrow, so I'll ask him then.'

Thea was able to console herself with the thought that she did, at least, do some things right.

On the point of saying something about flowers, she suddenly stopped to listen. Was that the rumble of aero engines in the distance? There was a murmur among the gathered WAAFs, and Pearl clutched her arm. 'What if he doesn't come back?' she gasped in a strangled voice. 'I couldn't bear it.'

Thea floundered for words, her own thoughts with Fitz drifting along the same lines. It was Jenny who answered, only the slightest shake in her voice betraying her own worry. 'He'll be back. With a crew as good as his, they can't fail to be safe.'

That reminded Thea of something she hadn't told them. 'And this time they've got Squadron Leader Price on the crew, no less.' And she filled them in on what had happened with Jack.

When she got to the part about Jack declaring he would go LMF in front of Group Captain Rhodes, Jenny clapped a hand to her mouth. 'Oh no! Poor Jack. He must have been in a terrible state for it to burst out like that. What did Rhodes say?'

'That's the good part. Price stepped in and acted like Jack hadn't mentioned going LMF. He just announced that he would be taking his place and told Fitz to take Jack to the MO.' Thea's thoughts drifted to how desperate Jack had looked. 'When I see Fitz, I must ask how he got on.'

'So you do plan to speak to Fitz, then?' Pearl asked, and Thea could hear the grin in her voice.

'It would be terribly unfeeling not to. Jack did help me out this afternoon. Yesterday afternoon. Oh, I always get muddled up over my days when I spend so many of my nights like this.'

But no one was paying any attention, because the rumble of Merlin engines had become a roar, and now the first Lancaster was coming in to land, and more were circling at varying heights. The first glow of dawn had lit the eastern sky in dove-like pale blues and pinks, and every now and again Thea caught the glint of the sunrise reflected in the windows of one of the returning Lancasters.

Pearl was gripping her arm again, and Thea hoped for the sake of her circulation that *C-Charlie* was in this first group.

There was only the most desultory conversation while they waited for the buses to ferry the aircrews to the operations block and the WAAFs milled around the kitchen, collecting trays of hot tea. The WAAFs were usually aware if ambulances had been requested, and thankfully there didn't seem to be any needed for the first lot of arrivals.

Glancing around the group, Thea saw Blanche, bouncing a little on her toes, and her heart went out to her erstwhile antagonist, knowing Blanche had been on the receiving end of bad news before.

The first bus rolled up, and the WAAFs surged around the doors. Thea, being slightly taller than average, had a good view of the occupants. Relief broke over her like an ocean wave when she saw Fitz's face in the window. 'It's *C-Charlie*!' she cried.

'Oh, thank God!' Pearl brushed away a tear, drew a steadying breath and then pushed her way to the front of the group. A moment later she was in Greg's arms, regardless of the tea that threatened to spill down his back.

Thea, however, hung back. Standing on her tiptoes, she counted each man as he climbed out of the bus, reassuring herself all had returned safe and sound. Her thoughts immediately flew to Jack and she wondered how he would react on hearing that, if he had flown, he would be another mission closer to the end of his tour. Then she remembered his agitation and decided that he really hadn't been in a fit state to fly. Her anxiety for Jack gave her the courage to approach the group, and she joined Pearl and Jenny. Pearl was still hugging Greg; Thea grinned to see a smear of lipstick on his cheek. 'Just one more op!' she was saying, tears streaming down her face.

One more op. Thea instinctively looked for Fitz, who also had just one more mission left to fly. One more mission before he would leave Fenthorpe and be out of her life for good. She was so overwhelmed by a wave of desolation that she nearly forgot why she had decided to speak to him in the first place. However, when she saw Squadron Leader Price climb out of the bus, it reminded her why he was there. Jack would remain in RAF Fenthorpe after Fitz and Greg had left, and she felt a sense of responsibility towards him.

Doing her best to ignore the yearning to fling herself into his arms, she approached Fitz and handed him some tea.

'Thanks,' he muttered without looking at her, and Thea had the feeling he hadn't even recognised her. He wrapped both hands round the mug and took a long drink. Thea was shocked by his pallor and the deep lines of strain scored at the corners of his eyes and mouth.

'You look awful,' she said. 'Are you hurt?'

His head jerked up when she spoke, and his gaze met hers. 'Thea!' The way he said her name brought to mind a man lost in the desert stumbling upon an oasis. 'I'm fine. Just a tough mission. How did it go with Group Captain Rhodes?'

He looked so shattered it was all she could do not to pull him into her arms and let him lean on her, but she had to keep her distance. 'What you'd expect, I suppose. He just told me to go straight to a senior officer if Billy approached me again.' She gazed into his face, allowing herself a tiny moment to drink in the sight of him. 'What happened with Jack? Is he going to be all right? Rhodes didn't mention him after you left, so I think Price's ploy worked.'

'Well that's something, anyway.' Fitz pulled a face. 'I made sure Jack reported to the MO, but then he couldn't go through with it at the last minute and told the doc he'd had bad stomach pains but was feeling better. I think the MO suspects something else was wrong but, unless Jack actually tells him, there's nothing he can do. I had to leave then, so I don't know what happened next.'

The rest of the crew were making their way towards the operations block, where they could shed their gear before going through to be debriefed. Thea battled with herself, knowing there was no reason to delay him, yet wanting to have Fitz to herself for a while longer. 'I'll try and find him when I get a free moment,' she promised.

'Thanks.' Fitz gave a stiff smile. He seemed to be looking at the other WAAFs as though searching for someone in particular. 'Is Blanche here?'

Thea felt an irrational stab of jealousy. 'Blanche? She's around somewhere.' Just then she saw Blanche moving towards the next bus that was just arriving, and Thea knew she would be looking for Sam. She pointed her out to Fitz. 'She's over there. Why?'

There was a pause while Fitz gulped his tea, then he said, 'We saw *D-Donald* go down. There would have been no survivors.'

'Oh God.' Thea couldn't take it in. The seven men Thea had worked with for months, all gone. Including Sam. 'Oh no. Poor Blanche.'

Fitz nodded. 'I know. I have to tell her. It'd be cruel to keep her waiting.'

Before Thea could even reply, he pushed past her and made his way to the next bus. Thea couldn't tear her eyes away, saw Blanche give Fitz a bright smile when he called her name, then that smile first freezing and then slowly fading as Fitz said his piece. Then Blanche shook her head, and, even over the hubbub of the crowd, Thea could hear what she was saying. 'No. No! You're lying.'

Fitz cast frantic glances over the heads of the people milling around, and at first Thea thought he was looking for her. But then she saw him beckoning to Greg and Squadron Leader Price. They clearly understood the situation and went to join Fitz and Pearl. Thea also moved closer in case Blanche needed her.

Price took command of the situation. Putting an arm round Blanche's shoulders, he spoke to her in a low voice, and Thea could see from the shaking of her shoulders that she'd finally accepted the truth. Thea took a step closer, thinking she might be able to offer comfort, but before she could reach her Blanche broke away from Price and fled. Thea toyed with the idea of going after her but on reflection decided that Blanche might need to be alone for a while. She went to rejoin Pearl and Jenny, telling them in a low voice what had happened.

'I think you're right to leave her be for now,' Pearl said. 'Poor Blanche. I don't suppose there's anything we can do at the moment that would be the slightest help. Let's finish giving out the tea and then go and find her afterwards.'

The others agreed, and it was two hours before the last of the Lancasters limped home and Thea, Pearl and Jenny were free to return to the Waafery. *D-Donald*'s fate hung heavily upon them, and they cycled back in subdued silence. Once they had parked their bikes, Pearl and Jenny went into Hut Three, expecting to find Blanche there. Thea hovered outside for a moment, wondering if she should go in, but, deciding she didn't want to crowd Blanche and thinking she would offer her condolences later, she turned away, only to stop when the door opened and Jenny stepped out, looking worried.

'Blanche isn't here,' she said. 'The others say she didn't come back. I think we ought to look for her.'

Thea went cold. This wasn't the first tragic loss Blanche had experienced, after all. What if it had pushed her over the edge? 'I'll help,' she said. 'I can't bear to think of her suffering alone. I wish I'd gone after her as soon as she ran off.'

Pearl had now emerged, wrapping a scarf round her neck against the chill dawn air. 'You weren't to know. I agreed that she could probably do with some time alone. I'm sure she's fine, but I won't be able to relax until we find her.'

'I hope you're right. I suppose we could try the rec first. Let me just drop my bicycle clips in my hut, then I'll join you.'

However, as soon as Thea walked into Hut Four she knew she had found Blanche. A drawn-out keening wail made the hairs stand up on the back of her neck, and in the dim light she could just make out a huddled form on the floor beside her bed. There was also an odd tearing noise.

Thea switched on the light, wondering why none of the other girls in the hut had gone to Blanche's aid, but then saw that all the beds were empty. Either her hut-mates were on duty or they had also volunteered to meet the returning aircrews and had not yet returned.

The figure by the bed was definitely Blanche. She knelt on the floor, her back to Thea, and didn't appear to notice Thea's presence. She rocked a little, still keening, as though in pain. The tearing sound grew louder.

'Blanche.' Carefully, as one would approach a wounded animal that was liable to lash out, Thea edged closer. When Blanche still gave no sign that she had seen or heard her, Thea dropped her cycle clips onto her bed and placed a tentative hand on Blanche's shoulder.

'Go away!' Blanche whipped round, her words more an animal howl than anything uttered by a human. Thea caught the glint of silver and instinctively staggered back, in time to see a sharp pair of scissors scythe through the air where her hand had been only a split second before.

The near-miss seemed to snap Blanche back to full awareness, and she gasped. The scissors clattered to the floor, and she stared up at Thea with wide, shocked eyes. 'I'm sorry. I wasn't trying to hurt you.'

'I know.' Thea glanced at the door, wondering if she should go for help, yet she couldn't bring herself to leave Blanche alone in such distress. She spoke in the soothing voice one would use on a frightened child and said the first words that came into her head, more to keep Blanche calm than because she wanted to know the answer. 'Why did you come to my hut?' She inched one step forward again. When Blanche didn't lash out this time, she took another step. 'Were you looking for me?'

And now she could see what Blanche had been doing, and the source of the ripping sound. Blanche held Pearl's gorgeous lace wedding gown crumpled in her lap, and several slits in the lace had left gaping holes in the bodice. Blanche hadn't come to Hut Four to find Thea. She had come to destroy the gown.

Chapter Twenty-Four

Thea stood, frozen on the spot, unable to get her horrified mind to take in what she was seeing. Some part of her told her she needed to offer Blanche sympathy and fetch Section Officer Blatchford, who would, no doubt, take Blanche straight to Sick Quarters. But the part of Thea's brain that controlled her actions didn't seem to be working, and all she could do was stare at the ruined gown. The gown Pearl had entrusted to her care.

The door burst open, and Pearl barged in. 'Get a move on, Thea. We—' Her words ended in a strangled gasp. 'My dress!'

But the sight of Pearl seemed to have reawoken the madness that had seized Blanche. Before Thea could intervene, she grabbed the scissors she had dropped and made another vicious slash through the delicate lace. As she did so, her face crumpled and tears dripped down her cheeks. 'It's not fair!' she wailed, her voice so distorted from her convulsive sobs it was hard to make out the words. 'Why is everyone I love taken away?' She raised a tear-streaked face to Pearl. 'Why did Sam have to die? Why couldn't Greg have been taken instead?'

Thea was aware that Jenny had now entered the hut, and she shot her a pleading look over her shoulder. 'Go and fetch Blatchford.'

Jenny gave a brief nod and dashed out. Thea let out a shaky breath, grateful that she and Pearl wouldn't be alone with Blanche for much longer.

In her moment of distraction, she hadn't noticed Pearl approaching Blanche or she would have warned her to step back. Now she grabbed her sister's arm and tried to pull her away, but Pearl resisted.

She stretched out a hand towards Blanche. 'I'm so sorry, Blanche. You're right. It isn't fair.' She took another step forward. 'Why don't you give me the scissors?'

Thea didn't wait for Pearl to finish her sentence and certainly not for Blanche to react. She lunged for Blanche just as the scissors swung up. But instead of lashing out at Pearl, as Thea had feared, Blanche's strike was aimed at her own thigh. Thea bowled into Blanche before she could land her blow, and she managed to knock her arm aside and close her fist round the scissors. A sharp pain shot through her palm, but she managed to wrench the scissors from Blanche and toss them to the other side of the hut. Then she fell to her knees beside Blanche and wrapped her arms round the girl's shaking shoulders. Blanche stiffened briefly, then relaxed and slumped against Thea, collapsing into racking sobs.

The door burst open, and Section Officer Blatchford strode in. She took in the scene immediately, supporting Blanche on her other side and saying, 'I see you've got things under control. Come on, Dalby, let's get you to Sick Quarters. Lend me a hand, Cooper.'

—

Two hours later, Thea, Pearl and Jenny were back in Hut Four. Blatchford had sent for an ambulance to take Blanche to Sick Quarters, for she had been unable to walk. Thea had then also noticed that her hand was bleeding rather badly and had ended up going in the ambulance with Blanche. It had needed stitches and, as a result, she had been relieved from duty until they were removed, as she would be unable to perform delicate repairs with a bandaged hand.

'I'm so sorry,' Thea told her. 'Is it just the bodice that got torn? Maybe we could make a sash out of parachute silk to cover it?'

Pearl simply shook her head and turned the dress, showing a long, straight cut in the skirt. She attempted to speak, cleared her throat, then tried again. 'It's not your fault.'

'But I feel responsible. I was supposed to be looking after it. And if I'd gone after Blanche as soon as she ran off, I could have stopped her.'

'You couldn't possibly have known she would do this. I thought you were right to leave her in peace for a while.' Pearl sighed. 'It was awful to see her like that. I'm upset about the dress, obviously, but I'd willingly have ripped it with my own bare hands if it meant Sam and the rest of his crew could still be here. The thing that makes me feel really awful, though, is that, while I'm terribly sad for Sam and Blanche, my overwhelming feeling is relief that Greg is still safe.'

'I think that's an understandable reaction. I feel the same way about F— about him and *C-Charlie*'s crew as well.' Thea thought she'd caught herself in time before saying Fitz's name, but from the arch look Pearl directed at her she guessed her sister had noticed the slip.

'You must be in pain, so I'll overlook that for now,' Pearl said, seeming to have regained some of her old spirit. 'But during your sick leave, I think you should take the time to consider your feelings.'

'If you can still dole out lectures, I know you're not too cut up about the dress, if you'll pardon the expression.' But Thea was too tired and heartsick to summon up any genuine indignation.

Jenny, who had seemed deeply shocked by Blanche's breakdown, finally spoke. 'This is all very well, but you're getting married in three weeks and you don't have a gown. What are we going to do?'

Pearl gave the lace another mournful caress. 'First things first, I've got to face Miss Honeycroft. I dread to think how she'll react.'

Thea thought of the kind woman who had seemed genuinely excited to be dressing Pearl for her wedding. She knew the

236

loss of one of the most exquisite gowns in her collection would be a terrible blow. 'We'll both go.' She held up her bandaged hand. 'I have to go back to Sick Quarters first thing for a quick check-up, but after that I'm free as a bird.'

'You don't have to.'

'I want to.'

'I wish I could come too, but I don't have any free time,' Jenny said. 'Are you going to ask Miss Honeycroft for another dress?'

Pearl pulled a face. 'I doubt she would let me within five miles of her gowns after this. To be honest, I don't think I could even ask. I might not have been the one who damaged it, but I still feel responsible. I'll probably end up getting married in uniform.'

–

Pearl's declaration that she would marry in her uniform haunted Thea as she tried and failed to snatch a quick nap before it was time to rise for breakfast. Despite what Pearl had said, Thea couldn't help but feel responsible for the dress that had been left in her care. Even without Billy Haywood's interference, she had already ruined her sister's wedding day. She also couldn't forget how Pearl had confided in her about her dream wedding and how she had longed to marry in a beautiful gown. If her sister wanted a fairy-tale wedding dress, then that's what she should have. The trouble was, Thea had no idea how they were going to arrange it in such a short time.

She rose for breakfast feeling heavy-eyed from lack of sleep and profoundly grateful that she wouldn't be required to work. Once breakfast was over, she made her way to Sick Quarters, having arranged to meet Pearl in Lincoln at midday.

The nurse who examined her dressing pronounced herself satisfied that the stitches were holding and then said, 'Blanche was asking to see you. Do you feel up to it?'

'Of course.' Although she was surprised that Blanche would want to see anyone who had witnessed her loss of control.

She found Blanche sitting up in bed, her face pale and puffy. Thea relaxed when she saw that she seemed drained of the violent despair that had seized her earlier.

Thea sat on a chair beside the bed. 'How are you? I'd have brought you a magazine or something if I'd known I'd be seeing you.'

Blanche gave a wan smile. 'I'm all right, I suppose. I've been put on sick leave for at least a week and I'm going home for a while. It will do me good to get away from here, I think.' Her gaze dropped to Thea's bandaged hand and, if possible, she turned a shade paler. 'Did I do that? I'm so sorry.'

Thea shrugged. 'It was an accident.'

'I don't know what came over me. Well, I do. But I can't believe I behaved that way.' Then her shoulders heaved. 'I can't believe Sam's gone, either.'

Thea didn't hesitate to wrap an arm round Blanche's shoulders. 'None of us can. He was a lovely man, and you made him so happy. This war is just so cruel.'

'The nurse asked me how long I'd been seeing him.' Blanche seemed to need to talk, and Thea, deciding that listening was the most helpful thing she could do right now, let her talk without interruption, just nodding or murmuring encouragement in the appropriate places. 'When she found out it was only for a few weeks, she said she was sure I'd soon find someone else. Can you believe that?'

Thea, who hadn't been altogether convinced about the depth of Blanche's feelings, felt a twinge of guilt and murmured, 'How awful!'

Thankfully Blanche didn't seem to need anything more as a response. 'Just because we hadn't been going out for long, it doesn't mean I don't have deep feelings for him. I'd fancied him for ages. He was so quiet and steady, not brash and arrogant like so many of the aircrew.' She talked on, pouring out her feelings for Sam, and it dawned on Thea that Blanche really had loved him and would most likely mourn him for the rest of her life, whether or not she eventually fell in love again.

A while later, the nurse approached the bed. 'The doctor will be in to see you shortly, and then you'll be able to leave.' She looked at Thea. 'Time to go now.'

Thea nodded and rose, but Blanche clutched her arm. 'Wait. Please tell Pearl I'm really sorry. I'll pay for the dress, of course. Have you got something to write on? I'll give you my address so you can send me the bill.'

Thea, who had been worried Pearl would be landed with a bill she couldn't afford, didn't protest but dug in her pocket for her latest letter from Deedee; Blanche wrote the address on the back of the envelope.

'Do you think the dress agency will have another dress she can wear?'

'I hope so.'

Blanche's cheeks turned crimson. 'I really am sorry.'

'I know. I'll tell Pearl.' Although how forgiving Pearl might feel was doubtful, considering the one thing she had dreamed of was to be married in a beautiful gown.

'I might be able to help.'

'How?'

'I remember reading somewhere that Gainsborough film studios have started hiring out their costumes. You might get something suitable from them.'

'Thank you. It's worth a try.' Thea doubted they would have anything in the short timescale available, but she would try anything to get Pearl her dream dress.

Deciding to act on the idea straight away, she hastily wrote a brief letter to the studios, asking if they had anything available in Pearl's size. It was a good thing she already knew Pearl's measurements from the last time they had gone dress-hunting; she included them at the end of the letter. As there was just time to take the letter to the camp post office before she had to leave for the bus, she got it posted off, sending with it her prayers that she would receive a favourable reply.

She decided not to say anything to Pearl about it yet, thinking it was probably a forlorn hope. And of course, if Miss Honeycroft did have another suitable dress, there would be no need to go to the expense of hiring a dress from a film studio.

–

Pearl looked up at the imposing door to Miss Honeycroft's house and released a shaky breath. 'I think this is the most difficult thing I've ever had to do.'

'This from the woman who's spoken to pilots in burning aircraft.'

As Thea had intended, this reminder of how she'd met Greg brought a soft smile to her sister's face. 'Anyway, *you're* not going to do this. You left the dress in my care, so it's up to me to break the news.' Before she lost her courage, Thea knocked at the door.

The same maid Thea remembered from their last visit opened the door. 'Hello. Have you got an appointment?'

Thea spoke up before Pearl could reply, determined to take the lead in this unpleasant task. 'We haven't, but we really need to see Miss Honeycroft. It's about the dress my sister hired.'

The maid's face lit up. 'Oh, I remember you. Do come in, and I'll see if Miss Honeycroft is available. You hired the Edwardian lace gown, didn't you? Does it need altering?'

'No, I—' Pearl began.

But Thea wasn't going to let her take the blame. 'I'm afraid it's more serious than that. The dress got torn last night. We really need to explain to Miss Honeycroft and apologise.'

The maid's hand flew to her mouth. 'Oh no! She's with another customer at the moment, but you can wait in the morning room.'

The morning room turned out to be a pretty, airy room on the ground floor, decorated in shades of green and primrose.

The maid invited them to take a seat and then left, saying she would make them tea and tell Miss Honeycroft they were here. The room contained comfortable-looking armchairs, but Thea chose to sit at a writing desk, on a high-backed wooden chair, feeling that she didn't deserve to wait in comfort. She held on to the dress box, unwilling to let it out of her sight for an instant. Pearl took one of the armchairs, although she perched on the edge.

'I feel like a schoolgirl again, waiting outside the headmistress's office,' Thea said. She waited for Pearl to make a remark along the lines of, 'You should know,' but her sister remained silent.

The door opened and they both sprang to their feet, only to see it was the maid bringing their tea and a slice of carrot cake each. 'Miss Honeycroft will be about a quarter of an hour,' she said as she left.

Thea and Pearl sank back into their chairs. Pearl stared at her cake. 'I don't think I can eat this. It would turn to ashes in my mouth.'

Thea nibbled the corner of her cake and closed her eyes in bliss. 'That is honestly the best carrot cake I've ever had. You've got to try it.' Then she frowned. 'Do you suppose it's poisoned?'

Pearl chuckled. 'I think they'd wait until after we'd paid for the damage.' She bit into her cake. Her eyes widened and, after she had swallowed, she wailed, 'That just makes this worse!'

'Why – did you chip your tooth on a walnut?'

'No. But this tastes so good. It's going to break Miss Honeycroft's heart to see the mess I've made of this dress, and yet she's been so kind to us.'

'The mess *Blanche* made of the dress,' Thea said firmly. 'And she's promised to pay.' She told Pearl what Blanche had said earlier, only omitting the news about Gainsborough Studios. This turned the conversation to Blanche's tragedy. 'I know she wasn't nice to Jenny at first, and she was only too happy to label me a thief, but I think I can forgive her. She lost two other boyfriends before Sam, remember. I'm not saying it excuses her behaviour, but who can tell how suffering those losses has affected her?'

'I think last night's performance gives a pretty good indication,' Pearl said. 'I don't think she really knew what she was doing. I hope going away on leave will help her.'

One good thing had come out of this mess, Thea mused. The MO had been revealed to be understanding and had realised that Blanche needed treating, not punishing. She recalled how he had also stepped in to help when Jack had blurted in front of the station commander that he wanted to go LMF. If only Jack could be persuaded to tell the MO the truth, she was sure he would be treated with compassion.

Pearl, unaware of the change in Thea's train of thought, said, 'At any rate, Blanche is trying to make amends, so I can forgive her. I just wish she hadn't taken out her grief on my beautiful dress.'

There was no time to rely to this, for the door opened and Miss Honeycroft walked in, greeting them with a smile that made Thea know it would be all the more difficult to explain what had happened. 'Good afternoon, girls. How lovely to see you again. Anna tells me there's been an accident with the dress.'

Thea opened the box. 'I'm so sorry, Miss Honeycroft. I'm afraid it was more than an accident.' And, after drawing a steadying breath, she explained the events of the night before. Only when she had finished, and their hostess's eyes were already clouded with dismay, did she unwrap the gown from its tissue paper, drape it over Miss Honeycroft's arms and point out the damage. 'Blanche is devastated at what she's done,' she concluded, 'and she's promised to pay. I've got her address. She says to send the bill there.'

'As if I'd charge that poor girl after what she's been through.' Miss Honeycroft carried the dress to the window, holding it to the light. She shook her head sadly as she examined the damage. She took her time, inspecting each tear, then turned the lace overdress inside out so she could see how the tears looked on both sides.

Thea and Pearl waited in silence. Thea held her breath in the irrational fear that any noise might make the damage worse. Pearl was twisting her hands, her gaze glued on Miss Honeycroft.

Finally the older woman spoke. 'Yes, I'm very sorry but I won't be able to mend the damage in time for your wedding.'

'It can be mended?' Thea wouldn't have believed it was possible.

'Oh, yes. The underdress wasn't damaged at all. Most of the tears were to the same panel of lace in the bodice.' Looking to see where Miss Honeycroft was pointing, she saw the section of bodice that had been ripped was a continuous band of lace that circled the dress from waist to just beneath the bust. 'These cuts are too jagged to be repaired, but I know an excellent lacemaker, and I think it would be possible to get a matching section of lace made that I can use. I never liked throwing away garments, even before the war.'

'What about the tear in the skirt?' Thea pointed to the long slice that laid open the lace from hip to mid-thigh.

'That's not as bad as it seems. It's mostly damage to the seam, and I'm confident Anna can make that as good as new.'

'I'm so glad it's not ruined,' Pearl said. 'But you must let us pay for the lace. And for any loss of earnings from not being able to hire the dress to anyone else.'

But Miss Honeycroft waved aside Pearl's protestations. 'Nonsense. I didn't start up this service to make money. My reward is to see brides' happy faces in the newspapers and know that, thanks to me, they got married in the dress of their dreams.'

'That's very generous of you,' Pearl said. 'It doesn't feel right not to make some kind of amends though.'

'My dear.' Miss Honeycroft laid a hand on Pearl's shoulder. 'I'm getting on in years, and there's comparatively little I can contribute to the war effort. Please let me do this one small service for young women like you who have sacrificed so much.'

There was little either Pearl or Thea could say to that. Pearl simply bit her lip and nodded.

'Now,' Miss Honeycroft went on, 'Many of the dresses you looked at last time won't be available for your wedding, but shall we see what we can find?'

Pearl looked as stunned as Thea felt. 'You mean you're still prepared to let me hire another gown after what happened to the last one?'

'Of course. It was an accident. I know it won't happen again. The gowns are upstairs in the drawing room. Would you like to see?'

Pearl cast a longing glance upwards, then shook her head. 'You've been so kind, and I'm sure I'd find another beautiful gown, but I can't. I couldn't wear it without being terrified I'd damage it or spill something on it, and I couldn't put you through that twice, no matter how understanding you've been.'

Thea could see Pearl meant every word. Miss Honeycroft studied her face for a moment, then nodded, clearly understanding. 'Very well. I won't embarrass you by trying to change your mind. I wish I could recommend another place, but I'm sure this is the only dress hire service in Lincoln.'

Pearl gave a sad smile. 'I've decided to marry in my uniform. Greg will be in uniform too, so at least we'll match.' Then she clapped a hand to her mouth. 'I just remembered I left the shoes and veil behind. I'll bring them back as soon as I can. They were untouched.'

Miss Honeycroft placed a gentle hand on Pearl's arm. 'Hold on to them for now. If you find another dress you might be glad of them.'

'That's very kind.' But from Pearl's downcast expression, Thea could tell she doubted that would be likely and was bitterly disappointed.

Chapter Twenty-Five

Pearl's look of desolation wouldn't leave Thea's mind and quite overpowered all of her other worries. She parted company with her sister at the bus station, for Pearl had said she needed to do more work on the next edition of the *Bombshell* before returning to Fenthorpe. Thea therefore returned to the village alone, brooding over the ill luck that seemed to be haunting the wedding. Still, she told herself, the main thing was that Greg survived his final mission in one piece. As long as he was there, Pearl would be happy to wed in a pair of overalls if they could finally be married.

When the bus arrived in Fenthorpe, Thea alighted in the village rather than at the stop nearest to the base, not feeling like facing life on the station just yet. The sun had beaten on her head all the way back from Lincoln and she was gasping for a drink, yet if she went to the NAAFI there was a chance she would bump into Fitz. She still hadn't got used to the lurch of misery that hit every time she saw him, and knowing it was self-inflicted was no comfort. Accordingly, she opted to visit the tearoom in the village before returning to the station. While she didn't often go there, considering it a little too genteel for her tastes, anything was better than seeing Fitz at another table and not being able to join in.

She lingered rather longer than intended at the Rosebud Tearoom, delaying the moment when she would have to risk bumping into Fitz. However, when all the other customers had left, and the waitress was walking around the tables, straightening the chairs rather more noisily than necessary, Thea took the hint and left. Her head was so full of Fitz that she completely forgot to watch out for Billy and was therefore too late to avoid him when she reached the junction at the end of Fenthorpe Lane and found him there, smoking a Woodbine.

'So you've finally turned up,' he said. 'Where were you last night?'

'I might say the same about you,' Thea retorted. 'I waited and waited for ages.'

Billy frowned. 'You were here?'

Thea rolled her eyes. 'No, I went to tea at the vicarage. Yes, of course I was here. You'd threatened to do all sorts of terrible things at my sister's wedding if I didn't do as you asked, so where were you?'

Billy shuffled his feet and gazed at a point over Thea's shoulder for a moment before replying, 'I knew you'd be coming through the hole in the fence, so when I didn't see you when I got here I wandered up the lane a little way to meet you.'

Thea knew he must be lying, because she would have seen him on the drive from the main gate. She couldn't tell him that, though, without giving away the fact that she hadn't been alone. Instead she said, 'Sorry – I managed to wangle permission to leave through the main gate. I thought you didn't know where the back door was.'

'Yeah, well, I overheard a couple of girls in the pub talking about it and worked out roughly where it must be.' Then his gaze hardened. 'Anyway, you still owe me. Next time they're flying ops at Fenthorpe, you'll just have to do the whole thing again.'

'If you know where the back door is, why not meet me there?' The lane closest to the hole in the fence was much more winding and had places where a car could pull right off the road and be concealed. She would be happier knowing that Squadron Leader Price, or whoever accompanied her next time, was nearer than he had been last night. More than ever she suspected Billy of some kind of trick, and wanted the reassurance of knowing help was at hand.

'Fine. And make sure you're there. This is your last chance if you want to save your sister's wedding.'

–

This was it. By the end of the night, Fitz would either have completed his tour or disaster would have struck and he would probably be dead. One way or another, today was his last day as aircrew.

The announcement that ops were on had arrived just after breakfast, and now the aircrews were making their way to the operations block to check the lists.

'What are you going to do if you're on the list?' Fitz asked Jack as they joined the queue of men waiting to see the notice-board. Jack just shrugged, so Fitz said, 'You should go to the MO. Price made it clear he understands what you're going through, and surely the MO has proved his worth to you by now.'

'I don't know.' Jack's voice was strangled. 'Let's just see who's on the list first.'

Fitz couldn't argue with that, so said no more until they had progressed to the front of the queue. His heart leaped with relief when he saw *C-Charlie* was on the list of aircraft flying that night and confirmed he and Greg were both down to fly. Another surge of relief hit when he saw that Jack's name wasn't there. Instead Sergeant Norton, from *J-John*'s crew, was down as their tail gunner.

A glance at Jack showed him pasty-faced, leaning against the wall as though he would fall without its support. When he caught Fitz's eye he muttered, 'I need the bog,' and bolted for the toilets.

'I'll see you in the locker room,' he called, then jumped as he felt a hand on his shoulder.

He glanced up to find himself looking at Greg. 'This is it, mate. You ready for a change of scene?'

'Absolutely. And you'd better make sure you get back safe and sound, because I don't want to have to explain to Pearl why you missed the wedding.'

'No worries.'

There was no chance to say more, for Squadron Leader Price came up to them, and they saluted. 'Just checking you noticed the change to your crew,' Price said after returning the salute. 'Whatever Knight may say, I'm not convinced he's fit, and besides, Norton is on his thirtieth op as well, and as *J-John* isn't serviceable I thought I'd put him on your crew.'

'Good idea, sir,' Greg said.

Fitz fully expected Price to end the conversation and so was surprised when he turned to Fitz. 'I suggest you try and persuade him to tell the MO about his real problem. The station commander will want to make a public example of him if he gets the merest whiff that Knight refuses to fly.'

It was no good protesting that he'd tried and failed many times, so he simply said, 'I'll do my best, sir.'

–

There was nothing he could do about Jack that morning, as he needed to collect his kit and join the rest of the crew for the night flying test. By the time that finished it was lunchtime, and the sergeants' mess was too rowdy for a serious conversation. It was only in the hour before the crew briefing that he managed to catch Jack alone. 'Let's go for a walk,' he said, thinking that it would be easier to talk freely in the peaceful lanes outside the base.

While Jack didn't resist, neither did he seem keen to talk about how he was feeling. Instead he chattered incessantly about the weather, last week's football match against RAF Waddington and even the possibility that they might get some real coffee in the sergeants' mess. Every time Fitz tried to steer the conversation towards Jack's state of mind, Jack immediately deflected it.

'Jack, I really think—' Fitz tried for what felt like the hundredth time, as they turned onto the lane leading behind the Waafery.

He broke off as Jack clutched his arm. 'What's that?' Jack was pointing at the bushes running alongside the wire fence. The section of fence, Fitz recalled, where the 'back door' was hidden.

'Why? What did you see?'

'I'm not sure. I thought it looked like someone hiding in the bushes, but my eyes must be playing tricks on me.'

'Probably a WAAF sneaking out without permission.' Fitz explained about the back door.

'I don't know. There was something furtive about it. Anyway, I'm pretty sure I saw a man, not a woman.'

'Could have been a WAAF in battledress. And of course she would be furtive – no one's supposed to leave the station without signing out.' Fitz was growing impatient with Jack now. He only had limited time before he needed to attend the crew briefing, and he still hadn't managed to steer the conversation to Jack seeing the MO.

'I don't think so.' Jack was craning his neck, studying the bushes with narrowed eyes. 'Yes, look – there's a man there. Behind that hazel.'

Fitz looked, and froze. Now he could see there really was someone there. Not entering or leaving via the 'back door' but standing there. He dropped his voice. 'You're right. It's almost like he's lying in wait.'

'That's what I thought. Think it's that Billy bloke who was bothering Thea? What should we do?'

Fitz wondered why that hadn't occurred to him. It made sense, because he couldn't imagine that two suspicious men would be hanging around RAF Fenthorpe in the same week. He thought quickly. For now the man was facing away from them, looking towards the Waafery, but he could turn and see them at any moment. A sensible voice in his head told him to report to Squadron Leader Price as he'd been instructed. But another voice warned him that the man might get away before they could return with Price, and then Thea still wouldn't be free of him. 'We should challenge him,' Fitz said. 'If it *is* Billy, we need to take him to Price or the station commander so we can sort this out once and for all.' Then he shot a glance at Jack. 'If you're up to it.'

Jack squared his shoulders. 'Anything to help Thea.' He strode towards the hazel bush where the stranger lurked, forcing Fitz to run to catch up.

Fitz kept his footsteps light so as not to alert the man, and he could sense Jack doing the same. They reached the hiding place at the same time; Fitz signalled to Jack to approach from the other side to hem the man in. When Jack was in position, he silently counted down from three on his fingers and they both leaped at the stranger at the same time.

'Who are— oh.' For the man Fitz had grabbed by the arm could not be Billy. Because this man was a sergeant in the RAF police.

The sergeant stared at Fitz and Jack gape-mouthed for a moment, then grabbed them both by the arm and steered them back onto the lane. 'What d'you think you're playing at? You could ruin the whole operation.'

'What operation?' Jack asked.

The sergeant looked them both up and down, taking in their aircrew brevets, then appeared to come to a decision. 'We've had reports of a WAAF smuggling mission-sensitive inform-ation out of RAF Fenthorpe, and we're waiting to catch the people involved.'

'But then you'd catch—' Jack broke off as Fitz, fearing he was about to name Thea, gave him a surreptitious kick on the ankle. Jack disguised his start with a cough before continuing, 'You'd catch the WAAF carrying the information out of the base, but would that be everyone involved?'

'We'd wait for her to meet the person she was handing the information to. Once we had them, we could question them to discover who else is involved. Now, move along before you ruin everything. I don't want to hang around here for yet another afternoon.'

Fitz and Jack returned the way they had come. Only when he was sure they were out of earshot of the sergeant, and any other members of the RAF police, did he speak. 'This doesn't make sense. The station commander already knows about Thea and Billy, and has made plans for how to act if Billy contacts her again. So why set the police to watch the fence when he already knows it's Thea who'll come through the back door, and she's innocent?'

'I still think it's strange Billy didn't turn up the other night. If he wanted the information so badly, why wasn't he there to collect it?'

'Unless he did.' Something the sergeant had said had been bothering Fitz, and now understanding dawned. 'The sergeant just now said he didn't want *to hang around for yet another night.*'

'So? If he'd failed to catch Thea today, he'd have to come back next time ops are on to do it all over again.'

Fitz shook his head. 'That's not how I interpreted it. The way he said it made it sound like he'd already done this before.' He put especial emphasis on his next words. 'And Thea didn't leave the camp by the back door last time, because Price took her through the main gate.'

Jack's face was a picture of confusion. Fitz took pity on him and spelled it out. 'I don't think this is a case of espionage at all. I think someone's trying to set up Thea.' Another thought struck. 'Yes! That's it!' He grabbed Jack's arm in his excitement. 'Billy wasn't at the meeting point, because he didn't think she'd be there. He thought she'd be caught at the back door. It's Billy. He's trying to set her up.' Fitz went cold. 'And she'd have got into serious trouble if she'd been caught smuggling out the location of that night's target.'

Jack was ashen-faced. 'That's awful. Why would someone want to do that to Thea?'

'I don't know, but I intend to find out.' Fitz struggled to remember what Thea had told him about Billy. He was a friend from her past whom she'd regretted hanging out with and who had ended up in prison. But she'd been vague about the precise reason why he had been caught. Could it be that he blamed her? If so, that would explain why he wanted to see her punished. *See her punished*. A horrible suspicion struck. While he had no proof, he was sure he was right. 'Jack, he's here!'

'Who?'

'Billy. I don't know why, but he's set her up because he wants to see her suffer. But that means he must be hiding here somewhere, waiting to see her get caught. That's why he wasn't at the rendezvous last night – because he was lurking somewhere he could see her being caught by the police. He must have been furious when she didn't appear.'

'We should tell Price.'

'Yes. No, wait. If he's seen us talking to the police, that could have spooked him, especially if he's ever seen us with Thea. I'd hate for him to bolt the minute we're out of sight. He might not be here yet, of course, but we should look for him if he is. The RAF police are nearby, so we can yell for help if we need it.'

'Okay. Where would he hide?'

In a flash, Fitz knew exactly where. He remembered seeing a hollow tree when he had walked this way with Thea what felt a lifetime ago. 'There's an old oak with a hollowed-out trunk near the junction. Billy would be able to see the police grab Thea from there and then make his own getaway before they came searching for him. This way.'

They were only about fifty yards from the tree – Fitz could already see it – so, if Billy was there, he would be watching them. Speaking in a low voice, Fitz said, 'We need to act like we're sauntering past and taking no notice of the tree. He's bound to be looking this way, so, once we're between him and the junction, we dash back and take him by surprise.'

There were probably a load of holes in the plan, but it was the best Fitz could come up with on the spur of the moment. He spoke in a loud voice about the eggs and bacon he was looking forward to after that night's mission, and Jack played along. Fitz was careful not to so much as glance at the hollow tree when they walked past, although it was almost impossible to keep his gaze from sliding in that direction. His heart thudding against his ribs, he waited until they were several yards past the tree so anyone hiding would hopefully be lulled into a false sense of security. Then he tapped Jack's shoulder in a silent signal and they both turned and made a dash for the tree.

Fitz saw the man immediately. As expected, their quarry was facing away from them, and he only turned when Fitz was about three paces away. He lashed out, striking Fitz on the cheek. Fitz staggered back and saw Jack leap into the fray. That was when Billy – for surely this could only be Billy – stuck his hand in his pocket and pulled out something that gleamed silver. 'Look out, he's got a knife!' Fitz yelled, then yelled again for the police and launched himself at Billy.

Jack had already grabbed the arm holding the knife, but Billy was bigger and stronger, and the arm was getting closer to Jack, the knife aimed at his throat.

Fitz had never been in a fight, but he wasn't going to stand by and let this man stick a knife in his friend. After assuring himself two policemen were running their way, he grabbed the arm holding the knife. He might never have been in a fight, but he was a dancer and strong enough to lift a ballerina with one hand. He twisted Billy's arm behind his back, and Billy dropped the knife with a cry of pain.

It was over in a few seconds. Jack kicked the knife out of reach while Fitz grabbed Billy's other arm and got him in a headlock. 'Billy Haywood, I take it?'

When Thea learned ops were on, her emotions were pulled in all directions. There was excitement that Fitz and Greg would complete their tour, and fear that, in the cruellest of all fates, disaster would strike and they wouldn't return. Added to that was the dread of repeating the rigmarole with Billy. Would he show up this time? Would she spot the WAAF giving her the information?

At least her injury meant she wasn't on duty, so there was no trouble going to the NAAFI at the allotted time. The handover happened as before, except this time Thea managed to catch a glimpse of the mysterious WAAF's face before she disappeared. Although she didn't know her name, she was sure she worked in the signals office. That made sense: the WAAFs working there received the messages from headquarters containing the inform-ation of that night's target. Sickened that anyone in Fenthorpe could be persuaded to betray their own comrades, Thea rose on shaking legs and went to report to the station commander.

No sooner had she rounded the corner of the admin block than she came face to face with a curious procession of RAF police, at the centre of which was Billy, being manhandled by a burly sergeant. Fitz hovered next to them, looking as though he would punch Billy at the first opportunity. Jack was also there.

She clutched Jack's arm when he drew level. 'What's going on?'

Jack gave her a triumphant grin. 'Fitz worked it all out. We caught Billy red-handed.' He stepped aside to let the sergeant restraining Billy go through the door. 'They're taking him to the station commander.'

Thea wasn't about to stand by while someone else dealt with Billy. 'I'm coming too,' she said. 'I was supposed to see the station commander anyway.'

Once in the station commander's office the police pushed Billy onto a chair and cuffed his hands then arranged themselves on either side. Price had been sent for and arrived within minutes.

'I've pushed the crew briefing back by thirty minutes,' he told Fitz, and only then did it dawn on Thea that Fitz had been in danger of missing vital operational information.

Rhodes approached Billy, towering over him. Then he frowned at Price. 'I don't understand. I thought we were supposed to wait to catch him handing the information on.'

'I can explain, sir,' Fitz said. 'You see, this wasn't about espionage at all, was it, Billy?' Fitz gazed at Billy, who began to squirm. 'You weren't selling secrets. You wanted to get Thea in trouble. I've no idea why you'd want to do that, but all this was a charade, to get your revenge on this sweet, innocent girl.'

To say Thea was startled at hearing herself described as sweet and innocent was putting it mildly. Then she saw the rage in Billy's eyes and worked out Fitz was trying to goad him.

'Sweet?' Billy sneered. 'You wouldn't call her sweet if she'd landed *you* in prison. Everything that's ever gone wrong in my life is because of her and of course I wanted to get my own back.'

Thea had heard enough. 'Your life went wrong because you're a crook,' she said. 'That's all your fault. Nothing to do with me.' With a sinking heart, she knew she would have to explain herself to the others. While she'd always intended to tell Fitz, she'd never imagined having to make her confession to so many people, including the station commander.

Nevertheless, it was Fitz who needed to hear this most of all, and she addressed her next words to him. 'I knew Billy when I was growing up in Shrewsbury,' she said. 'I was once stupid enough to fall for him, and when he asked me out I leaped at the chance. Only it turned out he just wanted to use me as a lookout while he broke into places—' Thea caught herself. They didn't need to hear all the details, how she had been so infatuated with Billy that she hadn't questioned why he'd wanted her to stand outside the tobacconist's while he went round the back, and shout if anyone arrived. She'd just been thrilled that he'd noticed her. In fact, it was only when she'd heard a cry and the sound of breaking glass that it dawned on her what he was doing. And she'd been enough of an idiot to let him make her an accessory to his crime.

'When I realised what he was up to, I telephoned the police and turned him in.' She hadn't given her name, but the police had taken the tip seriously enough to send officers to the scene, where they had caught Billy in the act. After the arrest, ashamed at how Billy had used her, she had volunteered for the WAAF, determined to do something useful with her life. 'I had no idea he was out of prison until he showed up in Lincoln, and he told me his brother had seen me make the call and put two and two together.'

Fitz marched up to Billy. 'Is that what this was all about – getting your own back on Thea for turning you in?'

Billy looked shrunken, all defiance gone. 'That and for my brother. He would still be here if he hadn't been killed on his way to meeting me when I was released.'

Thea tried to meet Fitz's gaze, looking for any sign he wasn't repelled by her past. Instead she saw nothing but hardness in his eyes. Her heart went cold. She had been right to break up with him because now he wanted nothing to do with her.

Chapter Twenty-Six

The meeting ended soon after that. The station commander pressed Billy for the name of the WAAF who had given Thea the target note, and Billy made no attempt to protect her but named a WAAF who worked in the signals office, confirming Thea's suspicions. When pushed, he admitted they had been going out together. Thea felt sorry for her, knowing she would likely be thrown out of the WAAF at the very least. Then Billy was taken away and the group dismissed.

Thea tried to catch Fitz's eye, but Price spoke to him first. 'Get a move on, Fitz, or you'll miss the briefing.'

Fitz nodded and was gone before she could even ask if they could meet before he left on the mission. She hated to think of him flying into danger and thinking the worst of her.

She found Jack by her side as she walked outside. 'Can I ask a favour?' he said.

Thea nodded absently, her mind still on the possibility of seeing Fitz before he left.

'Will you walk with me to Sick Quarters?'

All thoughts of Fitz fled her mind and she stared at Jack with growing hope. 'Of course. Why?'

'Ever since Mannheim, I've thought I was a coward and deserved to be humiliated if that's how Rhodes wanted to treat me.'

'You're not—'

'I know that now. I tackled Billy today, even though he had a knife. I didn't think twice. It made me realise that maybe what you and Fitz have been telling me is true. Anyway, I think I want to tell the MO about my… my nightmares and flashbacks. I don't know what he can do, but I can't carry on pretending I can cope, even if I do get called a coward.'

'No one could ever call you that. You've flown over twenty missions in that turret. I couldn't stick it for five minutes.'

'Thank you. There will be people who think I'm a coward for what I'm about to do, but I can face it. Because it would be irresponsible to fly when I can't control my fears any more.'

Thea felt tears prick her eyes, knowing how difficult it must have been for Jack to come to this decision. 'It's the right thing to do. And I've never said this, but I'm proud to be your friend.'

–

Thea sat with Jack for an hour before the MO had a spare moment to see him. 'I'll be here waiting until you finish,' she told him.

It was a long wait. Thea's imagination ran away with her as she tried to guess what on earth could be taking so long. Finally the MO came to find her. 'I've decided to admit him for now,' he told her. 'I wish other crewmen had had friends as good as you and Fitz. Now he's finally told me the trouble, we can get help for him. It will be a long process, but I'm sure he'll be fine in the end – there are some excellent doctors who treat this kind of illness now, and I'm going to pull some strings to make sure he gets seen by the best.'

Waves of relief rolled over Thea. 'So he won't be required to finish his tour?'

The MO shook his head. 'Nothing's definite yet, but I'm as sure as I can be. He asked if you would sit with him once he's settled.'

Thea squashed thoughts of finding Fitz. 'Of course.'

She had to wait another half an hour before a nurse came to fetch her. She found Jack in bed on a ward, looking very self-conscious and a bit nervous. His eyes were red-rimmed, as though he had been crying until very recently. Thea remembered what Fitz had told her about his fear of hospitals, and knew she had done the right thing by staying with him, no matter that her heart called out for Fitz.

'I feel a bit of a fraud, lying in bed when I'm not ill,' Jack said. He pulled at his pyjama top irritably.

'I suppose if you're having nightmares, they want you here where they can keep an eye on you.' And she guessed the MO was probably fearful that Jack might try to harm himself if left alone in his hut while the rest of his room-mates were on ops. Thea floundered for a subject that was nothing to do with hospitals or bombing missions, and remembered she was working on a crossword. She pulled out her notebook and together they passed the time, trying to work out words to fit the grid Thea had drawn up. Finally the nurse chased her out, saying it was time Jack got some rest.

The first thing Thea heard when she stepped outside was the roar of Merlin engines. The Lancasters were leaving, and she hadn't had a chance to say goodbye to Fitz.

–

Fitz squinted through the bomb sight, feeling the vibration of *C-Charlie*'s engines through his stomach. There were the marker flares, dead ahead. 'Steady... steady,' he called. His fingers hovered over the bomb release, itching to send the payload on its way. Orange puffs of exploding flak lit the sky, buffeting the aircraft, and Fitz knew the whole crew must be silently willing him to hurry up and drop the bombs.

Quivering with tension, he watched cross-hairs on his bomb sight approach the target with agonising slowness. Beads of perspiration dripped from his brows and onto the window beneath his face. Then, at last, the target was in his sights and he triggered the release. 'Bombs gone!' Fitz called.

As usual, the thirty-second wait for the photo flash was unbearable, and he wished they could turn and flee the scene, but without a photograph they couldn't claim a completed mission, and Greg, Fitz, Edwin and their rear gunner would be forced to fly yet another one before they finished their tour. Each second was a drawn-out study in agony. He had never known time to go so slowly. And while Greg held his steady course over the target, they were vulnerable to attack from anti-aircraft fire or night fighters.

Come on, come on. Where's the flash? Just when Fitz became convinced that something had gone wrong with the flash bomb and the camera would take a shot of nothing but blackness, it came. 'Get us out of here, Gramps!' he called, but Greg had needed no prompting, because *C-Charlie* went into a dive and banked before he'd completed his sentence.

Vaguely, Fitz was aware of the navigator calling out a bearing for the course home, but he didn't pay attention, overwhelmed that he and Greg had actually completed thirty bombing runs.

They weren't home safe yet, though, and Fitz gave himself a stern talking-to. It was a long way back from Frankfurt, and anything could happen before they reached Lincolnshire.

The thought had hardly crossed his mind before the bomb aimer's compartment was flooded with bright white light. His first thought was that another flash bomb had gone off, but then when the light didn't disperse it dawned on him with sickening horror what had happened. 'We've been coned!' he cried, scrambling up the steps to take his position at the front gun. From his new view he could see the two searchlight beams that had intersected on *C-Charlie*'s nose, lighting them up for the anti-aircraft gunners to aim at.

A second later he had to brace himself against the nose turret as the Lancaster seemed to tumble out of the sky. 'Hold on, everyone,' Greg called. 'I need to throw off the searchlights. Keep your eyes peeled for fighters.'

The lack of fear in Greg's voice – you would swear he was enjoying himself – gave Fitz faith that they could still escape. Greg had got them out of similar positions before, and there was no reason to suppose he wouldn't now. He swung his machine gun through a series of arcs, gazing out at the ever-changing patch of sky (and occasionally ground) that he could see from the nose turret, and looked for any sign of movement that might herald the arrival of an enemy fighter. His stomach rebelled as *C-Charlie* pitched and rolled, and he was relieved that he hadn't taken a drink from his soup flask yet this flight.

A loud bang made his ears ring, closely followed by several more; the anti-aircraft gunners had turned their guns on them. The turbulence from the explosions rocked the Lancaster, and Fitz's heart was in his mouth; he expected a mass of red-hot metal to strike the aircraft at any moment.

'Hang on. Not long now and we'll be out of range.' Fitz couldn't be sure if Greg was reassuring the crew or himself.

Then he caught a glint in the corner of his eye. He focused on the spot and saw what he had dreaded: a fighter flying directly for them. Swinging his gun towards the fighter, he cried, 'Night fighter at two o'clock!' He fired, and simultaneously a line of glowing tracer shot towards them. All the while, Greg was throwing *C-Charlie* around the sky in an attempt to evade the attack, but, as the air around them was now filled with orange bursts of flak, it would be a miracle if they escaped undamaged.

One of Greg's manoeuvres gave Fitz a perfect shot at the whole length of the fighter's fuselage. He wasn't going to pass up the opportunity, and fired a burst at the enemy. Although he couldn't see where he had hit, the fighter abruptly sideslipped and was caught by a searchlight, allowing Fitz to see it pitch into a steeper dive and then a spin. Flames licked the engine cowling. 'I got it!' he cried.

The flight engineer slapped his shoulder. 'Nice shot!'

Cheers came through the intercom as the other crewmen congratulated him.

'Stay alert!' Greg called. 'We're not out of the woods yet.'

A split second later, there was a crash, and *C-Charlie* gave a horrible lurch. At the same time a rush of freezing air whipped into the usually warm nose and sliced through his Sidcot suit.

'Flight engineer, get up here. A load of flak just came through the cockpit,' Greg called.

Fitz didn't dare look round to see the damage, because he needed to keep a lookout for more enemy fighters. However, judging from the gale blowing around him, the flak must have made a sizeable hole. Even while he scanned the sky, he listened in to what Allan Doughty and Greg were saying. From what he could gather, shrapnel had blown a hole in the windscreen and then exited again through the cockpit roof. Allan gave a running commentary as he inspected the areas around the holes for any damage, listing each one in turn, then reporting each undamaged. Gradually Fitz's muscles unclenched as the list ran from vital to less necessary, and all were reported undamaged. 'Looks like we got away with it,' Allan concluded.

'Not quite.' Greg's voice sounded strained, and immediately put Fitz on the alert again. 'Allan, take over the front gun. I need Fitz to take over from me for a while.'

The icy chill that seeped through Fitz's veins had nothing to do with the icy wind. He released the gun and scrambled up to Greg's position. 'What is it, Skip?'

Greg pointed to his sleeve, and immediately Fitz knew they were in trouble. A crimson stain was rapidly spreading across Greg's torn sleeve. 'Bloody hell!' Fitz exclaimed, abandoning any pretence at radio protocol. 'Wireless operator, we need the first-aid kit. Up here. The skipper's been hit.'

There was a chorus of dismay and 'How bad?'

'It's just a scratch,' Greg replied, although he was pale and a sheen of perspiration coated his face. 'Fitz is going to take over while I get patched up.'

Greg released his harness. 'You can do this, Fitz. We might be out of range of the flak, but there are still fighters out there. I've switched to George for now, but we need a human being at the controls, not George.' By 'George' he meant the automatic pilot, not the wireless operator.

Fitz knew there was no other option; Greg had clearly been hanging on while he steered them out of immediate danger, but now he looked so pale, Fitz feared he would faint while still at the controls. Between them, George and Allan heaved Greg out of his seat, and helped him back to where there was a bed where he could lie while Allan gave him first aid. Fitz, heart in mouth, slid into Greg's seat, made sure he was attached to the oxygen and intercom, then finally switched back from autopilot to manual control. Although he had taken over from Greg on other flights, this was the first time he wouldn't be able to hand control back over should an emergency arise. He'd never felt the weight of responsibility as acutely as he did now.

At first he flew with his gaze pinned to the artificial horizon, convinced the heavy Lancaster would pitch into a dive the moment he let his attention stray. Every muscle in his body was rigid, partly from the icy cold, now that he was sitting right beside the hole that was letting in the air, but mostly from the sheer terror that he was in sole control of this huge aircraft. Finally he managed to draw in enough air through his tight throat to speak. 'Course check please, navigator.'

Edwin replied almost immediately with, 'You're veering too far north. Correct to bearing three-one-five.'

Fitz tried to remember his flight instructor's instructions as he eased the controls to correct his course. Good grief, the controls weighed a ton. How did Greg manage to get out of bed the day after a long flight? A check of the compass revealed he was now flying on the right course, and he released a shaky breath. 'How's the skipper doing?' he asked.

'I think he'll be okay. He's lost a lot of blood, but I've got the bleeding under control now.'

'Is he up to flying?'

'Only if you don't mind him passing out at the controls.'

Great. If they came under attack again, Fitz had zero confidence in his ability to evade enemy aircraft. He had even less confidence in his ability to land. He had only ever flown a single-engined twin-seater, and landing that was as different from landing a Lancaster as rowing a boat was from sailing a five-masted clipper.

He tried to put his fears out of his mind for now. He would concentrate on getting *C-Charlie* to England and worry about landing later. If the worst came to the worst, he could order the crew to bale out before attempting to land. Hopefully Greg would be alert enough to pull his ripcord. One way or another, he would get Greg home for his wedding, even if he couldn't be there himself.

'That's the Lincolnshire coast ahead,' Edwin announced what felt like ten weeks later. Fitz's arms ached from keeping the Lancaster level and on course, and his palms itched from the vibrations felt through the control column.

'How's the skipper now?' he asked. 'Edwin can guide me to Fenthorpe, but there's no way I'm landing this thing.'

To his joy, he heard Greg's voice over the intercom. 'Get us to Fenthorpe and I'll do the rest.'

A short while later, Greg clambered to the front of the plane, assisted by Allan. 'How far out are we?'

'Ten minutes,' Edwin replied.

'Right, I'd better take over.' He still looked white and shaky, but Fitz knew they had a better chance of getting home in one piece with him at the controls.

Fitz relinquished his seat with a sigh of relief, but hovered nearby in case Greg needed help. 'Wireless operator – better request an ambulance,' he called. 'Pearl will have my guts for garters if I don't get her fiancé back in a fit state for the wedding.'

'Good job it was his arm and not his groin,' quipped the mid-upper gunner, and this led to a selection of increasingly ribald comments.

'Enough!' Greg roared, his ears looking suspiciously red. 'I need to concentrate.'

Fitz held his breath as Greg contacted RAF Fenthorpe's Flying Control. 'Causeway, this is Gabbro Lancaster *C-Charlie*. Do you read me?'

When the reply came through, everyone cheered. Fitz felt the coil of tension in his gut slowly unwind. They were really going to do it. He was really going to complete his tour. If anyone had said to him six months ago that he would be one of the select few who made it all the way through thirty missions, he wouldn't have believed them, having seen far too many good aircrews lost. Even so, he couldn't relax until he was sure they were safely on the ground, so, as Greg made his approach, he found himself gripping the back of his chair.

Greg glanced up. 'You'd better strap in. I'll be fine.'

Knowing there was nothing he could do to help Greg now, he took his seat and buckled his harness. If he was going to be killed it would be now. It was a sobering thought, yet, instead of focusing on Greg's communications with Flying Control, his mind wandered to Thea. Would she think any more highly of him now he had piloted *C-Charlie* all the way back from Germany? The trouble was, he still didn't understand why she had finished with him.

He knew one thing for sure, though. He blamed himself for letting her go too easily. If she genuinely didn't care for him... well, he would just have to learn to live with it. But something told him it had pained Thea as much as it had him when she had ended their relationship. If that was the case, he would find out what had gone wrong and see if there was anything he could do or say that would change her mind. When he'd heard her account of her past association with Billy, he'd wondered if she'd broken up with him because she was afraid he'd find out. He'd wanted to speak to her afterwards, but he'd been late enough for the briefing as it was. Anyway, he'd had to leave the room before he'd been overcome by his temptation to break Billy's nose. Not only had he dragged Thea into trouble in Shrewsbury, but he'd probably wrecked the W/T WAAF's career, yet he hadn't shown a shred of remorse.

The bump of the wheels striking the runway brought him back to himself. They bounced once, then the Lancaster settled on all three wheels and Fitz was pressed against his seat as they slowed. Then finally they were taxiing in a controlled manner towards their dispersal point. Fitz felt light-headed with relief, as if he had lost as much blood as Greg. As soon as they came to a stop, he released his harness and made his way to Greg, grinning so widely he was surprised his face didn't split. He remembered just in time not to slap his skipper on the arm.

'We did it!'

'We certainly did.' Greg addressed the rest of the crew. 'I'm handing *C-Charlie* over to you. Take good care of her and she'll see you right.'

Fitz was burning to get out of the Lancaster and see if Thea was waiting to meet them. However, he waited for Greg, who looked unsteady on his feet. Curbing his impatience, he helped his friend negotiate the bulkheads and then assisted him down the ladder. There was an ambulance waiting, but Greg refused to get in. 'I'm going in the bus with the rest of the crew. Pearl's waiting for me. You can pick me up at the operations block if you insist on carting me to Sick Quarters.'

The ambulance drivers reluctantly agreed. Before Fitz got on the bus, he looked around for Thea, but there was another fitter waiting to meet them. Allan told Greg he would deal with the ground crew and told the driver he would get another bus back to the operations block.

And so soon Fitz was climbing out of the bus. Immediately Greg was nearly bowled over by Pearl, who was sobbing. 'I was so scared. You made it.'

Greg flinched. 'You didn't think I was going to miss our wedding, did you?'

Fitz looked around for Thea. Surely she had come to support her sister, even if she hadn't wanted to see him. He thought he caught a glimpse of auburn hair, but when he turned to look he couldn't see her. With a heavy heart, he left Greg to his celebrations, secure in the knowledge that Pearl would insist on him going in the ambulance that had followed the bus. Then he trudged off to the debriefing.

Chapter Twenty-Seven

Thea rolled out of bed the next morning, bleary-eyed and feeling strangely tearful. Fitz and Greg were safe. Jack had agreed to ask for the treatment he needed. Billy was no longer a threat. She should be happy.

Who was she kidding? She couldn't be happy when Fitz was leaving. For he had finished his tour; he would be on leave now and then he would be posted elsewhere, probably as an instructor. His time at Fenthorpe was over.

She briefly thought of going to find him, but then she remembered his cold gaze when he had heard her tale. He didn't want to see her. She made the most of being on sick leave, taking her time over tidying around her bed and writing a letter to Deedee. When hunger got the better of her, she went to the NAAFI, half dreading to see him and half longing for it.

The first person she saw was Pearl, her eyes suspiciously red. 'What's happened?' she asked. A horrible thought struck that maybe Greg had been more badly injured than they'd first thought.

'Greg's just left.' Pearl pulled out a handkerchief and dabbed her eyes. 'I know I'm being silly. I've been wishing for this day ever since we first met, and I was so busy wanting his tour to be over, I completely forgot it meant he would be leaving Fenthorpe.'

'Where's he gone? Has Fitz left too?'

'Yes, Fitz went with him. They haven't gone far. Greg said they were going to get rooms in Lincoln while they wait for their next posting, and they've no idea how long they'll have to wait. The worst thing is, we've no idea where Greg will be posted next. It could be miles away.'

Pearl wiped her eyes again and then glanced at her watch. 'I must dash – I'm supposed to be at the Lincoln office this afternoon.'

Thea didn't feel like eating after that. So Fitz had already gone, without saying goodbye. She wouldn't see him until the wedding. Still exhausted from the events of the day before, she cycled back to her hut to get half an hour's sleep before returning to duty. Checking in at the guardroom on her way into the Waafery, she collected the post for her hut and discovered an official-looking letter for her. Once back at the hut, she saw her hut corporal was in, so she handed the other letters to her and then lay on her bed and slit open the envelope, skimming the letter inside. Then she sat bolt upright and read it through again.

> Dear Miss Cooper,
>
> Thank you for your enquiry. Although it is short notice, we do have one dress that would fit your sister and is available on the dates you specified. If you would like it, please complete the enclosed form and return it with a postal order for the sum of £2/12/6.

The remainder of the letter contained instructions on the care of the dress and how to return it. All weariness forgotten, she shoved the letter in her pocket, pulled on her shoes and jacket and raced for the door. She had a wedding dress to order! It was a good thing the other WAAFs were speaking to her again, because she would have to borrow from several friends if she was to gather enough money to cover the postal order.

'Wait!' the corporal called her back. 'There's another letter here for you. Looks like someone handed it in to the guard-room, because it didn't go through the post.'

Thea took it, barely registering the corporal's words. She crammed the envelope in her pocket and went to get her bike.

If she was going to collect enough money in time to catch the post, she had to act now.

It was only much later that evening, when she was sitting in the rec with Jenny, that she remembered the hand-delivered letter. Pulling it out, she swallowed when she saw the hand-writing on the envelope. She ripped it open and read.

> *Dear Thea,*
>
> *I didn't want to leave without speaking to you but you weren't around when I went to look for you. Thank you for how you helped Jack yesterday. It's a huge weight off my mind knowing I'm leaving him in good hands. I'm going to stay in Lincoln with Greg while we wait for our next posting. Wherever I am sent, I've arranged for leave for the wedding so I will see you there.*
>
> *Yours sincerely,*
> *Fitz*

Thea turned the page over to see if anything more was written on the back. Nothing. With all she wanted to say to him, it was clear he wasn't at all saddened by leaving her behind. Why bother writing at all if it was going to be as dull and lacking in feeling as that?

'What's the matter?'

Thea looked up from the letter to find Jenny gazing at her. 'Nothing,' she said, with a light laugh to show how unaffected she was. 'Just a little farewell note from Fitz that says nothing at all. I don't know why he bothered.'

'If it's any help, I saw Fitz in the NAAFI this morning. I think he was hoping to see you.'

'I doubt that. Not if the total lack of feeling in this letter is anything to go by.'

'Well, Greg came and chivvied him along, saying they couldn't waste time if they were to find a good place to stay. So Fitz got out some paper and dashed off a letter. I didn't know it was to you, of course, but it would explain why it was so terse.'

'Either that or he couldn't be bothered to spend any more time on it.' Thea wasn't in any mood to let him off lightly.

Every day passed, as dull as the one before. Pearl grew ever more excited about her wedding day, but Thea couldn't work up any enthusiasm. Her hand healed, her stitches were removed and she returned to duty, glad to get back to the Instrument Section, doing her best to ignore how wrong it felt to see a new bomb aimer on *C-Charlie*'s crew.

The only moment of brightness came three days before the wedding, when Thea was told a parcel had arrived for her. Parcels weren't delivered to the Waafery; instead, a parcel slip was sent with the other mail. The recipient then needed to bring the slip to the camp post office to collect the delivery. Thea went along, thinking it was from Deedee – some books, perhaps or maybe some toiletries. She presented herself at the post office, daydreaming of scented soap, and only when she was handed a box with *Gainsborough Studios* written on the outside did she remember the dress.

She practically sprinted all the way to the Waafery, and burst into Hut Three, feeling a thrill that had been absent for many days. 'Pearl, I've got you a dress!'

Pearl, who had been brushing down her best blues, replied, 'Don't tease me, Thea. I've just about reconciled myself to marrying in my uniform. Don't get my hopes up.'

'I'm not. Open this.' She thrust the parcel into Pearl's arms.

'If this is a joke…' But Pearl started to pick at the knots with trembling fingers.

Jenny, who appeared to have picked up on Thea's excitement, asked, 'What's it like?'

'No idea.' And she explained how she had written to Gainsborough Studios and been told there was only one gown available. 'But just imagine – it could have been worn by a film star!'

Pearl had become more animated as she heard Thea's tale, and she yanked the knots with increased enthusiasm. It seemed an age before she was able to prise off the lid and lift the top layer of tissue paper. Beneath was a mass of lace, even finer than the lace of the Edwardian dress. With trembling hands, Pearl lifted out the dress and held it up. All three girls gasped.

'It's beautiful,' Pearl said, her voice husky.

It was, indeed, beautiful. It was very different from the dress Blanche had ruined, although it, too, consisted of a silk under-dress with lace over the top. However, the Gainsborough dress was not old fashioned; it screamed film star glamour.

'Try it on,' Thea urged. 'I can't get a good idea of the shape until I see it on you.'

Pearl was unbuttoning her shirt before Thea had finished speaking. Once she'd stripped to her underwear, Jenny and Thea eased the dress over Pearl's head and tugged it into place. 'Breathe in,' Thea warned as she started to fasten the various hooks and eyes. 'This looks like a close fit.'

Then she and Jenny stood back to admire the effect.

'How do I look?' Pearl peered into the tiny square mirror on her shelf, although there was no way she'd be able to view more than a few inches of the dress at a time.

'Hold still. You're going to have to take our word for it, but you look stunning. It's the perfect shape for you.'

The neck plunged into a deep V front and back, and flutter sleeves fell to midway down Pearl's upper arms. Below the bust, the dress was divided into several vertical panels that clung from ribcage to hip, then flared so the skirt swirled around her legs.

Tears welled in Thea's eyes. 'You look like a film star. Greg's going to be bowled over when he sees you.'

'I don't know how to thank you,' Pearl said. 'Why didn't you tell me?'

'At first I didn't know if they would be able to send anything at such short notice, and when they wrote back to say they had a dress... well, I was rather distracted and I forgot.'

Pearl's eyes clouded. 'It's Fitz, isn't it? You haven't been the same since he left.'

'I suppose.' Thea couldn't see any point in denying it.

'How will you feel to see him at the wedding?'

Thea desperately wanted to tell her sister the truth and for once let Pearl be the mother-figure she had rebelled against for so long. But maybe Thea had finally grown up, because she realised she couldn't lay her problems on Pearl. Not when she was so close to her wedding. Afterwards she would tell her everything, but for now she had to pretend all was well. She forced a smile. 'I'll be fine. You know me – I never stay with one fellow for long.' Then, before Pearl could get suspicious, she said, 'Now, try on the shoes so we can see how they look with the dress. Aren't you glad you forgot to return them?'

Chapter Twenty-Eight

The next day brought a fresh distraction for Thea: Deedee arrived. Thea had been unable to get time off to meet her at the station, so Pearl had gone to accompany her to Fenthorpe, where she had a room at the White Horse. As Pearl had to work late to complete the latest edition of the *Bombshell* before her leave started, Thea had arranged to spend the evening with Deedee. She finished her shift at four and cycled straight to the village, not even bothering to change out of her battledress and into her smarter skirt.

Deedee was taking a walk down the main street when Thea arrived. There was no mistaking her – Deedee's dyed red hair shone in the afternoon sunlight, and her emerald-green dress competed with the new leaves unfurling on the trees.

'Deedee!' Thea cried, and hugged her. She was transported back to the days when Deedee would pick her up after she'd taken a tumble and, after Pearl scolded her for being careless, would bathe and bandage her scraped knees and give her a piece of barley sugar. If only today's problems could be solved so easily.

'How lovely to see you, Thea. Isn't this exciting? When I asked Pearl to tell me about Greg, she went a very interesting shade of pink. I think everyone should have someone in their life who makes them blush like that.'

'Pearl doesn't usually blush. What did you ask her?'

'I wanted to know if Greg made her go all tingly in her knickers.'

Thea choked.

'Oh, don't look at me like that, dear. You know how Pearl lets her head rule her heart. I wanted to make sure she felt attraction as well as love and friendship.'

Thea had to admit Deedee's methods were sound, if unconventional. 'I don't think you've got anything to worry about. I've had to watch her go all misty-eyed whenever Greg's around. Anyway, I hope you won't be interrogating me on any feelings in my knicker region if I ever meet someone?'

'Oh, no. I'd have no worries on that score. You're the other way round. I'd be asking if you could imagine an evening spent just talking.'

Thea burst into tears. Not the pretty, delicate kind that rolled one by one down the porcelain cheeks of a heroine in a film, but great, heaving sobs wrenched from deep in her core. She couldn't stop, even knowing that she was attracting curious stares from passers-by. Images flooded her mind of the walks she had taken with Fitz, arm in arm and talking of all the things that mattered to them. Of course the kisses had been wonderful too, and had set off a whole range of reactions, and not just in her knickers, but right now she would give anything to have a whole evening alone in his company, even if it was spent just talking. Vaguely aware that Deedee had wrapped an arm round her, she allowed herself to be guided to a nearby bench. Gradually the storm subsided, and she accepted a handkerchief from Deedee and wiped her face.

'I must look a sight,' she said, sniffing.

'Well, yes, but you seemed to need it. I take it this is over a man – that bomb aimer you wrote about – Fitz? Pearl did tell me you'd recently broken up with him, and she couldn't understand why because you were perfect together.'

'Yes, she's made her disapproval quite plain.'

Deedee gave Thea a sharp look but forbore to comment, simply saying, 'I'm sure you had your reasons.'

'I did. It was the right thing to do.'

'If you don't mind me saying, it doesn't seem to have made you very happy.'

'Happiness isn't everything.'

'Granted. I suppose in wartime we all have to make our sacrifices – but only if they're necessary. Did ending things make Fitz happy?'

This line of questioning was making Thea uncomfortable. 'Honestly, Deedee, you should work in Intelligence. They need people like you.'

'This isn't about me. Are you going to answer my question or are you too afraid to think about it?'

'Fine.' Thea gazed down at the handkerchief she was twisting in her lap. 'He wasn't happy at first, but he didn't have any problem leaving Fenthorpe without saying goodbye.'

'It didn't occur to you that maybe he couldn't face you because you'd hurt him so badly?'

'I... that's not...' Words failed her, and she could only shake her head.

Deedee patted her hand. 'Fitz is Greg's best man, is that right?' When Thea nodded, she continued, 'Good. He'll be at the wedding. If you want my advice, you won't let him leave again without telling him how you truly feel. Not about how you think you should feel, and don't make any assumptions about his feelings, either. Just be honest with him and ask him to be honest in return. I made assumptions about a young man's feelings once and thought I was doing the right thing by him. It was only when it was far too late that I realised I'd never given him the chance to say how he felt.'

Thea wiped away fresh tears. 'I don't remember you telling me about a young man. Was this before or after you met my grandfather?'

Deedee simply shook her head. 'It's a long story and buried in the past. Maybe I'll tell you another time, but right now I'm far more concerned about the present. Will you promise to speak to Fitz at the wedding?'

Thea shrugged, unable to understand the source of her odd reluctance. 'I don't know. What's the point? He's leaving, and he'll probably think it too much effort to stay in touch.'

'It isn't like you to be so defeatist. Has something else happened?' Deedee narrowed her eyes. 'Pearl also said something about a young man from home trying to cause trouble, although she couldn't tell me much. Is it anything to do with him?'

'Maybe. Yes. But not in the way you think.' The reason Pearl didn't know much was because Thea had been deliberately vague when telling her and Jenny what had happened with Billy. Although she'd explained that she'd known him before she'd joined the WAAF, she hadn't admitted that he'd tried to use her as a lookout and she'd glossed over the reasons why he'd wanted her to get information out of Fenthorpe, hating for them to know that he'd been trying to get revenge for her turning him in to the police. She didn't feel the same reticence now, however. She was suddenly overwhelmed with a desire to get the whole story off her chest, tired of trying to handle the whole mess by herself. She told Deedee everything, starting with her infatuation with Billy before she had joined the WAAF and continuing all the way to his arrest three weeks ago.

'The thing is,' she said, feeling hollow once she had poured out the whole tale, 'I just don't seem to have good judgement when it comes to men. I'm better off without them.'

'Poppycock.'

'What?' Thea blinked at her grandmother.

'I don't believe that for one moment and neither do you.'

'Haven't you heard a thing I just told you? I was in love with a criminal.'

'No you weren't.'

'How——?'

Deedee tapped the bench's armrest with a stern finger. 'Now you listen to me, Thea, and pay attention because your happiness depends on this. Deep down you knew exactly what this Billy was like, and you didn't feel the slightest bit of affection for him.'

'How can you know that?'

'Because I know you, Thea, and I saw you play out the same scene over and over when you were younger. The choices you made regarding friends and boyfriends had very little to do with love and everything to do with Pearl.'

'Pearl?' Had Deedee gone mad? 'What's she got to do with it?'

'Everything. Pearl smothered you, and you, understandably, rebelled. No, don't interrupt. You need to listen. Everyone you ever chose to mix with was invariably someone you knew Pearl would disapprove of. I don't think it was ever a conscious decision, but the pattern was clear. I spoke to Pearl several times, telling her she would lose you if she didn't stop trying to govern your life, but she can be every bit as stubborn as you. I did think she'd improved since joining the WAAF, though.'

'She has.'

'I'm glad to hear it. But it's clear you still hate taking her advice. Why is that?'

'I don't.' Thea squirmed a little. 'We get on well now. Anyway, I thought we were talking about Fitz.'

'We are. But if you're going to mend matters, you need to understand why you pushed him away.'

'I told you. I can't trust my own judgement when it comes to men.'

'And I told you that was rubbish.'

'I think the term you actually used was poppycock.'

Deedee's lips twitched. 'We're going round in circles, and I don't want to argue with you. This should be a happy occasion. But promise me you'll think about what I said.'

Thea didn't answer for a while, her mind buzzing with Deedee's bizarre theory. A light breeze whisked down the street, swirling the litter of old, dried leaves on the pavement and lifting a lock of Deedee's hair from her face. Deedee wasn't distracted, though, and kept her gaze pinned to Thea's face.

Finally Thea relented. 'Fine, I'll think about it.' Although she was sure Deedee was wrong.

'Good. That's all I ask. Now come up to my room and help me unpack. I've brought something for Pearl.'

–

Deedee packed Thea off to Fenthorpe at eight, claiming tiredness from her journey. Thea suspected it was more to do with Deedee wanting her to speak to Pearl, but she did as she was told. *For a change*, she wryly reflected as she mounted her bike. She couldn't imagine how Deedee had come up with her fanciful theory, but Thea would be the first to admit she resented being ordered around.

Once she'd signed in at the guardroom, she retrieved the package Deedee had asked her to deliver to Pearl and went to see if her sister was back. She found Pearl in Hut Three, pacing up and down. She was muttering to Jenny, the only other person present, who sat cross-legged on her bed. 'Something old, something new, something borrowed, something blue. The something new is my wedding ring. Something borrowed – the dress, shoes and veil. And the something blue is you and Thea in your best blues. But what about something old?'

'Easy,' said Thea, shutting the door behind her. 'That's you. You've just turned thirty, after all.'

Pearl, without pausing in her stride, picked up a pillow from her neatly stacked bed and flung it at Thea. 'I'm serious. The wedding's tomorrow! This is no time for jokes.'

'Who said I was joking?'

Pearl quelled her with a look. 'Why didn't I think about this before?'

'It's fine. Deedee gave me these just now.' Thea handed her the faded flat velvet box she had carried back from the village. 'They can also be your something borrowed, because she wants them back.'

Pearl opened the lid and gasped. 'These are beautiful.' She lifted out a string of seed pearls with a lustrous teardrop-shaped pearl pendant in the centre. Next came a pair of drop earrings, with matching teardrop pearls dangling from a circle of seed pearls. 'I never knew she had these.'

'I know. I nearly passed out when I saw them. They must be worth a fortune. Deedee clearly has secrets in her past.' Thea had tried asking Deedee again about the mysterious man she had let slip through her fingers, but Deedee had neatly deflected her questions.

Jenny came and cooed over them, then said, 'Actually, now might be a good time for us to give you your wedding presents from us.' She raised her eyebrows at Thea.

'Good idea! We'll be too busy tomorrow. Hang on while I fetch mine.' Thea raced off to her hut and returned with the frame she had wrapped in tissue paper. She looked at it mournfully. 'It's not much. But Jenny and I agreed we'd get you something better when you and Greg set up home. Why – what have I said?'

For Pearl's face had crumpled. She pulled out her handkerchief and dabbed her eyes. 'Greg found out where he's being posted.'

What about Fitz? Thea wanted to ask. Instead she said, 'Where?'

'Near Loughborough. 28 OTU.'

'But that's not far. It must be one of the closest OTUs.'

'I know, I know. Jenny's spent the last half-hour saying exactly the same thing. I suppose I've been so focused on the wedding and praying that Greg would make it that far, I completely forgot that we'd probably have to live apart for ages after the honeymoon.'

'It won't be so bad,' Thea tried to console her. 'You're mostly working office hours now, and Greg's not flying ops any more, so you'll be able to arrange plenty of weekends together. Anyway, it's a good thing you won't be living together. It'll take Greg longer to discover all your bad habits.'

Pearl laughed, as intended, and, after a final dab at her eyes, tucked away her hanky. 'Did you mention presents before?'

'We certainly did.'

Thea and Jenny handed them over, and Pearl professed herself delighted with the vase and photo frame. 'They're perfect and I'll be able to take them with me wherever I go.'

'I still wish I could have afforded something better.'

'Nonsense. You and Jenny are going to be with me on the happiest day of my life. I couldn't ask for better.' Then Pearl seemed to hesitate. 'Actually' – she shook her head – 'no. Forget it.'

'What?' Thea looked at her sister, who had given up so much to take care of her, no matter that Thea had resented much of that care. It suddenly seemed of vital importance to give Pearl the happiest possible wedding. 'Ask whatever you want.'

'That's just it. You've always hated me interfering, yet what I want most of all is for you to be as happy as me tomorrow. Won't you tell me what went wrong with Fitz? He was so right for you.'

Perhaps Thea was more aware of it after hearing Deedee's opinion, but her heart gave a distinct kick of resentment at Pearl's question. Why was that? Pearl hadn't told Thea what to do, or even given her advice. She had simply stated her opinion, which she had the total right to hold. Could it be there was truth in Deedee's theory after all?

She drew a shaky breath. 'It's fine. I'll tell you. I think I want to now.'

Jenny unfolded her legs and swung them to the floor. 'I can leave if you'd rather.'

'Stay.' Thea waved her back to her bed. 'You're as good as family and, if Pearl's going to hear the truth about me, I want you to know too.'

Jenny, looking gratified, scooted back on the bed and hugged her knees to her chest, regarding Thea with rapt attention.

Now she had an audience, agog to hear her tale, there was no way to go back on her word, even had she wanted to. Yet perhaps telling Deedee had helped, for Thea found she really did want to explain everything, including her association with Billy. She watched Pearl's face carefully as she related everything that had happened four years ago as well as the full story of Billy's planned revenge. Although Pearl looked troubled when Thea haltingly confessed how she had foolishly been roped into keeping watch for Billy, her face cleared when she revealed she had reported him to the police. A few times she looked as though she wanted to say something, but each time she closed her mouth again with a self-deprecating smile.

'I can't believe you went through all this without telling me,' Pearl said when Thea finally finished. 'I understand why you wouldn't want to, though. I do find it hard to keep my opinions to myself.'

'But I'm starting to see I was being unreasonable,' Thea said. 'Deedee was uncharacteristically stern with me.'

Pearl gave a reminiscent smile. 'She can be, sometimes. She had words with me when she worked out I'd joined the WAAF in the hope of keeping an eye on you.'

'So you admit it! I knew it was more than coincidence, you turning up in Lincoln like that.'

'Since we're being honest with each other, I suppose I ought to come clean. Deedee was right, I *do* smother you.'

'Did,' Thea corrected. 'I know I complain about you, but you really have improved. And to be honest, I can't have been an easy child to keep in check.'

'You can say that again. All I wanted was to keep you safe. You and Deedee were my only family, and I was terrified of losing you.'

'Keep me safe,' Thea repeated, feeling dazed. That was Fitz's excuse when he had tackled her over Billy that time. And now it dawned on Thea why his words had caused her to lash out.

'I promise to keep my nose out of your business from now on,' Pearl said.

Thea shook herself from her daze. 'Not completely, I hope. Because I've realised that, while I resent your interference, I really could use your advice.'

Pearl's beaming smile was Thea's reward. 'Now that's the best wedding present I could have asked for.'

'Good. Because I've finally got it into my thick skull that I was an idiot to break up with Fitz, and I really need to know how to win him back.'

Chapter Twenty-Nine

Thea burst into Hut Three carrying the box holding the gown and a selection of make-up. Jenny and Pearl were the only ones within, the other WAAFs all being on duty. Pearl was sitting on her bed and had her hair up in rollers. She wore nothing but a pair of silk French knickers and a camisole – the underwear the dressmaker in Lincoln had made from the parachute silk Jenny had managed to procure. Fortunately, although the camisole had been ordered to suit the gown Blanche had ruined, it was shaped with a deep vee back and front, low enough for it not to show beneath the film star gown.

'Today's the day!' Thea cried. 'How's the soon-to-be Mrs Tallis?'

'Thrilled, nervous, excited. I hardly know.' Pearl pressed both hands to her midriff and drew a deep breath. 'Someone told me this would help calm me down, but it's not working.'

Jenny cast her gaze to the ceiling. 'That was me. I read it in a book and I keep telling you, you're doing it wrong. After breathing in, you're supposed to release your breath slowly, not gabble away nineteen to the dozen.'

Thea flung herself onto the bed beside Pearl. 'You're not supposed to be calm. It's your wedding day.'

'You're right.' Pearl leaped up. 'I refuse to be calm and sensible today. I'll leave that to my bridesmaids. What should I do first – hair, make-up or gown?'

'Make-up first so we don't spill any on the lace. We should probably leave the gown to last to be absolutely certain it doesn't get dirty.'

Pearl snatched the make-up bag from Thea's hands. 'Make-up it is.'

A short while later, she peered over the top of her mirror and met Thea's gaze. 'And what about you – are you ready to meet Fitz?'

'I suppose so. I have to be.' Last night, after she'd explained her revelation and asked for help, she, Pearl and Jenny had discussed it from all angles. Pearl and Jenny had added their pleas to Deedee's that she would have a serious conversation with Fitz before the day was out. 'I lay awake all night, rehearsing what to say.' She took the powder compact from Pearl and dabbed some on her own face before saying, 'Anyway, I promise to do my best, and that's all I'm going to say. This is your day, and I'm not going to spoil it with my woes.'

And she was convinced her day would end in woe. She couldn't imagine Fitz wanting her back after the way she had treated him. Tears pricked her eyelids, and she blinked them back, trying hard to forget her gloom and help make Pearl's wedding day perfect.

Time flew, and, although they had thought they had plenty of time to do Pearl's hair and make-up, after a glance at Pearl's bedside clock Jenny gave a cry of dismay. 'We're supposed to meet Mr Haughton outside in ten minutes, and you're not even dressed.'

Thea and Jenny hastily helped Pearl into the gown and fastened all the hooks and eyes, growing more frantic as time ticked by. Fortunately, once that was done the veil was easy to fix, needing only a few hairgrips to secure the headband. When Thea stood back to view the final look, fresh tears pricked her eyelids, this time tears of joy. She felt a rush of gratitude towards Pearl for all she had sacrificed for her sake, and she was happy to see Pearl doing something to make her own life happy for a change. 'You look beautiful. You'll have to take care Greg doesn't rip that dress off you. I've already got one ruined gown on my conscience.'

Pearl blushed crimson. 'Honestly, you and Deedee between you are the limit. Anyway, are we ready? I feel like I'm missing something.'

'This.' Jenny picked up a pretty bunch of wildflowers she had picked early that morning. Thea spotted forget-me-nots, buttercups, white stitchwort and some fronds of greenery. Jenny had tied the stems with ribbon. 'Now you're ready.'

Jenny went out ahead but, when Thea went to follow, Pearl took her arm, halting her. 'I need to say something, and I don't want Jenny to hear.'

'Surely it can wait? We're running late.'

Pearl shook her head. 'This is important. I managed the whole maid of honour situation badly. I should have had more faith in you and asked you. I've regretted it ever since.'

'You were right, though. It would have been difficult with everyone not speaking to me.'

'Even so, I wanted you. I wanted to change my mind later, but Jenny was so pleased to be asked I didn't want to hurt her feelings. But if I could do it all again, I would have asked you. I just wanted you to know.'

Thea gave her a watery smile. 'Now look what you've done. My make-up will be ruined, and we haven't even got to the church.' She squeezed Pearl's arm. 'It means a lot to hear you say that, though. Thank you.'

Mr Haughton had arranged to meet Pearl and her brides-maids at the Waafery gate, and so they hurried out, Jenny and Thea helping Pearl raise her trailing skirts so they didn't drag on the gravelled path. The WAAFs who we off duty came out to wave Pearl off and wish her well. Even Section Officer Blatchford smiled and waved.

'Golly,' Pearl muttered once they had walked past. 'I was convinced she was about to put me on a charge for being out of uniform.'

Mr Haughton was waiting for them as arranged, beside the horse and cart the vicar had organised. He kissed Pearl on the cheek. 'You look beautiful, my dear. Now, shall we go and put your Mr Tallis out of his misery?'

—

For about the hundredth time, Greg twisted around in the front pew and gazed at the door.

Fitz placed a steadying hand on his arm. 'You'll do your neck an injury if you keep doing that. She's not even supposed to arrive for another five minutes.' Although he found it hard to follow his own advice, for a moment later he cast his own glance at the door. Unlike Greg, though, he wasn't anticipating the bride's arrival but Thea's.

Greg grimaced, running a hand under his collar. 'I can honestly say I wasn't this nervous even when I had to let you fly us home.'

'Now you tell me you don't trust my flying?'

'I was hardly going to say it at the time, was I?'

'Thanks for the vote of confidence. I'll remind you of this next time you ask me to take over.' Then it hit Fitz all over again that he wouldn't be flying ops again. For the foreseeable future, he would be training other men to be bomb aimers. And there would be no more looking for Thea's face whenever his aircraft landed, and no more cosy chats in the NAAFI. No more holding her in his arms while they danced a slow waltz, her body moulded to his...

'You're thinking of her again.'

'What?' Fitz started and saw Greg eying him with sympathy. 'Thea. She'll be here. You should speak to her.'

Fitz shrugged. 'I don't know what good it would do. She made it quite clear she wanted nothing more to do with me.'

'Honestly, mate, you need to try. Pearl says Thea's been miserable ever since you split up.'

'She has? Did Pearl say anything else?'

Greg shook his head. 'She's as puzzled as I am. That's why you need to find out what went wrong.'

There was another stir at the church door, and Fitz looked round as sharply as Greg. However, it turned out to be the landlady of the White Horse, accompanied by a lady in her late sixties or early seventies dressed in a creation of flowing orange silk that clashed with impossibly red hair. As she advanced to the front of the church, it dawned on him that this must be Thea's – and Pearl's – grandmother. He nudged Greg. 'I think that's Deedee. Thea hinted that she was eccentric. She looks fun, though.'

Greg didn't have a chance to reply, though, for Deedee only paused to place her handbag on the front pew on the left before she crossed the aisle and approached Fitz and Greg. They both rose. Greg held out a hand, clearly intending to shake hers, but Deedee ignored it, pulling him into a hug instead. 'You must be Greg. Pearl's told me all about you. It's wonderful to meet you at last.'

'Lovely to meet you, too, Mrs, er...'

'Call me Deedee. You're going to be family, after all.'

Greg indicated Fitz. 'This is—'

'Oh, I know all about you. You're Fitz.' Her gaze bored into him, although it was inquisitive rather than threatening. 'I had hoped to welcome you into the family too, but Thea can be too stubborn for her own good.'

Family. Fitz swallowed. 'I would have liked that too.'

Deedee's face softened, and she patted his hand. 'At least you're able to say what you want, unlike Thea. A good sign. Maybe you should try telling that to Thea.'

Before he could reply, the faint *clip-clop* of a horse's hooves drifted in from outside. A second later, Edwin dashed inside. 'They're here.' He slapped Greg's shoulder and took a pew behind him and Fitz.

Fitz wanted to ask Deedee what she meant, but she had already taken her seat. For the first time in weeks, he felt hope. He had feared Deedee would be cross with him for whatever imagined slight had caused Thea to break up with him in the first place. Instead she had been sympathetic and even encouraged him to speak to Thea. Surely she would only do that if she thought Thea would welcome his approach? He went to stand with Greg, grinning to see him fidgeting. Then he faced the doors, waiting for his first sight of Thea in three weeks.

Deedee had wanted to welcome him into her family. As he had explained to Thea, family was of utmost importance to him, whether that meant his mother or the family he had found in his dance company and his crew. To the point that, even when he'd had a chance to speak to her on the return from Berlin, he hadn't. Why? Because he had been worried about Jack and was more bothered about checking on his friend than trying to discover what he had done to drive Thea to her decision. He had put his friend before Thea, and he had cursed himself for his choice ever since. He had come to the wedding thinking it was too late to undo his mistake, yet here was Deedee intimating that Thea might be persuaded to change her mind.

He shot a sidelong glance at Greg, and bit back a smile. The man was practically bouncing on his toes in his eagerness to get his first glimpse of his bride.

Longing swept over him. One day he wanted to be standing in church, waiting for his bride to appear. And the only woman he could imagine ever wanting to marry was Thea. He would take Deedee's advice and find the first opportunity to speak to her. And he would win back her heart, even if that meant making a fool of himself in front of all their friends.

—

It didn't take long to reach St Margaret's Church. Elmwick was a pretty village with houses of pale creamy stone, and, in the morning sunlight, the church's tall spire gleamed gold. Several villagers came out to wave and wish the bride joy. The way through the churchyard was lined with blossoming cherry trees, and once they had left the cart by the gate they walked to the church door on a path of pale pink petals.

They paused by the door to arrange Pearl's veil. Thea smiled at Pearl, expecting to see her look nervous, but now she simply looked radiant. 'Ready?'

'Can't wait.'

Walking side by side, Thea and Jenny entered the church first, and Jenny nodded at the organist. As the notes of 'Jesu, Joy of Man's Desiring' drifted through the building, Thea stepped slowly down the aisle, keeping pace with Jenny. She had no idea how Greg looked; all she could do was gaze at Fitz. If anything, he looked even more handsome than when she had last seen him, and her breath caught in her throat. She wished he would look at her so she could smile at him, show him she still cared, but his gaze seemed to land anywhere but on her. He looked so serious; she longed more than anything for him to meet her eyes and smile a smile meant only for her.

The walk down the aisle seemed to last for ever, but finally they reached the front. While Jenny took Pearl's bouquet, Thea took her seat beside Deedee, who had been brought to the church by Norah Brumby. Therefore she happened to be looking at Deedee rather than the wedding party when Pearl and Mr Haughton stopped in front of the vicar. Deedee's face was frozen in an unreadable expression. Thea couldn't tell if it was joy or dismay. Fearing something was wrong with Pearl, she shot her a look, but all she could see was Mr Haughton helping Pearl lift her veil away from her face.

She whispered to Deedee, 'Is something wrong?'

Deedee simply shook her head and shushed her.

However, when the vicar began, saying the old, familiar words opening the marriage service, Deedee gripped Thea's arm. Tears trickled down her cheeks, but by this time tears were welling in Thea's own eyes to see the joy in her sister's face. Beside her, Jenny was sniffing.

As the vicar spoke, a golden glow seemed to surround the bride and groom; both too engrossed in each other to spare him a glance.

Thea had nearly forgotten her conversation with Fitz when she had told him her full name, but was reminded when the vicar asked, 'Aphrodite Pearl, wilt thou have this man to thy wedded husband, to live together after God's ordinance in the holy estate of matrimony?' For a fleeting instant, Fitz caught her eye and grinned, and in that moment she felt the old connection she'd felt with him from the start. It was over quickly but it gave her hope.

Finally, Greg slid the ring onto Pearl's finger looking as though he'd been handed the keys to Buckingham Palace, and there was an audible sob from Jenny. By the time the vicar pronounced them man and wife, Thea was viewing the proceedings through a blur of tears that made the scene sparkle and shimmer.

When it was time to sign the register, Jenny prodded Thea. 'Go on,' she murmured. 'You should be Pearl's witness.'

'But you're maid of honour.'

Jenny shook her head. 'It wouldn't feel right. Go on.'

So Pearl went into the vestry to join Pearl and Greg. And Fitz. Although neither of them spoke, she was aware of his gaze on her when she stooped to sign her name in the space set aside for the witnesses. Fitz had already signed, and it gave her a little thrill to add her name next to his.

The full consequences of Jenny's gesture only struck her when it was time to leave the vestry and process down the aisle. Because now Jenny took Mr Haughton's arm and nodded for Thea to do the same with Fitz, before nodding again to indicate that they should go before her and Mr Haughton. There was nothing for it but to take Fitz's arm.

Fitz spoke to her for the first time that day. 'You look beautiful, as ever.'

Thea swallowed the lump in her throat. 'So do you. Handsome, I mean. Not beautiful.' Although she thought he *did* look beautiful. There was a look of assurance in his eyes that hadn't been there when he'd been at Fenthorpe. She could only suppose it was the confidence that came with surviving his tour of duty. She wanted to say something to him then – apologise for hurting him – but they were out on the church steps, with blossom falling on the group like confetti, and they were surrounded by the off-duty WAAFs and aircrews who had also attended the ceremony. In the hubbub of congratulations, teasing and laughter, Thea lost her chance.

–

Only a small group returned to the White Horse for the meal. Mr Haughton excused himself, saying he had to return to work, and the personnel from RAF Fenthorpe also drifted off. It was just the bride and groom, Thea, Jenny, Deedee and Fitz, plus the rest of *C-Charlie*'s former crew, who were continuing the celebrations.

Much to everyone's amazement, when they went to find the horse and cart that had brought them here they saw Greg's motorcycle and sidecar parked beside it. Tin cans and colourful ribbons were attacked to the back on string, and a cardboard sign saying *Just Married!* had been fastened to the sidecar.

Edwin gave a delighted laugh at the dumbfounded expressions of the bride and groom. 'You didn't think the lads were going to let you get away without leaving you something to remember them by?'

'Congratulations, Gramps!' chimed in George Hepple. He, Allan Doughty and *C-Charlie*'s mid-upper gunner, Sid Eccles had all attended the wedding. Only Jack, who had been admitted to hospital, was missing.

'Did you hear we completed our tour yesterday?' Sid asked.

This prompted an enthusiastic round of congratulations, and then all of Greg's old aircrew insisted they needed to kiss the bride. In the flurry, Thea herself was kissed several times. This inevitably led to thoughts of Fitz, although when she looked for him she found him standing a little away from the group. She got the impression he'd been gazing at her and had only looked away an instant before she'd seen him. She tried to push through the crowd, but, before she could reach him, Pearl beckoned her. With a regretful look at Fitz, she went to join her sister.

Pearl was unfastening her veil. 'Take care of this, will you? It'd probably cause a terrible accident if we rode off with me still wearing it.'

Thea took the veil, then she and Jenny held Pearl's gown off the ground while Greg helped her into the sidecar. They tucked her skirts securely inside the car. 'For goodness' sake, go slowly, Greg,' Thea ordered. 'I doubt Gainsborough Studios would be as understanding as Miss Honeycroft if this dress got ruined.'

The crowd waved off the bride and groom, laughing and wincing at the clatter, then Thea, Jenny and Fitz climbed into their cart. Thea hesitated between sitting with Fitz and Deedee, and reluctantly decided she needed to speak to Deedee.

'Is everything all right?' she asked as soon as the cart moved off. The steady clopping of the horse's hooves and the rattle of the cart ensured their conversation wouldn't be overheard. 'You looked quite upset for a moment back there.'

Deedee regarded her for a while in silence, then said, 'Promise you won't tell Pearl today? I don't want to spoil her honeymoon.'

Thea's insides knotted; now she was really scared. 'I promise, but tell me. You're not ill, are you?'

'Oh no. I'm so sorry if I worried you. It's nothing like that.'

'Then what is it?'

'The man who gave Pearl away – who is he?'

'Mr Haughton. I'm sure we've told you about him. He's funding the *Bombshell*.'

'Yes, I remember. But you've never mentioned his first name.'

'Thomas.'

Deedee sighed, repeating the name on her exhale. 'Thomas. I thought so.'

'Are you saying you know him?'

'Know him? I—' Then she seemed to change her mind. 'Remember what I said about the man I let go?'

Thea stared at her in shock. 'That was Mr Haughton?' She could scarcely believe it, even when Deedee nodded in confirmation.

'Obviously, when Pearl first wrote to me about a Mr Haughton who had generously offered to fund her newspaper I thought of Tom, but she never gave his first name, and I didn't seriously believe it could be the same person. Tom wasn't in the newspaper business when I knew him.'

'Tom? I can't imagine anyone as old and correct as Mr Haughton ever being called Tom.'

Deedee gave a sad smile. 'He wasn't old when I knew him. Or correct.'

'Do you want to meet him?' Thea remembered a few times when she had seemed to remind Mr Haughton of someone. Now she realised it had been her grandmother. 'I'm sure he'd like to see you.'

'No. The past is in the past. I'll be going home tomorrow, so it's pointless to rake up old hurts.' Deedee's gaze sharpened. 'But new hurts, now those are things you can do something about.' She gave a significant nod towards Fitz, who was speaking to Jenny and not looking in their direction. 'Now he's a sight for sore eyes. I wouldn't let him go if I were you.'

Much to Thea's horror, Deedee's last comment had come when the driver had slowed the horse as they approached a junction, which quieted the various rattles and creaks. Fitz turned his head and their gazes locked. She was sure he must have overheard.

Chapter Thirty

Fitz, being the perfect gentleman that he was, jumped down from the cart himself first and then helped the women, swinging down Jenny and then Deedee.

'I do admire a man who can lift a lady without rupturing anything,' Deedee remarked when he set her down on the pavement outside the White Horse. She addressed Jenny. 'Be a dear and help me inside. I'm feeling quite stiff after being jolted around in that cart.'

Thea narrowed her eyes at Deedee as she skipped up the steps to the pub door, not seeming to have any trouble. Then she and Jenny were gone, leaving her alone with Fitz, for the driver had excused himself and nipped into the pub.

Gentleman that he was, he would probably offer to lift her down, but that would have been far too awkward. Instead she turned to lower herself onto the step, fully expecting Fitz to follow the others into the pub. She hoped so, because the view she was offering could hardly be flattering.

'Can we talk?'

She glared at him over her shoulder, one foot dangling, seeking the step. 'You're asking now?'

'Let me help you down.'

He reached up, but Thea baulked at the prospect of the uncomfortable, backwards lift and scrambled back up into the cart, where she perched on a bench. 'What did you want to say?'

She knew she was acting irrationally – hadn't she spent most of the morning longing for a chance to speak to him? But now she felt prickly and out of sorts, and it was all because she knew she was in the wrong. Worst of all, she was going to have to apologise and explain why she'd broken up with him, and after that he probably wouldn't want to see her again anyway. If it hadn't been for her promises to Deedee and Pearl, she would end the conversation now with a cutting remark and save time.

'Fine.' Fitz sank onto the step. His attitude was so dejected, Thea's bad humour dissolved like a mist, and she drew breath to apologise. But Fitz got there first. 'I'm sorry,' he said. 'I know you don't want to speak to me, but I might not see you again, and I wanted to apologise.'

'You? Whatever for?' She stared at him in shock.

'When I saw you with Billy Haywood that day, I must have done or said something to upset you but—'

'No, I—'

'Please, Thea. Let me finish.' He didn't shout or demand it, but simply voiced his request in quiet but determined tones. 'I've been rehearsing what I want to say all the way here, and if I don't get it out now I'll get myself in a muddle.'

Thea subsided, biting back the protest that everything was her fault. She hadn't let him speak when she'd broken up with him, so the least she could do was listen now. She simply nodded, giving him what she hoped was an encouraging smile, although she was so tense it probably looked like a hideous grimace.

Fitz rose and faced her. The brief instant during the service when they had shared the joke of Pearl's name was no more than a memory, because now his expression was grave and tense, with no hint of humour. 'I don't know what I said back then, but the point is, when I had the chance to speak to you after Berlin, I should have asked you to explain, tried to work out our problems. Instead, I chose Jack over you when I should have put you first.'

Thea couldn't let this go on. 'Seriously, you did nothing wrong. Of course you were worried about Jack. Everything is my fault.'

The corner of Fitz's mouth lifted. 'Surely not *everything*.'

Thea stood, then wobbled as the cart moved slightly beneath her feet. 'Look, there are things I need to explain, but I'd rather talk face to face.'

Fitz reached up and this time she put her hands on his shoulders and let him lift her down. Once her feet hit the ground it would have been so easy to lean in and kiss him. She swayed forward as though their bodies were drawn together by a magnetic force, was acutely aware of his hands on her waist and the feel of his firm, muscular shoulders beneath her palms.

No. She mustn't. It would be all too easy to kiss and make up now and avoid explaining herself, but Fitz deserved to know the truth. If he didn't know the worst of her then any relationship would be built on shaky foundations. She stepped back, and Fitz let his hands drop to his sides. She folded her arms to resist the temptation of touching him again.

This was it. Time to make the confession she dreaded. 'You know about my past with Billy Haywood now.' When he nodded, she went on, 'At the time I felt guilty and naive for being so taken in. I thought I'd dealt with those feelings years ago, but when Billy showed up again they all came flooding back. I thought if you knew what I was really like you'd despise me.'

'I could never despise you.'

'Wait. You don't know the worst. All this time, I've told myself that my judgement was flawed and used this as an excuse for never getting into a serious relationship. In Shrewsbury I was always going out with blokes that Pearl would consider unsuitable, and I carried on that way until I met you. But it's taken some home truths from Deedee and a conversation with Pearl to realise the truth.'

'Which is?' Fitz's faint smile had disappeared, and he looked worried again.

Thea struggled to organise her thoughts. This was even more difficult than she'd anticipated. 'It's no secret I've spent my life resenting Pearl's interference.' A small chuckle escaped. 'Although Pearl would call it *keeping me in one piece*.'

Fitz's mouth quirked. 'I'm sure it's a matter of perspective.'

'Well, Deedee kindly pointed out that a lot of my more foolish choices were not because I have poor judgement but because I'm a contrary so-and-so who really hates being told what to do. Although she might not have put it quite like that. In other words, if my sister told me to do one thing, I'd rush out and do the exact opposite. I was going out with unsuitable men not because I didn't realise that's what they were like but because deep down I knew, and I was rebelling against my sister.' Thea sighed. 'I didn't enjoy hearing that, but now I've had time to think about it, I can see it's true. The thing is, Pearl's really improved since coming to Fenthorpe – she doesn't mother me nearly as much as she used to. It's me who hasn't changed, to the extent that I even resented it when she tried giving me advice. Which brings me to why I was so awful to you.'

Fitz raised his eyebrows. 'Because Pearl told you to be nice?'

'Pretty much.' She grimaced. 'It sounds so childish, doesn't it?' She realised she was twisting her hands together, so she clasped them behind her back. 'It wasn't just that, though. When you helped me get rid of Billy—'

'Or *poked my nose in*, as you termed it.'

Thea winced. 'Yes. Sorry. But it was as though I'd spent my life trying to escape from Pearl's interference, only for you to take over.'

'And that's why you broke up with me?'

Thea could only nod, feeling very small. 'I didn't realise it at the time. I told myself it was because if you found out about my past with Billy, you'd despise me.'

'But, Thea, I love you. If I see you in trouble, I'm going to help.' He suddenly looked very tired and sad. 'I don't think I could stop myself.'

Thea blinked back tears. Why couldn't she have just kissed him? She'd known he wouldn't want her if she told him the truth. 'I know I was being unreasonable. If you'd only give me a second chance, I'm sure I'd do better.'

Fitz grasped her shoulders, and the light of hope in his eyes made her catch her breath. 'You want to try again?'

'Of course. I thought you knew.'

'I thought you just wanted to clear the air so we wouldn't spoil the party.'

'You mean' – Thea scarcely dared to ask the question – 'you still want me, even after I've told you what a contradictory mess I am?'

Fitz chuckled, the sound sending a quiver of anticipation from Thea's head to her toes. 'I explained how important family is to me, didn't I?' She nodded, and his features softened. Now he was looking at her with the loving expression she had missed so terribly. 'I suppose I might have idealised them before, but families are by nature contradictory and messy. Take my dance company: we trained together, supported each other and celebrated each other's successes, but we also bickered and vied for the same roles. Yet when push came to shove, we were family.' His gaze bored into hers, making her feel... well, various sensations that Deedee would be all too delighted to hear about. 'We've both got our faults, but that doesn't matter if we love each other. And I love you, Thea. I never stopped loving you.'

She gave a little sob and wound her arms round his neck. 'I love you too.' The next moment they were kissing, and she pulled him close, needing the reassurance of his body pressed to hers.

When they finally broke for air, she gave a little laugh. 'Is this really happening?'

'I hope so. If I wake up and find this is all a dream I'm going to be really annoyed.'

'Even if it is a dream, I'll come and find you when I wake up. I don't want to lose you again.' A thought struck her. 'I don't even know where you've been posted.'

'28 OTU. Same as Greg and Edwin.'

'I suppose I should be grateful it's only about forty miles away. I'll miss you, though.'

'It won't be easy, but I want to give us a chance.'

She traced the faint silvery scar on his face with gentle fingers. 'You're not afraid to be seen with a rebellious, contrary WAAF?'

'You forgot compassionate, enthusiastic, funny.' He punctuated each word with a kiss. 'Not to mention stunningly beautiful.'

They only broke the next kiss when someone cleared their throat loudly. It was the driver. 'Excuse me, but I need to take the cart back to Elmwick.'

Thea stepped away, feeling her face burn. 'I suppose we ought to join the others.'

They approached the pub door. Music drifted out through the snug's open window. The landlady must have provided a gramophone for the celebration, and now Bing Crosby's voice, low and melodious, sang, 'The moon was yellow...'

Fitz held out his hand. 'I don't feel like joining the others just yet. Care to dance?'

Thea melted into his arms and found herself being expertly guided in a tango on the pavement in full view of everyone in Fenthorpe High Street. 'You do realise everyone's watching?' And it wasn't only passers-by; someone in the wedding party must have seen them from the window, and now Pearl, Greg, Jenny, Deedee and the rest of Fitz's former crew were crowding around the open door, cheering.

Fitz dipped her before answering. 'I don't care. I came to the wedding thinking that, if I had to make some dramatic gesture to persuade you to take me back, I'd do anything. Let the whole of Fenthorpe know I'm a dancer, I don't care.'

And they danced on, Fitz steering them adroitly around pedestrians who stared at them as though they were mad. They only stopped when the last notes of the song faded. Then they were kissing again, and only broke apart when a shout came from the pub doorway. It was Jenny. 'Break it up, you two. We're all starving, and everyone's waiting.'

Laughing, they went to join the others. Jenny gave Thea a meaningful look and said, 'About time.'

When Pearl's gaze fell on Thea and Greg's joined hands, her smile beamed all the brighter. 'Now we've got even more to celebrate.'

Deedee got the last word, though. When Thea slipped into a seat beside her, she asked, 'How are your knickers feeling, dear?'

Thea shot her a grin. 'None of your business.'

It might have been a humble meal, consisting mostly of food that didn't require coupons, but despite the difficulties Norah Brumby had done them proud. There was also no shortage of drinks from the bar. What there wasn't was a great deal of was talk about the future, and Thea guessed everyone was avoiding thinking of the separations to come.

At the end of the meal, Fitz rose. 'I know you said you didn't want any speeches,' he said to Pearl and Greg, 'but I can't let the day end without at least proposing a toast.' He raised his glass. 'To the best pilot in the world, and the woman who saved more than one crew's life before turning her talents to producing the most entertaining and informative newspaper I've read. To the happy couple, Mr Greg Tallis and Mrs Pearl Tallis.'

Thea grinned. 'Mrs *Aphrodite* Pearl Tallis,' she reminded him.

Pearl shot her a glare. 'Careful, or I'll tell Fitz *your* real name.'

'It's the first thing I told him. There are no secrets between us. Not any more.'

Fitz sat back down and squeezed her hand under the table. In response, she pulled her chair closer so she could lean her head upon his shoulder.

'Happy?' he asked.

'Very.'

And as the afternoon passed, it was as though the war had paused. Thea knew there would be difficult times ahead, and long separations. But although the war might come between them, nothing could separate their hearts now they were reunited.

Author's Note

Rationing made it very difficult for brides to find wedding gowns and, if they couldn't borrow one, they often simply married in their best dress. WAAFs could marry in uniform, although they were allowed to request permission to marry in civvies, as Pearl does in the story. Rationing also created problems for theatres and film studios, as they were unable to make many new costumes for their productions. In response, Gainsborough Studios set up the Studio Hire Service, enabling producers to hire costumes from them. Although this service was eventually extended to women wanting to hire wedding gowns, I was unable to find evidence that it was available as early in the war as 1943. However, the thought of Pearl getting married in a film star's gown was too tempting to resist!

The label 'lacking moral fibre' or 'lack of moral fibre' did exist, and the intention of stigmatising aircrew who refused to fly was to dissuade others from doing likewise. While there are accounts of parades such as the one witnessed by Fitz and Jack at the start of the story, there seems to have been a lack of consistency in the way LMF cases were treated in different RAF stations, and men were treated more humanely elsewhere. I therefore chose the characters of Group Captain Rhodes and Squadron Leader Price to represent the hardline response and the compassionate one respectively.

After setting a series in Orkney, with its unrelenting wind, and now including ten days of gales in this book, some people (my editor included!) might be excused for thinking I'm obsessed with storms. Yet the records show gales really did sweep across Lincolnshire for ten days in March 1943, grounding many of the bomber squadrons. As I was desperate to keep Fitz in Fenthorpe for as long as possible, I was delighted to discover a genuine reason to prevent him from finishing his tour too early in the story.

The incident where Fitz is forced to pilot *C-Charlie* after Greg is injured was inspired by the true story of Australian bomb aimer Laurie Woods. After his pilot received severe facial injuries during the final operation of their tour – a raid on Wanne-Eickel – he took over the Lancaster's controls and flew it all the way back to England. When they reached RAF Manston, the pilot had recovered enough to be lifted into his seat, and made a safe landing. In recognition of his actions, Woods was awarded the Distinguished Flying Cross.

Acknowledgements

I couldn't have built up a picture of life in Bomber Command without the priceless archive of oral histories created by the International Bomber Command Centre. I spent days absorbed in the amazing accounts the centre has made available online, and it was only the need to meet my deadline that got me to stop listening and start writing the book!

A huge thank you to the wonderful authors of the RNA Cariad chapter. Our monthly Zoom chats really helped keep me sane while I was struggling to complete the first draft of this story, and knowing that I'd be meeting many of them in sunny Cardiff spurred me on to my deadline.

Thanks as ever to my editor Emily Bedford and the whole team at Canelo for their hard work, dedication and general behind-the-scenes wizardry. Also to Lina Langlee for being the best agent in the world.